Fifty is Not a Four-Letter Word

Fifty is Not a Four-Letter Word

LINDA KELSEY

ISIS
LARGE PRINT
Oxford

First published in Great Britain 2007
by
Hodder & Stoughton
a division of Hodder Headline

Published in Large Print 2007 by ISIS Publishing Ltd.,
7 Centremead, Osney Mead, Oxford OX2 0ES
by arrangement with
Hodder & Stoughton
a division of Hodder Headline

British Library Cataloguing in Publication Data
Kelsey, Linda
Fifty is not a four-letter word. – Large print ed.
1. Middle-aged women – Fiction
2. Life change events – Fiction
3. Large type books
I. Title
823.9'2 [F]

ISBN 978–0–7531–7928–4 (hb)
ISBN 978–0–7531–7929–1 (pb)

Printed and bound in Great Britain by
T. J. International Ltd., Padstow, Cornwall

For Christian

Grateful acknowledgement is made for permission to reprint from the following copyrighted works:

Simone de Beauvoir: *The Woman Destroyed*. Reprinted by permission of HarperCollins Published Ltd © Simone de Beauvoir 1969

T. S. Eliot: "The Burial of the Dead", from "The Waste Land" (1922), *Collected Poems 1909–1962* (Faber & Faber, 1974), reprinted by permission of the publisher

Gus Kahn: "It Had to Be You" (Bantam Music Publising Co. Keyes Gilbert Music Co., 1924)

Jenny Joseph: "Warning", *Selected Poems* (Bloodaxe Books, 1992), © Jenny Joseph, reprinted by permission of Johnson & Alcock Ltd

Elinor Wylie: "Farewell, Sweet Dust", *Angels & Earthly Creatures* (Alfred A. Knopf, 1929)

The door will open slowly and I shall see what
    there is behind the door. It is the future.
The door to the future will open. Slowly.
Unrelentingly.
    I am on the threshold.
        Simone de Beauvoir, *The Woman Destroyed*

When I am an old woman I shall wear purple
With a red hat which doesn't go and doesn't suit
me

                    Jenny Joseph, "Warning"

PROLOGUE

May 2003

Just as I was about to get it right, at the very moment I knew we were on the road to recovery, Jack walked out. I'd just got home from three days in Paris, three days which had changed me in ways I couldn't possibly have predicted. Olly had gone upstairs to do some last-minute revision for his A levels. Or so he said. His sudden studiousness, even at this eleventh hour, was suspicious. More likely he'd gone upstairs to get away from me. Or to download songs onto his i-pod. Or to surf for porn. Or to do whatever eighteen-year-olds do behind the closed door of their bedroom. I'm being unkind. But then we had just had a major row. I'm not sure who started it.

I'd planned the seduction of my husband of twenty years all the way from Gare du Nord to Waterloo. As soon as I'd cleared away the dishes, my femme fatale act would begin. I was already tingling.

Jack was hovering.

"What is it, Jack?" I asked, looking up over my shoulder from the saucepan I was scrubbing. "You look like a kid in infants, trying to catch teacher's attention. Too timid to speak, are we?" I grinned, chucking him mockingly under the chin with my rubber glove, depositing soap suds on his stubble.

I knew instantly it was the wrong thing to have done. I had been planning to seduce him, not eat him alive.

"Well spotted, Hope, that's exactly how you make me feel."

"But I was joking, Jack."

"Maybe you were, but I'm not." Jacked brushed away the suds with the back of his hand and breathed in deeply, as though bracing himself for a blow.

And then he let me have it. "I can't take it any more, Hope. I can't take *you* any more. Not your cynicism. Not your selfishness. Not your belief that you're the only woman in the universe who has had to endure the humiliation of becoming fifty. Or your self-pity. Or your sniping at me. Or the way you sabotage yourself with Olly. Or think you can challenge your mother to explain fifty years of bad parenting in a single afternoon, just because you're in the mood for an answer. And the fact that you freeze whenever I come near you. For the first time in our lives together, you've had six full months of opportunity to make it right between us. But it was all too much effort for you. Well, now it's all too much effort for me. I've had enough. It was never any secret that all these years I've supported you more than you supported me. But I didn't mind any of that. Because, despite your success, you needed boosting far more than I ever did. But I've had it. That's it. Finished. I'm moving out."

"Jack —"

"No, Hope, not now, I'm just too weary to allow this to escalate into another row."

He looked weary. *So* weary. Weary, ashen and old. For the first time, Jack, my rock, fifty-two and as fit as a man of thirty, looked old.

"There's a small flat above the clinic, and it's available, and that's where I'm going."

"Please, Jack, please, just one thing. Does Olly know?"

"Yes, Hope, he does know."

"And?"

"And he doesn't like it, but he understands."

"But that's unforgivable. How could you tell him before you've spoken to me about it? Before we've had a chance to discuss it."

"That's typical, Hope. I tell you I'm leaving and you're concerned only about who comes first in the pecking order. It's irrelevant. If I could actually speak to you about anything at all without it turning into a row or a monologue about how sorry you feel for yourself, then we'd never have got to this point."

I turned away for a moment, stared into the sink, as though the grease floating on the surface of the water, between the suds, might provide an explanation.

"Jack, is there someone else?"

But Jack had already left the room.

What use now for the Sabbia Rosa lingerie I'd bought on the Rue des Saints Pères? I tried to give the saucepan my full attention, scrubbing at it with wire wool. And then, with slow deliberation, I lifted the sopping scourer from the sink, squeezed it free of water and soap, and began to drag it along the inside of my left arm, bare except for the rubber glove. Again and again, back and forth, I scraped it along the soft skin of my inner arm, watched the scratches and the teeny pinpricks of blood appear. Then I leaned back over the sink and retched, vomiting chicken and ratatouille into the already unctuous water. My head was too heavy to lift. I don't know how long I stayed in that position, watching one tiny and forlorn tear after another plop into the debris, plop, plop, a drop at a time, like a tap in need of a new washer.

Did I deserve this? Looking back over the past six months I think perhaps I did . . .

PART ONE

Birthday Blues

Five months earlier, New Year's Day 2003,
late at night

He's on me, and in me. If a peeping Tom up a ladder
were to shine a torch through the window of our
bedroom, he would think he'd struck gold. Hope
Lyndhurst-Steele and Jack Steele, unmistakably mid-
coitus. But he'd be wrong. Appearances can be
deceptive. I'm not mid anything. Only Jack is labouring
away. Well, I suppose I'm doing *something*. I'm
thinking, after all. But my mind — as so often these
days — is elsewhere. My body has been embalmed,
while my brain is turbocharged. A question keeps
forming and re-forming in my head. IS . . . THIS . . .
IT?

IS . . . THIS . . . REALLY . . . IT? And I don't just
mean the sex, although it matters. It matters a lot. I
mean my whole life. Why does it feel so — over? So far,
so very good. And now suddenly so over . . . I have no
right to feel this jaded.

I really must try to concentrate. Even after almost
twenty years, Jack's a sensitive lover, and he can always

7

spot when I'm not paying attention. But with any luck he won't notice the fractional shifting of my head that allows me to see the LED on my alarm clock, illuminating the time at 23.53. It's a matter of honour — Jack's honour, that is — that we make love on my birthday, which just happens to be today, 1 January. With only seven minutes to go until it's over he has a deadline to meet. Sex on special occasions is one of Jack's quirks. My birthday. His birthday. The anniversary of the day we met. And the anniversary of the day our son was conceived (Jack's very precise with dates). Our wedding anniversary. Christmas, Jewish New Year, Chinese New Year and Divali. Well, the Jewish New Year anyway. And quite a few times in between as well. But who's counting?

I've been dreading this birthday for months. And now that it's almost over, instead of the relief that should come from realising that any given birthday is just another day, I feel increasingly agitated, little knots of nervousness gnawing at my solar plexus. As though something dreadful is about to happen. Something in addition to the one dreadful thing that's already happened.

I forgot to mention the F word. The *F* word. Not that F word. How about F is for fuming? F is for flabbergasted. F is for effing Fifty! And now, bitch that I am, F is for flaccid. Jack clocked what was going on, as I knew he would. Making love to an embalmed woman is few men's idea of fun. And necrophilia definitely doesn't feature in Jack's erotic repertoire.

He withdrawing. Me long since withdrawn. Jack looks at me, more quizzical than cross. "And where do you go to, my lovely, when you're alone in your bed?" Peter Sarstedt. Jack's a sucker for a good lyric.

"I'm sorry, darling," I reply. "The party. A new year. Being fifty. Wondering where on earth we go from here. I guess it's just all been a bit much. But you've been brilliant."

"Never mind, old girl, you'll soon get used to it." He kisses me gently on the cheek and squeezes my hand briefly as he rolls over to his side of the bed. "Sleep tight."

I turn onto my side too. We're back to back, with a couple of feet between us. Or maybe the Atlantic Ocean. But it's not Jack, it's me. It's my fault, this growing gulf. I am *so* tired. I fall into an uneasy sleep.

The previous month, December 2002

The party had been Jack's idea. "What's to celebrate?" I'd countered curtly when he suggested it. Honestly, I didn't used to be this grumpy.

"Come on, Hope, don't be such a misery. Just think of it as a New Year's Eve party, which it will be, a not-birthday party that just happens to begin the night before your birthday. By the time it gets to midnight, everyone will be too drunk to remember that half-a-century Hope has joined the Saga generation."

"It's a blessing you never planned a career as a salesman. You wouldn't earn a penny in commission."

"OK, look at it this way. If we have a really big bash, Claire will come from Australia and Saskia from Rome. And so will the rest of the clan. I could take you on a cruise if you'd prefer."

"A cruise! Very funny. I'd rather slit my throat. In fact, I'd rather slit *your* throat."

Jack was grinning, so I knew he didn't really mean it about the cruise. What clinched it as far as the party was concerned was the thought of all my émigré BFs turning up at the same time. I'm only moderately political, but there are two things that could get me signed up for an anti-globalisation campaign. One, the fact that Starbucks cappuccino sucks, and the other that so many of my friends have abandoned Blighty for a better life elsewhere. Thank God for email.

But I think it went deeper than that, this agreeing to a party that I didn't really want. I'm hardly the doormat type, so usually when I say no, I mean it. The weird thing is I'm not sure what I want any more. Over these past few months I've been suffering from a kind of mental vertigo. A sense of spinning, of disequilibrium, but entirely in the mind.

Take the business of confidence, for example. I spent the first thirty years of my life trying to acquire some confidence. *Feeling the fear and doing it anyway.* Going on courses to learn how to be assertive. Forcing myself to walk into crowded rooms alone without running straight out again. The next almost-twenty years enjoying that hard-won self-assurance. And now? Gone. Kaput. Like I'm the victim of a smash-and-grab attack. How on earth did this happen? If I'm being truthful I can't even decide in the morning what to wear for work, or what to cook for dinner. And as for my job, my precious career, I keep wondering if I'm good enough. And if I even care that much any more. Can I blame it all on the big 5–0?

"Officer," I want to shout at every passing policeman. "I've been robbed."

"Sorry to hear that, ma'am," I imagine the reply. "What did they take?"

"Just my confidence, officer. Probably not very valuable as far as you're concerned. But it meant a lot to me."

At least I still had the wherewithal to insist on conditions. I refused to allow any mention of the birthday on the invites, knowing all along it was a hopeless cause and Jack was bound to be briefing everyone behind the scenes. But I did make Jack promise no speeches, no cake, no male strippergrams. And he's a man of his word.

"Jack, why are *you* so keen to have a party?"

"I think it will do you good. Remind you that life's for living. You haven't been yourself for months."

Exactly. Jack got it in one. I've forgotten who "myself" is.

"You're right, my love. If we're going to do it, let's pull out all the stops and make it the best party ever," I said. "After all, it's the only . . . the only —" I was going to say the only fiftieth birthday I was ever going to have, but the words wouldn't come out "— the only New Year's Eve party we're likely to have for some time," I finished feebly.

"Champagne," said Jack, saving me.

"Laurent Perrier pink champagne," I countered, perking up a bit.

"Martinis," Jack added. "With an olive."

"Cosmopolitans for the girls," I suggested, practising a pout, but sounding more like Peggy Mitchell from the Square than Samantha in *Sex and the City*. I was getting into the swing of it.

"Mojitos," interjected a gravelly voice entering the kitchen. "I'll do the cocktails. And if it means free booze, James and Ravi will probably help too. Just so long as when things get really gross, like by the time the hall is clogged up with Zimmer frames, you don't mind us saying goodnight to the corpses and moving on."

Olly loped over and around me, wrapping me from behind in his skinny arms, and planting a big smacker of a kiss on the side of my neck. My darling boy. Seventeen years old and six foot to my five foot seven (unless I've shrunk a bit lately, which isn't beyond the realms of possibility). Still capable of unsolicited hugs and affection when I'm not annoying the hell out of him which, according to Olly, is most of the time.

"Mmm, talking of Ravi," I mused, "I feel a theme coming on. There's certainly not enough room in the house, so we'll need a tent. A tent with heaters. Otherwise we'll all freeze to death. Although, come to think of it, preserving our increasingly ancient friends in a cryology experiment might not be such a bad idea."

"Yeah, absolutely fascinating, but what's cryology and what's all this got to do with Ravi?"

"Well, what I really fancy is a cross between a Moroccan souk and *Monsoon Wedding*. I can just picture it. The whole tent lined with beautiful, jewel-like fabrics, like something out of the *Arabian Nights* —"

"Look, I don't want to be rude or anything, but I've places to go, people to see. Do you think you could get to the point?"

"Well, I was only wondering if Ravi's mum might know where to get cheap sari material."

"Muuum!" Olly changes moods as easily as flicking a light switch. "I do NOT, do you hear, NOT, want you ringing Ravi's mum."

"But I thought I might invite her to the party."

"You hardly know her, for fuck's sake!"

"Olly, language check." Jack speaking.

"Well, *she* swears all the time. What do you call it, Dad? Swearing like a trooper? You guys are such hypocrites. And don't you have enough friends already without getting together with my mates' mums all the time? It's so creepy. I know you just sit around yabbering about us, trying to gather information to use against us."

My eyes fixed on the impressive array of buffed and sharpened kitchen knives which dangle from the magnetic metal strip behind the cooker. Did Medea commit infanticide with a pointy knife? Or was it a blunt instrument?

"Forget it, Olly." I was trying desperately not to lose it. "I'll sort it on my own. Forget I even mentioned it."

13

"Anything to eat?" asked the boy, flicking the switch again. "I'm starved . . . Shit, I've just realised something. You're going to be fifty, aren't you? Fifty! That's what this party is really all about. We're going to have to all club together now and buy you a facelift. Last night James and I were watching this hilarious programme, *Makeover Mayhem* or something. Apparently, it's what every fifty-year-old wants. A new face. How much do these things cost anyway? Can you afford it? Will I still get to go on my gap year? You did promise you'd pay half. Will you look surprised all the time, like Anne Robinson?"

"And start telling me that I'm the weakest link," added Jack, sounding somewhat rueful.

I kicked Olly playfully in the shins, but when he screeched, "Ow, that really hurt," in a way that suggested it really did hurt, I found myself smiling.

My being born on 1 January is a mixed blessing, depending on who you're talking to. My mother, for example, says New Year's Eve is her worst day of the year, because when everyone else is celebrating she is reliving the nightmare of giving birth to me. If you were to go to a party on New Year's Eve where my mother happened to be as well, you'd spot her straight off. She'd be loudly and aggressively subjecting anyone within earshot to the story of my undignified entry into the world. Later, she'd be the one curled up in a foetal position in the corner, swigging gin straight from the bottle, getting more maudlin by the minute. You can imagine why relations between me and my mother sometimes tend towards the frosty. This year, to my relief, she and Dad are going to South Africa for Christmas and staying for the New Year, so at least we are spared her presence. My father's presence, by contrast, is always pure pleasure. He's the longest-suffering and cheeriest person I've ever met. And he still adores her and what he chivalrously refers to as her "engaging eccentricity". Even after fifty-five years of marriage. I don't get it, but neither would I dare to question it. It's not my business.

After twenty-seven hours in labour, by 10p.m. on 31 December 1952, Jenny Lyndhurst wasn't the slightest bit interested in the symbolic nature of the date. She didn't give a damn whether her offspring arrived before midnight, as the clock struck twelve — or never. The midwife, who'd been hoping to get off her shift at 10p.m. in order to join a group of nurses and doctors for the countdown on the hospital roof, with its panoramic views of the Thames, could barely loosen my mother's vice-like grip on her arm.

"You can't leave me, not now," my mother wailed. "I'm going to die if this isn't over soon."

Mary, the midwife, who was caring and Catholic and Irish, didn't have the heart to abandon my belligerent, albeit distressed, mother. As Big Ben began to ring out for midnight she exclaimed, "You're ten centimetres dilated! We'll soon be there, Mrs Lyndhurst. It's time to push; start pushing, Mrs Lyndhurst. We're nearly there."

An hour later, Mrs Lyndhurst was still pushing and still wailing and still ranting between wails about how she'd never wanted to have a second child and how Abe, my soon-to-be father, was to blame, and how she was going to have her tubes tied the minute the baby was out, and how all midwives were sadists. Not that any of it mattered, she insisted, because she was about to die anyway.

By this time the doctor had arrived — from the roof presumably — wearing a silly paper hat on his head and streamers around his neck.

"Get out of here," she screamed. "Mary, the alarm, get this intruder out of here."

"Calm down, Mrs Lyndhurst, and let me have a look," said the duty obstetrician. "Do we want to get this baby out now or not?" He bent down to look closer between my mother's writhing, ricocheting legs, jerking his head back then forward then back again to avoid being hit in the face by a flailing limb.

At the very moment he was thinking of forceps, Jenny Lyndhurst felt something rip her flesh apart and she let out a low, guttural groan that sounded nothing like the noise a human being makes. The crown broke through, and a bloody, big-headed baby slithered out of her, caught just in time by the triumphant doctor. He beamed, as though he — and he alone — had been responsible for the successful outcome.

"A beautiful baby girl, Mrs Lyndhurst. My sincerest congratulations. One of the first babies of the new year, born midway through the twentieth century, at the dawning of a new era of peace and prosperity. What a blessing."

If she'd had the strength my mother would have strangled the patronising popinjay. Instead, she snapped breathlessly, "Cut the sermon, Doctor. I'd like to see my baby, if it's all right with you." As I was lifted and placed on her belly, a wrung-out, torn-asunder Jenny Lyndhurst relented, just a little. "In the spirit of the good doctor's words, I name you Hope. As in Hope for the future. As in Hope that I never, ever, have to go through this again."

At which point my father, who'd been pacing and intermittently peeking around the curtain for what seemed like days, walked in clutching the hand of a sleepy, confused, curly haired two-and-a-half-year-old in a smocked dress and patent shoes and with a big ribbon at the side of her head. My sister, Sarah. She, in turn, was clutching a one-eyed teddy bear. Before my father could say a word, my mother was off. "You've no idea what I've been through. *And* I told you not to bring her. This is no place for a child. Why isn't she at her grandmother's?"

"My poor darling, you must be quite exhausted," he replied, refusing to be riled. "But look at the little mite, she's perfect. Look, Sarah, your lovely little sister." Sarah took one look at me — still attached to the umbilical cord, still smeared with slime — and began to scream.

"Congratulations, Mr Lyndhurst, but you're a little premature," said Mary sternly. "All is well. But it's nearly three o'clock in the morning, and Sarah should be in bed. According to hospital rules you shouldn't be here at all, and certainly not with your daughter. It disturbs the other patients at this time of night. There's clearing up to do. And then Mrs Lyndhurst and baby Hope need some sleep. So please go home and come back in the morning."

"Hope? I never . . . Oh, never mind. Hope, that's the prettiest name I ever heard. Next to Sarah, that is."

Sarah's head was buried in my father's overcoat. "Baby horrid. Mummy horrid," she sobbed. "Daddy and Sarah go home."

17

My dad smiled on regardless. He says he fell in love with both of us girls from the first second he saw us. I've never once had reason to doubt him.

Unlike my mother, I revel in having been born on 1 January around halfway through the twentieth century. It kind of puts me in the thick of things, gives my birthday an extra significance, a bit of historical context, as my dad would say. OK, this year it has a significance I could well have done without, but as a rule it has worked in my favour. Mostly, I've chimed rather well with the decades. As I came in, rationing was about to go out, and by the time Harold Macmillan, in 1957, told Britons that they'd "never had it so good", it was certainly true of my family. I managed to squeeze in about five minutes of swinging at the end of the 60s, I marched to a faint-hearted feminist tune in the 70s. In the 80s, I became a working mum and soared to the peak of my profession, although I never voted for Margaret Thatcher, and in the 90s . . . well, what did I do in the 90s? I just carried on doing what I'd done in the 80s, only minus the shoulder pads. Oh, and I took up yoga, to which I was totally unsuited, because my head steadfastly refuses to unclutter even when I'm asleep. My fight-or-flight mechanism is on constant red alert. I'm not even sure I see the point of relaxing. It's *not* doing stuff that makes me anxious. Lying on a mat with someone else's feet too close to my nose, trying to imagine the gentle swish of waves beside the seashore, makes my breathing go all funny — fast and short and shallow, instead of slow and deep and regular.

It seems to me that I've gone from 0 to 50 in about the same time as it takes a Ferrari Testarossa. One second I was slithering out from between my ill-tempered mother's legs, the next, whoosh, here I am weighing up whether to bleach or laser my incipient moustache. I don't care what those inane glossy magazines tell you — oops, I nearly neglected to mention that I am editor-in-chief of one of those very same glossy magazines — but fifty is not fabulous, it's not fun and it certainly isn't funny.

I do love giving parties, though, and I would have been thrilled to be giving one on New Year's Eve if it wasn't for the F-word.

Jack and I sat down to do the invites under various headings. First, Family.

"Well, that's easy," said Jack, "what with my parents both being dead and yours on holiday in Cape Town." I ignored him and wrote down my sister, Sarah, her husband, William, and their three girls, Jessie, Amanda and Sam. "Don't forget *my* delightful sister," Jack continued.

"As if I could," I replied glumly, adding Anita to the list. Anita, who hates me, and her husband, Rupert, who hates everybody, so at least I don't have to take it personally. Next up my cousin, Mike, who loves me, and his new boyfriend, a ruggedly handsome Slav called Stanko, whom I'm prepared to love, but only once Mike tells me he is definitely "The One".

Then Best Friends, mine, Jack's and Olly's (already resigned to the fact that Olly and pals will exit the party at the first opportunity), with marvellous, maddening, unpredictable Maddy, Dr M to her adoring patients, right at the top of the BF list; then the aforementioned BFs abroad. There are about ten of them in various parts of the globe, and they book flights as casually as they make restaurant reservations.

After that came the second tier. Colleagues and bosses, school mums and dads (Olly would have gone ballistic if he'd seen this category on the list), old school friends whom I see once a year, neighbours, so they won't complain about the noise, plus one set of neighbours who have been promoted to New Best Friend status. (Original BFs, like Original Pringles or Original Branston Pickle, have to have been around for at least twenty years to qualify; NBFs can be made in a week, although you'll never love them as much as your BFs.) What is it with me? I may be pushing fifty, but I still think like a small child. Fifty going on four. That's part of the problem, I suppose. When the numbers reached eighty-five, Jack declared a halt.

The guest list sorted, next came the question of food. If there's anything that marks me out as Jewish — apart from hair that frizzes at the mere mention of the word moisture — it's my attitude to food. It's one of the many reasons Jack's sister Anita hates me. I do food, all the time, and in copious quantities. My fridge is so full it keeps springing back open the second I shut it. Once a frozen chicken fell out and landed on Anita's toe, and it broke — the toe not the chicken. Some people have second homes on the Costa del Sol; mine's on the Finchley Road at Waitrose, quite a hike from there to the coast.

In the almost twenty years Jack and I have been together, we have been to Anita and Rupert's place for dinner maybe five times. Anita has been to us more like five hundred times. She thinks I invite her to spite her. And it's me who does Christmas too. Jack's a Christian (lapsed), and Olly is whatever suits him on any given day. It's not that I particularly like cooking but, for me, friends around a table groaning with food (even if the food has come straight from the deli) is one of life's great pleasures.

So the food was going to have to be fantastic.

I rang Pam. "Pam? Fancy doing a New Year's Eve party for eighty-five?"

A former sub-editor on my magazine who only left journalism six months ago to become a caterer, Pam was perhaps a bit of a risk. But she deserved a boost and if all went well she'd make lots of new contacts.

"Food stations, darling," she insisted, "so right for you and so right for now." I could swear Pam never called anyone darling before she went into the party-planning business. And I didn't have a clue what food stations were.

"Food stations? What exactly . . ."

"Grazing areas. Food stations are grazing areas, strategically placed so you can pick up delicious morsels of sustenance — some hot, some cold — as you go along."

"Aah, I see, grazing areas. Like cows. Or sheep. Now I get it. A kind of farmyard theme, although I'd been thinking more Moroccan myself."

Pam gushed on regardless. "You're so lucky to have the open-plan with that *divine* conservatory" (more like a lean-to, but never mind) "which is just perfect for parties."

I hoped I hadn't made a big mistake. Pam always was too creative to spend her days correcting punctuation, but maybe this was all getting a bit out of hand. *Delicious morsels of sustenance*, for heaven's sake.

"I think we'll have a shellfish station, a cocktail bar, and several hot-food stations with a choice of dishes. All served on these dinky little dessert plates I have at the back of my van. It's going to be quite *divine*."

Pam never used to use the word *divine* either. I'm mystified, but impressed. I learn that the correct nomenclature for this new style of serving is "miniature mains". Our miniature mains are going to be lamb with mash and mint sauce, Thai fish curry with jasmine rice, and roasted vegetables with pesto dressing for the food-combining bores.

"And a chocolate fountain, of course. With strawberries for dipping."

At least I'd heard of chocolate fountains. I think I'd even seen a picture in the paper of George Clooney dipping his strawberry at a premiere after-party. And I like a bit of pretension every now and then. It was all beginning to shape up.

I actually bumped into Ravi's mum, Nomi, in Waitrose. I couldn't resist asking her the fabric question, and I swear she immediately volunteered for the job of accompanying me to Southall. "Sari Central" she called it. Olly's right in a way about me and the other mums. I do like getting together with them, and we do talk mostly about our boys, but why shouldn't we? It's comforting to be told, "Ravi's so rude to me these days," or "James was found drunk in a gutter in Leicester Square." Less comforting to hear that a boy from Olly's year has been expelled for selling skunk to Year 9s. Why on earth didn't Olly tell me? What has he got to hide?

A Saturday morning spent in Sari Central was a great success. Thanks to Nomi's brilliance at bargaining, for fifty quid I bought enough material to drape the entire inside of the tent as well having some left over to cover four tall, bar-style round tables we'd hired to lend an air of louche nightclub glamour to the place.

All this displacement activity was definitely doing the trick. I had no time at all to get morbid about what was about to hit. Christmas came and went with me playing the role of whirling dervish. Friends arriving from abroad. Food, drink, talk, more food, more drink, more talk. No chance for real intimacies, just exchanges of information. More catch up than cosy up. Busy, busy, busy. Going to work is a lot less exhausting.

My mother says I bring it on myself. Not one to hold back, she's convinced I'm heading for a breakdown. She has been predicting it for the last twenty-five years. Anita hopes I'm heading for a breakdown. I overheard her saying to Rupert after I'd served Christmas lunch for fifteen: "Hope always has to be one better than the rest of us, but I can see it's beginning to take its toll." Jack hasn't mentioned breakdowns, but he has this new method of dealing with my more manic outbursts. "Whoah, girl," he says, as though reining in an overexcited horse. The only time he doesn't have to rein me in is in bed. In the meantime, my sister, Sarah, is a pillar of support. Claire, who's come all the way from Australia, would be a pillar of support if only we could manage twenty minutes alone together.

At 7.45p.m. on the night of the party, I'm standing in front of the full-length mirror inside my wardrobe. I should be pleased with what I see. For a woman who's just over four hours away from being fifty, just two hundred and fifty-five minutes less than half a century old, I'm really not that bad. I'm really not that real either. Tonight my hair is a dark, sleek bob. Left to its own devices it would be 85 per cent grey and 100 per cent frizz. I'm wearing a little black, knee-length, silk jersey dress. It has a halter neck, to show off my best feature — my shoulders. Well, doesn't everyone deserve a best feature? My breasts are not contenders (34A, almost), my nose is more Nefertiti than Nicole Kidman, my bottom I'd really rather not talk about. Can I be the only woman in Britain who has VPL even when she isn't wearing knickers?

But the overall package isn't bad. And tonight, with the help of the most extraordinary underwear ever engineered — I wouldn't be surprised if it had been designed and built by Norman Foster — I have a pancake stomach, a bum that would put Jennifer Lopez out of business and, most miraculous of all, a cleavage. People have often complimented me on my boyish figure. Finally, tonight, at borderline fifty, I look like a woman. But hang on there, I'm not wearing my glasses, so I'm missing some of the important detail, the stuff you can only see close up. I've failed to mention the deep furrows on my forehead and the angry vein that shoots from my eyebrow to my hairline, and not just when I'm angry. Then there's the Rift Valley that runs from the outside edge of each nostril to the corners of my mouth. And finally the neck. The neck that until two months ago was just a neck. A neck to which one never gave a second's thought. Then boom, overnight it collapsed into a heap, along with the chin, like a building hit by an earthquake, reduced to rubble.

There comes a point in your life when you may still fit into a Topshop 10, but that doesn't stop your new neck dictating the contents of your wardrobe. For example, it's a complete myth that a polo-neck sweater can disguise a neck that's lost the will to live. You can wear your neck flesh tucked in (but I guarantee you it will pop out), or you can let it all hang loose above the rim of the polo and hope small children in the street don't mistake you for a free-range chicken. Either way you lose: polo necks, along with mini-skirts and flesh-bearing midriffs are not to be entertained by a woman fast approaching fifty.

I need a drink.

"Wow!" I say as I enter the tent. It's totally transformed. While I've been off to have a bath and get ready, Jack and Olly have been lighting the candles. At six o'clock, it had looked the nadir of naffness, tacky even for a Footballer's Wife, with its clumsy cacophony of styles. What had I been thinking mixing Eastern exotica with American 50s glamour? Who would ever put a cocktail lounge in the kasbah? Mark, the editor of *Exquisite Interiors*, one of the magazines at Global, where I work, would have had me tried for treason for less. Fortunately, he's not invited. And now, in the glow of a hundred tiny, flickering flames, the atmosphere has become magical. The fabrics shimmer. Mounds of plums, figs, pomegranates and red grapes, dusted with icing sugar, sit in big glass bowls on tables, lending a Bacchanalian air. A Rod Stewart CD, Volume I of the *Great American Songbook*, plays mellow in the background.

Jack's already in the tent, dressed in a DJ and clutching a Martini. He snakes over with a big self-mocking grin on his face and hands me a glass of pink champagne. " 'It had to be you, it had to be you,' " he croons along with Rod.

> *"Some others I've seen, might never be mean,*
> *Might never be cross, or try to be boss,*
> *But they wouldn't do . . .*
> *It had to be you . . .*

"Gorgeous, Hope. Really gorgeous. The tent, the music, the mood, everything. Even you. Gorgeous."

Jack's a better person than I could ever be. For a start, he does something useful. He's a physiotherapist.

And he doesn't think his work is the be-all and end-all. He doesn't come home and bang on about Mrs Chadwick's sciatica or Johnny Philpot's latest sports injury. Whereas I go on endlessly about my job, my staff, the sales figures and the interfering suits on the top floor. He comes home and he relaxes. I come home and worry. He's strict, though: no smoking in the house, no ashtrays even, organic food, that sort of thing. And a bit anal when it comes to precision and making lists. But he also listens. I'm too busy talking or thinking to listen. The only thing in my favour is that at least I'm aware of some of my faults.

"You're gorgeous too." I smile. And I mean it. He's in great shape for fifty-two. Not a great deal of hair left on top, but shaved closely to his head it's not noticeable. In theory, I still fancy him a lot. In practice . . . Maybe I've just lost the knack. Maybe . . .

The bell rings and Jack races off to answer it.

Cocktails and laughter, but what comes after? Just for once, Hope, I tell myself, go with the flow. And I do. I start with the pink champagne, then move on to the mojitos. I snack on giant prawns with creamy mayonnaise and lamb chump with mash. I flirt with Rupert to annoy Anita, and because Rupert won't even notice I'm doing it, and with Mario of Mario's Greek down the road because he's sixty-two and still sexy and because he gives good kleftiko. Mario's forever-harassed wife, Sofia, is building up a business empire based entirely on her secret recipe for hummus. She started making it for the restaurant, now she's supplying Sainsbury's. "My very own Shirley Valentine," Mario laughs, as we attempt Greek dancing to "The Israelites" by Desmond Dekker and the Aces. "Come with me to Skyros, and I will introduce you to my favourite feta-producing goat. If she gives her blessing, I will divorce Sofia, carry you all the way to Thessalonika and wed you at the top of Mount Olympus."

"I accept," I giggle, skittering off towards more mojitos.

I see that Tony, the rat-catcher, who comes and gets rid of our annual ant infestation — and whose accounts of exterminating giant rodents utterly transfix — is doing some kind of chicken dance with Sharon, who waxes my legs and wanted to give me a Brazilian as a birthday treat. I said my husband would never forgive me, although in truth I never even asked.

I glance at my watch: 11.45p.m. and Olly's still here. He's being chatted up by local vamp Vanessa the Undresser, as she's known to the Neighbourhood Watch committee on which she and I both serve. I don't think half the men on the committee are even a teeny bit interested in traffic calming or the rise in muggings in the area; they turn up for the sole purpose of seeing how little Vanessa will be wearing on any given evening. If Vanessa were to resign from the committee, attendance would plummet, and the whole thing would fall apart.

In her early thirties and divorced with two kids, Vanessa sports a small tattoo on the swell of her substantial bosom, a bosom she's currently thrusting in

28

Olly's direction. Olly's not even looking embarrassed. Something altogether new has come over him. Instead of examining the floor as usual, he's looking straight into Vanessa's eyes. And now, glancing confidently down towards her breasts, he's casually sliding an arm around her waist and leading her to the dance floor. My throat catches. My beloved boy, my precious one and only son, the only person in the world for whom my love has never wavered, is becoming a man. When Jack's lovely, wise old mum was alive, she said to me, "A husband? Pah! He's just some man you met. But a child, no contest. A child is your flesh and blood." No offence to Jack, but it's exactly how I feel. He's mine, not yours, I want to scream at Vanessa, as jealousy slashes at me like a scythe.

The show must go on. Cuban *son* is filling the air, and I'm just about sozzled enough to have a go at salsa. Earlier in the year, as a team-boosting exercise for my staff, I organised a series of lunchtime salsa classes. They were a huge hit. I make a wobbly beeline for my cousin, Mike, who fancies himself as a bit of a Ricky Martin on the dance floor. I flare my nostrils, flick my bob in a poor imitation of Rita Moreno in *West Side Story* and grab him by the bottom. He winks at Stanko, who is looking particularly handsome in faded Levis and a tight, grey marl T-shirt, and whirls me into position. Tap 1, 2, 3. Tap 1, 2, 3. I'm not a natural at this, and the alcohol is beginning to play havoc with my counting. But Mike's good, and I allow him to lead. And soon the music and our bodies are in perfect harmony. "Dip!" commands Mike. I've seen dips, but have never so far managed one of my own. "Dip!" he orders again. And so I dip. And so I land on the floor, hard on my coccyx, with my dress drawn up around my waist, revealing my Norman Foster tights and no knickers underneath. Eighty-five people turn to cheer, except Olly, who's right in my sight line and has a look of horror spreading across his face as I start pulling frantically at the fabric rucked up around my middle. I see him whisper something into Vanessa's ear, and they are gone.

My coccyx is bruised, but no major damage has been done. I'm too far gone to feel embarrassment. Or pain. Mike pulls me up, both of us laughing dementedly, as Jack shouts, "Countdown!" Everybody starts counting backwards: *Ten, nine, eight, seven, six, five, four, three, two, one* . . .

"Happy New Year, my darling." Jack's lips meet mine tenderly, and then move away a fraction. "And Happy . . ." I put my index finger to my mouth in a shushing motion.

My stomach lurches to the rhythm of popping champagne corks. A new scary thought occurs to me. We vowed to be the generation that would die before we got old. Now it looks as though we're still going to be alive when the *next* generation gets old. The big 5–0 can no longer be denied. Can't go back and can't stand still. OK, half-century woman, time for your next act.

Office Politics

The first day back at work after New Year is a Thursday. I stride in through the open-plan office towards my private nook in the corner, trying to look purposeful, flinging casual hi's and smiles and happy new years at the few (*very* few, I note) staff members who've managed to make it in on time. My body feels leaden, and there's a brick that has lodged itself just behind my temples.

My PA, Tanya, has already been to the market to buy flowers — cut hyacinths in my favourite shade of lavender blue — and an extra-dry cappuccino, 99 per cent froth, a dribble of milk. The arrangement is that I ring her on my mobile five minutes in advance of arriving, and she scoots straight out for the coffee, so it's piping hot and ready when I arrive. Spoiled? Did I ever suggest otherwise?

Tanya's only twenty-nine, but she's a PA of the old school. She doesn't resent taking my clothes to the dry-cleaner's or popping out to do some shopping for me. My devastation of a desk is her greatest challenge, requiring ruthless culling and cleansing every single week, as it threatens to be submerged in an avalanche of clippings, press releases, unsigned invoices, unsolicited manuscripts and to-do lists which, once written, are never consulted again. Tanya would do her dump-and-Dettox routine every day if I let her. Putting my detritus into little piles with Post-it notes labelled in the neat copperplate she learned at evening classes is her favourite job of all. I know because she told me so at her last appraisal.

Unlike all my past PAs, who either viewed the job as a springboard to becoming editor a couple of weeks down the line or were secretly researching novels which would expose the bitchy world of glossy magazines while making them a mint, Tanya has worked for me for five years. She'd rather die than have my job. I think she feels sorry for me. Can't understand why anyone would want all that nasty responsibility.

"Simon wants to see you at ten o'clock," says Tanya. Simon is the MD and Global Magazines is the kind of outfit in which even the post-room boys call the big boss by his first name. It doesn't really signify openness and informality, other than in the most superficial way. Global is as hierarchical as any other big corporation — the execs have the share options and the bonuses and stake themselves out in their glass-walled offices on the top floor, the worker bees scrabble for space on the overcrowded floors below.

Simon and I aren't exactly friends, but we rub along. We know precisely where the line is drawn. So, for example, I invite him and his wife to the New Year's Eve party, certain (as is my intention) that they will refuse. "So sorry," will come the reply, "but unfortunately we have a prior commitment . . ." I've done the right thing by inviting Simon, he's done the right thing by not accepting. We've known each other for twenty-two years, longer even than I've known Jack, as I've worked my way around various magazines in the company, ending up — for the last eight years — on *Jasmine, the magazine for women who live life to the full.* Code for women who are knackered all the time.

"*Ten o'clock!* What can be so bloody urgent? I've got about a million things to do, and it means I'll have to cancel the ideas meeting. Why doesn't he ever ask if it's convenient?"

Tanya shrugs. "You know that's not how he thinks. Look, you've got no outside appointments today — I've deliberately stalled on everything external until next week — so it shouldn't be a problem to switch the ideas meeting to this afternoon. Say, three thirty, if that's OK with you. I'll send an email round while you're in the meeting."

"You're an angel," I reply. "How about scones with jam and cream as it will be almost teatime by the time we get going. That'll blow everyone's diet on their first day back, but at least it will liven us all up."

Tanya's eyes go all sparkly. A tea party to organise! I wouldn't be surprised if she does name cards and a seating plan.

"What did you think of *my* little gathering?"

"You looked amazing. No one would ever believe . . ."

The problem with personal assistants is that they get to know those things which are personal to their employer. All those forms they fill in for you, the ones in which date of birth is a compulsory field, are an instant giveaway. "I'm not asking you how I looked," I reply, trying not to sound as irritated as I suddenly feel. "What did you think of the party?"

"Completely brilliant. It was two o'clock before I could drag James away. And you know how much *he* loves parties. Not. The food was incredible. We spent ages talking to your friends from Australia. And did you see James on the dance floor, looking like a pretzel struck by lightning? It shouldn't be allowed in public."

I smile, feeling momentarily cheered at Tanya's graphic description of her adoring boyfriend. "Jesus, it's two minutes to . . . I'd better get going."

When I arrive in the outer chamber, Genevieve, Simon's PA, informs me he's on the phone and asks me to take a seat for a couple of minutes. I arrange myself on the white wrap-round leather sofa which, in a nod to modernity, has recently replaced the black wrap-round leather sofa. Sitting on this supermodel of a sofa, this Kate Moss of couches, makes me feel like a proper editor. Like the Kay Thompson character in *Funny Face*, circa 1957, who points a gloved finger at her staff, declares, "Think Pink," and, *voilà*, the entire set changes colour to fulfil her rose-tinted fantasy. The fact that I *am* a proper editor, and have no need to fantasise about the Hollywood version, is too hard for me to compute. Nah, not me. Surely not. Even after all these years, it surprises me that I do what I do rather well, have even won awards for doing it. I sometimes look around at my team, waiting for someone to make a decision, and then suddenly realise that they're all looking at me, waiting for *me* to make a decision. Being decisive isn't a problem, just remembering that it's what I get paid for sometimes takes me by surprise.

Here in the outer office, wooden floorboards have been imported at great expense. On top of the oak boards sits a vermilion shag-pile rug and on top of the rug a large, curved, smoky perspex coffee table. A huge marble-based arc lamp sheds its beam onto the carefully arranged magazines — from *Hot Property* and *Metro Girl* to *Exquisite Interiors* (whose exquisite editor, Mark, has been personally responsible for the ante-chamber refurb). It's all very seventies, and very modern. Not really the kind of look that would put Simon at his ease. His wife's a chintz and swags kind of woman, and Simon's office was equally traditional until recently, with its old-fashioned French-polished partner's desk and manly sofa, upholstered in burgundy and green stripes to match the upholstery of his office chair. John Lewis in a nod at Ralph Lauren.

Though not now that Mark has got his hands on it. Iconic black and white photographs, signed by Bailey, Avedon and Helmut Newton, adorn the walls. The Bailey is a photograph of the Krays, all harsh lighting and menace; the Avedon, an original print of the elegant model Dovima out and about in the African bush wearing inappropriate evening-wear and stroking an elephant's tusk; the Newton, a girl naked but for platform shoes, a whip and a monocle, standing beside an empty swimming pool. I think all this might be a bit much for poor old Simon, especially the Newton, what with him being a self-declared family man. My guess is that he would far rather have had a blow-up of himself shaking hands with Margaret Thatcher. But that Mark, the style oracle, stamped his Gucci boot.

The desk is a clean sweep of glass. My heels clickety-clack across the floor as Simon stands and gestures towards the seat facing his. Simon is what in a former age, the one I grew up in, you'd call dapper. Like Roger Moore in *The Saint*. He's quite a lot shorter than Roger Moore, but slim, tightly packed, like a well-wrapped parcel. His trousers have razor-sharp creases and never sag or bag, his tie never turns itself over to reveal the label or strays a bit to the left or right. There's always a handkerchief in Simon's breast pocket, one that looks as though its base might be a cardboard cut-out, with only the pointy triangular bit at the top made of cotton lawn, and neatly monogrammed. His hair never flops, it just sits there, as though lacquered into place, so abundant it could almost be a wig. He's how I imagine a Stepford Husband might look. Except for the flaky skin. The flaky skin which sometimes sheds like first snowflakes onto his navy pinstripe lapels. I never did get the chance to tell him about Eve Lom's Cleanser, the miracle cream that cleans, exfoliates and tones all at the same time.

I sit, crossing my legs and tugging at the hem of my skirt in order not to expose too much thigh beneath the transparent glass. I think I preferred his old desk.

I'm uneasy, and I don't know why. I have this strange sensation, as though my legs are beginning to sweat under my 7 denier tights, the moist warmth starting somewhere around mid-calf. My legs have never spontaneously sweated in their entire lives. It's not what legs do, unless they're manacled to a giant radiator on full blast. I think Simon has started talking, but this strange warm rush, like a tidal wave, is surging through my body, and now the little indentation between my breasts and my ribcage (still not substantial enough, thank heavens, to hold a pencil — I only checked last week) is wet. And now my armpits are distinctly clammy, and now my neck is hot beneath my hairline, and now my face is hot, hot, hot, as if it's burning. And I feel shaky, and I know he's talking, but I don't know what he's saying.

"Are you all right, Hope? You look a little . . . flushed . . ."

"Yes, fine. I mean . . . I'm fine, Simon, thank you. I just felt a little odd for a moment."

"Perhaps Genevieve could get you a glass of water."

"Yes, that would be lovely." I'm all-over damp, but recovering, although from what I've no idea. Simon presses a button and says over the intercom, "Be a love, would you, and get a glass of water for Hope?"

"I'm so sorry. Most peculiar. I feel absolutely OK again now. I'm afraid I may have missed something you said."

"Not to worry. It happens to Harriet all the time. And you must be just about the right age for . . . for — what does Harriet call them? — power surges. That's it, power surges."

My mouth hangs open. I've been outed in the middle of my very first hot flush, and it took a man — not just any man, but my boss, for heaven's sake — to tell me what was going on. My humiliation is total.

"You didn't miss anything important," he continues, as though his previous pronouncement has never been made. "I was merely enquiring after your Christmas break."

Get a grip, woman. "Oh, yes, it was lovely. Absolutely lovely." I sound totally moronic.

Genevieve walks in with the water, and I sip gratefully.

"Now, Hope, I want you to listen very carefully to what I am about to say."

"I always listen carefully to what you say." Me failing to bring a touch of levity to the exchange after our disastrous opening scene. Discombobulated. I love the sound of it, but not how it feels.

A sharp intake of breath from Simon. "For eight years now you have been one of my star editors." Oh, no, it's a new year's state-of-the-nation speech. "You took *Jasmine* to new heights of circulation and created a wonderful buzz about the magazine."

"Thank you." Simon is being unusually complimentary. Being a glass half-empty sort of person I focus on the word *took*.

"But in the last three years . . ." There, I was right. "In the last three years, things have not been going so well. Times are changing, Hope, but you're not, and neither is the magazine."

"Of course times are changing, and so am I, and the magazine is —"

"If you could let me finish, Hope."

"Of course."

"For three years now sales have been slowly sliding. Very slowly, I admit, but the advertisers are beginning to lose faith. It's not so much the bottom-line sales figures that are worrying me as the fact that the magazine has begun to look fusty and old-fashioned. Always banging on about working mothers and their rights and childcare problems, and all those lurid stories about the sex lives of married women. Women want to escape all that. Women are returning to more traditional values, they're fed up with feminism. Think Nigella. A shining beacon of modern womanhood. That's who women want to be. Domestic goddesses, not workplace warriors. Stains, my dear Hope, are the new sex."

I laugh so hard I involuntarily snort. I'm sitting in the MD's office, oinking like a pig. I'm wishing today could be cancelled.

"Stains are wh-wh-what?" I stutter helplessly.

"Stains are the new sex. Mark and I have been discussing it and a lot more besides."

"Stains?" I ask again, my laughter not yet fully run its course. I really have not got the faintest idea what he's talking about. And what have stains got to do with Mark? I'm unstoppable now. "Stains? As in wet patch? As in who sleeps on the wet patch? That kind of thing?" I'm still laughing, even though it's not funny, and another snort escapes.

"Hope, is this really necessary? Why does everything have to come back to smutty sexual innuendo? That's your problem. Sex, sex, sex. It's so very last century."

39

So very last century. That's not a Simon phrase. It has a distinctly Mark flavour to it. Something nasty is about to happen.

"But I'm still not getting it, Simon. Stains are the new sex. What the fuck does that mean?" Olly is right about me and swearing. I may have Tourette's. Why can't I keep myself in check?

"It's a metaphor, Hope, a metaphor for the new domesticity. The new domesticity that is going to be at the core of a revamped *Jasmine*. A *Jasmine* that celebrates women's unrecognised desire to demonstrate their domestic skills in traditional pursuits such as baking and needlecraft. A twenty-first-century take on traditional values. And stains are part of it. In a recent survey conducted by *Disappear*, stain removal — be it grease from cooking or flower pollen on a silk shirt — is a burning issue in households up and down the country."

My mouth is opening and closing like a fish. First, I was a pig, now I'm a fish. I catch some words, like a fish snapping at a fly. "No, we're not having this conversation. Not seriously having this conversation. Of course a survey for *Disappear* would say that. You're kidding me, aren't you? Please tell me this is some kind of early April Fool." The laughter has dissolved. I'm feeling another tidal wave surging up. This one is neither pre-, peri- nor post-menopausal. This one has the three Furies riding on its crest.

"Has it not occurred to you, Simon, that it's *Disappear*'s job to be obsessed with what the nation thinks about stains? If there were no stains to deal with,

Disappear wouldn't have a business. It would simply *disappear*. But even I, who have about as much desire to become a domestic goddess as I do to become Saddam Hussein's personal handmaiden, want to know how to get rid of stains. But a whole magazine dedicated to the subject of stain removal and tapestry cushions because the manufacturer of a stain-removal stick has done a survey . . . You can't honestly expect me to take this seriously. You don't really want me to turn *Jasmine*, which has become nothing short of a bible for working mothers, into a . . . a . . . journal for domestic drudgery."

Simon edges back in. "No, Hope, of course I wouldn't expect that from you. Not from our resident, unreconstructed, dyed-in-the-wool feminist. Which is why I know you will understand when I tell you that Mark will be taking over as editor of a new-look *Jasmine*. I've taken the decision that, rather than allow the valuable brand that is *Jasmine* to simply fade away over time, we will take Mark's marvellous idea and superimpose it on *Jasmine*. After all, the core audience for the new magazine — women aged thirty to fifty — is exactly the same age group as *Jasmine*'s dwindling readership. Our new strategy will save *Jasmine* and . . ."

". . . lose me my job and my career and probably result in half my staff being fired as well. This isn't really happening. We've not once even discussed it. And sales have only fallen by about two per cent. By July they could be up again — we've got some great issues coming up. Please tell me that you are not replacing me with a man who, just because he likes to potter around his apartment in a pinny while icing fairy cakes for his fairy friends —"

I come to a halt. This may be the most surreal thing that has ever happened to me, but nevertheless it is happening. And then this image of Tanya pops into my head: she is seated at her kitchen table poring over a copy of the newly domesticated *Jasmine*, emitting teeny yelps of delight as she snips out all the useful little tips to store in a box file marked S for Stains. Tanya, who never reads a single word of *Jasmine, Jasmine* just being too, well, strident, I suppose. And then something else occurs to me. All this creeping uncertainty I've been feeling — maybe it was some kind of premonition, only I didn't recognise it as such.

"Hope, we need to sort out terms. This is not personal, it's business. I admire you as an editor and I appreciate what you've done for the company. But I have to make the business decisions that will keep our shareholders satisfied and our customers happy."

"But what about my staff? Are you going to fire them all? All twenty-five of them? You can't just get rid of all those hard-working, talented people; it beggars belief."

Simon visibly stiffens. I notice his flaky face is even flakier than usual. And so it should be.

"Mark must be the one to decide. He needs to have a core team of people who can turn his vision into reality. All those who aren't on-message will either be made redundant or, if there are suitable vacancies on other magazines within the group, be transferred. It's going to be a painful transition for everyone. *You* will get a year's pay and a wonderful reference, and everyone else will get the redundancy to which they are entitled."

On and on he drones. I look up. There's a dark brown mark in the corner of the ceiling next to the window. It seems to be growing as I stare at it. I wonder whether it's coming from the flat roof. What extraordinary synchronicity. A stain.

He's still talking. "We have to run three more issues of the old *Jasmine*, much of which I'm sure is already planned, before relaunching with a big promotional splash in May. I would be delighted if you would stay to see the last issues through but will understand if you find your position untenable."

I could swear the stain is spreading right before my eyes. Bet the new *Jasmine* would know just how to deal with such an emergency.

"I won't hold you to your notice period. In which case Megan, as your deputy, can keep things running until Mark and his team take over."

He's still going at full throttle, but I'm not keeping up. The words come at me in spasms, with bits missing in between. Must mention the wet patch on the ceiling when he's finished. Inexplicably, I remember we've run out of salt for the dishwasher.

". . . announcement . . . staff . . . three thirty . . . not . . . speak . . . advance. Can . . . word . . . this."

He's finished. I say nothing for a long while. At least a minute. And when I do speak, I'm not sure if the words are coming from me or if I'm just a ventriloquist's dummy and someone else is talking for me.

"I really do have to go now. I'm late for a meeting. And by the way, there's something very nasty happening to your ceiling."

Simon says, "I don't think you were listening, Hope. I said I am going to come and make an announcement to your staff at three thirty and am instructing you not to say anything to them beforehand."

"Well, I shall give that some serious consideration." No, I damn well won't. "And now I am going to stand up calmly and leave the room."

Calmly? *Calmly?* Why even contemplate calmly? The Furies have shifted position. They're lined up behind Simon, giving me the thumbs-up, egging me on. I stand up to my full five foot nine in my kitten heels, put both hands firmly on his glass desk and lean forward to face him straight on. So close am I to his face that I could easily flick off a flake of skin that is trying to part with his nose. "Fuck you, you stupid bastard," I shriek. "You stupid, stupid, stupid bastard." The Furies are smiling now. "You dumbed-down advertising salesman in a Savile Row suit." The Furies are jumping up and down in excitement. "You pathetic philistine who has read only two books in his entire life — and both of them by Jeffrey Archer." The Furies are swaying, in an ecstatic trance. I swing round and clackety-stomp out of the room. Holding the door wide open and in full view of Genevieve, I deliver my final insult over my shoulder, demonstrating my incontrovertible superior intelligence and sangfroid. "You, you, you complete and total fuckwit . . ." The Furies sigh in unison. Not a memorable exit line after all. I've disappointed them. They dissolve into the ether.

Over towards the fire exit, stumbling. Clunk, clunk, clunking down all eight flights of stairs to avoid bumping into anyone. I wrench down the metal door handle at ground-floor level and turn sideways to heave the door open. Can't catch my breath. Think I'm hyperventilating. How badly did I blow *that*? Telling the MD he's a fuckwit and reminding him that he left school with one O level, will not have helped my case. Not that it matters, I suppose; it's all over anyway bar the black bin liner.

I'm standing in a grim alley around the back of Global's glitzy offices, among the rubbish bins and broken glass. Cats are eyeing me suspiciously. Coatless, jobless and too numb to feel the cold. But not quite so numb as to forget the effect the sleety drizzle will have on my 8 a.m., pre-office blow-dry. I race back round to the revolving doors at the front of the building and try to compose myself.

"Hi, Stan," I say to Stan on reception. "Bit parky out there, but I needed some fresh air."

I head for the lift and press the up button. It grinds its way up from the garage in the basement, where editors and publishers and the top-floor boys are allowed to park their cars. The lift shudders slightly as it comes to a halt and the doors part dramatically like the Red Sea. Standing there in an immaculate, lemon cord Paul Smith suit with a pink shirt and a burgundy kipper tie with garish ruby lips printed all over it, is my nemesis.

"Happy New Year, Hope," Mark smirks. Stepping to one side to make way for me is this, this boy — not yet thirty, prettier than I ever was in my heyday and, loath as I am to admit it, talented too. "Hope you had a good one. Little birdie told me you've just been celebrating a rather important birthday."

I want to say something clever and cutting and deeply homophobic. I want him to be struck down by AIDS and suffer a long, lingering death. I want to ask him what right he thinks he has to snatch away my beloved magazine and set about destroying it. I want him to explain how he can possibly believe himself qualified to know what women want. I want him to justify how he's going to be able to live with himself when perhaps fifteen, or even twenty, of my staff get fired, because of him. If this had been a month ago, I'd probably have wanted to ask him where he gets his tinted moisturiser. Now I'd like to squirt a tube of it straight into his aquamarine eyes fringed by those unbearably silky black lashes.

The lift is almost at the sixth floor, where I'm due to exit. *Exquisite Interiors* is on the seventh. In a few seconds I will escape, and he'll continue his journey, unable to help admiring me for reining in all emotion. For a split second I am Katherine of Aragon, proud and indomitable at the court of Henry VIII, even after being dumped in favour of Anne Boleyn. So how come tears are suddenly gushing out of me like a geyser? How come my sobs are reverberating off the walls? Mark is no longer smirking. As the doors open I shove my fist into my mouth to stifle the sound of weeping. I head for the sanctuary of the toilets, lock myself into a cubicle, sit on the closed seat and bury my face in my hands.

Time passes. I'm still sitting in the cubicle. Twenty-somethings come and go, exchanging stories of all-night benders, one-night stands and the hell of going home for Christmas. Animated talk of New Year diets and sales bargains in the stores. Little cries of "God, I'm humongous," and "I'm so fat I'm disgusting." One girl's got engaged, her temporary squirty ring, presented on a beach in Mauritius, soon to be swapped for a little something from Stephen Webster, Madonna's favourite jeweller. The girl she's sharing this with has just discovered her boyfriend's screwing someone else. The reassuring sound of lipsticks and mascaras and eyeshadows being jiggled in make-up bags. Thirty-somethings with their altogether different agendas. Hassles with babysitters and child-minders, and even: "Do you think Hope would let me go part-time? I'm so tired I can hardly stand up." "Well, she can hardly say no, when that's exactly what *Jasmine* campaigns for every single issue." Forty-something? All the forty-somethings are on the top floor. Fifty-somethings? You've got to be joking.

And then Tanya, lovely, ever-discreet Tanya. "Where's Hope?" I can hear the fashion editor ask her. "Oh, she just popped up to see Simon. Be back soon." In fact I've been gone for fifty minutes, which is highly unusual as Simon has a twenty-minutes-only policy for all but board meetings. Tanya has been asking herself,

"Where's Hope?" for at least half an hour and is beginning to worry, in the manner of a mother whose child is late home from school.

I can't stay here all day. I've got to get to my girls before he does. My girls. Even the two boys among my staff are my girls.

All is quiet. I peek round the door of the cubicle, step outside and grab a paper towel. After dousing it with liquid soap I remove the mascara smudges from underneath my eyes. My handbag is in my office and I can't do full repairs without my kit. I look awful. I run the cold water and sloosh my face, then dab it gently with another paper towel, trying to avoid removing the last vestiges of make-up. OK, this should be enough to get me into my office. This time, as I stride purposefully back through the open-plan, I fling neither casual hi's nor smiles, keeping my eyes straight ahead.

"Just give me five minutes, Tanya, no interruptions, then come in and see me."

Tanya looks at me, her face a question mark, then merely nods.

I close the door and get out my armour. Eye whitening drops, lip- and eye-liner, YSL Touche Eclat to deflect light from the shadows under my eyes. A comb. Looking the part helps. This time I really do have to be strong. Not for me, but for them.

Five minutes later, Tanya knocks quietly and enters before I can answer.

"Close the door, please."

She sits down with me at the small round conference table, hub of the magazine, home — over the past eight years — to hundreds of discussions, debates, heated arguments and heart-to-hearts.

"Something awful's happened." My right hand is resting on the table and Tanya instinctively reaches out to cover it with hers. "*Jasmine* is to be relaunched with Mark as editor. I've no idea how many of the staff will lose their jobs, but there is one thing I am absolutely determined to make happen. Mark will need a PA. We both know he's using a temp at the moment. And you're the girl for the job. He'll let you fuss over him to your heart's content but, more important, I really think that the new *Jasmine* will be right up your street. Promise me, Tanya, promise me you'll give it a go."

Tanya's lower lip is trembling, her eyes are welling up.

"But, Hope, this is too terrible. I couldn't even begin to think of working for Mark. Not after working for you. Why are they doing this? What's going to happen to you?"

I gently remove her hand from on top of mine and place it between both my hands, taking control of the situation.

"Tanya, it's just the way of the world. It's unfair, it's unjust, but it's business. Although bad business, I can guarantee. I'll fight all I can to save as many jobs as possible. Me? God, I could do with a break. I've been doing this for nearly thirty years. Who knows, I may decide to become a geologist. The world will hardly be

49

a poorer place if Hope Lyndhurst gives up being an editor."

I'm fully in charge again. This is what I do best. "Look, we'll have plenty of time to talk this over later, but now I have to brief Megan. Then, at midday, I want everyone to gather round, and I'll make the announcement. Make sure everyone who's in today stays here; all appointments, however important, are to be cancelled. Simon's coming at three thirty. Ring that bar in St James's and, if it's available, book the private room in the basement for six o'clock. Tonight we're going to get hammered. Drinks on me. Or rather, drinks on Global. Let's see if I can give my company Amex a heart attack."

My tears are all dried up; everyone else's have only just begun. Megan, when I tell her, cries. The fashion editor, the beauty editor, the art director and — probably just because these things are catching — the work experience girl who only started this morning, all cry. The junior features assistant, my current candidate for penning a secret bestseller about the bitchy world of women's magazines, doesn't cry. She has started taking frantic notes, and she's grinning. I had her sussed right from the start. My features editor, Ally, and my two boys — Saul and Cosmo, picture editor and style assistant respectively — are looking shifty. That suggests to me that Mark has already had "words" and that all three are moving camp. In Cosmo's case extremely camp. Saul, on the other hand, is a father of three and as straight as Fifth Avenue. He can't afford not to have a job, not even for a fortnight. Their early absconding suits me fine, that's three less to worry about.

The rest are genuinely shocked, deeply upset, for me, for the magazine, for themselves. I tell them to be ready to fire questions at Simon about their future, but to be prepared for him to prevaricate. Dig out your contracts when you get home tonight, I say, so you get a clearer idea of where you stand. I promise to talk first to HR and, if I don't get any answers, to an employment lawyer who is a family friend. I promise to do everything I can on their behalf. Write references, recommend them to other editors, give them time off for interviews — whatever they need to get themselves sorted. "And remember, tonight we're going to get hammered. Until then, try and make it business as usual."

I leave them standing in forlorn clumps, like the wilted specimens on the last day of the Chelsea Flower Show. Back at my desk, I dial Jack.

"Jack Steele is either on the phone or with a client. Please leave your name, number and time of call and he will get back to you as soon as he's free."

"It's me, darling, with some not so good news for the new year. I've been put out to grass. Like the old mare that I am. Just like that. Try and call, but if I don't pick up it's because mayhem has broken out. I'm taking the whole team to Baz's Bar later, so if you want to join the wake, you'll know where to find us. Otherwise, I'll be home late — very late and very drunk. Tell Olly — and tell him I'm fine."

I've passed the first hurdle. I've not let my team down. I've not let myself down. Now what the hell am I supposed to do?

Thursday night is just as I knew it would be. Everyone gets rip-roaring, rat-arsed, out-of-their-brains, off-their-faces hammered. I know, these are not genteel descriptions for a woman of my age. They're not words I normally use to describe a state of inebriation — I pick up the cool vernacular from Olly and the kids but never use it for fear of shaming Olly to death — but, in the circumstances, rat-arsed sounds about right. I've told everyone who wants to invite their partners to do so. The thought of a giant, hormonal gathering of hens, with Saul and Cosmo muttering on the sidelines, is more than I can handle. As it is, the tears flow as freely as the champagne, girls hug girls and swear undying love for one another; and my fashion editor announces to the entire room that if only Cosmo would let her shag him once, he would convert to heterosexuality for life. Saul and Tanya get just a little too familiar in the corner (Saul's wife isn't here because she couldn't find a last-minute babysitter), but then it occurs to me that if Saul and Tanya are both going to be working for Mark they obviously have a lot to talk about.

I drink far less than I'd expected, determined to keep my wits about me. Jack arrives around eleven o'clock, looking haggard. "It's all right, darling, no one's died," I tell him brightly. "In fact we're having a lovely time." Tanya, Cosmo and Ally have just burst into a spontaneous rendition of "I Will Survive" and everyone else is whooping and Mexican waving.

"Jack," I whisper, feeling a wobbly moment coming on, "please don't say anything nice. I'm doing very well considering, but one nice word from you and I'll fall to pieces. What I really want right now is to go home to my bed."

"Our bed, sweetheart." Before the floodgates have time to open, Jack wraps an arm around me and leads me, as though I am an invalid, slowly up the stairs.

On Friday I go straight to HR to see what transfers might be possible. I email Mark to recommend Tanya to him, making no reference to our encounter in the lift. "Tanya's a great PA, the best I've ever had. Give it some thought, Hope." I call round some of the other editors in the company and some editors I know at other publishing houses. Then I brief Megan. In the afternoon, Tanya and I go through my office sorting things into chuck piles, Megan piles and take-home piles. I am on automatic pilot, responding but not feeling, reacting but not thinking. Better that way. Then the flowers start arriving, each new bouquet more stylishly sumptuous than the one before. Burgundy roses with winter berries from Estée Lauder. Chicly clashing tulips in reds, oranges and pinks from Lancôme. A succession of single orchids in ceramic pots from various fashion houses and PRs. It's called insurance. If I were to pitch up in another editor's seat in the near future, they would have already oiled the path to my office door. If I didn't turn up elsewhere, case dismissed. I'd never hear from them again.

The biggest bouquet of all comes from my publisher, the person responsible for the advertising and marketing strategy of the magazine. Janet is a good publisher, pragmatic and ambitious. And a terrific salesperson. She could sell a shop-windowful of cream cakes to a bunch of schoolgirl anorexics. Yes, that good. So flogging fiddly fondant fancy recipes to time-poor working mothers will be a cinch as far as Janet is concerned. I have neither the desire nor the strength to berate Janet for not keeping me in the picture about Simon's plans, which clearly she was in on. The difference between editors and publishers is that good editors love their magazines, they believe in them; for publishers it's just a job.

What I don't want to do is fill my home with these flowers. It would feel like being present at my own funeral. So I distribute the bouquets among the staff. Around 4.30, I am presented with my leaving card, or rather "the book of condolences" as Olly dubs it later. The art department has performed a miraculous artistic feat in next to no time, being far too hung-over to do any proper work. It's an album of images of my greatest moments, receiving awards, meeting various celebrities, curtseying to Princess Diana on the polo lawn at Windsor. And as is customary with these things, a mock-up of the front cover of the magazine with the departing member of staff as cover-girl. In this case, yours truly photo-shopped so heavily that I've almost morphed into Jennifer Aniston.

At 5p.m., I suggest everyone calls it a day, and the hugging and the kissing start all over again. I hang on by a thread. By 5.30, I am ready to leave, just me and Tanya to go. "Tanya, please don't say anything more. I may be old enough to be your mother, but I'm also young enough to be your friend if you'd like me to be. We can meet for coffee, you and James can come for dinner, and if Mark gives you trouble he'll have me to deal with."

"Oh, Hope . . . .?"

"Oh, Tanya, you soppy thing, come here and give me a hug."

I act almost normal over the weekend. After all, it is the weekend, and I wouldn't be at work anyway. The nights are tricky. Sex, of course, is out of the question. I don't think Jack is much in the mood himself to be honest. Sleep would have been out of the question too, but half a Zopiclone sends me straight into a blissful, dreamless eight-hour coma.

Olly is angelic. He takes me and Jack to a matinee of singalong *Grease* at the Prince Charles Cinema. Incredible how a 70s film about a bunch of American high-school kids in the 50s can stand the test of time. Olly and his generation are as big fans of the movie as our lot were. He played the Frankie Avalon part in a school version of the show last year, greased-back hair, padded-out front, totally hilarious. But I still think Olivia Newton-John's a drip: even dressed head to toe in leather for the finale she looks about as sexy as a bar of soap. Whereas Stockard Channing, as the plucky

Rizzo — what a great girl. From now on Rizzo will be my role model.

"Greased Lightning". "Summer Nights". "There are Worse Things I Can Do". For 110 glorious minutes I forget fifty, I forget being fired, I even forget my sweaty legs. And when we go for a Chinese in Soho after the movie, I keep the conversation strictly neutral. Every time I'm tempted to mention Vanessa the Undresser, I shovel a mound of rice into my mouth, and chew and chew and chew until the temptation goes away.

Jack agrees to field all phone calls for me, except for any from my sister Sarah, or my friend Maddy. My sister is psychic where I'm concerned, and she's already suspicious.

"Something's up, isn't it? I can tell," she says when she rings on Saturday morning. All I've said is "Hello."

"Everything's fine," I reply. "I'm just grumpy about being so old."

"Fine means not fine," she says. "Whenever you use that word I know you're not fine at all."

"Just shut it, Sarah. Just this once. Give me a break. OK?"

Now she can be absolutely certain that I'm keeping something from her. But she'll have to live with it until I'm ready to talk.

I tell Sarah everything (usually), and I tell my friend Madeleine almost everything, but her sister is in a hospice, dying of melanoma that has spread to her bones, and the last thing she needs to hear about is my troubles. So when she calls we just talk about the party and catch up on her sister.

Whenever anyone else rings, Jack tells them I am out. In fact, I am curled up in the corner of the sofa in my dressing gown, aimlessly plucking hairs from my legs, my fingernails standing in as tweezers. It's tricky at first, but with practice you soon get the hang of it.

Sunday is a write-off. I lie in bed until 10 a.m., staring at the ceiling. I wash my hair and iron tea towels in the basement. Ironing tea towels, I find, is extremely therapeutic. The rest of the ironing I leave to my cleaner, but tea towels are my personal province. I listen to *The Archers* omnibus, then leaf without much interest through the papers. In normal circumstances, I'd be scrutinising them intently, circling stories with magic marker for ripping out later in the day, when Jack and Olly have done with them. Although I'm not sure Olly ever gets past the sports section.

And that's about it. I try starting to read *The Little Friend*, Donna Tartt's first book for ten years since her bestselling *The Secret History*. But it's a terminally depressing story about a twelve-year-old girl determined to avenge the death of her older brother who was found hanging from a tree in the family yard. I snap it decisively shut. The most decisive thing I've done all day.

Olly announces he is going out. "Out anywhere in particular?" I ask casually.

"Just out," he replies. Images of Olly being suffocated by Vanessa the Undresser's enormous bosoms float across my vision. Jack tries to get me to talk to him, but for once I am all talked out. I hit the vodka bottle. Jack goes to the study, sits at his computer and hits Google. I manage to down three big ones, neat, except for ice, before falling awkwardly asleep with my head scrunched up in the corner of the couch.

By the time I wake up with a cricked neck at 1 a.m., Jack is in bed. I creep upstairs so as not to wake him. Passing the closed door of Olly's bedroom, I wrap my hand round the doorknob and start to slowly turn it. *He's seventeen, Hope,* I chide myself. *Home or not home, it has nothing to do with you.* I hold on to the doorknob, then slowly, reluctantly, unwrap my hand. Redundant editor, redundant mother. All I need to hear now is that Jack is having an affair. Then I can be a redundant wife as well.

Neighbourhood Watch

I used to think Bob Geldof had got it wrong. When I was working I absolutely loved Mondays. Couldn't wait to start the week, although I looked forward to weekends as well. My life was like a sandwich. Weekdays were the bread, two sturdy slices of healthy wholemeal on the outside, protecting the weekend, that delicious, indulgent filling in the middle. But the thing about a sandwich is that even if the filling is the best bit, it wouldn't be a sandwich without the bread for support. Without the bread as ballast, the filling would lose its form and its lustre. Without the filling for contrast, the bread would become prosaic, necessary but dull. Now weekdays and weekends are indistinguishable: now it's all bread, or all filling, depending on your point of view. But definitely no longer a sandwich. And in my case, just a stale old loaf. I miss my old life as a sandwich and have no idea if I'll ever get it back. Or even, which strikes me as strange and disconcerting, if I want it back.

There are certain things I've learned since giving up work. I should say since work gave me up. For a start, the world is full of other people who don't work, at least not during daylight. Young people, old people, in-between people. Everywhere you go there are people *not* working. After twenty-eight years of slogging full-time in an office, I find this a revelation.

Hundreds of thousands of them are out there, millions for all I know, buying stuff they don't need and, because they're not working, probably can't afford. Chatting casually in cafes, arms resting on the back of banquettes as if settling in indefinitely. And I thought you were *meant* to knock your coffee back in one gulp, coat still on, then leap up and out of the door quicker than you can say double espresso. I've even witnessed people reading newspapers at a leisurely pace, story by story, one at a time. This is all so new to me. I used to whizz through three broadsheets and three tabloids quicker than a virus scanner. I was all done in the time it takes these people to read the front-page headlines.

There's *loads* of pre-watershed violence and swearing going on. It's women mostly, threatening small toddlers and large dogs, usually both at the same time.

Another thing I've noticed is men loitering up against lamp posts, talking into mobiles cradled in the crook of their necks and making weird hand signals to other lamp-post loiterers further down the road. I'm not sure if this is a national phenomenon. I live on the borders of Kilburn, and Kilburn is teeming with loiterers. I suppose it could be work they're doing, just not the kind of work I'm familiar with.

Kilburn is also home to the sleight-of-hand merchants. Now these cool young dudes in shiny sportswear are definitely doing some kind of work, but I don't think they get PAYE slips at the end of the month. They have this way of skimming by one another, in an arcane version of pass the parcel, only in this case the parcel's so small as to be invisible to the average passer-by. Funny what you notice when you stop running. It's even crossed my mind that I could retrain as a narc. Well-dressed, fifty-year-old woman. They'd never suspect.

Where I actually live is West Hampstead. Or South Hampstead, as estate agents have recently attempted — and failed — to rename it, in a bid to rid the area of its student-bedsit image, an image which is at least twenty years out of date. But there does remain something determinedly scruffy about the area, as though the locals had banded together and made a populist proclamation to disdain gentrification. And this despite the area's broad leafy streets, and huge houses ranging from elegant, early Victorian white stucco to the comfortably sprawling Edwardian villas built for middle-class professionals. Nowhere is West Hampstead's indifference to going upscale more pronounced than in West End Lane, a high street with about as much charisma as Delia Smith demonstrating how to boil an egg. Which is why I tend to venture further afield for my investigations into the strange new world of people not chained to a desk.

I'm starting to feel at home in grotty, gritty Kilburn with its pound shops, bingo halls, and Irish pubs, and the recent fashion phenomenon that is Primark. Primark is where you hand over twenty pounds, leave the shop with two head-to-toe outfits that are dead ringers for Marc Jacobs, and then spend the rest of the day feeling guilty about the worker exploitation required to produce decent clothes for so little money. Or so people tell me. My shopping urge has gone the way of my sex drive.

Before this latest instalment of my life, Kilburn was an area I avoided like avian flu. What I like best of all about Kilburn now is that you don't have to dress up for it. Hampstead and St John's Wood, my other local stomping grounds, are a different matter altogether. A lot more effort is required in terms of grooming (French manicures *de rigueur*), but the people-watching is equally fascinating. In Hampstead, the only people who loiter are the traffic wardens. Traffic wardens do great business in Hampstead. The place is teeming with yummy mummies who overrun their meter time, being unavoidably detained in Whistles or Carluccio's. When Olly was born, yummy mummies hadn't been invented. Mummies went back to work, and did something called juggling. Some still do, but not this lot, that's for sure.

You'd never believe these women had borne babies at all from their model-perfect bodies, air-brushed faces and shiny, flicky hair. But you do know they're mothers because they're sitting in Carluccio's, on their mobiles, and issuing instructions to their au pairs about what Skye or Mia or Orlando should be having for lunch. Since most of these lunches seem to consist of jars of ready-made mush, organic of course, I'm not sure why the au pairs can't be left to decide between the chicken and rice or the turkey and carrot on their own. I used to let Olly's nannies make lots of their own decisions. Which is how Olly became an early prison visitor, when one nanny decided to take him along when she went to visit her boyfriend, who was doing three years for armed robbery. She told the prison officers that Olly was her son, and her boyfriend the father. I found out because the nanny told one of the other nannies, who told her boss, who told me.

Meanwhile, sitting alone at the next table pretending to read the *Guardian*, I feel like an interloper in a warren of chic rabbits, all nibbling happily on rocket leaves with just a touch of balsamic, while I clumsily tuck into scrambled eggs with bacon, field mushrooms and fried tomatoes.

At Waterstone's you get a different crowd. Yummy mummies not really being the reading type. It's always busy in Waterstone's, even mid-week, but I reckon that's because there are so many authors living in Hampstead who spend their days anxiously checking up on how their books are selling. I only know they're authors because I keep overhearing them telling the sales assistants that they'd be more than happy to sign some of their unsold copies as a gesture of goodwill. I wonder when they actually get down to any writing.

When all other activities are exhausted, I head for St John's Wood High Street. If St John's Wood had been used as a template for multicultural society by the likes of Bush, Blair and Saddam Hussein, the term "clash of

63

civilisations" would never have been invented. Here's where rich Arabs, rich Jews and rich Americans live side by side in perfect harmony, triple-parking their Mercs, their SUVs and their Aston Martins with total disregard for the law and East — West politics. Just moments away are a couple of synagogues, the Regent's Park mosque and the American school, a melting pot of wealth and cultural mores. Admittedly, the school and the synagogues are swarming with security guards, which is understandable in these uncertain times, and the mosque may well be fomenting terrorists in its basement. But, any day of the week, pop into Panzers, the local deli cum greengrocer, where a single lettuce can set you back four quid, and all seems right with the world and its warring factions. St John's Wood women certainly don't work.

Yes, I've had a lot of time on my hands this last month. Noticing things around me and eavesdropping are about as much as I can handle. Right now I'm sitting in the Coffee Cup, a Hampstead coffee shop of the old school, one that smells of grease and cigarette smoke as it's supposed to. I'm munching on the first of three slices of extremely buttery raisin toast. That Topshop size 10 I said I could still fit into? Let's call it a 12.

I take a book out of my bag. *Feeling Good: The New Mood Therapy*, by someone called David D. Burns, MD. I picked it off the shelf at home, although I can't ever remember buying it, so it was probably sent to the magazine for review. It promises "a drugfree cure for anxiety, guilt, pessimism, procrastination, low self-esteem and other 'black holes' of depression". I don't know whether it can cure me, but it certainly knows exactly how I feel.

The bit I'm hooked on at the moment is the Beck Depression Inventory. It's a kind of quiz that can rate your mood and diagnose the presence and severity of depression. Each question has four possible answers, scoring 0, 1, 2 or 3, depending on the answer you choose. The higher you score the worse you are in terms of psychological health. I do this quiz every other day, which I'm sure is not the idea at all. It's stopping me reading past page twenty-three. I'm certainly suffering mood swings, and I was definitely in need of professional treatment a couple of days ago, according to Beck's Inventory. I've cheated a bit today, so I'm more borderline than off the scale.

I genuinely think this is a very useful quiz, but it's not infallible. On the question of food, for example, if you have completely lost your appetite, you score a 3. This would suggest a low mood. On the other hand, if your appetite is no worse than usual, you score 0, which is a good sign. But there's no score at all for someone like me, who didn't have time to eat before, and now is completely ravenous twenty-four/seven. Seven pounds! Seven pounds I've put on since 1 January.

"More raisin toast, please," I say to the waitress as she passes.

I also scored well on the suicide section. I agreed with the statement, "I don't have thoughts of killing myself" (thus scoring another healthy zero), versus the statement, "I would kill myself if I had the chance" (score 3). But I could have done with an option which read, "I don't want to kill myself, but there is someone else I'd like to kill." Like Simon. This Beck really knows his stuff, he's a world authority on mood disorders, so why, if I now know I'm not especially depressed, do I feel so — well, depressed is the only way I can think to describe it?

A lot has happened in the last month, not to me but to those around me. Olly is definitely hanging out with Vanessa. I suppose she's every FHM fantasy come true. A bit chav in her pink trackie suits with Ugg boots, bare midriff and back handles. Blonde hair pulled back *à la* Croydon facelift. Cleavage and Tiffany silver heart necklace. Olly's into the Indie band grunge look — early Pete Doherty in skinny jeans and an Oxfam shop T-shirt. More Glastonbury than bling. And he's such a twig that you fear he might break if you squeeze him too hard. I hope she's gentle with him. Vanessa's certainly had a lot of experience, and I just have to accept the fact that she's sharing it with my boy. Jack thinks it's hilarious. I just worry that Olly's looking wasted and not revising for his A levels.

"How's the coursework going?" I asked him at breakfast this morning.

"Mum, I'm reading the sport."

"I can see that, but how's the coursework going?"

"What coursework?"

"All of it — English, history, French. I thought it all had to be done by now."

"Actually, it has all been done. And now do you mind if I read the newspaper?"

"Oh, sorry. I mean, that's marvellous. Why didn't you tell me?"

"Why should I? It's *my* coursework, isn't it?"

"I only asked. Is it really necessary to be so rude all the time?"

"Well, you keep asking me the same questions, again and again. It's like *Groundhog Day* in this house. Maybe you should be looking for a new job. Are you looking for a new job?"

"Actually, not at the moment."

"Well, maybe you should."

"I promise you'll be the first to know. Just one more thing and I'll leave you alone, I swear. Could you *please* tidy your room this evening after school. There's so much stuff lying around that I can't even get through the door."

"Exactly as intended. You're not supposed to get through the door."

I hate this constant sniping. I know I'm an incessant nag. I know Olly needs to separate from me and that if he doesn't he'll turn into a mass murderer when he's thirty-five. I know it's normal. But I just can't accept it. It really hurts.

"Look, I'm not nearly as awful as you make out." This is pathetic, I know. "Have I even once asked you about Vanessa?" I can't believe I'm doing this. "Have I even hinted that going out with a woman almost twice your age might not be such a bright idea . . ."

Damn it, damn it, shit, bugger and damn it. Now I've totally blown it. Me and my big bloody mouth.

Madeleine's younger sister, Ruth, died, as expected. She was just forty-one. Madeleine was so brave at her funeral. If Sarah were to die, I think I'd die too. I certainly wouldn't be brave.

The funeral took place at the Hoop Lane crematorium. Ruth's twin sons, aged six, flanked their father, Ed, sitting bolt upright, one hand in each of his throughout the service. Until he stood, went up to the podium and read *Farewell, Sweet Dust* by Elinor Wylie:

Now I have lost you, I must scatter
All of you on the air henceforth;
Not that to me it can ever matter
But it's only fair to the rest of earth.

Now especially, when it is winter
And the sun's not half so bright as he was,
Who wouldn't be glad to find a splinter
That once was you, in the frozen grass?

Snowflakes, too, will be softer feathered,
Clouds, perhaps, will be whiter plumed;
Rain, whose brilliance you caught and gathered,
Purer silver have reassumed.

Farewell, sweet dust; I was never a miser:
Once, for a minute, I made you mine:

Now you are gone, I am none the wiser
But the leaves of the willow are bright as wine.

We all wept. And while we were weeping, to my teary-eyed astonishment, Olly passed by me in the aisle clutching his acoustic guitar. He sat down on a stool at the front, fixed his gaze in the middle distance, adjusted his strings and began to play "Thank You", Dido's first hit single. It's the chorus everyone remembers. The sweet simplicity of it: "I want to thank you for giving me the best day of my life."

I was moved, and I was amazed. Olly had babysat for the boys, at least once a week, from the age of fourteen to sixteen. I knew he thought Ruth and Ed were pretty cool, and he'd sometimes just pop in to see them to discuss new bands he'd discovered and thought they might enjoy. But I had no idea Ruth meant so much to him. I suppose he considered her as a friend rather than a parent figure, and she was the first person that close to him who had died. By the time Olly reached the second chorus, everyone was joining in.

Maddy, my BF, who is divorced, no kids, was sitting next to me. She was too dazed to be distraught. When the service came to an end, she whispered urgently in my ear: "I have to talk to you, Hope. Alone."

"Let's go round to the garden at the back. Everyone else will be gathering out front so we should be able to find a quiet spot. Be back in five," I said to Jack, who was sitting on my other side.

There was a bench, and we sat on it. Maddy immediately broke down.

"That was so beautiful," I said. "Ruth was so loved, and she knew it, even at the end. You'll be a rock for the boys, I know you will. And for Ed too."

Maddy sniffed and tried to speak, her voice barely above a whisper.

"I'm so wicked. So wicked. I will never be able to live with myself."

"What are you talking about? Wicked? What's with wicked? You need a large brandy when we get back to Ed's."

"But that's just it. I can't go back to Ed's. I can't go back to Ed's or see the children ever again."

"Please, Maddy, you're not making sense. You're still in shock. Of course you can see Ed and the children. They'll need you more than ever now."

"I loved her so much, and I betrayed her. Can't you see what a terrible thing I've done?"

"What terrible thing, Maddy? You were there for her; all the time you were there for her."

When she next spoke, Maddy's voice sounded different, cold and hard.

"Not after lights out in the hospice, I wasn't. Not when I was staying over at Ed's to help out with the boys and make sure they got to school in the morning. Not when I was staying in the spare room. Or rather not staying in the spare room and sleeping in Ed's bed, fucking my brother-in-law while my beloved sister was dying. That's what I mean by wicked, Hope. Do you get it now?"

"I, I . . . Jesus, Maddy, what am I supposed to say? I just don't know what to think. But I do know you're coming back to Ed's right now, for the sake of the boys. And if I have to tie you up and bundle you into the boot of my car to get you there, that's exactly what I'm going to do." I grabbed her, not at all gently, by the arm, and practically dragged her down the pathway to the car park. "In!" I demanded when we reached the car, and gave her a little shove towards the back seat. "Over here, Jack," I shouted, slamming the door on Maddy and waving at him across the car park.

When he got to the car, I simply said, "Maddy was feeling a bit too wobbly to face everyone. She'll be OK by the time we're all back at the house."

It's Friday night. The gathering of the clans for the start-of-Sabbath family dinner. Sarah and I take it in turns to share this task since my mother decided — about fifteen years back — that life was too short to chop liver and onions. In fact, she has given up cooking altogether since discovering her local Dial-a-Dinner. From Chinese, Indian and Italian to British cod and chips, there is no cuisine from anywhere in the world that can't be delivered by a boy on a motorbike within thirty minutes of ordering, and served straight out of nice, shiny aluminium cartons. "If you add up the time I save in shopping and cooking and washing up, and calculate what I could get paid for those hours, you will come to realise that takeaways are far more economical than doing it yourself."

"Yes, Mummy," I replied the first time she expounded the Jenny Lyndhurst Theory of Domestic

Economy, "but you don't actually have a job or a pay packet, so your theory doesn't really work."

"I gave up work, if you remember," said my mother frostily, "to look after you and your sister, so you wouldn't have to be poor little latchkey children. Sometimes your ingratitude beggars belief."

"But, Mummy, I'm not criticising you for not working. I'm just questioning your theory in light of the fact that you don't get paid anyway."

"My theory makes perfect sense. You're so literal, Hope, you need to look at the broader picture. Daddy has always said that I have a great head for business. Whether or not I work is beside the point. And in any case, Daddy and I are so enriched from having developed our taste buds over the years. There is life beyond roast chicken, you know. With such traditional attitudes, Hope, it amazes me how you can be so successful in such a fast-moving world as the magazine industry."

There's no use arguing with my mother. She never did make sense and never will do. Although, in retrospect, and in view of my recent professional demise, her criticism verges on the prescient. But give up work for Sarah and me she did not; she gave up working as a salesgirl in Harrods the day she married my father in 1949, when she was nineteen.

My mother fancies herself as a bit of an artist, a bit of a Bloomsbury person. Instead of work, she has *projects*. And instead of making any sense, she has style and an air of expensive dishevelment. The fact that her projects never come to anything doesn't seem to bother my father one bit, but it bothers me a lot, and probably accounts for why I'm so fixated on seeing things through.

Sometimes her projects would involve the entire family. When we were small, I think I was about five, there was the summer-of-the-stately-home project, when we were dragged round all the grand houses of England, forced to ooh and aah at bits of old porcelain and swords and hedges shaped like swans. One stately home might have been fun. Seventeen in six weeks?

Then there was the actress project. For about a year, my mother went to classes at something called the Actor's Space. She gave up all pretence at normal conversation and took to quoting Shakespeare over dinner. When my father bought her a bunch of roses, she declared, predictably, "A rose by any other name would smell as sweet." But then she added, "So from now on in this household we're going to call them thistles." And from then on — and even now — she has always referred to roses as thistles.

This may be funny for all I know — my school friends thought she was hilarious — but believe me, it's not easy to live with.

Her sense of style, though, is indisputable. As are her good looks. Her hair used to be as fair as mine was dark — I inherit my swarthiness from my father's gene pool. When her hair changed colour with age it didn't go the dull grey of industrial scaffolding like mine, exposing ugly metallic roots, but segued seamlessly from fair to brilliant white. If I didn't dye my hair I'd look about a hundred; my mother turned white, and it was barely

73

noticeable. When I was a child she looked like Gwyneth Paltrow in dress-down mode, and favoured floppy hats, and crocheted tops and peasant skirts. Now she shops only in Egg, a little boutique in Knightsbridge, and looks like a rather chic monk, in layers of linens that twist and tie and drape and cost a bomb, and has cropped white hair which suits her still well-defined cheekbones.

My father does his own thing a lot of the time and leaves my mother to do hers — for him it used to be work, golf, bridge, *The Times* crossword and reading; now he's retired, it's golf, bridge, *The Times* crossword, reading, the Internet and gardening — but when they're in each other's company they're like newly-weds. If he's not touching her arm, or planting little kisses on the side of her face or on the top of her head, he's praising the way she looks. "As beautiful as the day I met her," he's prone to saying. "And such style." When they leave my house, I watch them walking down the street towards their car, hand in hand. Of course it drives me demented. It's not normal. Look at me and Jack.

On Friday nights there's always quite a crowd. This Friday it's Jack, Olly and me; Sarah and William and Sam, their youngest (Jessica and Amanda are away at college); Anita and Rupert; Jenny and Abe; and Maddy.

I suppose I'm more Jew-ish than Jewish. Not at all religious, but I find ritual reassuring and relish the sense of continuity it brings. So I'll light the two candles and say the Sabbath prayer in Hebrew, words I've learned by rote but couldn't translate. And then each person will kiss everyone else and wish them a good Shabbat. And then I'll cut the chollah bread and then we'll eat.

It would have been so easy to let things go when my mother gave up cooking, but it's the only time the family really gets together. My mum's seventy-three now, so I suppose pushing sixty was a fair enough age to hand on the Friday-night mantle. But I resent her having done so all the same. She's in perfectly good health and has little else that's pressing to do with her time as far as I can see, although she always purports to be extremely busy, what with the t'ai chi and the life-drawing class and all the holidays she and Abe have to plan.

The truth is that my mother barely has to open her mouth to wind me up and turn me into an instantly petulant child. Sarah's so much more forgiving than I am. She's grounded and sane and sensible and just lets everything my mother says wash right over her. I'm neurotic and nasty. It has occurred to me that maybe I have exactly the same effect on Olly as my mother does on me, but I regularly pray — yes, I really do pray, although it's less a conversation with God than a cry in the dark — that with Olly and me it's just a teen thing he's going through. I try and take comfort from the fact that Olly and I remained umbilically attached until he was at least ten. With me and my mother, it has been like civil war from the very beginning.

I serve up the usual. Chicken soup with lokshen (that's noodles in English), and knaidlach, which is a kind of dumpling made with matzah meal; roast chicken with crispy roast potatoes, broccoli, peas and lots of oniony gravy. Followed by apple and blackberry crumble with ice cream. My father murmurs his appreciation. "So nice to have a good roast." I take particular pleasure in this, certain that he prefers my home-cooking to my mother's international takeaways.

"Last night we had something called Bali Hi, and I choked on some peanuts. Mind you, it was delicious, wasn't it, dear?"

"Not Bali Hi, Abe, Pad Thai. I think you do it on purpose." My mother giggles, skittishly. Unbelievable! I could swear she's flirting with her husband of fifty-five years. My dad looks at her like a smitten young suitor, taking away the advantage I scored with the simple, wholesome roast chicken.

"Pad Thai, you must all try it if you haven't already," my mother continues, as if opening up a whole world of exotic possibilities to the assembled crowd. "And, yes, it was delicious. We've discovered this marvellous new restaurant that's opened locally and Dial-a-Dinner are featuring it as their restaurant of the month." My father grins back at her as if he's the luckiest man in the world.

"Anyone going on the march tomorrow?" asks Olly.

"I should hope not," says Anita.

"Why's that?" asks Jack.

"Because, quite clearly, if you are against the war you are for Saddam Hussein. It's that simple. Isn't that so, Rupert?"

"Yes, dear."

"Oh, dear," says my mother. "I was planning on going on a little shopping expedition to Knightsbridge tomorrow. Perhaps not such a good idea after all. Do you think I'd get through? Will the march be very big?"

"Could be as many as a hundred thousand, according to the news," says Jack. "Hope, Maddy and I will be there, though we'll probably head straight for the rally in Hyde Park, rather than walk the distance with the crowd."

Anita sighs loudly. Rupert wrinkles his nose as though a bad smell has just wafted by. I look at Olly. He looks pleased at Jack's response. I want to say to Olly, "Be careful." I don't. Instead, I casually ask, "Who are you going with?"

"There's a bunch of about twenty from my year. We're all meeting up in Camden first."

That's a relief. I didn't think Vanessa would be up for it. She doesn't have the right shoes for marching.

"Anyone for more crumble?"

About five hands shoot up; they're like a bunch of enthusiastic school kids. If I'm catering for ten I make enough for twenty. It's a simple enough calculation.

"Sarah? William? Sam? What about you?"

"March or crumble?" says William.

"Both."

"March not possible," says William. "We're invited to lunch with friends in St Albans. And, in any case, the jury's still out as far as I'm concerned. I'm undecided, and I'm certainly not ready to engage in an all-out protest. But I'm definitely up for more crumble."

"Pass your plate. Maddy, you need fattening up."

She looks so pale and thin and sad, though she's trying desperately hard not to let her emotions show.

"Mum," says Olly, "I'm meeting Ravi. Mind if I go in a minute?"

Before I can answer, my mother launches in.

"There's something I need to tell you all," she announces, pushing aside the remnants of pudding and lighting a cigarette. My mother is the only person Jack officially allows to smoke inside the house. The deal is that she brings her own ashtray.

"I could take each of you off into a corner and tell you one at a time and try to break it to you gently, but what would be the point? What's got to be said has got to be said." And then she coughs. The coughing goes on for a full minute.

Oh, no, not again, I think, waiting for the cough to subside. Not some new bandwagon that she's about to jump on. Last time I saw her she was rabbiting on about the Kabbalah, having read an article in the *Daily Mail*. And tonight she's sporting one of those mangy little red thread bracelets that the Kabbalah people wear to ward off the evil eye or some such mumbo-jumbo. Or perhaps she's decided to take daddy off to an ashram in India.

My father, sitting next to her — as he always does — squeezes her hand supportively.

She has stopped coughing. "I'm dying," she says, without a trace of tremor in her voice. "Six months at most. Nothing interesting or original, just cancer. First,

Maddy's poor sister, now me. This cancer business has got quite out of hand. It's my own fault, of course."

I find I can't chew the crumble that's in my mouth. At first it was delicious, now it just sits there, gloopy and sticky, like newly mixed cement. I can't swallow it, but neither can I spit it out.

Instead of shock or sorrow, what goes through my head is this: *Trust my mother to make a spectacle of herself. To put herself centre stage as usual. To turn the whole thing into a performance as if she's Meryl Streep in a Hollywood weepie.*

My own mother has just announced she's dying and this is how I react. It's disgusting, I know. I look at my father, who's opposite me. His eyes are watery with age, but with tears too.

I want to race round the table and take him in my arms to comfort him. To tell him that it will be all right. That I'll take care of him. I look at my mother and feel oddly empty. Who is this dying woman I hardly know?

At the back of my mind I'd always had this idea that one day my mother and I would sit down and talk and talk and talk and I'd ask all the questions that I so desperately craved answers to. Like, why haven't you ever loved me? Why haven't you ever supported me? Why haven't you ever taken an interest in Olly? Why have you always been the centre of your own universe? Why, if daddy was the only person who ever mattered to you, did you have children? And the answers would make some kind of sense. And the difficulties between us would be resolved, and the distance bridged, and closure — as the therapists say — would be reached. But now, none of that is going to happen. The mother I never had will simply die. And that's something else I will have to come to terms with in the year of turning fifty.

Maddy, being the doctor in the house, asks sensible questions. The rest of us are incapable of saying anything coherent. We learn that scans have revealed a large tumour on her lung. My mother has smoked thirty a day since she was a teenager. When Sarah and I were young, we didn't know that smoking was bad for you. We just used to laugh along with my father when she drew one of her chic Du Maurier cigarettes from their distinctive red packet, and join in his chanting: *It's not the cough that carries you off, it's the coffin they carry you off in.*

Despite what you read about smoking ravaging your skin, my mother looks ten years younger than her age. Recently, however, she has had a persistent cough. The tumour, which is called a non-small cell cancer, is already very advanced, and the cancer has also spread into the chest wall and the oesophagus. Palliative radio-therapy is about the most the medics can offer.

"I took your mother to the doctor as soon as we got back from South Africa," says my father, "but she didn't want to worry any of you until she knew for sure."

This is a side of my mother I've not seen. The side that wants to shield us from unnecessary concern, to avoid burdening us with her problems. My mother has never held back from complaining before. But maybe it's always been small things she's made a big fuss about. Inconsequential stuff, like the impossibility of getting a decent cleaner or the appalling seat pitch in economy on long-haul flights.

Sarah walks round the table to my mother. "I want to hold you," she says simply. And does. She always knows the right thing to do. When she lets go, Sam does the same and, looking awkward and upset, Olly follows suit. I stay where I am. My mother draws deeply on her cigarette. "That's enough of that. Let's change the subject."

I start gathering up the pudding plates. Olly says his goodbyes and leaves. Anita and Rupert file reports from their absent children. For once, Anita rushes around being helpful, offering to make teas and coffees.

Soon they all start to leave. I find it so hard to touch my mother spontaneously, so I get her coat down from the peg and help her into it from behind, it's the nearest to physical contact I can manage. She starts to button herself up. "Let me do that for you," I say. But my hands are shaking, and I fumble with the buttons, prolonging the process. My mother pulls away impatiently. "I'm not dead yet, Hope," she says, then reaches out her arm and cups her hand around my cheek and chin.

"Oh, Mummy," I say, as the tears begin to pour down my cheeks, "please don't die."

"Don't be such a baby, Hope, my love," she says. "You're fifty, for heaven's sake. And how many women are lucky enough to reach the age of fifty and still have two living parents? And think of the upside. Now you'll have Daddy all to yourself. Come on, Abe, I'm exhausted."

The Best-laid Plans

Get Maddy back on track
Talk to Daddy about the future
Try and square things with Mummy before she dies
Make it up with Olly
Have sex with Jack — or at least dinner and a movie

I wrote this list at three o'clock this morning. I'm trying
to wean myself off the pills, but no Zopiclone means no
sleep. Since January, without the help of a little something
to induce a reasonable approximation of a coma, I barely
doze off before jerking awake with my heart knocking
wildly against my chest, clamouring to escape. Jack
assures me it is anxiety, rather than an incipient heart
attack. But I don't find this especially reassuring. Anxiety
feeds itself. And serious or not, the palpitations are
frightening. They can strike half a dozen times before I
eventually pass out properly, around 3 a.m., sometimes
even later. Which is why last night I decided to cut my
losses and get up, make myself a mug of Ovaltine, and
do something constructive. Hence the list.

I'm definitely in denial about work, and I need an
outlet for my pent-up energy. For the first few weeks

after getting fired I would compulsively check my answering machine and my emails after being out, even if I'd only popped out to the postbox for two minutes. Now I don't bother with either. The offers haven't exactly been flooding in since January, or even trickling in. I glance cursorily at the *Guardian* media pages on a Monday — there are lots of magazine jobs going in the United Arab Emirates. I'm thinking more Soho Square or maybe Mayfair. It's not urgent, at least as far as money's concerned. A big fat cheque has gone into my bank account, and my firing has been fiddled to look like redundancy so I'm entitled to a substantial tax-free sum on the pay-out. As long as I don't start buying bling or playing poker on the Internet for large stakes, I'm financially fine for the time being. Work can wait. There are more important things to think about right now.

At 3a.m., the list looked like the perfect antidote to anxiety — something that would give me back a sense of purpose, and prove what a good friend slash daughter slash mother slash lover I could really be. Reading it again at nine in the morning, the list looks preposterous, the wish-list of a woman with seriously deranged hormones — or maybe Pollyanna. I'm no longer confident of completing one of these tasks successfully. And even dinner and a movie's looking a bit of a long shot from where I'm sitting. None of which stops me getting straight on the phone.

"Maddy, how about supper at Mario's, just you and me, Wednesday, eight o'clock?"

Maddy hesitates.

"Hope, I'm not sure. It's late-night surgery on Wednesday, and I'm exhausted. And as you know, I'm pretty useless company at the moment."

"That makes two of us. I'll book."

"Daddy, it's me. Hope. How about a round of golf? I'll be your caddy, just like I was when I was eleven."

"That would be wonderful, but I can't manage more than nine holes any more. And in any case, I don't want to be away from Mummy for too long. Not with her so poorly."

I have this problem with my father. I think he's invincible. I don't want to hear him saying *I can't manage more than nine holes any more*. It means he's getting old, something I steadfastly refuse to acknowledge, even though he's eighty-one. When I think of my dad on the golf course, I think of Jack Nicklaus. When I imagine him playing a game of bridge, I visualise Omar Sharif. In the days when he mixed a mean Martini, I used to think Sean Connery as James Bond. In other words, my father is my hero. He hasn't really even done anything to warrant his hero status, other than be kind and clever and not at all like my mother. You don't want your heroes to have faults, so you don't look for them, and consequently you don't find them. My dad's my hero, free of flaws, and that's that.

"Mummy," I ask, "shall we send Daddy to the golf club for a game of bridge?"

"Good idea, he needs some time off from me, but he's so reluctant to leave me on my own. You and Sarah might have to take it in turns to baby-sit." Her voice is hoarse, has a rasping edge to it. "Will you get me some

Elizabeth Arden eight-hour cream and a Dior lipstick in Cointreau? I'm running out."

Running out of time, I think, but, extraordinary though it is, not running out of steam. My mother's vanity has not forsaken her, which I suppose is a signal of her inner strength. I've been wandering round looking like a bag lady since the beginning of January.

"I'll bring them. No problem. How are you feeling?"

She coughs.

Nearly all set. What can I offer Olly? An apology? Money? I'd better tread carefully with Olly; I don't want to make things worse than they already are. Perhaps best to say and do nothing, just wait as long as it takes for his general disdain and disappointment in me to pass. I'm afraid I may have to wait longer than I can cope with. Patience may be a virtue, but it's not one of mine.

That evening I greet Jack with a copy of *Time Out*.

"We haven't been to a movie in months."

"You haven't wanted to."

"But now I do."

"OK. Great. Look up that new French film, the thriller, the one that opens next week. I think it's on in Russell Square. Do you fancy that?"

No, I do not fancy that. I bite my lip. I do like French movies, but I generally prefer Hollywood or Working Title rom-coms with Hugh Grant. And I like thrillers, but not when they're claiming to be intellectual as well, which this one is almost bound to do.

"Sure, I'll call the cinema. Shall we go to the seven o'clock performance, and then afterwards maybe we can go for a Japanese?"

"Japanese or that new steak place?"

This is marriage for you. If I'd fancied the new steak place I would have suggested it, and I wouldn't have suggested the Japanese. But it is supposed to be his treat, not mine, and I'm building bridges.

"Steak sounds good. I think it's called Rib-Eye. I'll look it up and book."

This has to be better than moping. The planning has gone to plan. But it's a long way from successful execution.

I arrive early at Mario's because I fancy a little pre-dinner flirtation and because frankly I don't have much else to do. I even make an effort with my appearance for the first time in two months. My hair is washed and blow-dried, I'm wearing hipster Earl jeans with a wide leather belt, a vest top under a tight-fitting, bright pink V-neck cashmere sweater and pointy, kitten-heeled boots. Fashionable but not flash. Suitable for a woman of fifty? Now that I'm half a stone (OK, nine pounds) heavier, I have my doubts. The extra pounds cause my vest and my sweater to part with the top of my jeans. It is not deliberate. But it probably is disgusting.

"Hope, you make my night." Mario is upon me before I'm even properly through the door. He doesn't seem at all disgusted. He kisses me enthusiastically on each cheek and then squeezes me in a bear hug.

It's early, and the place is still almost empty.

"Sofia," he shouts into the ether, "Sofia, it's Hope. Bring the hummus and the pitta. And a bottle of her favourite retsina from Kourtaki. Be quick."

"You really shouldn't treat Sofia like a slave," I tell him. "Where would you be without her?"

"Without Sofia and her hummus, I would probably still be herding goats. With her I am a happy man. But with you, I could go straight to heaven."

I love this corny stuff that goes on between the two of us, and probably between Mario and most of his other female customers. Sofia puts up with it because it's good for business, and she knows she's the boss and that Mario would never leave her and the children. Mario flirting in his restaurant is Ealing comedy meets *Zorba the Greek*.

A super-sized Sofia appears looking hot and bothered.

"Good to see you, Hope . . . it has been too long. But only my husband has time to talk. I only have time to work." With the inside of her wrist she flicks back a thick slick of dark, wiry hair from her damp forehead, wipes both her hands on her apron, and stomps back towards the kitchen, her substantial bottom quivering as it goes. I tuck straight in. Sofia's hummus, spiked with charcoal-roasted red peppers and fresh coriander, makes me see blue. Santorini blue. The bluest blue in the Mediterranean. The wine, which most of my friends would sneer at, tastes like a bracing walk in a pine forest.

88

"Delicious. You two do know how to raise a girl's spirits." I smile.

Maddy walks in, and Mario proceeds to put on a performance equally enthusiastic to the one he has just entertained me with. Only Maddy's not quite so responsive. She looks wiped out.

She gives Mario her coat, plonks herself down, slumps her shoulders and sighs.

"Exhausted. Shattered. Completely dead."

I attempt to pour some retsina into her tumbler, but she places her hand flat above the glass to stop me.

"Oh, I forgot, you hate retsina."

"No, it's not that. I'm not drinking."

"Not drinking? Not possible. I'll order something you'll like."

"No, really, I've got a headache. It will only make it worse."

"Poor Maddy. How about you and me sneaking off to a health farm for a few days? I'm loaded at the moment; it will be my treat."

"I can't, Hope. We've already got two useless locums at the surgery. Max and I are the only ones who know what we're doing. It's chaos as it is, without me going off and landing Max in it."

"But you'd only miss a day or two at the most."

"It's out of the question."

"You do need to think of yourself, Maddy. You're still grieving, and that business with Ed . . ."

Maddy breaks off a piece of pitta and stabs it into the hummus. I bet she's not seeing Santorini blue. There's a silence between us. It happens all the time with me and Jack. With Maddy it never happens.

I'm six years older than Maddy, but it doesn't mean a thing as far as our friendship is concerned. We met on a flight to Venice in 1983. I was with a bunch of journalists heading off on a press trip; she was going to meet her younger sister, Ruth, an art student, who was spending a term studying Tintoretto, Titian and the rest of the great Venetian school of painters. Maddy and I hit it off immediately — I'm a hypochondriac, she's a doctor, a perfect match. I hate flying, and she talked down my nerves during the turbulence and advised me not to have a second double whisky. It also turned out we lived quite close in north London. During that weekend I was rounding a corner in some quiet backstreet, gazing up at a particularly handsome *piano nobile*, when I literally bumped right into Maddy again, this time with her sister. We took ourselves off to St Mark's, and bought outrageously expensive hot chocolates while the orchestra musicians, in evening dress, serenaded us with arias from Italian operas. As the pigeons massed appreciatively and the sun settled on the white-limestone and pink-marble facade of the Doge's palace and the tourists walked across wooden planks to avoid getting soaked as the *acqua alta* rose perilously in the square, I thought: Lucky me.

That weekend is etched forever in my memory. I met Maddy, the only person who could begin to substitute for my friend Claire, who had already emigrated to Australia. And I met Jack too, but that's another story.

Maddy may have been six years younger than me, but she had already crammed in a lot of living, too much by most people's standards.

From early childhood, Maddy had known she wanted to be a doctor. Her path was clear. What she couldn't have foreseen was that her parents would die in a car crash when she was twenty and Ruth was seventeen, that she'd marry a man twelve years her senior when she was just twenty-one, and that at twenty-four she'd be on the verge of walking out on him. This was the point she was at when I met her.

When Maddy's parents had died, they'd left behind a sizeable house in the suburbs of Manchester, from the proceeds of which Maddy was able to buy a flat in London for her and Ruth, which meant that she could continue her studies at UCL and at the same time keep an eye on her younger sister who had just won a place to do a foundation course in art at St Martin's. David was the solicitor she found to look after the conveyancing on the flat. As he was already a junior partner at a law firm, she felt she could rely on him totally to make sure nothing went wrong while the purchase of the flat was going through. When the sale was complete, he invited her out to dinner. He offered to go through her parents' papers, which were in a terrible mess. Over the next few months he lifted all the burdensome, practical problems off her shoulders, freeing her to concentrate on her studies. He even read and commented on her essays and tested her when she was revising for exams. He was kind to Ruth. And best of all, he made her feel safe. It lessened the pain, having David around.

When he said, "I want to marry you," she replied, "I want to marry you too." Her response was significant, she realised later. She hadn't said, "I love you." She'd said, "I want to marry you." Maddy moved into David's flat and Ruth moved some art student pals into hers.

What Maddy wanted was a security blanket. What David wanted was a wife. Maddy's studies, and later the all-night shifts as she continued her post-graduate medical training, took all her energy. Eighteen months after the small, register-office wedding, David announced he wanted to have a baby. "But I'm not ready, nowhere near ready," she told him.

"Look, you don't need to carry on with this, you know. We should have kids, and later on, when they're older, you can retrain for something. This is too much for you. Being a doctor and raising a family just don't go together, I realise that now. I'm earning plenty for the two of us. And we ought to start having a proper marriage. We're not like other couples. We never do anything together. And we never entertain. It's time I started bringing my partners — and even some of my clients — back for dinner. You can't cook, Maddy. Don't you think it's about time you learned? What's the point of being able to do open-heart surgery if you can't boil an egg?"

Maddy felt crushed. David looked at her sternly, without humour, and she was filled with fear. *He'll leave me. He'll go off with someone who can't wait to have babies.* And she thought about the loss of her parents, how it was only her and Ruth now. Children would mean they'd be a proper family again. Parents and children, as it should be. Not just one lonely, horizontal generation of orphans.

So she carried on with her studies and her clinical practice and threw out her contraceptive pills. And after six months she still wasn't pregnant.

"You're not doing this on purpose, are you?" David challenged her one night when her period came.

"What do you mean, on purpose?"

"Using something. Still taking pills."

"David, you can't possibly think I'd ever do that to you. Six months isn't long, it's normal. If still nothing has happened in three months' time, we'll talk again."

Three months later, Maddy still wasn't pregnant. Again it was David who brought up the subject.

"I really think you should get yourself checked out," he said, quite harshly.

"You do know they're going to want to check you out first," she replied. "They didn't used to, but now they always check the man first. Such a simple test, whereas if the problem lies with me it might take months of investigation."

"Madeleine, you can be absolutely sure there's nothing wrong with me." He'd called her Madeleine when their relationship had been on a solicitor/client basis. Then, after that first dinner, he'd started to call her Maddy. And now she was Madeleine again. It made Maddy feel desperately uneasy.

The letter from the consultant was to the point. "I regret to inform you that you have a condition called azoospermia. This means that there is no sperm present in the ejaculate and therefore you are infertile. There is no treatment for this condition at present, although current research indicates some possible cause for optimism in the future. I would rather not predict how many years in the future this might be. If you would like to come and talk to me about assisted reproduction, please call my secretary to make an appointment."

"Well, that's let you off the hook," he said coldly, flinging the letter at her across the table where they were sitting.

"David, you can't mean that," she said, shocked, reaching out to touch his hand which he abruptly pulled away.

And that was the beginning of the end. David wouldn't even discuss it. Wouldn't talk about adoption or artificial insemination by donor or anything to do with it. He dismissed the idea of going back to the consultant as "a waste of time and money". He went completely inside himself. Their sex life came to a halt, but Maddy found pornographic magazines under the bed. She suggested counselling. He went out drinking and came home crashing into things.

I'm twenty-four, she thought; I don't have to ruin my life just because he's determined to ruin his.

And that's how things were for Maddy when I met her. Orphaned and on the way to a divorce at twenty-four. An almost doctor, with green eyes, tumbling auburn hair and pale freckled skin, and the kind of small but curvy figure that men, Italian men in particular, couldn't resist. Their eyes went out on stalks when Maddy went by. But she couldn't see it.

Soon after getting back to England, Maddy left David and got on with her life. She hadn't counted on falling for Ed a few years later, and Ed falling for Ruth and the two of them getting married and having the twins. But she didn't begrudge Ruth her short-lived happiness. Ruth was her little sister and, in any case, Maddy wasn't the begrudging type.

I order the kleftiko, as I always do. Maddy orders some chicken kebabs, but after one mouthful excuses herself from the table to go to the toilet.

When she comes back I ask, "Maddy, are you OK? You've gone green."

"Yes, I feel better for having thrown up."

"It can't have been the chicken, you've only had one bite. Must have caught some beastly bug from one of your beastly patients."

"What I've got you can't catch."

"Maddy, don't do this to me. You're talking in riddles again, and when you talk in riddles I know something's up."

"The thing is, Hope . . . the thing is, I'm pregnant."

"You? Pregnant?"

"Yes, little old me."

"You? At forty-four? Oh, my God, I don't believe it. It's wonderful. No, I mean, it's terrible. I don't know what the fuck I mean. For God's sake, tell me what I mean . . ."

"Calm down, Hope, Mario's watching. Shall we start at the beginning?"

"Yes, please."

"OK, I'm pregnant. And there's only one man who could be the father."

"Not Ed, surely not Ed . . ."

"As I said, there's only one man who could be the father."

"Have you told him?"

"You are joking, of course."

"But you've got to tell him. If you're going to keep it, that is."

"Keep it? What do you think I'm going to do with it? Flush it down the toilet? I'm forty-four years old, Hope, as you so helpfully pointed out. Forty-four years old and this is the first time I've been pregnant in my life. I thought it was all over years ago. I'd resigned myself to never having a baby. I actually thought I was having an early menopause. My periods have been haywire for months. And now some kind of miracle has taken place. I'm overjoyed. I'm terrified. I think I'm going to be sick again."

And she's up and gone once more, leaving me to try to take it in. Maddy having a baby. Having Ed's baby. Having Ruth's husband's baby. The twins' aunt providing them with a baby brother or sister. Except they won't know they have a brother or sister because Maddy will keep it from them, and from Ed too. Maddy, forty-four, my best friend, having her first baby. Not an elderly primagravida. A positively ancient primagravida. My best friend having a baby and my own son about to leave home. Why doesn't anything happen when it's supposed to any more? Why do I feel my life has turned into a soap opera, with shocks, confessions and cliff-hangers at every turn?

By the time Maddy gets back, tears are dribbling down my face.

"Hey, Hope. I'm supposed to be the one in a state. What's with you?"

"I really don't know. I'm happy and sad and stunned . . . Just ignore me," I sniff. "Tell me the plan."

"There is no plan. The scans so far are fine. I'll have all the tests and, providing everything goes well, the baby will be born in October. I shall be a single mother, and you shall have to make yourself useful for a change."

"And Ed?"

"For Ed, I do have a plan. I'll tell him when I get to twelve or thirteen weeks. I'll do it casually, make up something about this guy I was seeing at the beginning of the year, but am no longer seeing. He's not going to start counting forward from my last period and putting two and two together. Men don't think like that. I'll just say the guy who's the father has gone away and that I have no intention of telling him about the baby."

"And are you still in love with him?"

"What difference does that make?"

By not answering, Maddy has told me all I need to know.

"So it's all settled. You really are having a baby."

"I really am having a baby."

"And you really want this baby."

"I really want this baby."

"And you think you can cope with being a single mother."

"Not a clue, but I've coped with everything else."

"So shall we have a drink?"

"Anybody there? Drink? Pregnant? I don't think so."

"So you really are going to have a baby. Maddy's going to having a baby."

"She sure is."

"Well, I can have a drink, can't I? I could do with one. Mario," I squeal, waving and smiling, "a glass of Perrier for me, please. And make hers a double." And at last we both burst out laughing.

My father and I are walking towards the ninth-hole tee together for the start of our half-round of golf, me dragging the trolley with the clubs, which feels heavier than I remember it. I must be seriously unfit. On the last occasion I did this, I was seventeen, around the time I started driving lessons. Thirty-three years ago! What had seemed a treat at eleven, at seventeen had become faintly embarrassing. However much I adored my father, I was too grown-up and too busy to spend my precious Saturday mornings trailing after him around the bloody golf course while he talked business to his friends and ignored me. When I told him I wouldn't be coming any more, he simply said, "Quite right, you're a big girl now," which briefly made me wonder whether he had ever wanted me along in the first place. I'd expected him to put up at least a bit of a fight, that's how insecure I was back then. I relied on him for the approval I didn't get from my mother.

And now I'm back on the same golf course, remembering how I felt when I was eleven, when I was his new caddy, so proud to have been the person chosen to accompany my father on his early morning round of golf. Not my mother, not my sister, but me. And I'm thinking that I don't just want to remember how it felt to be that little girl, I want to actually be that little girl again, eleven years old, Daddy's favourite, if only for the day, the girl whose daddy would always make everything all right. Life was so much simpler then.

Mummy. Daddy. Is it charming to still call your parents Mummy and Daddy when you're fifty? Or is it a classic example of infantilism? I suspect the latter. Sarah doesn't do this, to her they're Mum and Dad. But do you ever grow out of wanting to be approved of by your parents? I'm not sure you do.

I'm thinking about how Daddy used to get Sarah and me to film him with his cine-camera, over and over again, as he practised his golf swing in the garden. We'd take it in turns to be cinematographer and director and argue endlessly about the best angles and where the light was coming from. Around teatime, at the weekends, we'd unroll the foldaway canvas movie screen that we stored in the cupboard under the stairs, set up the hefty projector on a card table and fix the fragile rolls of film onto the projector's spools. We'd draw the curtains and turn out the lights. Our very own home cinema. Barnet goes to Hollywood. Even our wobbly efforts at recording our father hitting an imaginary ball seemed Oscar-worthy to us.

If we nagged long enough, he'd let us watch our holiday movies as well, and the films of us when we were even younger, jumping in and out of our little blow-up plastic pool in the garden, splashing each other mercilessly, getting more and more excited until inevitably one of us ended up in tears. Sometimes there'd be a shot of my mother, smiling seductively for the camera, ice-blonde and glamorous in a slightly mussed-up way, in a blouse and skirt nipped in at the waist with a wide, elastic belt. But there were never any shots of her joining in with Sarah and me playing.

My father's swing is still firm and accurate. The ball goes straight down the fairway, although not as far as it used to. He sets off at a terrific speed. "Come on, girl, stop dawdling." He grins. His shot is shorter, but his teeth are longer. "There are people coming up behind us from the eighth."

From his time in the army in the Second World War, Abe can still walk at the Light Infantry pace of 140 steps per minute. As I'm the one pulling the trolley, I have to beg him to slow down.

"Wait for me; this trolley weighs a ton."

"Well, you did offer. Want me to take over?"

"No, I do not."

He slows down, and I catch up, a little breathless.

"What are you going to do afterwards?"

"Go home to your mother, of course."

"I don't mean after this. I mean after . . . after she dies."

"Well, I'm not going to move into some awful old-age home that smells of wee-wee, that's for sure."

"But you can't live in that big barn all on your own either. I'd like you to move in with us. Olly's going on his gap year, then on to university. There's the spare room. We'll do it up; you'll have your own bathroom."

"Move in with you, Hope?" He looks genuinely startled. "What on earth are you thinking of? I'm perfectly capable of looking after myself, and I fully intend to. I haven't got Alzheimer's, have I? Unless I've forgotten . . ."

He pauses for me to get the joke. I titter obligingly, but without real enthusiasm.

"I've been teaching myself to cook a bit, lately, making soups for your mother, things that are easy for her to get down. After she's gone, I'm never going to have a takeaway again. It would be just too . . . sad."

"Oh, Daddy . . ."

I go to embrace him.

"Not here, sweetheart. Not on the golf course. The foursome behind are already snapping at our heels. I think I'll take a chance on a three iron."

I give him the club and wait quietly while he takes the shot.

"Damn, I've sliced it."

"Sorry, Daddy, I didn't mean to upset you, but when else are we going to get to talk?"

"It's OK, Hope. I just hate to see your mother suffering like this. And I shall miss her so much when she's gone."

"I know you will." Will I, I wonder?

101

"Fifty-five years. Almost every day for fifty-five years we've been together."

We're quiet for a moment while we head off towards the rough. We go through the club-passing ritual again; this time the shot is good.

"Hope, by the time you get to my age, you've seen a lot of people die. And I lived through the war, remember, so death's hardly a surprise. But I should have gone first, I never expected it to be this way around."

"You know I'll worry if you're on your own."

"If you insist on worrying, Hope, why don't you worry about your mother for a change? Or at least try to forget your perceived slights and gripes and show a bit of compassion."

I feel I've been hit in the face by a stray golf ball. This isn't how he talks to me. Not ever.

"But . . ."

"Hope, I know you've got this ridiculous idea that your mother never loved you, but she did. In her way. Think how frustrated she must have been. She had so many talents — musical, artistic — but she didn't know how to channel them. She married young, and straight away had Sarah and then you. And I didn't particularly encourage her in her endeavours. I just thought as long as I brought home the money, provided a nice house and pretty clothes and holidays, she'd be happy. I probably stifled her, even though I didn't mean to."

"But she adores you. Always did."

"Yes, because I rescued her from her life as a Harrods shop girl. I think she thinks I saved her, and

102

she never forgot it. But I do feel that had she been born twenty years later, around the time you were, she would have made something of herself. Become a something. Like you have done."

The foursome behind us are shouting now. We can't hear them, but we can imagine what they're saying.

My dad takes another shot. It lands on the green, close to the hole.

"Good one, Pops." My tone is falsely light.

"Haven't completely lost my touch, have I?" he says, as if cross words never passed his lips. "Don't need to be locked up in the old folks' home just yet."

We've never talked about my mother in this way before. I'm still smarting from his surprise attack. It's been an unspoken agreement that I don't bleat about her to him. It wasn't even me who brought the subject up. There would never have been any point in me complaining about my mother openly, because, like now, he would most certainly have leaped to her defence. But while I was growing up, I never blamed him for his failure to criticise her; I blamed my mother for manipulating him and holding sway over him. I can see now it was something of a weakness on his part. A little chink in his heroic armour. Maybe not quite perfect, after all.

We're not going to get any further down this particular path today. And neither do I want to spoil this precious time together. Daddy won't be coming to live with us and that's that. Which is probably just as well as I suddenly realise I haven't even consulted Jack on the subject.

The early morning haze has dispersed.

"Twenty-first of March," my father says. "The first day of spring."

We walk on, companionably now. It's not possible to remain entirely unaffected by this season of rebirth, the daffodils fanning out under the oak trees, the first buds. I think of Maddy and her baby. A seven-spot ladybird lands on my left-hand knuckle, a sure sign of spring come early. For a while, we're each suspended in our own thought bubbles.

"Are you all right for money?" my father asks, out of the blue. I sigh with relief. We're back on safe ground now. "I don't know what physiotherapists earn these days."

"We're fine, Daddy, just fine. I got a year's money, remember. And if we do run out before I get myself a job, we'll just move in with you and rent our house out to pay the bills."

"Over my dead body," he says, potting a long putt with a satisfied smirk.

My parents' house isn't at all what you'd expect. It's not one of those stone-clad retirement bungalows with lots of mod-cons and a taste bypass. It's a stunning eighteenth-century converted barn, filled with twentieth-century art and sculpture, stone floors covered with colourful rugs bought on holidays in Mexico and Peru, African wood carvings and one-off pieces of furniture by Le Corbusier and Eileen Gray.

My mother had a Frank Lloyd Wright moment after Sarah and I had both left home. She discovered "organic architecture" on a trip to Arizona, where she visited Wright's architectural commune at Taliesin West. When she got back to England, it was curtains for the suburban semi in which we grew up. Her new project was to find a unique home for her and Abe and furnish it in a way that would, in the great architect's words, "promote harmony between man and nature, create a unified whole". If this search for a unified whole, in which building, furnishings and surroundings would integrate seamlessly with one another, required swapping a set of well-upholstered dining chairs for two stone benches that gave you a sore bottom, it was a small price to pay for aesthetic harmony.

Even our old suburban semi had been quite avant-garde as suburban semis go. My mother's taste had always been different from that of the other mothers — just as she didn't dress from Jaeger or John Lewis, preferring shops like Granny Takes A Trip or designers like Ossie Clark, she never went in for moquette or swirly carpets, favouring wooden floors and clean lines long before Habitat flagged up the concept of contemporary design. Chintz had always been a dirty word in the Lyndhurst household.

At the time I was rather partial to swirly carpets. Round at my friends' houses, I would sit on the stairs and trace the patterns with my eye with such determined concentration that I'd forget where I was for minutes at a time, until I was dragged off to play hula hoops or jacks or Monopoly, or whatever game was the current craze.

There was a cocooning quality to swirly carpets that our house lacked. Looking back, of course, I can see how those comforting swirls were something of a metaphor for the overall sense of welcome I felt in my friends' houses, the kind of homes where mothers seemed more interested in their children's day at school than in the way light fell on a vase, or the perfect shade of oyster for the architraves.

In the absence of other work, my mother has put real passion into her housing projects. Frankie's Barn, as the family dubbed the home where my parents have lived for more than twenty-five years now, has been her *magnum opus*. It has appeared in dozens of interiors magazines over the years, both here and in the US and the rest of Europe. Even in *Exquisite Interiors*. It's a great source of pride for both my parents. And it's remarkable, truly remarkable. I, of course, do not love it, cannot love it. But it's no wonder my father could never bear to give this up, I think, as I enter the vast living area with its terracotta floors and huge central fireplace, lit and glowing, and its twelve-foot-high windows, overlooking the benign Hertfordshire hills.

"I'm off then, Jenny, my love," says my father almost the moment I arrive. "If you need me, I'll be on the mobile." He leans over the sofa, where she's sitting with her legs up and with her back against the plumped-up ethnic cushions, to kiss her tenderly on the lips.

I look at my father's back as he exits through the front door, willing him to turn round and decide to stay, even though it was me who'd set this whole thing up in the first place. It's the two of us now. Just me and my mother.

"Can I get you anything?"

"Some camomile tea would be nice."

The kitchen is in the corner, solid wood and simple Shaker style. I go to switch on the kettle, playing for time as I get out the cups and the tea bags, busying myself unnecessarily, searching for a tray and biscuits. I barely take breath between biscuits these days.

"No biscuits for me; they just get stuck," calls my mother, her throat catching as she does so. "And it might be a good idea if you don't have any either. Has Jack said anything about your weight since you've stopped work?"

I pretend not to have heard her and put three chocolate biscuits on a plate. I've been here less than five minutes, and my mother has already as good as told me that I'm fat, unemployed and that my husband must find me unattractive. How am I going to get through this?

I pick up the tray and return to the living area, placing the tray on the rough-hewn slab of granite that has been fashioned into a coffee table.

I pour the tea and take a biscuit. I make a decision to eat all three, even though I'd be quite satisfied with one, or maybe two.

"You shouldn't let yourself go, Hope," my mother continues.

"I'm not letting myself go; I'm having a biscuit."

"What does Jack say?"

"Jack doesn't say anything. It's got nothing to do with Jack."

"Men are vulnerable at his age."

"We're all vulnerable. But I wonder what exactly you mean by that? If you mean vulnerable to an affair, I don't suppose nine pounds is going to be the deciding factor. Ten or eleven maybe," I say sarcastically, "but surely not a mere nine."

"There's no need to be sarcastic, Hope. I've always made the effort to look my best for your father. As should you for Jack. To the best of my knowledge, Abe has never strayed." I hate it when she emphasises a point by calling me by name. It's like being ticked off by teacher.

"That's because you've never had anything better to . . ." I hate this. It can only be downhill from here. "Stop it, Mummy, please stop it," I plead.

"Stop what?"

"Stop criticising me. I've put on weight because I haven't got a job and I'm fifty and I feel bad about it. It doesn't mean that Jack will have an affair. He's really not that shallow."

"You can't stand me speaking my mind, can you, Hope? Was I really so bad a mother that my opinion counts for nothing?"

"Please let's not do this. Not now."

"But we need to be honest with one another, Hope. Don't think I don't know you'd like to clear the air before I die."

"Clear the air?" The woman's crazy. "Clear the air in an afternoon. How do you do that? How do you clear

108

the air of fifty years of stinking smog in a single encounter? Where do you want to begin?" She's pressed the right button, she always does.

"You never saw it from my perspective, did you?"

"I was a child, for heaven's sake. How was I supposed to see things from *your* perspective? Even now I don't know what your perspective was or is. But I do know the truth. I've always known it. You just didn't love me; it's that simple. You didn't want me around. Sarah was more than enough. The only person you ever truly wanted was Daddy, and I got in the way."

My mother's face doesn't change expression. I don't mean for us to be doing this, not now, not ever. I can't get this sorted before she dies, I realise; it was a ludicrous idea. I can only make it worse.

"You have no idea how I felt," she says.

As usual, once I start I can't stop. It was the same when I got fired.

"No, but I'll tell you how *I* felt. Like I was some bad-taste ornament someone bought you as a Christmas present. Only, unlike an ornament, you couldn't put me to the back of the cupboard then dust me down when the friend who bought it came to visit. And you certainly couldn't take me down to the charity shop. You were stuck with me. But unfortunately, I didn't fit into your design scheme. I was clutter. All uneven edges and uneven emotions. Neither organic nor minimalist. Just a messy blot on your personal landscape. And, unlike Sarah, I didn't fade into the furniture. I didn't put up with everything and let it all wash over me like Sarah did. I know the truth, Mummy, I don't need you to tell me it."

I'm shaking, she's not.

"You're wrong," she says quietly. Is that a hint of regret I detect in her voice? I doubt it. It's probably the cancer eating away at her lungs and maybe now her larynx too. I feel cruel, but I don't think I'm a cruel person. "You just don't understand."

"What's to understand?" I'm suddenly overwhelmingly weary.

"The war. Marrying so young. No career."

"You never wanted a career."

"It's not that I never wanted a career. I never wanted to be in any situation that made me unavailable to your father. He rescued me."

"But you could have worked. Later. When we were at school."

"As what, with no qualifications? In a shop? That's exactly what I'd escaped from. And no one was going to pay me to be an artist. As an actress, of course, I was pretty hopeless."

"Well, that's an admission. You gave the impression you thought you were Grace Kelly. Are you telling me you were unhappy?"

"No, not unhappy. I had your father and Sarah and —"

I butted in before she could lie. "Don't you dare lie to me, don't you dare say you had me. What was the good of having me when you didn't want me?"

"If you could just hold your tongue long enough to listen, I'll attempt to tell you." She's breathless now, but

110

her anger is helping her through. "I'm trying to tell you that I was a little bit jealous of you. A lot jealous, actually," she says, raising her hand to her chest and wincing as she coughs.

Jealous? Of me? Impossible. This is some kind of ruse to get her off the hook. Maybe it's my duty to help her get off the hook, as none of this is going to make anything any better. And she looks as though she might be in pain.

"You're not up to this," I say. "Why don't we watch Richard and Judy? This isn't doing either of us any good."

She waves her other hand at me, dismissing my remark.

"Your father adored Sarah, but you and he always had something extra special. You made him laugh. You had such an easy rapport. You were quick with your tongue, like him. He always said you'd do something with words when you grew up. But you were such a fierce and focused little girl, you used to frighten me sometimes. I didn't recognise you as belonging to me. I couldn't find any of me in you — not in your looks, your manner or your approach to life. You were like a little stranger. But you charmed the pants off your father."

I'm shivering, despite the fire. What I want my mother to tell me is that it was all a ghastly mistake, that she did love me, that I had misunderstood, that all my life I'd been labouring under a terrible misunderstanding. But she's not saying any of that. This is even worse than I feared.

"Why was it so hard? Why couldn't you just love me for being your daughter? For being me. I don't love Olly because he walks or talks or acts in a particular way. I love him because he's my flesh and blood, because Jack and I created him, because how can you not love something to which you have given life, nourished in your belly for nine long months? A tiny human being who utterly depends on you for survival. What was it that made me so unlovable, so unbearable to be around? It can't just be that my father liked me. Fathers do tend to like their daughters, it's not an aberration."

"I don't know, Hope, I really don't know. I didn't want to hurt you. That's never been my intention. I'm sorry."

I shut down. Suddenly and without warning. Like a crashed computer. "Would you like some more tea?"

"No more tea." She's really breathless now. "Too tired." Her chest is rising and falling rapidly. "I'm not used to . . . Would you mind if I dozed for a while?"

"Of course not." This means it's over. Thank God.

My mother closes her eyes, and her breathing slows. I take a throw from the armchair and place it over her lap. While she sleeps, I watch her. Going over my childhood. Wondering what made me unlovable. Thinking how different it might have been. I watch her face, looking for clues or understanding, finding neither. I sit and watch her for two whole hours until my father's key sounds in the lock, and she stirs.

"Had a good time, you two?" he asks.

"Yes, darling," my mother replies sleepily. "Good bridge game?"

"Yes, we won. I'm going to blow the tenner I made on an extra portion of spare ribs and some won-ton soup with tonight's takeaway. So what have you two been up to?"

"Not much," I reply. "Just chatting, and then Mummy had a little sleep. I'd better be going."

I pick up my handbag from the floor and prepare to leave.

"Good choice, *mon amour*," I say, as we leave the cinema.

"But you really didn't want to see it, did you?" says Jack.

"I never said that."

"No, but I saw the look on your face."

"It's just that the French do seem to make more than their fair share of poncy, pseudo-philosophical and pretentious movies. But this one was great. Sexy and smart and stylish. I think I held my breath for the whole last half-hour. Did you fancy her?"

"Who?"

"You know exactly who. Chantal whatshername. She's definitely over forty but totally amazing."

"Mmm, but not really my type."

"And your type is . . .?"

"Oh, you know me, I like them younger. Chantal whatshername is too old for me by at least fifteen years."

The restaurant is walking distance from the cinema, and we're almost there.

"I could never lead a double life like that. If you can tell from one look at my face that I don't want to see a particular movie, imagine how guilty I'd look if I was having an affair."

"Would you like to?"

"Have an affair? Why, do you have someone in mind for me?"

"I'm working on it."

"My procurer. I like the sound of that."

Jack takes my hand. This feels nice. For the first time in ages.

We've arrived at Rib-Eye, and the aroma of steak sizzling on the wood-fired grill wafts over appetisingly as we remove our coats. The contrast of the cold night and the warm restaurant makes my face tingle.

I decide quickly on an entrecote, medium rare, a salad and no chips. When the waiter arrives, I order the fillet with chips and creamed spinach, but I stick to medium rare. Jack looks as though he's about to say something, then changes his mind.

"My mother was asking if you'd commented on my weight," I say, when the waiter's departed with our order.

Jack shrugs. "Well, I haven't, have I?"

"She says I've turned into a fat, ugly cow."

"Is that a direct quote?"

"Well, not exactly, but that's what she was implying. And she's probably right. I am a fat cow, aren't I?"

"No, you're not a fat cow, but you are a bit of a silly cow. I will not deny that I've noticed you've put on a few pounds. A few pounds don't bother me. What bothers me is that they bother you."

"Why are you always so incredibly reasonable?"

"Because if you'd married someone as unreasonable as you, you would have been divorced before the end of the honeymoon."

"So how do you know they bother me?"

"I know because for twenty years your weight has never fluctuated more than a couple of pounds, and because your ability to stay slim with the passing years has been just one of your many self-imposed disciplines to prove to yourself that you are an OK person."

"So now you're not just a physiotherapist, but a therapist therapist."

"I'm only telling you the truth. And I'm with your mother on this one. Yes, I would like you to lose a few pounds because it may just make you feel better about yourself. Personally, I don't care. You don't look that much different, and as for whether you feel any different to the touch, I wouldn't know. We don't seem to go in for that kind of thing any more."

"Jack —"

"Shall we change the subject?" Jack never loses his composure before I do. Tonight is an exception. "I think we ought to talk about what you want to do about work; you must be getting bored out of your mind at home all the time."

"No, not work, Jack, let's not talk about that."

"OK, what about you and Olly? We do need to talk about you and Olly."

"No, not Olly either, not tonight. I never stop thinking about Olly, and I need a break. You have no idea how I feel about the idea of Olly going off for a year on his own, and then to university. Olly leaving home is unimaginably awful."

"So you think I've no idea. I'm mystified as to what makes you think that. What is it that makes you think you have the monopoly on feelings? Do you perhaps think that I love my son less than you do? Is your love more special, more real, than mine? Is that what you think?" Jack really angry is as rare as me really chilled.

"Of course I don't, Jack. Please calm down. But maybe it just doesn't hurt you as much as it hurts me. Maybe it's the difference between being a man and being a woman."

"So now you not only have the monopoly on feelings, you have the monopoly on pain. I can see you don't want to talk about Olly, what you want to talk about is *you*. You and your unique feminine feelings."

"Fuck you, Jack. This is almost as bad as trying to talk to my mother."

"I never thought the day would arrive when I would remind you of your mother."

"You don't remind me of her, you idiot, it's just that I can't seem to get through to anyone any more. It's all no-go zones and *Danger: do not enter* areas. And then I walk through the wrong door, and the whole place fucking explodes. Can't we just be kind to one another?

Like we used to. When Olly goes, it will just be you and me. Then what?"

Jack takes a sip of wine and picks up the menu, which he has already read and from which he has already ordered. I glance at the couples at the other tables. Nobody appears to be listening in. The waiter is approaching with food. I focus on my chips. I eat them all, and then half of Jack's portion as well. We order the bill. We've only been in the restaurant forty minutes. I judge a successful dinner out by how much time passes without you noticing it. When you order your bill then look at your watch and say, "Two and a half hours. I can't believe we've been here that long," it means the enterprise has succeeded. Jack and I used to do four-hour marathon meals when we first met. They'd be piling chairs upside down on top of the other tables before we'd get the hint. Forty minutes is a pitiable performance. Jack moves to stand up. I put my hand to my over-stuffed belly and resolve to do something about it. Tomorrow. We walk back to the car, Jack's hands deep in his pockets, mine hugging myself against the cold.

Another 3a.m., another night of not sleeping. I review my list.

Get Maddy back on track

Maddy's so far off track as to be outside the stadium. But this baby might yet turn out to be a good thing, so definite cause for optimism here. Score out of 10: 4

Talk to Daddy about the future

This went relatively smoothly. And even the outcome, although not what I was aiming for, is perhaps for the best. Score out of 10: 6

Try and square things with Mummy before she dies

Unmitigated disaster. Score out of 10: 0

Make it up with Olly

Deferred until later. Scoring deferred likewise.

Have sex with Jack — or at least dinner and a movie

Sex, didn't even try. Score out of 10: 0. Movie, best result of the month. Score out of 10: 10. Dinner — chips, nicely crisp; steak, cooked to perfection; bridge-building, aborted. Overall dinner score out of 10: 2.5, for the steak and chips.

What does this tell me? Other than that I should go more often to the movies? I really think I'm going to have to do better than this.

Body Issues

Maddy isn't even showing. I'm the one who looks pregnant. For a while in the bathroom last night I entertained the idea of a phantom pregnancy. I'm a bit hazy about how phantom pregnancies come about, but I know they have something to do with unfulfilled psychological needs. Might not projected loss (of Olly) and envy (of Maddy), mixed in with a few menacingly menopausal symptoms (sweaty legs again the other day, this time in the supermarket), be psychologically needful enough to trigger sore breasts and a belly full of air? It's not that I really want another baby, I just want to go back in time and relive the good bits all over again. And being pregnant with Olly was one of the best bits of all.

The real story is that I'm getting fat, and the only things my belly is full of are chocolate biscuits, chips and cashew nuts. And rather more vodka than I care to admit. I actually dream of cashew nuts, twice so far this week. The second time was a nightmare in which I'd swallowed a whole mouthful at once. I awoke, coughing and clutching at my throat, convinced I was choking. Jack had to bash me on the back and get me a glass of water. There are only two ways to interpret this. It was either nature's way of telling me to go on a diet or a subconscious response to my mother's worsening condition. Both demand the same course of action: cut the cashews.

I've moved on since March. Having faced the fact that I have no positive influence whatsoever on my friends and family, I have decided to revert to trying to sort out the wreckage of my own life.

While I examined my ever-expanding flesh in the bathroom mirror last night, I had an unbidden poetry moment. Quite suddenly, while prodding an unruly batwing, I found myself reciting T. S. Eliot.

April is the cruellest month, breeding
Lilacs out of the dead land, mixing
Memory and desire, stirring
Dull roots with spring rain

That's all I can remember of my sixth-form studies. And I don't suppose T. S. Eliot had a disgruntled middle-aged woman in the buff in mind when he wrote the opening to *The Wasteland*. He wasn't thinking body brushing in the shower and a good workout to stir dull skin and flabby flesh out of winter complacency. But as I looked in the mirror those words spoke to me, succinctly summarising my current state of mind and suggesting a kind of limbo land, in which things were neither dead nor fully living. Which is pretty much how I feel. Not dead. Not living. Pulled between memories of the past and a desire to move forward. Exactly. But how? I guess the gym might be a good place to start.

As a VIP member, I'm entitled to a free fitness assessment and two personal training sessions per annum. I fully intend to use up my quota this week. What makes me a VIP is the fact that I've been a member of this particular gym, located on Abbey Road, a few doors down from the famous studios where the Beatles recorded their even more famous album, for five years.

I'm deeply embarrassed about this but, apart from the first month when I went religiously three times a week, I haven't been back since. My membership has been paid by direct debit for exactly *five years*! Which makes it four years and eleven months since I last went to the gym. And yes, I know I could have given the money to starving children instead, or built a dozen schools in Africa, for all the use I've made of it — and even claimed some tax back on the side, which could have been passed on to Amnesty International or Médecins Sans Frontières — but I haven't. It's all gone into the coffers of Fit For The Future, an organisation which floated on the stock market last year, entirely thanks to the likes of super-saps such as me.

Fit For The Future looks more like Fit For The Scrapheap. It's gone badly downhill in the last four years and eleven months, and despite what I read in the papers about it going public, it looks to me as though it must be in some kind of financial trouble. The basement, where the changing rooms are located, smells of drains, keys to most of the lockers are missing and there are brown marks on the walls, at both floor and ceiling level, suggesting rising damp and even, perhaps, leakage from the swimming pool above. On the spur of the moment, I put a note in the suggestions box advising the management to ring the editor of the new *Jasmine* to find out how best to get rid of the stains. I leave Mark's name and his direct line, the one that bypasses Tanya. I know, I know, but it makes me feel better.

I should probably be banned from going anywhere near a gym. Or a beach. Or any department store where there are communal changing rooms. I have this problem with bodies. The problem is staring. I'm no closet lesbian, but I am totally and utterly fascinated by other women's bodies — fat, thin, good, bad or ugly, I simply cannot resist looking and — of course — comparing. The unstated first rule of gym etiquette is that you mind your own body business, especially in the changing rooms. I spend more time in the changing rooms than I do working out, because I'm clocking all the other members.

I try to stare subtly, pretending to fiddle in my purse for the coin that will enable me to use the locker, at the same time as surreptitiously glancing at the naked woman to my right who is relatively slim, but has enough cellulite to keep a lipsocutionist in business for the next fifteen years. Jerry Hall has cellulite too. More useful information gleaned in my long career as a magazine editor.

There's a gorgeous young black girl to my left. Legs like Naomi Campbell, a bottom so pert you could rest your teacup on it. But are they stretch marks I see on her thighs? I believe they are, and on her tummy too. She gives me a hard look. I avert my eyes and march exaggeratedly towards the toilets where they used to have a decent pair of scales. Unfortunately, they still do.

While I'm sitting on the loo, a considerable amount of door banging suggests a couple of women are entering the adjoining cubicles.

"Hey, V, there's no loo paper in here. Can you spare a square?"

"Comin' right under."

"Thanks, love . . . Ooh, that feels better. Now I don't mind weighing myself. That must've got rid of at least a pound or two."

"Too much information, Sandr."

"You're probably right. How's that toy boy of yours?"

The sound of toilets flushing simultaneously and bolts being yanked back.

"Ooh, he's gorgeous," says the one called V, switching on the hand-dryer, making it hard for me to hear what they're saying. "Bit of a skinny kid, but I love him to bits. Even the bony bits."

"Really?"

"Well, not really really. It's just a bit of fun, isn't it? But he's as cute as a puppy. And a quick learner. And so eager to please. I've had enough of brutes to last a lifetime. He's even good with my kids — I mean, he's more their age than mine." The two of them titter like five-year-olds. The dryer switches itself off.

"Good on yer, Van. Does he have a playmate for me?"

V? Van? *Van?* I knew I recognised that voice. It's her. It's Vanessa the Undresser. And that's my boy they're talking about. How *dare* they? Talking about my precious Olly as if he's just a piece of meat.

I storm out of the cubicle as Vanessa and her pal Sandr are adjusting their lipstick. It beats me why women wear make-up to work out. Or maybe I've just been too complacently married for too many years.

"Morning, *Van*," I say. "Having fun making fun of my son, are you?"

"Blimey, it's you." Vanessa drops her lipstick in the sink and a little chunk of it falls off. I have magical powers! I feel like Samantha in *Bewitched.*

"Oh, bugger, that's my new Mac lippie." She picks up the lipstick container and the bit that has detached itself and tries to weld them back together with her fingers, but only succeeds in squishing the surviving part of the lipstick and having to scrape the whole lot into a tissue and dump it in the bin.

"But we weren't making fun, were we, Sandr?" says Vanessa, trying to compose herself and wash off the lipstick that's smeared all over her hands. "We were just saying what a lovely boy your Olly is."

She looks at Sandr for support.

"You the mother? Olly's mum? Nah, not possible. Doesn't look old enough, does she, Van?"

Good try, Sandr, whoever you are, but it's not going to work.

"Vanessa, I've nothing against you personally — if I didn't like you I wouldn't have invited you to my bir — I mean, our New Year's Eve party. But surely you must agree it's just not appropriate. You're a mother with two kids. He's a boy."

"You're wrong there, Hope. He's just turned eighteen, and he's a man. A *real* man. My kind of man. And, from what I hear, it's not me who ought to be leaving him alone, it's you who ought to be getting off his case."

What *nerve*. What bloody nerve. There I was, trying to be reasonable. To discuss things objectively. Woman to woman. Adult to adult. And she throws it all in my face. Where would she even get an idea like that from? Surely Olly wouldn't complain to her about me. The idea of him talking to her about me makes me feel physically sick.

"You're unbelievable. Who the hell do you think you are, telling me how to behave towards my son? You're the one with the problem behaviour. At least I won't have to put up with it for much longer. Once he's on his gap year he's sure to meet someone his own age."

Vanessa places her hands just above her substantial hips and, legs apart, tilts one hip up to the side so she looks like an aggressive, overgrown teenager. "So now you can't wait to be rid of your son. That's a new one on me. I was under the impression that you were going to fall to pieces when your *one and only* flew the nest. The only reason you don't want him to be with me is because you want him to be with you. Still tied to your apron strings. Still a mummy's boy." Sandr stifles a giggle.

I know when I've been beat. She's got him, and I haven't. But I'll get him back. I will. Sandr passes

125

Vanessa her lipstick, and the two of them go back to concentrating on their *maquillage*. Vanessa's hand, I'm pleased to note, shakes a little as she attempts to draw a Cupid's bow.

Flapping my hands vigorously to dry them (I won't go near those air-dryers, they're absolute breeding grounds for Legionnaire's disease), I suck in my stomach as much as I can and flounce off and upstairs to meet my fitness assessor. By the time I get up the two short flights of stairs, I'm puffed out and on the verge of tears.

"Take a seat and we'll have a little chat," says a perfectly ordinary-looking girl in her mid-twenties with a New Zealand accent and no obvious musculature or designer sportswear. "I'm Callie, and I'm here to sort out a programme for you. But first you need to tell me what you'd like to achieve and the areas you'd like to work on."

"What's a punchbag good for?" I ask, trying not to breathe as heavily as my lungs would like.

"Well, it's great for upper-body conditioning . . . arms, chest and shoulders. Abs too. But why don't you tell me the areas you want to shape up, and we'll sort the equipment for you to use afterwards."

"Just ten minutes, please, just ten minutes. Afterwards we can come back and fill in all the forms and stuff."

"Need to release some pent-up energy, do we?"

"We do."

I've never used a punchbag before. I'm tentative at first. I feel a little foolish in my sparring gloves. Who the hell do I think I am? Rocky? Hilary Swank? I'm not the sort of person who goes round hitting things. I'm so *not* physically aggressive that I don't even want to hurt this bag. But I'm getting into the rhythm of it. I'm feeling the warm blood circulating in my arms and chest and it's a good feeling. I punch a little harder, jabbing and punching, jabbing and punching, until I forget where I am, until I forget everything except the uncontrollable urge to punch harder, faster, harder. And now this big black plastic thing that I'm beating the life out of has taken on human form. My old boss Simon flashes before my eyes and at my next punch I grunt out his name under my breath. It feels fabulous. And then the name Mark. And another punch. And then Vanessa. A perfect left hook. And then . . . and then . . . and then the name Jenny. The black bag has become my mother. Yes, even my mother feels the force of my fist, although I have to close my eyes as I punch. One almighty punch for all those years of not loving me. Harder, faster, harder . . . Simon . . . Mark . . . Vanessa . . . Jenny . . . Simon . . . Mark . . . Vanessa . . . Jenny . . . until my hair is soaked, the water is running down my body in rivulets and I'm gasping for air.

"Slow down now," says Callie at my side, bringing me back to the present. "That's more than enough for your first try. Seems to be what you needed, though. I'll build it into the programme as a regular ten-minute warm-up."

I'm high. Exhilarated. Endorphined to the max. The feeling stays with me for at least five minutes.

★ ★ ★

"Saturday morning you're coming with me for a walk," says Sarah when she rings.

"Whatever for?" I reply.

"Because I don't like having a fat-arse for a sister, that's what for."

Only Sarah can get away with this kind of thing. She can say anything she wants to me, and I won't take offence. It works the other way round as well.

"But how is a walk going to help?"

"I'm not talking about the kind of walk you're already so good at. The one that involves getting from the taxi to the kerb. Or poodling down Bond Street between Donna Karan and Nicole Farhi, musing on how you're ever going to spend that ginormous clothes allowance."

"That was then."

"I know that was then. Which means you're doing even less exercise now."

"But you've no idea how much time I spend walking up and down Kilburn High Road and Hampstead High Street."

"Yes, and instead of stopping every two minutes to try on a little blouse or pair of boots, you're stopping every five seconds to stuff your face with cappuccinos and croissants and raisin toast."

"But I've started going to the gym."

"Good, but not good enough."

"You're such a bossy cow."

"And you're such a control freak."

"Yeah, a control freak who can't control anything any more. Not a good situation."

"You're coming."

"Once."

"Once to start with. And then again."

"Once."

"I'll pick you up at ten to eight."

"You must be mad. It's out of the question."

"I thought you couldn't sleep anyway, so what difference will it make?"

"You don't get it, do you? I can't *get* to sleep. Often not until nearly four o'clock. But once I'm asleep, then I can't wake up. And since I've nothing to get up for, it doesn't matter. Ten to eight is not a good moment of the morning for me."

"Too bad. And wear an anorak and some decent walking shoes."

"Will trainers do? And a denim jacket?"

"Fine if it's dry. Useless if it isn't."

"But doesn't it get called off if it's raining?"

"Do you have a problem with rain? It's designed to make things grow, you know, not just to make your hair go frizzy."

"I don't have an anorak."

"Then buy one. You're loaded, remember?"

"I could bring a brolly."

"It's not that sort of walk. If you take a brolly, you'll just end up poking your neighbours in the eye with the spokes."

"Neighbours? Which neighbours?" Since my recent encounter with Vanessa, I panic even at the mention of the word *neighbour*.

"The rest of the walking group, ninny. I've told you about the walking group. Not listening as usual, I suspect. Anyway, enough of this. See you Saturday at ten to eight. Bye."

It's true, Sarah has mentioned something about a walking group to me before. I just thought she got together with some pals and went strolling over Hampstead Heath with them. This sounds rather more serious. No umbrellas! Anoraks! How peculiar.

I refuse to speak to Sarah during the ten-minute ride to Hampstead Heath. It's been larks and owls with us throughout our lives. She is so perky first thing in the morning that all I want to do is thump her. I often tried to when we were little, but I was always groggy first thing, and she was always too nimble for me. But by 9p.m. midweek she's in her dressing gown reading herself goodnight stories.

When I was working, the only way I could get through the first couple of hours of the morning was with coffee. A black coffee the minute I got up, another after my shower and the cappuccino when I got to the office. Plus coffees at half-hourly intervals until mid-afternoon. After which I'd be raring to go until midnight, which is about how long it must have taken to get the caffeine out of my system.

Sarah turns right into the Kenwood car park, and backs into the nearest space. Over in one corner is a large clump of people, about thirty it looks like from here.

"I don't suppose we could . . ."

"What? Go home?"

"Well, no, I wasn't thinking of going home. I was just wondering if we might walk on our own, without the rest of them. It would be good to talk."

"That's a joke. You've not talked to me properly for months. If you really want to talk — and you've been avoiding me since the first of January right up until this very second — we can do it some other time. Like this afternoon. But they're my friends, and they're expecting us."

"What, all of them? Your friends?"

"Well, in a way, yes. They're my walking friends. You don't have to talk to anyone if you don't want to. It will just confirm that you're the snobby, stand-offish bitch they expect a glossy magazine editor to be."

"Thanks, Sarah, for giving me the big build-up."

"Come on, you big lump of lard. What's happened to the old sparkling personality? Why not give it an outing?"

"Even if I hadn't lost it, I wouldn't be able to bring it out at this time of the morning. Let's just get this over with."

We walk towards the crowd. My God, they're noisy. Everyone's talking at once. It's like a bloody cocktail party. People are actually kissing one another. Some are even dressed for a cocktail party. There's a woman over there wearing gaberdine trousers, a velvet blazer and Tod's loafers. The only missing item is a Hermès handbag. She looks ridiculous. I'm starting to feel rather grateful for Sarah's advice on the dress code.

131

I sincerely hope I don't bump into anyone I know. For what possible reason could I want to hang out with a bunch of geriatrics who need to be taught how to put one foot in front of the other?

"There can't be a single person here who's a day less than forty," I hiss at Sarah.

"Yes, little sister, and you can't be a day less than fifty, remember?"

This is seriously depressing. And who is that woman over there wearing head-to-toe Lycra, clasping a clipboard and blowing a whistle?

"Registration, over here," she's booming. "All new members of the group must register over here."

I look at Sarah for help. She nods and points. "And have your fiver ready."

"What fiver?"

"The fiver for Henrietta. Henrietta, also known as Henri, is our leaderene. Where she goes, we follow. When she blows her whistle, we shut up and listen."

I'm stumped.

"This fiver. Is it a one-off? Or every time? Does it go towards the upkeep of the Heath?"

"No, it's not a one-off, it's every time, and no, it doesn't pay for maintenance, it's how Henri makes her living. When, that is, she's not walking other people's dogs, doing distance Reiki healing and running her 'Blobby Bellies' empire."

"Oh, I see," I say, not seeing anything.

For protection I put on my sunglasses. Henri greets me with what seems to me an unnecessary amount of *joie de vivre*.

"So lovely to have you with us," says our gracious hostess. "And not to worry if you fall behind. I have Nick here as back-up, and we're in constant communication on the walkie-talkies." She gives Nick a little wink and a thumbs-up. Nick does a thumbs-up back. "He'll keep pace with the slowest of the group and file regular progress reports. That way everyone can walk at the pace that suits them best, and I can relax knowing that you're safe and sound."

Have I got this wrong? Is this Hampstead Heath or the Himalayas? Is Henri concerned I might get altitude sickness or find myself cut off from civilisation somewhere around Parliament Hill?

"You seem to be going to an awful lot of trouble . . ." I start to say. By way of response, Henri turns her back on me and blows her whistle. Everyone stands to attention, or at least a little straighter than they were before.

We're off.

I look round for Sarah, but she's deep in conversation with a couple I take to be husband and wife as they're wearing matching fleeces and baseball caps, and both have pouches round their waists with various flaps and pockets, from one of which protrudes what I suppose to be a water bottle. It's like some weird sect. With uniforms and rules and secret hand signals.

I try not to catch anyone's eye. I'm deciding between hovering near the back and trusting to luck that I don't get noticed, or striding off towards the front and proving that I'm fitter than the rest of them put together and that I don't need someone to teach me how to walk. It has to be the latter.

We're heading down towards a small gate, beyond which the Heath opens out into a large meadow, green as far as the eye can see. I take long, fast strides, but no matter how long and fast my strides, I seem not to be able to make it to the front. The only possible way I can get into the lead is by breaking into a jog. This would bring attention to myself, which I most definitely don't want to do. I'm getting very warm and we haven't even reached a hill yet. I try to remove my hideous new anorak and tie it round my waist, without slowing down. This proves impossible. I've now slipped into last place and Nick is glancing over at me with a slightly worried expression.

"You OK there, Hope?"

"Great thanks. Just trying to sort this anorak out."

"I'll hang back with you, if you like. It's not a problem."

"No need." I smile stiffly, trying to tie the arms of my anorak at the front of my waist, and surging forwards at the same time.

"Whoops!" My right foot has caught on my shoelace and I lunge towards Nick, arms outstretched.

"Gotcha!" he shouts triumphantly, saving me from falling.

I extract myself from the arms of this stranger, who's smiling at me with nicely crinkly eyes.

"Ever so sorry. I've clearly forgotten just how complicated this walking business is."

134

"No worries," he says to me. "May I suggest a double-knot might be a good idea." For some reason I don't take offence. Must be the crinkles.

There's no way I can carrying on walking while tying my shoelaces, and I'm quite grateful to be getting my breath back. Nick updates Henri on his handset while I get my laces in order.

We set off and fall into step with one another. We're approaching a hill. If I can get him to do most of the talking — and even I realise it would be rude to refuse to speak to him after he's been so courteous — then he won't notice me getting out of breath. As we begin to mount the hill I bark out questions, keeping them as brief as possible, and hoping he'll respond expansively.

"So how did you get started on this?"

"Sally and I — my wife, that is, and I — are planning on trekking in the Atlas mountains in the autumn. We're raising money for this charity we run, and this is part of the training to get us into shape."

"Tell me about the charity," I puff, looking for the top of the hill, but it hasn't yet come into view. This should keep him busy for a bit.

"Well, when our little girl died . . ."

"Oh, God, how awful, I'm so sorry."

"I know it always comes as a shock when I say it so bluntly, but there's no other way to put it really. Our sweet Cat — Catherine — was only six when she died of cardiomyopathy."

"Car . . .?"

"Cardiomyopathy. She caught this virus, which went to her heart and set off an inflammation. It's not inevitably fatal, but in her case it led to complications, and we lost her. Six years ago now."

So much for the cocktail-party chatter.

"And the charity?" I can barely breathe, and my thighs are killing me, but compared to this . . .

"It was about six months after Cat died. It was Sally's idea in the main. She kept saying how she couldn't communicate with anyone any more, how no one understood what we were going through because no one we knew had been through a similar experience. She got it into her head that what people needed when a child was terminally ill, or after that child had died, was a safe haven — somewhere to go, possibly away from the family, or even as a family group — where they could meet up with others having to face this particular, and particularly devastating, loss. And so she conceived the notion of nationwide family drop-in centres."

"What a wonderful idea."

"Yes, it is a wonderful idea. And thanks to Sally's incredible determination, we're almost there. We've bought a building, started the conversion and with a few more fund-raisers we'll be ready to open. It will be totally unique. We'll have bereavement counsellors, family therapists, yoga and meditation; a games room for the older kids and a play area for the younger ones; a coffee and snack bar. And when that's up and running we're going to try to get another one going in Edinburgh, Sally's home town."

I've been so engrossed in Nick's story that I've forgotten about my own physical discomfort. We're almost at the top of the hill, and the rest of the group is waiting for us. "Well done, Hope," shouts Henri. "Time for a stretch."

"Yes, well done, Hope," says Nick. "Pretty good for a first timer."

"Thank you for looking after me," I say.

"All part of the soft sell," says Nick, smiling again in his nice, crinkly way.

"Meaning . . .?"

"Meaning, by next week we'll have you signed up for that trek in November."

"No way."

"Are you willing to take a bet on that?"

"Oh, yes, please," I gasp gratefully, as Henri proffers her water bottle. "That's very thoughtful of you."

Nick waves and wanders off. For the next five minutes, Henri has us lined up in front of a long sweep of railings, stretching our muscles according to her instructions. We all grab the railings for balance as we wobble around on one leg while trying to grab the foot of the raised leg and bend it backwards from the knee. "This will release tension in your thighs and prevent stiffness," says Henri authoritatively.

"Fry-ups all round when this torture's over," whispers a particularly plump woman to my right.

"Fancy sneaking off into the bushes for a fag?" asks an even plumper bloke to my left, as he produces a pack of Marlboros from the back pocket of his shorts. "*Heil* Henri doesn't let us smoke," he grins, "but we have ways of escaping her instructions." He pats the side of his nose a couple of times with his index finger.

137

"I don't smoke, and I'm on a diet. Life's barely worth living, is it?" I reply.

Marlboro Man chuckles and turns in the direction of a small wooded area. "Once more into the beech," he shouts over his shoulder.

"Beech, breach, get it?" says a rather bent old gent of at least seventy. "You get lots of bad tree jokes when you coming walking with us. Wait for it," he says, "she'll be having us walking up hills backwards in a minute, it's our punishment for misbehaving."

"And what exactly constitutes bad behaviour?"

"Oh, the usual stuff," says the plump woman who's looking forward to her fry-up. "Talking too much, dawdling, not having the exact money for the walk and demanding change."

On cue, Henri announces, "See that hill over there? We're going to walk up it backwards."

And we do. Muscles scream in agony, and those of us not blessed with eyes at the back of our heads are constantly craning our necks behind us to avoid collisions. Collisions occur anyway, with fellow walkers, stray dogs and Hampstead Heath strollers going the conventional route and walking down the hill in a forward direction.

"Bloody ramblers," says a man to his beagle as we file past backwards. "It shouldn't be allowed."

By the time we eventually arrive at Kenwood House, close on two hours after setting off, the sun is shining and we plonk ourselves down at three adjacent round tables in the walled garden behind the cafe.

"Still alive, are we?" asks Sarah.

"Just," I reply.

"Seeing as it's your first time, I'll stand you breakfast. What would you like?"

"Sausages, eggs, ba — On second thoughts, make that brown toast and marmalade and a cup of tea. And hold the butter. Thanks, Sarah."

"So when's the next walk?" I ask Henri, as Sarah trots off to get breakfast.

"Tomorrow, Sunday. You coming?"

"Well, actually . . . I just might."

"Good on you, girl," says a woman opposite me. She's wearing a jade-green anorak and a baseball cap, her hair hidden inside it except for a small blonde ponytail which peeks out from behind her cap when she turns her head. "I'm Sally, and I know you've been talking to my husband, Nick. It will be my pleasure to escort you around tomorrow."

I feel like a fish who's just spotted some tasty bait. If I take it I'm asking for trouble, but something tells me I'm going to take it anyway. It's not an entirely unpleasant feeling. And the funny thing is, this lot don't look nearly as old as they did at eight o'clock this morning.

On the way home, Sarah quizzes me, but I'm not giving anything away.

"See, they're not such a bad bunch, are they?"

"Who, the Hampstead Over-the-Hillbillies?"

Sarah snorts. "Hey, that's a pretty good name for us. I like it. Headlines always were your thing, weren't they? I think the rest of the guys will like it too."

139

I lean back against the headrest and close my eyes to avoid further questioning.

"Thanks for the lift, Sarah," I say, as she stops outside my house to drop me off. "How about if I pick you up tomorrow morning? Ten to eight. And I'll buy breakfast."

Sarah leans over the gearstick and gives me a hug.

"Hate you."

"Hate you too, you cow."

"Mooooo."

Jack and Olly are out. After a long, hot shower I go and lie down on the bed. I fall into my first peaceful sleep since the start of the year.

I take the Jubilee Line to Baker Street. I fail to concentrate on the newspaper, still full of stories about the Iraq war and on this particular day the capture of former Deputy Prime Minister Tariq Aziz by the American forces. It's impossible to reconcile the fact of Britain at war with daily London life continuing business as usual. However current the news coverage, however graphic the images on Sky News, it still has a kind of not-really-happening aura about it. I'm reading today's headline stories, but at the same time, I'm noticing my thumbnail is split. Damn, I think, it will take weeks to grow out. I examine my nail for a few seconds, then my eye wanders round the carriage, barely focusing on a succession of random images. Trainers with flashing lights, Walkmans clamped to heads, a young couple who can't take their hands off one another, his hands down the back of her jeans, a woman hanging on to the rail above her and one-handedly reading a Maeve Binchey novel, a red-and-blue-nosed drunk swaying perilously, men in suits, women in suits, students with rucksacks, a fat middle-aged man opposite, legs wide apart, his grey prinstriped trousers straining at his crotch as he tucks into a giant baguette and a small piece of tomato dribbles onto his tie. He picks it up, unperturbed, and pops it straight into his mouth. As the train pulls into Baker Street Station, my tummy is telling me I am not looking forward to my appointment.

It's just a few minutes from here, past Madame Tussauds, the queue of tourists already snaking round the block, across the busy Marylebone Road with its bumper-to-bumper traffic and onto my Harley Street destination where Dr Olivetti and I are due to meet. I've not told anyone about this appointment. Not Maddy. Not Sarah. Certainly not Jack. When I rang last November, the brisk secretary told me that there was a five-month waiting list for a consultation. "Lucky it's not an emergency, then," I said breezily.

"Dr Olivetti is very much in demand," the secretary responded. "Of course if you'd sooner look elsewhere . . ."

"Not a problem, I'll take the date you offer."

"We look forward to seeing you, then, on 25 April at ten o'clock. Thank you for calling."

That particular day last November I'd been in the fashion cupboard approving handbags for an accessories shoot. Bags had become the hot new accessory ever since celebs had been spotted sporting Hermès "Birkin" bags and Fendi "Baguettes". Now practically

141

every designer bag worth its £700-plus price tag has its own personal name attached to it. Like Croissant. Or Alma. I was admiring a bag in buttery, plaited leather by Bottega Veneta, when I had something of an epiphany. *I don't have to put up with it any more.* For the price of two top-of-the-range designer bags I could probably get rid of mine altogether. While fashion victims across the UK are forking out fortunes for a bag that lasts a season I could take five years off my looks. My bags — the kind you carry under your eyes rather than over the shoulder — could be history. That's when I decided to give Dr Olivetti a call on a number I just happened to have cut out and kept from last issue's cut-out-and-keep guide to cosmetic surgery.

But now the moment of truth is here. And I'm scared. Very scared. At least last November I could have justified it on the grounds that I might have to go on TV to talk to Lorraine Kelly or Natasha Kaplinsky about stress and the working mother. And it wouldn't do to look stressed out myself.

What excuse do I have now? Apart from vanity — and desperation. Supposing Dr Olivetti thinks my face is beyond repair. "It's important for healing," I imagine him saying, "to have a degree of elasticity left in your skin. Unfortunately, you don't seem to have any." That would be just too awful.

I'm giving myself the full interrogation now. Will fewer wrinkles really change my life? Get me a job offer I can't refuse? Get my sex life going again? Wasn't there a time — back in the dark ages of the late 1980s — when I refused to carry ads for cosmetic surgery in the magazine I edited before *Jasmine* because it so thoroughly went against my feminist principles? Because I thought it immoral to encourage women to undergo dangerous surgery just in order to conform to male standards of beauty? Well, sod that. Times have changed. Even so, I'm not at all convinced. And what if it all goes wrong and I end up looking like the Bride of Wildenstein?

As part of my new fitness regime, I decide to walk up the three flights of stairs to Dr Olivetti's consulting room. The name Dr Olivetti, MS FRCS, is etched on a shiny brass plate on a well-polished wooden door. I know this man to be a highly respected plastic as well as cosmetic surgeon. He's renowned for the reconstruction work he does on burns and other accident victims. But maybe wrinkles are what bring in the cash.

I knock tentatively. Almost immediately the door opens.

"Good morning, Mrs . . . Hope? My goodness, so it is you. What a surprise."

Not as much of a surprise to her as it is to me. My luck really has run out.

"I only started working here last week," she twitters, "and when I saw your name in the appointments book I did think it unlikely that two Hope Lyndhursts . . . On the other hand, you're the last person I'd have expected to . . ." She trails off.

It's some kind of curse. Or divine retribution.

"Don't you worry now, Hope, your little secret is safe with me," says Vanessa the Undresser, a look on her face so jubilant that I could be forgiven for thinking she'd just won the lottery roll-over.

Dr Olivetti is silver-haired, handsome and patrician.

"How can I help you?"

"I, I . . ."

He waits patiently. His forehead is remarkably smooth for a man who must be in his late fifties. Gordon Ramsay could do with some of what he's been having.

"I, I . . ."

"It can be hard to get started; take your time."

"Well, when I booked this appointment back in November I had been expecting to be doing some television work, as part of my job. But I'm not doing that job any more so I'm not sure . . ."

Dr Olivetti's left eyebrow rises a fraction, but his forehead remains static.

"The thing is, it's my face. It's, well, basically it's collapsed. And I just hate the way I look. I used to think I was OK. Now I look in the mirror and wish I had cataracts so I didn't have to see the truth."

Another uplift of the eyebrow.

"Everything needs doing. My neck is like chicken skin. My upper eyelids are drooping and my lower lids are disappearing. The bags under my eyes are these hideous watery pouches. I'm a mess."

The tears are welling up again.

"I don't wish to contradict you, Mrs Lyndhurst, but for a woman of your age — let's see . . ." Dr Olivetti refers to his notes, "you were born in 1953, so that makes you fifty — you are holding up remarkably well. Everything you describe is part of the normal ageing process, but there is a great deal we can do to counteract the visual signs of ageing, if that's what you wish."

"I'm a mess," I repeat quietly, almost to myself.

"Would you mind coming over and sitting in this chair so I can take a quick digital photograph of your face."

I go to the allocated chair and sit down. Although I want to cry, I immediately smile instead for the camera. It's a Pavlovian response. Camera. Smile. All those years of directing magazine photo shoots.

"No need to smile," says Dr Olivetti, looking not at all like Mario Testino, "this one's not for the cover of *Vogue*." At least he's trying to make me feel comfortable. He takes a picture, walks back to his desk and starts fiddling with his computer.

"Come and sit back down over here and relax. This will only take a moment."

The next thing that happens is my face quite suddenly appears vastly magnified on the wall. This seems to me both unnecessary and unkind. Dr Olivetti starts drawing with a kind of pen mouse on what looks like a lightbox on his desk, and the marks are appearing — as if by magic — on the image of my face.

He's showing me exactly what can be done to the bags under my eyes, to the drooping upper eyelids, to my disappearing jawline. I obviously had "worst-case scenario" written all over me. But instead of a fresh and smooth new me all I can picture is barbaric metal instruments of torture and Sylvester Stallone's mother. I look down at my lap.

Dr Olivetti has put down his pen and walked around to just behind the chair where I'm sitting. He places a hand on my shoulder, and I jump and swivel round. Why is he touching me?

"The thing is, Mrs Lyndhurst," he says, "we can make you feel a whole lot better about how you look, but we can't make you feel better about yourself as a person. Surgery will enhance your appearance, but not your life. I don't say this to all my patients, but I think you may have more important issues to deal with at present. Am I right?"

I sniff miserably and nod my head.

"I'd put all this on hold if I were you. If you still feel the same about your face in a year, come back and we'll arrange for surgery. I won't refuse you, even now, if you insist, but the advice I'm giving you is with your best interests at heart."

Relief floods over me. I'm not going under the knife. I'm not. "Thank you, Doctor," I say. "Thank you so much for putting things in perspective. You must be a really good doctor if you turn people away rather than just take their money."

"I have patients queuing up for my services, Mrs Lyndhurst, so one more or one less, and I can still pay the children's school fees and holiday at Christmas in the Caribbean. But it's important to have realistic expectations about what surgery can and can't achieve. You're an intelligent woman, I'm sure, and I want you to consider your options carefully."

I love this man. If ever I do decide to have surgery, he's the only one for me. We shake hands, and I thank him again before I leave the room.

On my way past Vanessa's desk I say, "Nothing doing. He thinks I look fine just the way I am."

"That's excellent news, Hope," she smirks, "but there's really no need for this. I said it before, and I'll say it again: your secret is safe with me."

I'm so grateful to have been let off the hook that I consider a little visit to Bond Street for some summer clothes. Instead, I find myself heading north, towards Regents Park. It won't take me much more than an hour to walk home, it's a beautiful day and it's an absolute age since I fed the ducks. Only an hour! This is surely progress. Only a month ago an hour-long walk would have seemed like a twenty-six-mile marathon.

The one place I know around here with a bakery is Marylebone High Street. In the posh patisseries of Marylebone High Street they've never heard of sliced white. But bearing in mind that I've just saved myself up to ten grand for the full facelift, I think those ducks deserve a treat. I'm not saying the ducks would know the difference between Sunblest and Poilâne in a blind tasting, but whatever's left I can have for lunch with my daily blast of cholesterol-lowering mono-unsaturates. In other words, half an avocado. Poilâne for the ducks and Poilâne for me. This is the life. I've lost four pounds this month, and I could swear that's a muscle I can feel in my left upper arm. Things are looking up. Even my face feels less slack as I head jauntily for the park, a nice loaf of Poilâne tucked under my arm.

147

Sally, wife of Nick of the crinkly eyes, has asked me to meet her for a chat. I suggest the Coffee Cup. This is partly a test for me, to see if I can resist the raisin toast and butter.

Out of her walking gear, I hardly recognise Sally. Her hair, no longer hidden under a baseball cap, is honey-blonde, shoulder-length and swingy. She's wearing tight, beige cord jeans with a creamy-coloured silk shirt tucked in and a funky knee-length embroidered coat. It's Sloane meets Boho, and it really works. Mid-forties, I guess, but she could easily pass for thirty-five.

"Gosh, you look great in mufti," I say.

"You scrub up pretty well yourself," replies Sally, dropping elegantly into the chair opposite me and crossing her long, tapered legs. "Have you ordered?"

"Not yet, but I'm just having a coffee. You?"

"I'll have tea and some of that raisin toast. I hear it's the best."

I wince slightly, but when the waitress comes I hold firm.

"One cappuccino, one tea and one round of raisin toast, please."

"Look," says Sally, "I have a meeting at the site at eleven, so shall we get straight down to business?"

"Business? I didn't know we were going to be talking business, but fire away . . ."

"Well, first, here's the form for you to fill in."

Between that first walk on Hampstead Heath and now, a mere two weeks later, I appear to have agreed to

148

go trekking in the Atlas Mountains in Morocco in late November, sleeping under canvas and with absolutely no possibility of plugging in a hair-dryer. *Plus*, no plumbing for more than a week! I have also promised, apparently, to put down a deposit of £500 and raise at least two grand in sponsorship money. I can't recall a moment when I actually agreed to do this, but Nick and Sally are two of the most persuasive people I've ever met. And just thinking about Sally — her courage, her commitment, her grace — fills me with guilt. I hope I'm going to be up to this and not make an almighty fool of myself.

"OK, hand it over."

"We're going to have such fun," says Sally. "And think of all that lovely money we're going to raise."

I smile back weakly, envisioning myself at the bottom of a ravine having broken practically every bone in my body, waiting for the emergency helicopters to airlift me to a filthy hospital in downtown Casablanca where I'll probably die of blood poisoning caused by unsterilised instruments.

"But now for business . . ."

"Oh, you mean that wasn't business."

"Look, Hope, I know you're not working at the moment, and I don't want to twist your arm or anything . . ." Not much, I think, wondering if perhaps Sally is about to take just too much advantage of my guilty conscience. "But I wondered if you might write a few press releases for us in your spare time . . ."

"Press releases? I can do press releases with my eyes closed. I'd be delighted to help."

". . . and I thought maybe you'd like to join our committee . . ."

I hate committees. In fact, I've just resigned from the Neighbourhood Watch committee I hate them — and Vanessa — so much. On committees everyone has to pretend to be democratic and agree on everything, but in my experience they're all petty infighters and fifth columnists.

"Well, I've never really been one for committees, but I suppose . . . Yes, of course, in this case it would be an honour . . ."

"Terrific. And there's just one more thing . . ."

There can't be just one more thing, this is what's called seriously taking the mickey. I can't let myself be manipulated like this.

Sally hesitates. "I hope you don't mind my asking, but I was just wondering if you would give me your husband's work number. My back is killing me, and I need a physio to look me over."

Why am I always so suspicious? She's as good as she looks and it is uncharitable of me to think otherwise.

"Jack would be delighted to help you, I'm sure."

"Thanks for everything, Hope. I'm so glad we've met."

"And I'm glad to have met you too."

An American in Paris

Jasmine is about to be relaunched. Tanya, my former PA who is now working for Mark, is being admirably discreet, which is exactly how I would expect her to behave if she were still my secretary. On the other hand, I wouldn't have thought any less of her if she'd let slip one *tiny* morsel of gossip by way of demonstrating her loyalty to her old boss. But that's not Tanya's way. Fortunately, Megan, my deputy, who has been kept on by Mark but is convinced he's conniving to get rid of her, and who will, in any case, be off the second a decent opportunity comes along, is my personal fly-on-the wall, my very own Google news alert. Not everything I now know about Mark is of enormous interest, but I want to know it anyway. For example, I have become aware that Mark is wheat-intolerant and that his poor little tummy blows up to enormous proportions if he so much as looks at a grain of flour. On the rare occasions that Mark doesn't have a four-hour lunch date, Tanya has apparently been commissioned to make his sandwiches herself, from a menu of allowed ingredients that Mark has provided.

I am reliably informed that Mark has split up with the boyfriend who designs wallpapers for Colefax &

Fowler, and has started dating a young Royal College of Art fashion graduate whose degree show was an S&M fantasy, entirely in rubber. I also know that Mark thinks I was a rubbish editor who should have been fired five years earlier. He refers to me as "Hope-*less*" and laughs helplessly at his audacious originality. Meanwhile, the incredible, exquisite, creative powerhouse that is Mark has replaced features such as "How to grab a little me-time" with "Eight ingenious ways to fold a napkin". "Thirty-minute suppers" have been mangled in the waste-disposal unit to be substituted with "The return of elegant dining — why shop-bought pastry won't do in the noughties." "Sex tip of the month" (tongue-in-cheek and very funny and at one stage in my life even rather useful) has been dumped in favour of "Out damn spot", which focuses on one especially recalcitrant stain per issue (*very* useful but not exactly entertaining). All the columnists and most of the freelance writers have gone — "I want the pictures to *brrrrrreathe*," has become, according to Megan, Mark's favourite phrase. This means there is no room now for intelligently written features, only captions. *Jasmine's* last cover under the old order featured Kristin Scott Thomas. Mark has decided that all celebrities are chav (he's probably right there) and for his relaunch issue has gone for a still life of Cath Kidston's latest pinnies and matching biscuit tins. But pinnies and biscuit tins don't do marriage, divorce, wear shoes you'd kill for and go into rehab. Which does make me wonder if there is as much mileage to be had from a Cath Kidston pinny as from even the most chav of celebrities. I have to keep reminding myself that it's no longer my problem.

I wouldn't mind seeing a video of the relaunch party. All the waitresses will be wearing Nigella wigs and Nigella padding if their breasts don't naturally make the grade. Canapés will be served in cup-cake holders. Mark calls this "post-modern irony" and thinks the advertisers will lap it up. He is wrong. The men who buy space do not know what post-modern irony is, but they do like large breasts, so Mark may yet be seen to be onto a winner. Instead of a speech, Mark is going to auction himself as a prize. The money will go to a monkey sanctuary in Cornwall, and the winner will get to take Mark home where he will do a Susannah and Trinny on their interiors. The going-home goody bag is more ironing than irony — a DVD of *Pillow Talk* starring Rock Hudson and Doris Day, a tea towel (Cath Kidston, again), a lemon drizzle cake and a stick of *Disappear*.

The atmosphere at home is horrible. Whoever came up with the idea that the family that eats together, stays together, obviously hasn't been dining with Hope Lyndhurst-Steele and her jolly brood lately. There are no complaints about the food, in fact my culinary imagination knows no bounds since I've been unemployed. But once we've exhausted talking about the brilliance of my lentils with the herb, red onion and mustard dressing, and the sheer deliciousness of my pan-fried cod in ground almond batter served on a broad bean puree, the conversation grinds to a halt.

153

This is because there are so many taboo subjects that even opening one's mouth, other than for the purpose of popping food into it, is fraught with danger.

Subjects not up for discussion when Jack, Olly and I are all present at the table:
Vanessa the Undresser
Revision
Exam timetable
Gap-year arrangements
State of Olly's room
State of Olly's wardrobe — i.e. number of socks with holes, number of T-shirts in threads, jackets with no visible fastenings, buttons or zips
Recent acquisition of tongue stud (not Olly, Jack)
My next job
My mother — other than to enquire about her health
Who might be the father of Maddy's baby
What I do all day long

Subjects not up for discussion when Jack and I are alone:
All of the above, plus
Our non-existent sex life
Why all conversations end in an argument
Life after Olly leaves

Allowable topics:
The war — this is possible only because all three of us agree it should never have happened. But

because we all agree, it's not much fun as a topic for discussion. Everyone just nods.

Computers — not a bad one this, as Jack and Olly can exchange companionable glances every time I say something which demonstrates my profound ignorance of anything remotely technical. A perfect opportunity for ganging up on me.

Football — I don't even try

So my sitting here announcing that I fancy going to Paris for a few days — on my own — is the best thing that has happened to conversation in this household for months. At the moment of saying it, I haven't even considered it as a serious proposition. It's just a vague thought which I've aired to try to lighten up the atmosphere. But the second it's out there, in the public domain so to speak, it starts to feel real, and I begin to feel excited.

"Cool," says Olly.

"Great idea," echoes Jack.

"I can hardly believe it, but apart from work-related trips, when there have always been people to meet up with day and night, I've never been away on my own in my life." So much for the independent woman.

"It's not something I'd ever have thought about," says Jack. "But, if that's the case, it will do you good, and Paris is an ideal place to start. We wouldn't want to drop you solo in the middle of the Gobi desert, or deep inside a rainforest in South America, but Rue St Honoré I reckon you can handle." When Jack smiles, he gets a tiny dimple on his left cheek. I fell in love with that dimple, among other things.

"How long you going for, Hopey?" This is the first bit of enthusiasm I've seen from Olly in relation to me for some time. Calling me Hopey rather than Mum is what he does when he feels relaxed and well-disposed towards me. If I tell him I'll be gone for a month I think he might hug me. I'm tempted.

"Just about three nights, I should think. Unless you'd like me to stay longer."

I say this with what I hope sounds like good humour, but it could be the cue for an Olly-hates-Hope fest. Instead, Olly looks at his watch.

"Thanks, Mum, that was delicious. See ya . . ."

"Just put your plate . . ." Too late, he's gone.

Jack seems to genuinely approve of the idea. I suppose it will be a relief to have me and my mean spirits out of the house, but he has always been generous in the sense of wanting other people to enjoy themselves. By midnight, I've booked the Eurostar, phoned a little hotel in the Marais that we wrote up in *Jasmine*, and ordered my *Time Out* guide to Paris on Amazon.

I pick up the first edition of the new-look *Jasmine* at Waterloo, at the Eurostar terminal. Refusing, on principle, to buy a copy, I waste five minutes flicking. I nick the cover-mount, which is a stick of *Disappear* in a chic black container that could easily be mistaken for a Bobbie Brown lipstick. Other than in name, the magazine is in every respect brand new. A brand-new throwback to the 1950s. The strapline "*for women who live life to the full*" has been replaced with "*celebrating the new domesticity*". Fuck domesticity, I think, what about equal pay and maternity rights and part-time jobs for working mothers and supermarket pizza and putting your feet up and saying, "Sod the housework"? Who wants a life reduced to reducing sauces? Or to start stencilling one's husband's ties rather than buying him one that already has a perfectly acceptable pattern printed on it? I will not even consider drying pomegranate seeds and fashioning them into a necklace.

As a final act of defiance I pick up three copies of *Vogue* and place them on top of the pile of *Jasmine*. So even if there does exist a woman foolish enough to want to buy a magazine with stains on the brain, she won't be able to find it at Waterloo.

The whole of the journey from London to Paris is spent planning my schedule and poring over a map. It's one of those nifty, gloss-coated origami maps which folds into an oblong no bigger than the surface of a cigarette pack, but opens out in different ways to reveal the various districts of Paris in manageable chunks. Except, however many times I practise, I can't seem to fold it back the right way. Just as we enter the tunnel, I hurl it at the window in frustration, knocking over the paper cup in front of me, which splashes hot liquid and a soggy tea bag onto my lap. Bugger! It was wise to have ignored the collective sneers of Jack and Olly and to have brought with me a wheelie suitcase containing at least eight changes of clothing. As the train draws into Gare du Nord, I am slightly damp. So are my spirits.

Through the window of the taxi, Paris presents itself to me in shades of grey. What the writer Saul Bellow, who lived there for some time, described as "the native Parisian *grisaille*" is reflected in the streets, the buildings and even the people. I've always felt that Parisian women dress to match the muted colours of their city — rejecting colour in favour of black and grey with accents of white. How pared-down and sober they are compared to their London counterparts, hinting at sexiness only in the slightly tighter cut of their skirts, the low-key coquettishness of their leather ankle boots, the gamine-but-not-quite-groomed quality of their cropped hair and pale skin. Nothing's in your face like it is in London; there's not a single bobbing cleavage or back-handle out there on the boulevards, whereas at home there's an epidemic of midriff-mooning. French women are sexy, it seems to me, because they understand the art of insinuation. Their sexuality is a subtle, slow-burn thing rather than a here's-my-booty, take-it-or-leave-it *fait accompli*. Sex. Whatever happened to sex? It's like someone has locked up my sexuality and thrown away the key. I don't like this feeling one bit.

The woman who checks me in at my little hotel in the heart of the Marais, which is on the right bank and home to the Jewish quarter, the gay quarter and some of the best museums in Paris, is as friendly and charming as my taxi driver. She even seems to appreciate my faltering O-level French, although it takes only a couple of painful attempts on my part at asking, "Do you have a map? *Avez-vous une carte?*" for her to start addressing me in word-perfect English. I don't know why everyone says the French in general, and the Parisians in particular, are so rude. So far, they're being delightful.

"I wonder if you could book this restaurant on the left bank for me," I say to her. "It's called Brasserie Colette, and I'd really like to try it."

"Aah, yes, a very good restaurant. My pleasure, madame. I will call you in your room to let you know. My name, if you need me, is Madame Maripol."

The lift takes me up to my eyrie on the top floor. Paris is renowned for its tiny hotel rooms, and this one is no exception. Not enough room to . . . I try to pirouette with one arm outstretched, imagining myself swinging a cat. I knock against the bed and fall onto it, chuckling at my inanity.

The double bed — just about big enough for me — takes up almost the entire floor space. I jump up onto my knees on the blanket and reach out to the wardrobe, which is so tightly packed in that its door scrapes the side of the bed as I attempt to open it. I haul up my suitcase from the floor and then crawl over it to the other side of the bed, which is almost right up against the double windows. Flinging them back, I let out a yelp of delight. Grey, my new favourite colour! I'm in Paris! I'm going to have a ball!

It's all so very . . . French. Down at ground level on the narrow street are three cafes right next to one another, with chairs and tables lined up in rows on the pavement and, above, a stone building dotted with tiny wrought-iron balconies. An adjacent building is so imposing that it must be one of those eighteenth-century mansions the French call *hotels particuliers*, once home to wealthy aristocrats. I can just glimpse inside to a pebbled courtyard framed with stone arches and with low-lying topiary at its centre.

All the heaviness that has been clogging my head for months has lifted, like clouds parting to reveal a chink of brilliant blue sky. Grey skies, grey buildings, but suddenly it feels like sunshine.

For once I'm relieved to be middle-aged and invisible, wearing sensibly well-padded walking shoes and not having to impress anyone. Every few minutes, I have to stop to consult the map. This involves a delicate conjuring trick of removing my glasses to read the map close up, then putting them back on to read the street signs and then removing them again to check the map. All this while also trying to keep the guide book open to the relevant page and avoiding dropping my handbag.

What surprises me most about Paris is how little it seems to have changed since I first visited when I was eighteen years old. This is both its best and worst asset. Best in the sense that not every shop is part of a global chain, not every cafe a facsimile of one in New York or Tokyo. Paris has hung on doggedly to its legendary romantic charm. But there's a kind of arrogance too, about this refusal to move with the times. Paris could certainly do with a clean-up. I find myself playing hopscotch around the dog shit and wondering if all the cigarette butts on the pavement might soon join up to form a unique Parisian street carpet. And except for the occasional iconic piece of modern architecture — such as I. M. Pei's the Louvre Pyramid and Nouvel's Fondation Cartier — it has nothing new to match London's dynamic rebirth in Docklands and the Square Mile.

It's the old stuff that's unbeatable. I'm standing right in the middle of the perfectly symmetrical Place des Vosges, built from 1605, all arcaded red brick and stone facades and steeply pitched roofs, the oldest square in Paris. This garden at its centre was once a setting for duels and romantic trysts. A famous French courtesan, Marion Delorne, lived on this square at number eleven, running one of the most popular salons of her era. I'm swept away by the visionary simplicity of my surroundings and the stories these buildings could tell. What makes my mood so different, here in Paris, is that I'm in the moment, the here and now. I'm taking time to stand and stare. I'm not even thinking about the what ifs and the what nexts, and it feels like liberation. Jack would love this, the casual mooching and meandering. We mooch and meander well together. Or at least we used to.

Underwear. I've decided that underwear is the answer. Even though I haven't yet formulated the question.

I've done the Picasso museum, I've done a goat's cheese salad, and I've been walking up and down Rue des Saints Pères on the left bank for twenty minutes now, peering into the windows of the plethora of lingerie shops for which Paris is so famous. I read in a newspaper recently that while women in the UK buy an average of three bras a year, the typical Frenchwoman tallies up more than a dozen. This is underwear I can relate to. Not like Agent Provocateur. I'm not really the crotchless-panty type, however nice the fabric and neat the stitching.

Sabbia Rosa says the name above the shop. I take a deep breath and walk in. *"Est-ce que je peux vous renseigner?"* asks the assistant as I unzip my black puffa jacket to allow in a little air. *"Je regarde juste, merci,"* I reply without hesitation. I've looked this up so I know I've got it right. "Aah, Engleesh," she says, as if that explains everything, from the puffa jacket to the frizzy hair.

Nothing can break my mood, not even a snooty shop assistant. The underwear is having the same effect on me as Picasso's portrait of Dora Maar. I want it, and I want it now. I can't have the Picasso, but I might just be able to take home some of this. This is the real McCoy, serious, sensual underwear for serious, sensual grown-ups — for politicians' mistresses and the likes of Catherine Deneuve. French politicians' mistresses, that is. I mean you wouldn't want to go to the expense for a John Prescott or a Jack Straw . . .

Row upon row of sheeny, slippery satin slips and camisoles in vibrant, jewel-box colours. I feel like a child let loose in a sweet shop. Everything in this boudoir of a boutique is irresistible. I try on a slip the colour of emeralds, with insets of creamy, hand-woven lace. I haven't suddenly turned into Anouk Aimée or Fanny Ardant. I still look like me, only much more sultry and sophisticated, especially after the second twirl when I decide to take off my towelling sports socks to get the full effect.

For perhaps a quarter of a second, before my inarguable logic sets in, I baulk at the £300 price tag. Then I rationalise that a garment that costs me £300 but makes me feel a million dollars has to be a once-in-a-lifetime bargain. Yes, I'll take it. And because I can't possibly wear it over my M&S five-to-a-pack briefs, I buy a pair of matching panties — small but not invisible and with crotch intact — and a discreet, matching push-up bra. Then I buy the whole thing again in the blue of lapis lazuli. The bill comes to not far short of a thousand quid.

A thousand quid spent on underwear in the time it takes me to remember my pin number! Does anyone — other than Catherine Deneuve and the mistresses of French politicians — even wear slips any more? Oh, what the hell. Outside the shop I feel like dancing. I lift up the carrier bag to my face and plant a kiss on it. Me and my lingerie need a little snack. We head off in the direction of a patisserie which, according to my guide book, makes the best macaroons on the planet.

Madame Maripol has managed to get me a reservation at Brasserie Colette, but I have to get there by 7.30.

That gives me less than an hour to wash, flop and get dressed again.

163

I run the hot water, but the water is cold. After a couple of minutes the water is still running cold. I dial reception and Madame Maripol answers.

"*Mais, oui*, it eez the plumbing."

"I know it's the plumbing, but I do have a restaurant reservation, and I do need to have a bath."

"It eez not a problem, madame. Leave the tap to run for ten minutes and the water will be perfect."

"Ten minutes!"

"Yes, madame. *C'est normale*. This is how it works."

No apology, no excuse, just a French-style statement of the facts, a telephonic Gallic shrug, as though it's perfectly acceptable for water to take ten minutes to warm up, which perhaps in Paris it is. So I wait, too cheerful to be irritated. She's right, though; after ten minutes the water is sufficiently steamy for me to sink into a hot bath into which I squish the entire contents of the hotel's complimentary shower and bath gel. I'm living it up, after all. I'm also *un peu fatiguée* and my feet are aching after seven hours pounding the Paris pavements. But it's been a wonderful day. An early dinner and early to bed will round it all off perfectly.

For the sheer indulgent pleasure of it, I decide to wear my new underwear with the one skirt I have brought with me. The slip slithers silkily over my head. As I move around the bedroom it travels in opposition to my skin, caressing it like a lover. I get a sudden reminder of what it's like to feel sexy. If Jack were here right now, I might even be able to locate that dormant repository of desire. Maybe, just maybe, Paris and Sabbia Rosa will do for me what Kilburn and Primark can't. Kick-start Jack and me back into something physical which might, in turn, over time, lead us back to the intimacy we've lost.

As the lights twinkle along the Seine and the taxi transports me over the bridge and back into St Germain, I lean back against the upholstery and smile.

Arriving at Brasserie Colette, I am surprised to find it completely packed. Filled with young lovers in cosy twosomes, friends in foursomes, and a large group who must be having some kind of family celebration. I feel very alone. It's not that I mind eating by myself, not at all, but it does make me think about Jack and Maddy and how it might be even better to share this experience with someone I cared about.

My table turns out not to be a table at all, but a bar stool jammed between the cashier's counter and the window. There's no room for my legs so I have to sit sideways on to the counter. I'd be more comfortable eating my dinner standing up.

"I am zo zorree, madame, but we are full up," says the *maître d'* apologetically.

"Never mind," I say, remembering how often Maddy has had to put up with single people being treated as second-class citizens in a world designed for pairs. "I'm sure the excellence of your food will make me forget about the cramp in my thighs." My sarcasm is lost on the *maître d'* who nods uncomprehendingly.

I'm too busy trying to make sense of the menu to notice him when he walks in. My first consciousness of a new male presence is when he's trying to drape a

165

chocolate suede jacket over about fifty other coats piled onto the wooden coat stand adjacent to the counter.

By the time this newcomer has picked up various coats that have been dislodged in the process of attempting to add his, the *maître d'* has marched over and blocked my sight line, gripping him by the shoulders and kissing him vigorously on each cheek.

"Danee, *mon ami*, welcome back to Paris. It is zo good to zee you. And where eez your delightful wife?"

"Hey, buddy, good to see you too. My wife couldn't make it this time, I'm afraid, too busy with work and the kids. I've flown in for three days for a conference, and then it's straight back home to Boston. But I couldn't come to Paris without visiting my all-time favourite restaurant and the incomparable Monsieur Arnaud, my all-time favourite *maître d'*."

"But why did you not telephone? We 'av no table, only zis one, by the bar, next to zis most unfortunate lady."

The American is unfazed. "You have to remember you guys weren't this popular three years ago when you'd just opened. I never expected it to be so crowded so early on in the evening."

They launch into French. The American's is perfect, except for the accent, which is even worse than mine.

I stare at my menu, trying to guess what the starter *Effilochée de queue de veau tiède, glace à la moutarde à l'ancienne* might be. Something to do with old mustard is as far as I can get.

The poor guy must be at least six foot three. How he's going to sort his legs out at the side of the counter, which is at right angles to mine, I can't imagine. And it's going to be embarrassing, the two of us sandwiched in like this. He's going to feel obliged to talk to me and me to him. This is not turning out as well as I expected.

I look up at a jowl-free jaw, Quink Ink eyes and a J. Crew catalogue grin.

"Food's too good to miss," he says amiably, sitting sideways on as I had to do, so we're now directly facing one another. As he manoeuvres himself to avoid an avalanche of coats I realise that every time I look up from now on I will be looking straight into those ink-stained eyes.

"Oh, boy, this is so great. Only Paris has the power to send me as high as a flag on the fourth of July."

"Nellie. *South Pacific*. 'A Wonderful Guy'," I smile back tentatively.

"Hey there, you're a fan of the Great American Musical. Just so happens I teach a class at my college on the history of American musical theatre. It's a kind of hobby of mine. So what's your all-time favourite?"

"*West Side Story*."

"And then?"

"*Singing in The Rain*."

"After that?"

"*Grease*."

"Not bad choices. How about *An American in Paris*?"

"The jury's still out. You're the first American I've met in Paris."

Jesus. Was that me just answering a question? Or was it flirting? I didn't think I knew how any more.

167

"Gene Kelly or Fred Astaire?" he asks. He has great teeth.

"Gene Kelly."

I'm pretty good at this sort of game, though I'm rather surprised to be doing it with a guy I met five seconds ago.

I try one of my own. "Jets or Sharks?"

"Sharks, of course." Yes, he's definitely a Shark. Too dark and intense to be a Jet.

"Right answer." Now I'm taking charge. As usual. "Was *Gigi* American or French?"

"It was Lerner — Loewe. Their first musical after *My Fair Lady*."

"I *so* loved Leslie Caron, wasn't she gorgeous?"

"Yes, I don't care much for blondes."

My hand goes instinctively to my dark hair. Idiot! It's not a compliment.

"Something's just occurred to me. We're sitting in Colette's Brasserie. Didn't Colette write *Gigi*, the original story, I mean?"

"Hey, English lady, you're quite the expert."

The waiter has come to take our orders. He looks first at me.

"I think I need some help," I say, looking at the American as there really isn't any other place to look.

"Well, if I'm going to be your culinary adviser, I think we should introduce ourselves first. I'm Dan."

"And I'm Hope."

"I like your name."

"My mother liked it too. Although she was none too keen on me."

168

As the waiter looks on, Dan patiently takes me through the menu dish by dish.

"I want everything," I sigh, "it all sounds delicious. But as I have to choose I think I'll go for the calamari with red peppers and shrimp sauce followed by sea bass with spinach and *saucisses de morteau*."

"Good choices. I guess you'll be wanting white. How about us sharing a bottle and seeing how it goes?"

For some reason, this suggestion puts me on edge.

"Look, I'm sorry, Dan, I know this must be awkward for you. You really don't have to talk to me. I'm quite happy to just enjoy my food and read my guide book. You've been really kind, but I can manage perfectly well from now on."

"Do I take that as a brush-off? Or are you just being charmingly English, apologising for something that you haven't done and which certainly isn't your fault? Tell me honestly, have you ever come across an American who doesn't like to talk?"

I feel myself blushing.

"Hey, English lady, if you'd rather commune silently with your sea bass, that's fine with me. But if I can seduce you with a discussion on the semiotics of the *Wizard of Oz*, or the rise of tap-dancing in the McCarthy era . . ."

I'm blushing deeper. *Be reasonable, Hope. He's not really on a mission to seduce you, it's just a figure of speech.*

When I finally look over into the restaurant, I become aware that all the other customers have gone. It must be because we're seated in the leper colony that Monsieur Arnaud didn't need to turn us out for the restaurant's second sitting. My watch says 11.30.

"My God, the time. We've emptied the place out. So much for my early night."

"Yes, we do seem to have driven everyone away. But I can't imagine why anyone would want to sleep in this enchanted city."

"You have a point, but I need to find myself a taxi. I'm staying on the opposite side of the river. It's been a lovely evening, though."

"A cab may not be so easy to find in this part of town," says Dan, glancing out of the window and onto the deserted side street, "and you probably shouldn't wander too far on your own at this time of night. Let's look for one together."

"That would be great. Thank you."

We pay our separate bills and turn towards the coat stand. Our jackets have become entwined in an awkward embrace. Dan untangles them and helps me on with mine.

Monsieur Arnaud smiles beatifically as we leave the restaurant together.

"I have a great idea," says Dan once we're out on the street. "Just look at this glorious night, so warm I don't even need this." He swings his jacket over his shoulder, hooking a finger through the loop on the inside of the collar. "How about an exclusive Paris By Night tour? I lived here for three years as a student, and it would be my pleasure to be your guide."

"Dan, seven hours! That's how long I've walked for today."

I pause.

"Oh, well, I guess a couple more won't make much difference."

This is not the answer I should have given. I must be crazy. What am I thinking of? I'm standing here with a complete stranger in a foreign city in the middle of the night. His next move is probably to drag me down some stone steps beside the Seine, steal my jewellery (well, my watch, which is the only jewellery I'm wearing), rape me at knifepoint and dump me in the river, as good as dead. Or dead.

"Shall we head for the Seine?"

There, I knew it.

"It's so beautiful to walk along the Embankment when all the traffic and the fumes have gone. There'll be hardly anyone about. Except for lovers, of course."

We're heading towards the scene of the intended crime. But I'm a little drunk — not so far gone as to not know what I'm doing, but just far enough gone not to care — and for some reason, I trust this man, this easy-going college professor who wears J. Crew sweaters and teaches English Literature at a prestigious university in Massachusetts, is crazy for corny musicals and has a beautiful lawyer wife and two small children back home.

We walk and we talk. I tell him about my mid-life crisis, but only the bits that make me sound interesting. I don't mention my age or my dodgy relationship with my husband or my dying mother. I explain how I'm at a crossroads in my career, looking for a new creative path to follow, taking my time to think and travel and reflect before I throw myself into something new. None of it's actually a lie, it's just not nearly as true as it might be. We talk about books and movies and plays we've seen and countries we've been to and why he loves Paris and why I love New York and why Bush should be hanged, drawn and quartered. He's less enthusiastic about this last idea than I am. He tells me about his clever wife and how little time they seem to have to talk these days. And I look at my watch, and it's now 2a.m. and I'm about to say, "I think we'd better find that cab," when he says, "Would you like a nightcap? The bar at my hotel will still be open, and it's only a ten-minute walk from here to the Rue de l'Université."

I hesitate. "Well, let's head in that direction and if we don't see a cab, I can call for one from your hotel."

"I really must go," I say again, after the second brandy, sinking deeper into the burgundy velvet sofa.

"And I think you really must stay," says Dan, moving deftly from the armchair, taking my hand and pulling me to my feet. He traces my cheek with his fingers.

"You're quite something, little English lady."

He keeps hold of my hand as we walk across the bar, through the deserted lobby and single file up the narrow staircase. A zillion contradictory thoughts are racing through my mind. This can't be happening. Jack. Jack! *Jack!* I've never been unfaithful to Jack. Never even seriously considered it. My God, this Yank is handsome. And so young. Ten years younger than me at least. Don't do it, you fool, says the voice of reason in my head. *You'd be a fool not to,* says the voice of temptation. Twenty years of fidelity, about to be nuked in a single night. But what about my marriage? says the voice of reason. *Yeah, what about it? What has this got to do with marriage?* says temptation. It's not too late to turn and run. *Oh, yes, it is. Much too late.* And now I want it to be too late. I need it to be too late. As long as the lights stay out. As long as he doesn't see the real me. The me that's fifty. Oh, Jack, I really never intended . . .

I feel like a nuclear reactor about to pop. I blame the underwear. I've been carried away by my underwear. A key is turning in a lock. As the door slams behind us and he presses me up against it, his lips on mine, his tongue investigating the inside of my mouth, his hands roaming over my body, lifting my skirt, tearing at the buttons on my blouse, my hands pulling his shirt from his trousers, grappling with the buckle on his belt, unzipping him, all thoughts are finally extinguished. The sexual famine is officially over.

I awake, in a cold sweat, a shaft of light beamed across the bed into my sore eyes from the crack between the wooden shutters. I'm lying in a pool of something. Is it blood? Have I been stabbed? Is that what happens after a fantastic fuck with a total stranger? First he fucks you, then he fucks you again, then he stabs you. But there's no pain, just me covered in sweat lying on a soaking sheet. I feel along my body, too scared to look. I'm still wearing the slip, but the bra and panties seem to have escaped. I gingerly place my hand beneath the arch of my back, praying that the six foot three inches of all-American boy lying on its belly to my left won't wake up, and that I'm not haemorrhaging eight pints of blood. I bring my hand back round to my front. It's even wetter than before, but there's not a spot of blood.

Slowly, terrifyingly, it dawns on me. I am lying on a hotel sheet in a Sabbia Rosa slip, drenched in the watery excretions of a menopausal sex siren. I have been awoken from post-coital slumber by the kind of night-sweat that can only be induced by plummeting levels of oestrogen. The stabbing scenario seems almost attractive at this point. If he wakes and sees me lying here like a beached jellyfish, I shall simply have to jump straight out of the window.

The bed creaks as I roll over and onto the floor on my hands and knees, before carefully, quietly, standing up and tiptoeing my way to the bathroom, picking up bits of discarded clothing as I go. If only I can escape this hotel bedroom without waking the American (I can't even remember his name at this point I'm in such a state of panic), all will be salvaged. I sloosh myself with water from the sink, rub myself dry on *his* towel and dress in last night's much-mussed clothing. The American stirs as I turn the doorknob. Safe. Thank God. Out in the corridor, I take my notepad from my handbag and start scribbling.

174

Dear American,
Thank you for showing me Paris at night. Very,
very much appreciated. Have a nice life.
Yours,
Hope

PS My email, should you ever want to get in
touch, is hopelyndhurststeele@hotmail.com

I know I should feel guilty, but I don't. I know I'm trying to repair my relationship with Jack, not destroy it, but I don't see why this should get in the way. I'm walking on air. Despite my age, despite the hot flushes — and now the night-sweats too — I'm still a fully functioning sexual being. I came not just once, but three times! It was award-winning stuff. I didn't think about tomorrow's to-do list once, I didn't have to conjure up a fantasy about a dark and dangerous stranger to get my juices flowing, I had my dark — and potentially dangerous — stranger right there on the bed with me, lapping expertly at my labia and making me bite hard into my own hand to stop me Oh-My-God-ing at the top of my voice and waking the occupants of the next room.

I don't suppose sex with Jack will ever again be like this. It changed, after Olly was born, both in frequency and intensity. It stopped being a priority. But we both knew that was normal and natural. Our lovemaking still had the ability sometimes to surprise us, to teach us something new about our bodies and what gave us pleasure. I'm not sure exactly when I just lost the urge, when it became a chore rather than a pleasant diversion, when I started going to bed after Jack was asleep, just to be sure. But that would all change now. Armed with my Sabbia Rosa lingerie and the knowledge that my sexuality had been merely sleeping rather than killed off completely, I could surely find a way back to Jack.

Over two more days and nights in Paris, I walked for hours at a time, learned to navigate the metro like a local, ate and drank in endless cafes and *salons du thé*, exclaimed at the beauty of my surroundings and slept soundly. I did keep thinking about Dan, wondering whether I might bump into him by chance, and what might be the consequences if I did. He didn't know the name of my hotel, so it would have been up to me to get in touch. But I was too scared to, in case he had no interest in a repetition of our one-night stand, in case it hadn't been nearly as good an experience for him as it had been for me, in case I got in deeper than I dared. Keep it in perspective, I kept telling myself. Which didn't keep me from looking and hoping that chance would bring us together again, that he'd turn up at the same cafe or gallery as me, or that we'd find ourselves sharing a carriage on the metro.

By the time I checked back in to Gare du Nord, it all seemed something of a dream. Cherish it for what it was, I told myself, putting my bag into the X-ray machine and looking back over my shoulder one last time. Cherish it as a magnificent one-off, an experience intensified by its very singularity, one that repetition would only dissipate and dilute.

And so I settled into my seat on the Eurostar and planned my seduction of Jack, the start of my campaign to sort out what had gone wrong between us, and to face up to all the issues which I had spent the first half of the year avoiding.

I suppose it's what happens when a couple has lost the art of communication. One thinks everything's going to be OK. The other thinks it's all over. So when Jack told me that night he was going, that's when I really went to pieces.

PART TWO

Midsummer Madness

I'm being stalked by a big, dark cloud. It hovers just behind my left shoulder and if I turn my head a little, I can see it in my peripheral vision. Soot grey and fuzzy-edged, it threatens to engulf me, like the London smogs I remember from the 1950s, which would swoop in and swallow me up on my way to school. There's a difference, though. Those early morning fogs, the pea-soupers of my childhood, made every journey an adventure. The strange, ghoul-like figures emerging eerily from the mist, wrapped up in scarves and hats on their way to offices and factories, excited and intrigued me. Time teaches us to be fearful.

This cloud, my sooty stalker, is more menacing, mirroring my mood. At home, out on the streets, when I wake up in the middle of the night or first thing in the morning, wherever I am, it has become my unwelcome companion. Like the nerdy kid at school, the one you least want to be your friend, but who latches onto you anyway, and won't go away, however badly you behave.

Sometimes I try to punch it away with my fist, but it won't budge. My fist merely enters the cloud and disappears, until I pull it free. I have a constant pain in

181

my left shoulder, as though the cloud is pressing down its weight. I rub my shoulder all the time, but massaging myself is no substitute for Jack's healing hands. Jack's skill as a healer is that he knows instinctively, within seconds of touching you, where the problem is located. His hands emit a natural heat, burning almost in its intensity, which enters straight into the marrow of the pain. That very first time we met in Venice, I mildly twisted my ankle. He pressed into the sensitive area with his thumb, lost in concentration, and the soreness miraculously melted away under the heat radiating out from his own flesh.

The cloud is not the only strange new sensation in my life. My mind and body seem to have become detached from one another. I can be in a room, talking to someone, but I have this feeling that I'm somewhere else, over in the corner, for example, or floating up near the ceiling, watching the proceedings from a distance. My speech feels mechanistic. The words exit my mouth as usual, but in an automatic way, like a speak-your-weight machine, rather than flowing from thought or feeling. When people address me, their words too seem to be coming from afar, through a long tunnel. Meanwhile, my body behaves like a computer program, primed to respond to a set of codes. I shower, dress, shop, cook, eat, walk, drive, read a newspaper, all unaware, and then wonder how I have managed to complete tasks I have no consciousness of having engaged in. It's almost as if there are two of me — the one that speaks and acts and appears to the outside world as normal, and the other one, the one that watches, barely interested, observing dispassionately, distancing me from myself. I wonder if I'm losing my grip on reality. Or if this *is* my new reality.

Most troubling of all, in this strange new world I seem to inhabit, is the ever-present anxiety, the little mouse nibbling away. It has been there all year, lodged inside my solar plexus, but is more insistent now, hungrier. This hungry mouse eating away at my insides is doing what the diet and exercise failed to do, and the pounds are falling off. I am beginning to look gaunt.

There was a bad moment in the supermarket this morning. I was carrying just one small wire basket — no need for the trolley now it's only me and Olly, and more accurately only me, as Olly is finding excuses to be busy most nights. I was contemplating a can of chick peas. I fixed my focus on a solitary can of chick peas and was about to reach out for it, when I became unsure it was what I wanted. I kept looking at the chick peas in the hope that by looking for long enough the dilemma of to buy or not to buy would resolve itself. And then, quite suddenly, it seemed as though the chick peas were looking back through the can at me, transformed from inanimate objects into dozens of miniature eyeballs, jiggling, jostling and sizing me up aggressively, taunting me, as if to say: *Take us or leave us, what do we care? You're nothing to us. Nothing, do you hear?*

And then I couldn't breathe. My chest was being squeezed between giant pincers, and my hand jerked awkwardly towards the can, sending it skittering from the shelf with perhaps a dozen others. People turned to stare. I let my wire basket drop to the ground where I stood. A glass jar shattered inside and oozed red lava, like frothing blood, through the basket's wire mesh. Had this happened any other day I would have picked up what I could, apologised to everyone within earshot, and replaced the cans carefully and neatly back on the shelf. But the floor had moved, it was receding from me at a terrifying speed and, unless I escaped, the ground beneath my feet might disappear altogether. I raced towards the exit like a shoplifter caught in the act of stealing, faces, bodies, shelves piled high, all a disorienting blur. Outside, I fell back against the glass window of the store, hands to my chest, trying to catch my breath.

"Need help, missus?" I hadn't noticed the store detective chasing me or the shoppers who had stopped to witness the rare spectacle of a sprinting, middle-aged madwoman with a plain-clothed security guard hot on her tail.

"I didn't take anything. I didn't," I gasped desperately.

"Don't worry, love; I didn't think you had. You're not well, are you?"

My breath was finally beginning to find a more natural rhythm. "I felt so weird; I needed fresh air," I stammered. "Really, I'm all right, but I've left a hell of a mess in there."

"That's OK, don't you worry now. I've seen you dozens of times, you're a regular, aren't you?"

I managed to nod.

"You sure you're all right?"

184

I nodded again.

As he turned to go back into the store, I allowed my body to sink slowly to the pavement, with my back to the window. Sitting on the cool stone, knees up, elbows on knees, head in hands, bewildered, I thought: I'm one of them now. Hardly different, in appearance at least, from the dozens of homeless people with their begging signs and mangy dogs, the ones I'd passed countless times and mostly ignored over the years. And yet totally different. Unlike them, I did have a proper home to go to. What was I thinking of, sitting here on the pavement, imagining myself as one of them, as if my petty problems could be compared to theirs? But then again, perhaps the parallel wasn't so far-fetched. The slide from control to chaos can happen to anyone, regardless of their circumstances. It seemed to be happening to me. As for sitting there, in full view of passing shoppers, I was beyond caring if anyone I knew walked by and recognised me. *Hope Lyndhurst-Steele, glossy magazine editor, wife and mother turned pavement vagrant.* Quite a story to repeat at the school gates, over coffee or round the dinner table. To the rest, I'd be barely visible, just one more unfortunate bag lady to avoid tripping over.

I don't know how long I sat there, but I noticed an old woman with a hearing aid and a stick tottering out of the supermarket. She was having great difficulty juggling her shopping, her bag and her cane, and her plastic wallet was jutting perilously from her open handbag. So that's what's waiting for me, I thought. A little further along from me a sallow, straggly haired girl sat cross-legged with her sign on the ground in front of her and one hand outstretched, the other clutching a fat paperback that she was reading intently. She glanced up and over at me, blank-eyed, and returned to her book. Confused old ladies and homeless young girls. Why did they seem to be so much closer to my new circumstances than all the bustlingly efficient middle-aged women on their way to the car park, giant trolleys laden with groceries and self-assurance? Why did those women, so resembling me just a short while ago, seem so alien?

After what may have been five minutes or half an hour, I stiffly heaved myself up from the pavement. I dropped some coins into the straggly girl's outstretched hand. She looked up at me and then at her hand and then up again, nodding her thanks. Slowly I began to trundle home down the hill. I had become a wraith, a mere apparition, a woman of no substance. I wasn't even certain I existed.

"Cheer up, love, it may never happen," shouted a labourer high up on some scaffolding on a house at the end of my road, proving definitively that despite my uncertainty, I did indeed exist.

"Well, fuck you, mister, it already has." That's what I would have said, if I hadn't been a wraith. I said nothing and hung my head yet lower. The cloud was closing in on me. I fancied I could see it now without even turning my head. Oh, Jack, where did I go wrong?

Tears were trickling down my face, and I was nearly home. I was looking sightlessly at the cracks between the paving stones when I heard the click of heels coming towards me and felt myself assaulted by a whiff of designer scent. J-Lo, I registered, without looking up, and without curiosity. I recognised it from another life, the one that featured "perfume tastings", the life that thought that "perfume tastings" mattered — like the one my beauty editor organised towards the end of last year, which caused heated arguments among the staff as to which was the sexiest of six new scents out of a maximum score of ten. As J-Lo whooshed up my nostrils, making me momentarily light-headed and causing me to sway unsteadily, a pair of strong arms and a soft pillow of bosom enveloped me.

"You're in a right state, Hope. Just look at you. What the hell . . ."

I stood unable to move, locked in by the overwhelming fragrance, the cushiony breasts and Vanessa's unbidden embrace. At that moment I wanted her to never ever let me go.

"Argue all you like, love, but you're coming home with me. I'm going to make us both a nice cup of tea, or a strong pot of coffee if you'd prefer, and then you're going to start at the beginning and spill the beans. All of them . . ."

I didn't put up any kind of fight as Vanessa led me over the road and round the corner to her small terraced house with its glossy pink front door and cut-outs of stars and moons and animals and birds and trees stuck to the insides of the ground-floor windows. Having made it through the door behind her, I stood in her hallway, limp and motionless, until she removed my jacket for me. When she'd done that and I failed to follow her into the kitchen, she came back to collect me and took me by the hand.

I'd never been inside Vanessa's home before . . . our encounters had mainly been restricted to the Neighbourhood Watch committee, and I'd missed the meeting when it was her turn to have it at her place.

If I had happened to visit previously, I would probably have silently sneered at her poor parody of a country-style kitchen with its sunny, yellow walls, blue wood-effect cupboards stencilled with flowers. The floors and surfaces, strewn with plastic toys and Lego and video cartoons and Connect 4 counters and tricycles and tiny trainers, would have confirmed what I had suspected of Vanessa's sluttish ways. But in my distressed state, with my defences down, what I registered through the fug inside my head was the all-embracing warmth of a loving, child-centred home. Here was a house not so different from the ones I used to visit as a child, the ones with the swirly carpets that were so much more welcoming than my own pristine surroundings. My thoughts switched to Olly. *Maybe Olly feels about his home the way I felt about my mother's.* But hadn't our house, when Olly was small, been full of toys and mess? I tried to picture it, but couldn't. All I could see was me letting myself in through the front door at 7 p.m., after a long day in the office, Olly all washed and clean and smiley in his pyjamas, and his toys all tidied away by the nanny.

I shook my head to jolt myself back to the present.

"Drink up, then 'fess up," said Vanessa, placing a Thomas the Tank Engine mug filled with milky tea in front of me.

"But I don't know where to begin. I mean, I hardly know you. I mean, I do know you, but not intimately. And I've been so rude to you every time we've met lately. Maybe I should just have this tea and go home. I'm not even sure I have the energy to talk."

"Look, like it or not," said Vanessa, "I'm already well up on your family business. I get to hear quite a lot about what's going on from my little friend. He's been having a hard time of it lately what with Jack walking out and you being so in the dumps. You know what boys are like. They don't talk to their mates, not about proper stuff. And Olly's no different. But he does talk to me . . ."

I was grateful for Vanessa's matter-of-fact tone. Too much sympathy and I'd start blubbing uncontrollably.

"You know it's me who's created this disaster. It's my fault entirely."

"Not for me to judge. But according to Olly, you've had a lot on your plate to deal with this year."

"Olly said that? He said I had a lot on my plate?"

"Well, he didn't use those exact words, more like that you had a lot of shit to wade through, something like that . . . But whatever words he used, and I can't remember, it boils down to the same thing."

"But he never seems to notice anything. Teenagers are so much the centre of their own universe."

"Of course he notices. He's clever, like you, and he's got feelings like the rest of us. And you're his mum,

189

after all, so naturally he picks up when you're not yourself. Your problem is . . ."

"Is what?"

"I shouldn't have said that. It's not up to me; you're the one who needs to work out what your problem is. But talking can help. And as your husband has just walked out on you, you might want to start by talking about him."

"I just want him back."

"Do you know *why* you want him back?"

"Because we've been together twenty years and we're a family and I can't cope without him. And because I'm falling to pieces . . ."

"Mmm, I think you can do better than that."

You're going to start at the beginning and spill the beans, Vanessa had said to me when she accosted me on the pavement. If I was going to do this at all, I should really be doing it with Maddy, or Sarah, or Claire, if only she were in the country. That would have made sense. Sitting in this car-boot sale of a kitchen with Vanessa the Undresser, Vanessa the Vamp, Vanessa the Tramp, Vanessa the Seducer of Innocent Boys, made no sense at all. And yet sitting at Vanessa's kitchen table, my hands wrapped around a chipped Thomas the Tank Engine mug, I felt momentarily safe. I believed Vanessa when she said she wouldn't judge me or force her opinions down my throat. And I wasn't sure Sarah or Maddy would be able to do the same. Sometimes your sister and your best friend are just too close to you, too enmeshed, too involved with the minutiae of your life, to be able to offer objective

190

advice. They think they know everything about you, and they think they know what's good for you. And they don't hold back from telling you. There was always the possibility that Vanessa had an ulterior motive. I couldn't be sure my son's lover didn't want ammunition in what had escalated into a war between us. But I didn't think so. And now that peace seemed to have broken out, Vanessa seemed prepared, eager even, to listen to the ramblings of a foolish fifty-year-old who should know better. But where do you start, how do you begin to describe a marriage of almost twenty years? I figured starting at the beginning might not be an altogether bad idea.

Venice 1983. The weekend I met Maddy for the first time, on the flight over to Venice, I was staying at the swish Bauer hotel, a pigeon's skip from St Mark's Square. My arduous assignment for *Sapphire*, the magazine on which I was deputy editor at the time, was to soak up the atmosphere, take in the sights, check out some Venetian shops and restaurants and write a thousand words of copy. In other words, it was a dream assignment.

You couldn't get more motley than me and my fellow journalists on the press trip. There was an obnoxious and drunken crime reporter from a tabloid newspaper, who had stepped in for the travel editor at the last moment and refused to shift from the bar except for meals and sleep. A rather grand fifty-something freelance travel writer for a broadsheet, who complained non-stop to the PR girl assigned to nanny us about the service, the thread-count of her sheets and the intermittently pungent odours drifting up from the canal, as if the poor PR girl were personally to blame for Venice's sometimes disturbing aroma. And finally there was the photographer who'd come to take pictures of Venetian prostitutes for a Sunday supplement, who disappeared the moment we arrived and only reappeared for the water taxi back to the airport, behaving all enigmatically and refusing to share his experiences.

I pitied the hapless Clarissa, the way-beyond-her-depth PR girl acting on behalf of the luxury hotel marketing group which was financing our stay. Between warding off the lunges of the inebriated hack and fielding the broadsides of the broadsheet travel writer, Clarissa was mostly in tears. I know it wasn't exactly supportive of me, but I couldn't stomach the idea of spending mealtimes with the groping crime reporter and the evil harpy, she who had been everywhere and appreciated nothing. So I made my excuses to the much put-upon Clarissa about how I needed to strike out on my own for the story, and left her to manage as best she could.

I was having the loveliest time. I had risen, uncharacteristically, at 6a.m. to explore the city, shrouded in early morning mist, and stepped right into a Turner painting. With hardly another person around, the narrow canals that lace Venice, with its weather-worn residences in all shades of ochre, rust, pink and terracotta, and strung across with washing lines, looked as they would have done centuries before. I listened to the music of the gently rippling water, lapping against the candy-striped pylons that stand sentry outside faded palazzi, and enjoyed a far more melodious serenade to that of the singing gondoliers who'd soon be fleecing their willing victims in the theme-park atmosphere of daytime Venice. I'd sneaked in to a service at the synagogue in the ghetto, not for spiritual sustenance, but to imbibe the atmosphere of the world's oldest Jewish quarter, which had remained almost unchanged for five hundred years. And I had returned twice to the Scuola Grande di San Rocco to see Tintoretto's emotional depictions of scenes from both the Old and New Testaments. I'd taken the *vaporetto* out to the Lido and wandered barefoot along the empty beach, past the Hotel des Bains, where the mournfully beautiful *Death in Venice* was filmed more than a decade earlier. It was late October, and although Venice itself was still thronged with tourists, the Lido had been purged of holidaymakers. Empty seaside towns make most people feel wistful, a little sad even. I like nothing better than a clear stretch of sand and the sense of everything else around me — people, hotels, restaurants, shops — being sound asleep for the winter.

I'd returned, on the second night of my stay, from a noisy restaurant in a backstreet close to the Rialto, where I'd gorged on Parma ham and melon followed by *fegato alla veneziana*, meltingly tender calves' liver sautéed with onions in butter, finishing with a hefty chunk of creamy Taleggio cheese and a handful of Grissini sticks. A single woman on my own, I'd attracted waiters like a magnet; they'd fallen over themselves to explain the menu. A glass of wine — compliments of a trio of Italian businessmen at a nearby table — arrived within moments of my sitting down. I did a lot of gracious smiling, but I refused the offer of the businessmen to join them over a glass of post-prandial grappa.

I had a little plan of my own for when I got back to the Bauer. I was going to find a good spot on its famous outdoor terrace, overlooking the Grand Canal, and indulgently order myself a Bellini, that perfectly balanced equation of peach

193

nectar and sparkling Prosecco, which had, in fact, been invented in Venice.

The Bauer has perhaps the best terrace in the city. On this night an almost-full moon, like a silvery disco ball, lit the lagoon, sending diamonds skimming across the water.

It surprised me how good it felt to be thirty, independent, moderately successful, and OK — for the moment — about being single. Unlike so many women I knew, I had no sense of being about to pass my sell-by date, or of my biological clock ticking towards midnight. At thirty I'd finally hit my stride, although my anxieties, never more than a wafer-thin layer of skin from the surface, would seep through my pores, unbidden, without warning, and in an instant replace all my certainty with fear.

Not tonight, though. Tonight I felt invincible. Free and happy and hopeful for the future.

I was still basking in the glories of Venice and my success over dinner with the waiters and the businessmen. For once I was even feeling happy with my appearance. I was going through something of an Audrey Hepburn homage phase, wearing a simple, sleeveless, black linen shift dress to the knee, with a red cardigan around my shoulders and flat red ballet pumps. My big sunglasses, Audrey-style, were perched on top of my head, holding my hair back from my face.

I sipped my cocktail and stretched out a leg. Hmm, I thought, with my bordering-on-chunky calves and more than hand-span ankles, I'd never cut quite the elegant figure I aspired to.

My built-in smugness detector was already highly developed. Whenever I find myself getting pleased with myself — then, as now — I stop myself short and focus on a fault — in my figure, my personality, my performance at work. It's a kind of superstitious habit that accompanied my tortuous route to confidence. As long as I didn't start to think I was special, the fates would be kind to me. I let out a little giggle — very little, or so I thought.

"Must be an excellent joke for you to be laughing there, all on your own. Are you in the mood to share it?"

I hadn't even noticed the man at the next table.

"God, how embarrassing. I must look quite mad. But you'd think I was even madder if I told you what was making me laugh."

"Try me."

"No way."

"I'm prepared to overlook your insanity on this occasion. Would you like another of whatever it is you're drinking? Unless, of course, you're waiting for someone, or if you've had enough of the local Lotharios, one of whom I may just turn out to be."

And because the moon was so bright, and because it was Venice, and because I wasn't waiting for anyone, certainly not the hack or the harpy, I said, "You don't look especially Lothario-like. And I'd love another Bellini."

"Care to enlighten me?"

"If you've never had a Bellini, you haven't truly lived. The Bellini is sublime. It was invented here, in Venice, in 1931, by Giuseppe Cipriani, the founder of the famous Harry's Bar, which is just around the corner from where we're sitting. And it's made with Prosecco, Italian sparkling wine, mixed with ripe white peach puree. You can make it with champagne, but it does rather spoil the point of the champagne."

"Mmm, cocktails are a bit girly for me. I think I'll stick to lager, but I'd love to buy you a Bellini and watch you drink it."

"You're not girly, then?"

"Well, I get no kick from champagne. And I don't love to shop. But I have been known to cry at the opera, and people tell me I'm a decent cook. I was even caught on one occasion washing up afterwards. And if it helps to hear this, I think strong women are very sexy." His eyes took me in from head to toe and back up again in a single sweep. "Which, when you add it all up, probably does make me quite a girly sort of bloke, whatever that may mean."

"Would you like to marry me?" I laughed. "You seem just too good to be true . . ."

" 'Can't take my eyes off of you.' "

"What?"

"Oh, it's from an awful Frankie Valli song. When you get to know me better you'll discover I'm only as good as someone else's lyrics. But it's true about not being able to take my eyes off of you."

"Isn't 'I get no kick from champagne' someone else's lyric too?"

"Guilty as charged. Now let's find ourselves a waiter. And by the way, since you asked, I'd be quite happy to marry you."

"Only quite?"

"Well, let's not rush things. Let's have a drink and see how it goes from there."

While he was waving somewhat ineffectually at passing waiters, I got the chance to look at him. I liked what I saw. His straight, thick hair was just below jaw-length and fair, kind of streaky blond, parted in a random, zigzag fashion on one side. I said a silent prayer that those highlights were natural, otherwise this could be the start of something very small. I've always had a thing about good-looking guys with long hair, ponytails included; it gives them this androgynous quality I find really sexy. But highlights would be pushing it. As he ran his fingers through his mane, revealing a tiny silver hoop earring, and I watched his hair flop forwards again as soon as he released it, I felt the hairs on my arms stand to attention. He could have the benefit of the doubt as far as highlights were concerned. There was still the long, straight nose to consider, the mouth that stretched right across his face when he smiled, and the pale but bright and mischievous eyes (I couldn't tell what colour in the glow of the flaming torches surrounding the terrace). He was wearing crumpled linen trousers, sandals but no socks, and a nondescript T-shirt revealing slim but muscled arms and elegantly long fingers. The overall impression was of a lean-bodied man, about my age, comfortable in his own skin, and with legs that seemed to stretch out over a fair distance, although I couldn't tell how tall he was because he was sitting down.

"You don't seem very English," I said, as he finally caught the waiter's attention and ordered our drinks.

"How not very English?"

"Well, there's a trace of an accent for a start and there's something about the trousers you're wearing. I really don't know, it's just an instinct."

"Trousers, yeah, a dead giveaway. But your instinct is good." He smiled directly at me, and a single dimple appeared on the left-hand side of his face. "My name is Jack, the English version of Jacques, which is what my French mother wanted to call me. My father is English, but he's a diplomat, which is a far less fancy job than it sounds, so we moved around throughout my childhood . . . West Africa, Greece, Egypt. They didn't want to send me to boarding school, my mother made it a condition of her marriage that she could keep her children with her, so my sister and I were educated all over the place — often by private tutors — until my A-levels, when my dad was posted back to England. So I guess I am English, but I've never really absorbed Englishness. Unlike my sister, Anita, who has never thought of herself as anything other than a debutante and would die rather than get down and dirty with the natives. Me? You could dump me anywhere from Kinshasa to Kentucky, and I'd call it home."

"And how have you come to be dumped in Venice?"

"I'm here teaching English until Christmas. Then I'm going back to school myself to become a physiotherapist. I did drama at university the first time round, but the acting profession doesn't seem to be inclined to recognise my skills. So after too many years 'resting', with the odd — very odd — part in rep, and mostly working in bars and teaching, I've finally decided to grow up."

"Good for you, that makes me very proud," I said in a mock motherly tone that made us both laugh.

I didn't feel at all as though Jack and I had just met, but then foreign places always do weave a particular magic round me. I could pick up men in foreign parts far more casually than I'd ever do at home. So it could just have been Venice or the almost-full moon or the second Bellini rather than the Jackness of Jack that was making me feel I was on the brink of something important.

Maddy had been on the same flight home as me. We checked in together so we could get adjacent seats, and I spoke non-stop about Jack all the way to Heathrow. About how he'd magically cured my twisted ankle, about how the day after we met we shared a bowl of spaghetti at lunch which somehow he managed to spill onto my lap. Instead of being embarrassed, he'd just said, "I really am sorry, but it's too delicious to waste so, unless you object, I'm just going to carry on," and then proceeded to twist the spaghetti expertly round his fork from its new position on my skirt. Jack had a kind of childlike spontaneity about him that was perhaps the result of his own peripatetic childhood. I told Maddy how he'd escorted me back to my hotel room and asked, "Do you mind if I watch while you change?" And how that comment had sent a shiver right through me. How he'd not even tried to touch me, even though I'd been hoping he would, and how exposed, but also turned-on, I'd felt as he sat on the edge of the bed watching me step out of my stained skirt before I disappeared into the bathroom for a shower.

I told Maddy how Jack had asked me about the men in my life and I'd talked about Finlay, with whom I'd had an on-off relationship for five years, and who wanted me to go to Tokyo with him when his company transferred him there, which was when I had realised I didn't love him enough to move countries for him. And how Jack had said, "I'm so glad you didn't go to Tokyo, and especially glad you didn't go with Finlay."

And then I told Maddy how Jack had suddenly announced that I would love his mother, which for an instant had made me worry that he might be too much a mother's boy, prattling on about her so soon after we met; but then a moment later

I'd thought how unusual it was for a man to be so openly and uninhibitedly affectionate about his mother, and it was probably a very good sign indeed. So then I'd said he'd probably hate my mother, and we'd laughed and moved on from mothers to a million other things. And he wrote down my number and promised to call as soon as he was back in England at Christmas.

Poor Maddy must have wondered what she'd let herself in for, becoming friends with me. I was so excited, so very high, that I hardly gave her the chance to say a word. But it clearly didn't trouble her, because we've been best pals ever since. And I think Jack loves Maddy as much as he loves me. I should say loved, because now he probably loves her a great deal more than he loves me.

"Well, that wasn't too difficult, was it?" says Vanessa.

"I'm so sorry, I got completely carried away. I've no idea how long I've been rambling on. You know, I haven't thought for ages about what it was like when we first met. All the good things that brought us together. I seem to only ever focus on the bad."

"Yes, I remember some good beginning bits of my own. I'll tell you about them some time. Your tea's gone all cold, let me make another pot."

"Thanks, Vanessa, you're very kind."

"Did Olly tell you I'm thinking of becoming a psychotherapist — marriage guidance, couple counselling, that sort of thing? I've enrolled on a course starting in September."

"Olly and I don't talk. And we especially don't talk about you."

"No, of course not." Vanessa, without her usual eight layers of make-up, is extremely pretty. "But I'm a bloody good listener. Which is half of what it's all about. And I've been through the mill myself a few times, which is important. I get so pissed off by all these rich women with perfect husbands and perfect children who get themselves trained up as counsellors because they're bored with themselves. I mean, what do they know about life?"

"Mmm, you're right about that. But it's a serious slog, isn't it? There's a lot of long, hard study involved."

"What, you think I'm not smart enough? Not got the right accent?"

Vanessa narrows her eyes at me, as if issuing a warning.

"Oh, Vanessa, that's not what I meant, not at all. It's just that being a single mother with two young children and a part-time job, you must already have your work cut out. And don't you have to go into therapy yourself to become a qualified psychotherapist?"

Vanessa's face softens again. "I'm ready for it, and I reckon it would do me good. I'm a good listener, as I said, but I can also talk the hind legs off a donkey."

I smile at her pragmatic appraisal of herself. She smiles back at me, and for the first time I can begin to see what Olly sees in her.

"Look, Vanessa, there's something I need to say to you."

"I thought you'd said quite a lot already." She grins. "But go on, spit it out."

"I'm sorry."

"Sorry? Is that it?"

"Yes, I'm sorry. I'm sorry for being a snob. I'm sorry for being patronising. I'm sorry for trying to break you and Olly up. I'm sorry for being jealous. And I'm sorry for not realising what an excellent person you really are."

"Well, in that case, Mrs Lyndhurst — or should I say Mrs Lyndhurst-Steele? — your fifty minutes are up, that will be eighty quid please, and I'll see you the same time next week."

I look startled.

"God, you are in a bad way. I do hope you have a sense of humour lurking somewhere. And think about this. You may need to do a bit more than chat to me. I don't know, proper counselling, perhaps, just to get you through the worst of it. Or pills. Speak to your friend Maddy, she knows about all that stuff. But now I have to go and get the kids from school — Damien's finding it hard to adjust to big school, and he goes mental if I'm even thirty seconds late to pick him up. And I have to get Poppy from nursery before I get Damien, so the timing's pretty tight."

"Of course. I should have thought. Off you go. Look, we don't have to mention this to Olly, do we? I don't want him to know what a state I'm really in."

"That might just be one of your problems, Hope. Keeping it all to yourself."

"I really would like to talk some more."

"Well, we've hardly begun. I love a good 'how we met' story, but it's the 'how in the hellhole that is marriage we stayed together' that's the really interesting

202

bit. You're on. It will be good practice for when I sign up for the real thing."

"I like your perfume, by the way. It's J-Lo, isn't it?" Actually I find it totally overbearing, but Vanessa deserves to be appreciated.

"Yes, Olly bought it for me. He's such a sweetheart."

Olly bought it for her! So that's why he's always running out of pocket money. And me paying for it. *Me!* Funding his unsuitable mistress's lavish lifestyle. I can't help it, I'm back to being furious.

"He is a sweetheart, yes," I manage to utter, unconvincingly.

"Maybe he's inherited his generosity from you," says Vanessa cheerily.

"On that, Vanessa, you're seriously wide of the mark. But thank you for thinking it."

I shuffle home, shattered from the day's events. From my scene in the supermarket, from my therapy session in Vanessa's kitchen, from the sheer effort of not collapsing in a heap and staying there for the rest of my life.

In the shower, I run through the business of Olly blowing his pocket money on perfume for Vanessa. I'm like a windscreen wiper at full speed. Veering wildly in my opinions from one extreme to the other. Of course I can now see Olly's generosity in buying Vanessa perfume with his paltry pocket money. Vanessa's generosity in coming to my rescue after I've been so rude to her. My lack of generosity towards absolutely everyone. It all looks different now. Once I've handed over the money to Olly, it's his, to do whatever he likes.

It's so obvious, I shouldn't even have to think about it. But why didn't I see that right away? Why didn't I go straight to that conclusion? Telling Vanessa that I'm sorry for having been jealous doesn't seem to have killed the green-eyed monster. It didn't even send it to sleep.

No wonder Jack left me and Olly would leave me if he had the chance.

After showering and tidying myself, I psych myself up to ring my father.

"How's Mummy?"

"Not so good. She was pleased that Jack popped in yesterday — cheered her up. She's so fond of him."

"How's Jack?"

"What do you mean, how's Jack? You live with him, don't you?"

I haven't told my parents about Jack and me separating. I wouldn't be able to take my mother's admonitions or even my father's gentle sympathy. We both agreed not to say anything for the time being.

"I'm a bit doolally at the moment. I meant how are you, not how's Jack."

"Bearing up. When are you coming over?"

"Definitely later in the week."

"I'll send your love to Mummy."

"Yes, you do that. Bye for now."

That evening, when Olly comes in from school, I say, "Hi, Ols. Anything to report?"

"No, nothing," he replies, heading straight for the stairs and his bedroom.

"Mind if we have a word?"

Olly sighs.

"Look, I'm really tired, Mum. I've just had triple history with that idiot Elfenberger, and it did my head in. Can it wait?"

"Yes, I guess it can. Are you in for dinner?"

"I did say yesterday. Ravi's mum invited me round for a curry, and Ravi and I were planning on revising the Russian Revolution together. I did tell you."

"Yes, you did. I just forgot."

"Look, how long will this take?"

"Two minutes."

Olly drops his rucksack and coat at his feet, halfway up the stairs, and comes back down again, following me reluctantly into the kitchen.

"So . . ." he says.

"Can you just sit down? It really won't take more than a couple of minutes."

Olly positions himself on the edge of the chair, as if ready to sprint out of it if he doesn't like the way the conversation is going.

"I owe you an apology, Ols . . ."

"For anything in particular? I mean, the list's as long as my arm." Olly attemps a wry smile, but he needn't have bothered: the arrow hits the target.

"About Vanessa."

"Let's not go there. All right, Mum?"

"Give me a chance, Olly. I want to say I'm sorry."

"There, you've said it."

"No, I haven't. I want to say I'm sorry for being such a bitch. For interfering when I shouldn't. For not trusting your judgment. For being so shallow as to let

205

the way someone speaks and the way they dress influence my opinion of them. And, I suppose, for being the crappiest mother in the universe."

Olly is looking at me goggle-eyed.

"Shit, man, have you been taking something?"

"Only a dose of common sense."

"Do you really mean all that stuff you just said?"

"Want me to repeat it?"

"No. NO. Please don't do that. And anyway there are far crappier mothers than you about."

"You think so?"

"I know so. Look, that's cool, Mum. Really cool."

Olly stands up and goes to the fridge.

"You won't find anything in there. I didn't feel too good in the supermarket this morning and had to leave without the shopping. So it's a good thing you're going out for supper after all."

"Are you OK? Your eyes are a bit piggy."

"Yes, fine now."

"Any chance of a biscuit?"

"Yup, they're in the tin. I topped it up a few days ago."

Olly opens the cupboard, grabs the tin, and heads out of the kitchen, leaving the cupboard door wide open.

"You know something?" he says, as he disappears down the corridor, "I think the therapy's working."

"What therapy? I'm not having any therapy."

But Olly and the biscuits are gone, Olly bounding up the stairs, three at a time, crunching on double-chocolate-chip cookies.

★ ★ ★

Maddy's five months pregnant, and she has some colour back in her face. We're in Lupa, a maternity shop, one of the few places that make fashionable clothes for pregnant women. She buys great cargo pants and jeans with adjustable side panels for the weekends, a couple of flattering jersey wrap dresses for work and several tops, skirts and trousers which will mix and match.

"It wasn't like this when I was pregnant with Olly," I recall. "The only stuff you could buy were hideous maternity smocks and tents. It was fortunate that leggings were really fashionable at the time. I lived in them throughout my pregnancy. Leggings with sweaters, leggings with T-shirts or leggings with silky tops, depending on the occasion."

"Yeah, I remember, but leggings were completely hideous too."

"True, but we didn't know it at the time. Leggings, shoulder pads, big hair, what were we thinking of?"

"I know what you were thinking of. Storming the boardroom in your pinstripe trouser suit. Becoming the most successful editor in the universe, ever. Having a baby in your lunch hour."

"God, I sound ghastly. But what about you?"

"Oh, I was just signing sick notes for people who weren't sick, writing prescriptions to soothe the nerves of the very same working mothers you said could have it all, and catching colds from my patients. Nothing's changed, of course."

"Coffee?"

"Just make sure you keep your eye on the time. I'm taking the twins out for tea later."

"So how are things with you and Ed?" I ask over coffee and lemon drizzle cake.

"I'm keeping my distance, but I'm doing my bit for the twins, as I promised I would."

"Has he said anything about this pregnancy?"

"Like what?"

"Like whose baby is it anyway?"

"I told him exactly what I told you I was going to tell him. That I'd been having this relationship with this other guy, and how I'd forgotten my pill one night, and that was it."

"Did he even ask if it could possibly be him who'd made you pregnant?"

"I think maybe he was going to, but I kind of cut him short."

"Are you still sure this is how you want to play it?"

"To be honest, I don't see what choice I have. Let's say I took the risk — and it would be a huge risk — of telling Ed the baby was his. The last thing he could cope with right now is another baby. He's in mourning, for heaven's sake. And our few-nights stand was some kind of wild aberration that neither of us wants to think about. So say I tell him he's the father, what's he going to do? Offer child support? Tell the twins? Ask me to marry him? Can't you see it's impossible?"

"How do you know he doesn't love you?"

"Because he loves Ruth."

"But supposing he does have feelings for you —"

"Well, if he does, he has a funny way of showing it. He asked me to babysit the other night when he went out on a date."

"And how did that make you feel?"

"How do you think it made me feel to have the father of my child going on a date? It felt bloody awful. But he's not to know that."

"But if you told him, things might change."

"And if they didn't, I'd feel even worse. I need to keep myself together for this baby. This baby is the only thing that matters any more."

"Doesn't the baby deserve to know who the father is?"

"One day maybe it will. Just not for a very long time."

"I bumped into Ed the other day."

"And?"

"And he said the twins don't see you as often as they'd like to. But I got the feeling that he was telling me he didn't see you as often as he'd like."

"And what gave you that impression?"

"Nothing, really. Just a feeling."

"Case proven. Ed's not interested in me as anything other than a stable female figure in his children's lives. And when he remarries, or moves in with someone, he won't have any use for me at all."

"I can't believe that."

"You'll just have to take my word for it. Now, what about you?"

"Well, things are calmer with Olly. We seem to have had a bit of a breakthrough."

"That's a start. How are you feeling?"

"Awful."

"How awful?"

"As awful as it's possible to feel. I know it's probably all psychosomatic, but I feel so physically ill all the time; the only time my head clears is when I'm out walking. But the anxiety, the brick in my head, the nausea, the funny dizzy feelings, the panic attacks, the pain in my gut . . . sometimes I think I'm going quite mad."

"Hope, you know these are classic signs of depression."

"Of course I'm depressed. My life's shit."

"I'm talking clinical depression. You may need some help."

"I won't take pills. I won't. The odd sleeping pill, yes. Prozac, forget it. I'm miserable because my life has gone pear-shaped. Those pills steal your personality, turn you into a zombie. And I'm already close enough to being a zombie to know it's not a good position to be in."

"That's not what the pills do, I promise. They just take the edge off the pain. They give you the respite you need in order to start sorting out your problems for yourself."

"But I know what my problems are. They're common, boring, everyday problems. I'm not exactly a single mother of seven living on benefits in a dilapidated high-rise, or a battered wife. I have no right to be depressed."

210

"Hope, sorry to be so brutal, but you're not always what I'd call emotionally intelligent, are you?"

"Thanks a lot, Maddy. And I suppose you're an emotional genius. I mean, the way you're handling things between you and Ed — not exactly mature, is it? The man has a right to know, for God's sake."

"How dare you?"

"How dare *you*?"

"Maybe you're right, Hope. Maybe your problems are of the common or garden variety. Whereas I've got two dead parents, one dead sister, no husband and no prospect of one and now a baby on the way at the age of forty-four. Were you always so self-absorbed and selfish or is this a recent development?"

I slam a fiver down on the table, grab my jacket from the back of the chair and march out of the cafe without a glance back. Maddy and I have been best friends for twenty years. And now, just when we need each other more than ever, we have fallen out.

Big time.

Dog Day Afternoons

There are four messages on my answering machine.

"Hi, Hope, Sally here. The press releases were great. Could you get to a committee meeting on the twelfth? Eight o'clock, my place. We need to discuss the celebrity fund-raiser."

Why, when I hear the word *celebrity*, do I always want to weep? I'm wondering if the nightmare of trying to persuade celebrities to appear on the cover of your magazine and having to sweet-talk their poisonous agents and PRs and give in to their preposterous demands can bring on post-traumatic stress disorder. I'm wondering if, for the rest of my life, the word *celebrity* will trigger an anxiety attack. No need to check in my diary. Of course I'm free.

"This is a message for Hope Lyndhurst. My name is Harry Sharp, and I'm a headhunter for Creative Talent Search. I would be grateful if you could call me back on this number . . ."

A headhunter? Someone actually interested in employing me? More likely he wants me to recommend someone or give a reference to some bright young thing. Definitely not urgent. I scribble down the number for later.

"Jack, here. I'd like to pop by for some of my stuff. Ring me back when you get the chance." I call back straight away. I leave a voice message to say he can come by any time after six. When he comes be nice, be calm, I tell myself.

"I miss you, my friend. Can we please just kiss and make up? In any case, I've had this rather brilliant idea and I need to share it with you." Trust Maddy to be the brave one, the one to make the first move. We haven't spoken for two weeks and three days — it feels like a lifetime.

I go to pick up Maddy from the surgery. After a quick hug, I press my hands to her bump. Obligingly, the baby wriggles, as if to remind me that I'll be having to share Maddy with a new little person quite soon. We stroll off down the street, arm in arm.

"So, Maddy, are you my best friend again?"

"Well, seeing as I haven't had any better offers, I suppose I am."

"I blame the hormones — they're plummeting even as we speak."

"I blame the hormones too — only mine are heading for outer space."

"Show off."

"Misery."

"I love you."

"I love you too."

"Well, now we've got that sorted, what's the brilliant idea you hinted at?"

"You need someone to hug."

"Too right."

"You need a dog."

"A what?"

"A dog."

"Maddy, my mad friend. Puerperal psychosis I know about. Prenatal psychosis is a new one on me. You may need to see a doctor."

"Me being mad is nothing new. It doesn't take away from the fact that you need a dog."

"I don't even like dogs. I've never had a dog in my life. And look at your dog. Certifiable. Vicious. A tiny little mutt with a Napoleon complex who can't leave the house without a muzzle *and* a halti in case it attacks the nearest Alsatian."

"But Mozart's a rescue dog," argues Maddy. "He was an abused child. He has issues which we're working through."

"Oh, so that excuses him biting Sarah on the knee last year and the fact that she had to go to A&E for a tetanus jab, pouring with blood. Poor little Mozart's got issues. Mind you, with a name like Mozart I'm not entirely surprised."

"Look, it would do you good. Give you something to think about other than yourself."

Give you something to think about other than yourself. Didn't Jack say something similar just before he walked out? This seems to be becoming a bit of a theme.

"Maddy, I know you're suggesting this with my best interests at heart, but can you really see me with a dog?"

214

"Well, you were a wonderful mother to Olly. I can't see there's much difference."

"A wonderful mother. If only. I was always in the office. I seem to have spent almost my entire life in the office."

"Come on now, just because Olly's been behaving like a typical teenager doesn't mean that you were a bad mother and neglected him as a child. Do you know something? I'm not even going to apologise for calling you an emotional illiterate just before you called off our friendship."

"I forgive you anyway."

"Surely you can remember what it was like? Every second of your spare time you were glued to Olly. I don't think you went to a restaurant or a movie for years. And if you came to me, you'd bring him with you. Remember when I used to want to pop in after work and you'd reply, 'Well, all right, but don't expect me to talk to you. Olly and I are playing tea parties until bedtime.'"

I'm remembering tea parties. The little red plastic cups and the blue plastic tray and the yellow plastic teapot and the brown plastic biscuits. And my body so heavy with tiredness that I could have lain flat out on the carpet where I was sitting with Olly and fallen straight to sleep at seven o'clock in the evening.

"It's all so odd. When I was working, I didn't feel guilty. Now I'm not, I seem to have taken up guilt as a full-time occupation. Retrospective guilt. I keep trying to work out where I went wrong."

"Maybe you're looking in all the wrong places, Hope. With Olly you did everything right. He'll get over himself, already is getting over himself as far as I can make out. I'd focus on Jack if I were you. But there's no time for that now. I said we'd go straight round to Marge."

"Marge?"

"Yes, it's only a few minutes from the surgery. She's one of my patients. Her Labrador's just given birth to nine pups, and we're going to meet them."

"You're impossible."

"There's no harm in looking, is there? A little window-shopping. Marge says they're all adorable. She decided to mate the Lab because each pup is worth a few hundred quid, and she's really strapped for cash. Oh, look, we're already here."

We stop in front of a well-kept council estate with several large blocks of flats and a half-dozen rows of small houses around the perimeter. Maddy rings on the bell of the only house in the row with a sun-burst door. A man's voice booms out: "Get that, will you? I'm up to my ears in piss and shit."

"Be there in a jiff," we can hear a woman calling. "Comin' in a sec, don't go away," she calls again a minute later. Eventually, Marge appears, slightly out of breath. She's of indeterminate age with dark circles under her eyes and a bulk that takes up almost the entire door frame. Two small children and a large black Labrador are trying to squeeze by her to get a look at us. Nestled in the crook of her substantial arms, fast asleep, is a sleek and shiny ebony pup.

"'Scuse the mess. It's bleedin' chaos here. We've got rid of four pups, but there are five of the little darlings still to go. Mitch'll kill me if we don't get rid of the rest of them soon, but I tell you this, a little bit of my heart breaks every time I have to say goodbye to one of them."

Maddy and I are led into a small kitchen and out through the back, which takes us into the yard.

Mitch looks up from poop-scooping and growls good-naturedly, "You can have the lot for nothing as far as I'm concerned. It's like living in a sewer." He extends a hairy arm towards me. The name M-A-R-G-E is spelled out on the tattooed knuckles of his five fingers. "I'm Mitch," he says, shaking my hand, "and these little blighters are killing me off. Good to see you, Dr M. Here," he says, scooping up a pup and thrusting it at me. "This one's a proper scamp. Would chew your leg off if you gave him the chance."

"You are so cute," I say, stroking his silky pelt, although my body language betrays me.

"Look at you," says Maddy laughing. "You've gone all stiff."

Something warm and wet is dribbling down my front. "Yeuch," I screech, causing the pup to leap from my arms in fright and hit the ground with a yelp. "Ooh, this is horrible. Your dog has just peed all over me. Now I know for sure why I'm a pet-free zone."

Maddy is doubled over with laughter, or as doubled over as it's possible to get with six months' worth of baby lodged in your belly. Marge is looking a little bit desperate, and Mitch is snorting his approval. "Well, if

217

you're buying, you might as well know what you're letting yourself in for."

"Come back inside, love," says Marge sympathetically, "and I'll give you a cloth to wipe yourself down."

They're so good-natured these two, I can't allow my natural prissiness to override my manners. The little black bundle curled up in Marge's arms looks like she's settled in for life.

"Are you keeping any of them?" I ask politely, trying to save Marge's embarrassment, and thinking about how soon I can escape the menagerie and flee home to a nice hot shower and clean clothes.

"I would, but we can't afford to. And one dog's more than enough, what with the three kids and my fat bum and Mitch's fat gut taking up all the space. 'Ere, rub yourself down with this."

I mop up as best I can, but the sour smell won't go away until I've given my top a thorough wash.

Maddy comes back into the kitchen.

"They are the most adorable creatures I've ever seen. What do you reckon, Hope?"

"Yes, adorable and a handful too, I imagine," I reply, looking at Marge. "Does this sweet little mite have a name?"

"Sleeping Beauty is what we've called her for the minute. Though when she wakes up, she's a lively enough little thing."

"And the price?" asks Maddy.

"Three hundred quid. They're pure pedigree, mind, and you'd have to pay a lot more from a breeder. Well, you know where to find me if you want me. Good to see you looking so well, Dr Maddy, and apologies for the wet T-shirt, Hope."

"Well, what did you think?" asks Maddy, the minute we're out of the house.

"Seem like a nice couple," I say. "Considering what they've got to deal with, it's practically an oasis of calm in there."

"You know that's not what I meant."

"And *you* know that the idea of me having a dog is quite preposterous. But cute they most certainly are. Thank the Lord you're back in my life, Dr M," I say, as we reach the corner and prepare to go our separate ways. "Just one more feel before I go."

This time when I touch Maddy's belly, the baby ignores me. Without thinking I bend over and give Maddy's tummy a kiss. Maddy musses the top of my hair. My tear ducts, already on red alert, go into overdrive. If she notices she doesn't comment.

As Maddy goes off down the street, the hint of a waddle in her walk, I turn and watch her. Mad, maddening, marvellous Maddy. I wonder if she knows just how dramatically her life is about to change.

Just before Jack's due to come round, I open a bottle of white wine and pour myself a glass. I've already applied some lipstick, mascara and eyeliner and put on a clean vest top and some earrings. I don't want to look like I'm overdoing it, trying too hard, but neither do I want to look as much of a wreck as I feel. By the time the doorbell rings, I'm on my second glass of wine and have emptied a bowl of olives. On my way to open the door, I pass the hall mirror, wincing slightly when I catch sight of my face, flicking at my hair to no particular effect, and leaving my glasses on the console table.

"Hi, Jack," I say casually. "Come and have a quick drink if you've time — there's a bottle already open."

He pecks me on the cheek.

"Olly in?"

"No."

Jack actually takes a step backwards, as if deciding whether or not to leg it while he has the chance.

"Didn't he tell you? Now that he's finished his exams he's got himself a job in that new bar on West End Lane."

"Yes, of course he told me; we speak every day. It's just that I wasn't sure what hours he worked."

The atmosphere is already prickly. Jack needing to let me know that he and Olly are constantly in touch with one another, that he's left me, not Olly. Olly's presence this evening would have been Jack's safety net.

"I know what you're thinking. It's all right, Jack. I'm not going to start howling or attack you with my best Sabatier knife."

"I didn't think you were."

"Not much you didn't. Come and have a drink."

"I can't stay long."

"Got a hot date, have we?"

Jack ignores me.

I pour Jack a glass of wine and we sit on two high stools against the kitchen breakfast bar.

"So what's new, Hope?"

"Some headhunter rang, but I haven't bothered to call back yet."

"Why not?"

"Oh, it's probably just to get a reference for someone. I'll get round to it."

"Hope . . ."

"You've no right, Jack. You've left me, remember?"

"Anything else?"

"I'm thinking of getting a dog."

"You're not. That's hilarious."

I think it's hilarious too, but I'm not telling Jack that.

"Why hilarious? I've got the time. All I seem to do is walk, so exercising it won't be a problem."

"What about the dog hair on your white sofa? What about the restrictions it will place on your going out? What if you get a job? And what about the patience you'll need to train it? I'm telling you, Hope, it's like having a baby all over again."

"Well, if Maddy can be a single mother, why can't I?"

Jack lets out a laugh that sounds more like a sigh, disbelief mingled with exasperation. "But you don't even like dogs. Most of them you're terrified of."

"I'm thinking it might be like aversion therapy. You know, that technique they call flooding. You expose yourself to your greatest fear — snakes, walking across bridges, sitting for a day in a confined space or whatever — and stay with it until your fear dissolves. Boom, just like that, you're cured."

"You can't be serious, Hope. You'll be giving it to Battersea within the month."

"You know something, Jack? I didn't actually ask for your opinion. You asked me what was new, and I said I was thinking of getting a dog. You don't think much of me, or my staying power, do you?"

"Why is it that we can't have a simple, rational discussion?"

"Because, unlike you, I'm not a rational person."

"Let's just change the subject, OK? I saw your mother. I think she suspects something's up between us."

"Let her suspect. I just don't want to involve her in this. I'm not protecting her, I'm protecting me."

"Your dad is being his usual saintly self."

"Yes, he is, but my impression is that it's getting harder every day for him to cope. You know Mummy wants to die at home, and Daddy is determined to look after her, but eventually she may have to go to a hospice. In the meantime, I've been trying to get things moving on the help front. Doing stuff like getting on to the district nurse who's promised to arrange some visits from a Marie Curie cancer nurse."

"Ironic, isn't it, that after spending so many years avoiding her as much as possible, you're round there all the time."

"Well, if I were working I wouldn't be able to be there. But she is my mother, and I'm doing it as much for Daddy as I am for her. Sarah sits with her for hours. She has this infinite capacity for sweetness and sympathy. She holds Mummy's hands and talks endlessly about happy memories. I can't think of anything to say, and none of my happy memories involve her anyway. So I just make phone calls and soup. Which is better than nothing, I suppose."

We're silent for a moment. Jack leans in towards me, as if he wants to get close, then he pulls back, shifting his bottom on the bar stool and sitting up, straight-backed.

"Things are better between Olly and me," I say.

"I'm glad."

"Much better. Oh, yes, and I've changed my mind about Vanessa."

"In what way changed your mind?"

"Vanessa's all right, take my word for it. More than all right, actually."

"You are so unpredictable, Hope."

"I miss you, Jack."

Jack looks down at the hands crossed on his lap.

"Look, I'd better be getting my stuff."

"Of course. Your hot date. I abhor her, whoever she is."

When Jack stands up, I catch a familiar aroma, lemony and mossy at the same time. I've never tired of the smell of Vetivert. Jack was wearing it when we first met in Venice, and he wears it still today. But in Venice it filled me with the sense of possibilities; now it fills me with an all-over-achy kind of longing, a sense of something precious lost. I close my eyes for a second and say to myself, *Hug me, Jack, hug me.*

Jack walks towards the kitchen door. "I'll be down in a minute, just need to pick up a couple of shirts and my linen suit."

Well, it could have gone worse, I suppose, but I wouldn't exactly call it progress.

The next morning, at ten o'clock, I'm standing outside the book shop, waiting for the door to open. At two minutes past I'm already beginning to get impatient. Through the glass I can see a sleepy assistant coming towards me, imitating a particularly languid snail. When she finally opens the door with a great sigh, as if having to deal with a customer so early in the morning is the harbinger of a very bad day, I raise my elbow and look at my watch in the passive-aggressive way people do when they want to make a point but not a scene.

"Do you have a pets' section?"

"Down there on the left," she says miserably, with an expression that suggests this is beyond the call of duty.

I'm amazed. The pets' section is almost as big as the fiction department. There are hundreds of books on dogs and cats and fish and hamsters. I come across something called the KISS guides, acronym for Keep It Simple Stupid, which is about my level. I hone in on the KISS guide *Living with a Dog* by a Dr Bruce Fogle. I flick through it. It has lots of big pictures and short sentences. Perfect.

I take up my usual position at the Coffee Cup and spend the rest of the morning learning all sorts of fascinating information. Like the fact that there are more dogs in the UK than people. I read something flagged VIP for Very Important Point:

The most common reason for the popularity of dogs is also the most basic: we humans have a unique need, different from perhaps all other animals, to nurture, to care for other living things.

It goes on to tell me that dogs are almost perfect for nurturing because, in their own particular way, they are "children" from puppyhood to old age, and that "although outwardly we look after dogs, in a hidden way, by allowing us to nurture them, they also look after us".

This makes me cry. Ridiculous, but it does, just for a moment or two. Labradors, I discover, are active, amusing and with a gentleness of spirit. I could learn a thing or two from a dog like that.

"What have you been up to?" asks Maddy, when she calls early evening, after surgery.

"Nothing much, reading mostly."

"My day was shite. Ninety-nine per cent of my patients are depressed. I don't have time to talk to them, so I prescribe anti-depressants. But they don't really need anti-depressants, they just need someone to talk to."

"Great. That's really great. You have no time for your patients so you give them pills you say they don't need. And yet you have all the time in the world for me. I get all the talk-time your patients don't, so how come I'm one of the few who actually *need* the pills? I don't get it."

"It's not so difficult to understand, Hope. It's because I reckon you've been in pretty much this state for over a year. Way before Jack left. And that's too long."

This path is going nowhere.

"Do you think a crate is a good idea? Just in the early days."

"A *crate*? A crate of what? I'd rather you took pills than drowned yourself in alcohol."

"Not a crate of anything. Just a crate. For the dog."

"I don't believe it."

"I don't know why you don't believe it, it was your idea. Jack thinks I'm barking."

Maddy titters. "Well, someone will be."

"He says it will be in Battersea within the month. I'm determined to prove him wrong."

"Hope, this is a big commitment — you can't get a dog just to prove a point to Jack."

"I'm going to call her Susanna."

"You've chosen a name already! You have been busy. But why Susanna? Isn't that a bit of a silly name for a dog?"

"Huh. You accuse me of being emotionally illiterate. You, on the other hand, are just ignorant."

"I'm a doctor, remember."

"A woman of your education should know this. Susanna is the maidservant in *The Marriage of Figaro*, the pivotal character of the whole opera. And since your dog and mine, once you've taught your dog some manners, are going to be best friends, I thought it appropriate that my dog should be named after one of your dog's creations."

"Aah, I see. Like everyone's going to get that."

"What would you prefer? Fido?"

"On second thoughts, Susanna's perfect. This is so exciting. Which one are you having?"

"Little Miss Sleeping Beauty, of course. Better go, I was right in the middle of a fascinating chapter on fleas. And thank you. Thank you for being my friend."

I ring the headhunter.

"Ah, yes," he says, when I get put through. "Very good of you to call back, Hope. Your name came up in a conversation about potential candidates to head up a new launch. I wonder if you'd be interested in having a chat."

"Well, yes. Can you give me some idea of what it's about?"

"It's extremely hush-hush, and I can't say too much at this point — we'd need to get you to sign a confidentiality agreement first — but I can tell you it's glossy and upmarket and monthly and will appeal mainly to women."

"I don't suppose it's a celebrity magazine, is it?"

"Spot on," says Harry Sharp, "but that really is all I can say for now."

This is as bad as it gets. Not just a magazine featuring the odd celebrity — that I can cope with — but a *celebrity magazine*! I make a decision not to blow my chances before I've even met this Harry person.

"Would you be free at three o'clock on Wednesday to meet me and the publisher, Annelise Hopkins?"

I'm picking up Susanna at five, and I don't want to be late.

"As long as I'm away by four thirty that should be fine. I have another appointment at five."

"No problem. In the meantime, would you mind quickly emailing me your CV?"

In thirty years of working in magazines, I've never written a CV. I've gone from job to job via the grapevine, and no one has ever asked to see my CV. And then it dawns on me. This Harry Sharp doesn't have a clue who I am. I'm just the name on some list, and he's probably twelve years old.

"Sure, Harry. Just needs a bit of updating; you'll have it first thing tomorrow. One more thing. You didn't actually mention the name of the publishing company."

"Oh, it's very prestigious. It's Jackson International."

"Aah, Craig's outfit. I know Craig Anderson, the MD, very well indeed. Did he put my name in the frame? And if he did, I'm wondering why he didn't ring me personally."

"I really can't comment further at this stage. Craig is leaving the first-round interviews to us."

I'm not getting good vibes about this. Craig should have rung me direct. And shouldn't I already be on the shortlist? What's the point of going to be interviewed by some know-nothing graduate with a 2:2 in "human resources"? Craig knows me well enough to decide on his own whether I'm the right person for the job. I'll probably be expected to do one of those trendy psychometric tests to suss out my leadership style. And then, when the pre-teen Harry asks me to describe my strengths and weaknesses, I'll have to act as if it's the most probing, penetrating and Paxmanesque challenge I've ever been presented with. By the time he asks me what kind of "package" I'm expecting, if I don't watch myself I'll find myself saying, *oh, a jiffy bag will do*. I hate the word *package*, I hate celebrities and, even though I haven't met him yet, I hate the overgrown baby that is Harry Sharp.

The first thing Sally says when I go through the door of her house in Kentish Town, is: "Thank you for Jack."

"My pleasure."

"I'm pain-free for the first time in months. He's a miracle worker. Sorry, though, to hear about your separation."

The *bastard*. He's told her. It's one thing Maddy knowing, and now Vanessa too. But Sally is almost a stranger. Why is Jack talking about us to his clients? It's so unprofessional. And so unlike him. The more people who know, the more definite it all feels, somehow. The more like finished business. And I don't want it to be definite. I want to it to stay hazy and amorphous. It's not as though he's said he's never coming back. It's a trial separation, just to give us both a breather, until we can sort something out.

"Yes, I'm sorry too," I say, "but it's all a bit raw at the moment, so I'd feel rather more comfortable *not* talking about it. I hope you understand."

"Of course. There have been plenty of times these last few years when 'talking about it' was the very last thing I wanted to do. Let's go through and meet everyone."

There are five people sitting on sofas and various chairs around a big wooden coffee table.

"I want you all to meet Hope," says Sally, smiling. "We are so lucky to have someone with her reputation and experience on board. She has already transformed the quality of the press releases we've been putting out, and I know her contacts and powers of persuasion are going to be a huge contribution to our celebrity fund-raiser. She has even promised to write a newspaper story for us about the Atlas Mountains trek."

"Well, I've promised to try to place an article," I say. "It's not actually in the bag."

"I have complete faith," says Sally. How can someone who has suffered so much be so eternally upbeat? It has to be a gift.

We go round the table, one by one. Everyone says a few sentences about themselves and explains their role in the charity. Sally's husband, Nick, who's an accountant by profession, looks after the money. Melissa is admin. Ron, an architect, keeps an eye on the contractors who are converting the house in Hammersmith for "Cat's Place", as it will be called. Katie coordinates fund-raising events, and Sven Olson is a heart specialist who treated Cat and is on the advisory board, along with a dozen or so eminent absentees. Sally runs around doing something of everything, event-management, drumming up publicity, talking to health professionals, writing to potential donors. The rest of the work is done by part-time volunteers, and with the charity's offices taking up the top floor of Sally and Nick's house, which is way too large for the two of them, I can already feel that this charity is something that entirely dominates Nick and Sally's life. I'm suddenly struck by the fact that Nick and Sally didn't have more children. I wonder why.

I arrive at the grey concrete, New Brutalist, 60s tower block that is Jackson International's headquarters at 2.50p.m. A receptionist hands me a badge and directs me to a waiting area, where the walls are banked with the company's magazine covers. There must be a hundred different publications ranging from glossy fashion titles to *Laptop Gazette* and *Anglers' Weekly*. I didn't expect my sooty stalker, the one that's been following me around since Jack left, to accompany me here, but that's the thing with stalkers, they have no concept of personal space.

A pale-faced young man with spiky fair hair approaches me. "You're Hope, aren't you? Just arrived myself. We're both a few minutes early, but someone will be down to collect us shortly. Pleased to meet you, by the way."

We make very small talk. Within five minutes, I've found out that Harry Sharp has just exchanged contracts on his first flat, that he has become an avid reader of interiors magazines and that he's not sure where he and his girlfriend, who's supposed to be moving in with him, are heading, as ever since he found the flat they've been arguing over the decor. His opinion is that since the flat's in his name, and she won't be contributing to the rent until she's finished her MA and got a job, her predilection for white-painted floorboards and sparkly, home-made chandeliers can be ignored. I am about to offer him some motherly advice when a young woman comes up to us.

"Oh, hello," she says, "follow me." She doesn't really look the part of a publisher's PA. Her hair is lank and in need of a wash, she doesn't have even a hint of make-up on her face and she's wearing a plain navy-blue suit that's seen better days. Better decades, by the looks of it. On the journey up to the eighteenth floor, neither she nor Harry say anything, so neither do I.

The PA leads us down a corridor, through a scruffy open-plan office and into a meeting room. There's a long, rectangular table with a notepad and biro placed down one side in the centre.

"Shall I sit here?" I ask, pointing to the place exactly opposite the notepad and biro.

"Yes, I suppose so," she says limply, and I sit down and arrange myself, fully expecting her to leave the room and collect her boss. Except she doesn't. What she does is seat herself opposite me, behind the notepad and biro.

"Shall we begin with you telling me a little something about your career?"

No, this can't be right.

"Um, er, of course. I'm sorry, I had no idea. I mean, we weren't formally introduced."

"You didn't think I was the secretary, did you! That's the kind of reaction I expect from a man, and even then, only the ones who are dying out."

This is excruciating.

"No, I mean, no, that's not what I was thinking. It's just that we've never met, and I wasn't sure what role . . ."

Harry is glaring at me. Really I might as well leave now.

"OK," I say brightly, watching myself watching me from the far corner of the room. "I can do the long version or the short, but I think I'll do the short and you can ask me any questions afterwards."

I launch into a litany of my career highlights, emphasising my various successes, awards, circulation-boosting campaigns and, because I know we're here to talk about a celebrity magazine, the various celebrity exclusives I've nailed over the years.

"Impressive," says Annelise Hopkins, and then there's a silence, as though she's trying to think what to say or ask next. Or it could be a little psychological trick she's picked up. To see if I'm the kind of person who can handle silence, or whether I'll jump in out of discomfort and incriminate myself.

"Are you willing to sign this confidentiality agreement?" she asks, passing over a typed document.

"Of course." I barely glance at it before scribbling my signature.

"Well, we're very excited about this new launch. Celebrity magazines have become two a penny, but we really feel we've found a gap in the market. It's such a simple idea. And isn't it true that the simplest ideas are always the best?"

If this were a competition for the best cliché, Annelise Hopkins would win, no contest.

"What are the two things women are obsessed with?" she asks, her weaselly little eyes gleaming now she's come up with her ace in the hole, the killer question to catch me out.

"Oh, I can think of lots. Shoes. Handbags. Wrinkles. Chocolate Hobnobs. Writing lists. Stains, or so I've been told." Annelise is yawning. I'm clutching at straws. "Making sure their kids eat a decent breakfast and do their homework on time. Ageing, now that's a big one. Cosmetic surgery." I feel I've failed an important test.

"Anything else?" asks Harry.

I hesitate. There's something I've forgotten, something that stands between me and this job.

"Body hair?" It's my last offer.

"Not body *hair*." Annelise sniffs. "Body *fat*. Weight. Hip-to-waist ratios. Obesity charts. Calories. Cholesterol. Exercise regimes. Atkins. GI. Pedometers. Cellulite. In other words, *diets*."

"But of course; it just slipped my mind. You know how it is, you're taking part in *Who Wants To Be A Millionaire?* and if they'd asked you yesterday you'd have been able to give the answer to the million-pound question even without the multiple-choice answers on the screen in front of you. But today, your mind's a blank, and you've already used your fifty-fifty and your ask-the-audience —"

"Celebrity Diets," says Harry, interrupting my flow. "What do you think?"

"You're right. Deliciously simple. Yes, I think you're onto something. It could definitely work." What I'm thinking is that if I don't leave soon, I'll be late for Susanna. Marge and Mitch will think I've changed my mind.

Harry looks at me thoughtfully. "Hope, I'd like to ask you what you regard as your strengths and weaknesses."

I suppress the urge to giggle.

"Well, Harry, this is something to which I've given a lot of thought over the years. On the strength side I'd have to say that I know how to lead and make decisions. I can tease out ideas from people and develop them. I like to mentor young talent, and I always give people credit for any good work that they do. I work like a demon, I'm never short of ideas myself, I'm good on the PR and promotional side. Oh, and I know how to suck up to the advertisers." I thought this last comment might prompt a smile, or a conspiratorial exchange of glances, but the two of them are looking at me stony-faced.

"And any weaknesses?"

"My greatest weaknesses are a tendency towards impatience and a compulsive need to tell the truth. And to be absolutely honest, I'm not really interested in celebrities, and I'm certainly not interested in their diets because celebrity diets can't possibly work. Not for mere mortals who don't have personal chefs and personal trainers and personal stylists to keep them on the path of diet-righteousness. I could never successfully edit a magazine cynically, so I couldn't possibly edit a magazine called *Celebrity Diets*. But I'm sure the magazine will be an enormous success, and I wish you luck with it."

Annelise has turned a funny colour, kind of greige. Harry looks like he's just been mugged. "Well, unless you have any questions . . ."

"None at all, thank you."

Harry stands and extends a hand. "So very nice to meet you, Hope. We'll be in touch."

Annelise is gripping the arms of her chair as if to prevent herself falling off.

"You have such a reputation, Hope. I'd like to thank you for . . . for your honesty, I suppose."

I smile at the two of them. "Must dash, or I'll be late for Susanna. My baby. My brand-new baby. Thank you both so much for your time." Annelise emits a little noise, like a strangulated gasp.

"Oh, I see. I mean, congratulations." Annelise must be wondering when this surreal encounter will end. I have to admit I'm enjoying watching them squirm.

"I was aware that you had a teenage son," she blunders on, "but not that you'd just had another baby. How old are you? No, I mean, how old is she?"

"Eight weeks, ten weeks, I don't yet know for sure."

"You don't *know* how old she is?"

"Another one of my weaknesses. Never was much good with figures. As I said, must dash. And thanks again for your interest in me."

I exit with a deliberate bounce to my step. As soon as I'm out of the door I run through the open-plan and leg it down the corridor to the lift.

I've read the baby books. I've bought the layette — food and water bowl, collar, lead, ID tag, brushes, canine toothpaste and a selection of toys. The crib, or rather crate, in which Susanna will sleep to start with, is already set up in the conservatory, and the dog guard has been fixed in my car. I've even committed myself to a hand-feeding programme for the first few weeks, a radical new approach to training that will apparently have Susanna obeying every command as she eats, quite literally, out of my hand. So I'm as prepared as I can be for my "first night".

I'm nervous, more nervous than that first night with Olly. I'd already bonded with my beautiful boy at my breast, as I recovered from an emergency Caesarean section in the hospital where he was born. Getting home was bliss, even if I didn't get a decent night's sleep for the next five years.

The trouble with Olly was that he was always ill. From the moment he was born he seemed to catch everything going, from ear infections to salmonella poisoning, from molluscum contagiosum (a nasty wart virus that for a time covered his entire torso) to whooping cough, despite having had the vaccination. So many nights interrupted by Olly, that even when he slept right through, I didn't. Sleeping, like sex, was something that just seemed to slip off my agenda. Olly grew far more robust as the years went by, but the art of sleeping easy was lost to me. Not once, though, did I resent those interrupted nights, our precious boy lying between me and Jack, as one or other of us soothed him to sleep in our arms.

Olly was just three months old when I went back to work full-time. I was driven then, by both a desire to succeed and a dread of failure. I was suffering a bad case of what two American psychologists had recently identified as Imposter Syndrome. Often high-achievers, usually women, sufferers of Imposter Syndrome are convinced they're flying by the seat of their pants, about to be unmasked at any given moment and found wanting, not really worthy of their elevated positions or their impressive salaries. And the longer I stayed away from the office the more likely, it seemed to me, that someone would realise they didn't need me at all.

However much external proof of our abilities we imposters receive — academic qualifications, job promotions, salary hikes — we put all our success down to luck or timing or contacts, anything, in fact, but our own abilities and perseverance.

I suppose, as a child, I just never thought I was good enough, even though I was way above average at school. My mother took no interest whatsoever in my academic achievements and my father — to make up for my mother — did precisely the opposite, praising me wholeheartedly whether I got an A or an E. But if an A was OK, how could an E be equally acceptable? It was confusing to say the least.

Academically, I was up and down like a yo-yo. At nine I was so way ahead of my peers that the headmistress of my primary school put me in for my 11 Plus. So I was sent to grammar school with kids a year older. I struggled for two years to keep up, and by the end of the second year was almost bottom of my class. Because of my age, it was decided that rather than putting me into the next class in a lower stream, I should repeat my second year. This may have been a smart educational move, but it played havoc with my social life. My older friends couldn't handle being pals with a girl in the year below who still wore ankle socks; my new peers had already formed the kind of close-knit girl gangs that were impossible to penetrate. What little confidence I had was shattered. I'd wander round the school grounds alone at break, trying to look as though I was heading somewhere. Round and round I went — popping back to the classroom to "fetch something", going to the loo when I didn't really need to, anything to use up the time before classes would begin again. So I worked hard, caught up, and went back up again to the top of the class. "Well, what do you expect?" the girls whispered, but loudly enough to make sure I could hear. "It doesn't take a genius to be top of the class when she's already done the whole year once before. Not exactly fair for the rest of us."

I'm catapulted back to the present by the sound of whining.

I rush to Susanna's crate, scoop her up and out through the conservatory to the back garden. She races around manically for a minute or two, then circles on the spot a few times, before squatting to relieve herself.

"Good girl," I say. "Good girl, Susanna. I hope you're going to be happy in your new home."

When Olly gets in, he finds me and Susanna enjoying a game of tug-of-war with a short rope I've selected from her green plastic toy box, the very same toy box that many years ago belonged to Olly.

"Come and meet your little sister, Olly," I say.

"What a beautiful girl." He grins, his face alight with pleasure. And in the next instant Olly's down on the floor with us, Susanna is licking Olly's face, and I'm thinking this feels just like a proper family. I do wish Jack could see us now.

That night, while Susanna sleeps in her crate, I sleep on the sofa in the conservatory next to her. Apparently, this arrangement will accelerate the bonding process and ensure Susanna gets to know who's leader of the pack while she adjusts to separation from her doggie family. When Susanna wakes in the middle of the night and cries, rousing myself isn't a problem. I am already wide awake, staring through the glass roof to the stars, and trying to work out why I so deliberately sabotaged my job prospects at Jackson's. I put on the dressing gown and rubber shoes I've left by the back door, and stumble back outside again with her. It's 2a.m. and I'm fifty years old and I'm standing in the garden in a dressing gown and blue rubber shoes and haven't a clue where my life is going. But one thing is certain. Little

240

Susanna is going to have a happy home life, even if the rest of her housemates are more like something out of *Big Brother* than *Little House on the Prairie*.

An American in London

There are two new emails in my inbox. The first is from Creative Talent Search. I double click on "interview" in the subject box. As I read, I can feel all the little thread veins in my cheeks rising to the surface.

Dear Hope,

Thank you so much for your interest in the position of editor of the new launch at Jackson International.

Your track record is one of the best we've come across, but after a great deal of consideration and having seen all the other potential candidates, we have decided not to proceed to second interview stage.

Annelise and I wish you luck in finding a position to suit your considerable talents in the near future.

With all good wishes.

Yours sincerely,

Harry Sharp

The little creep. The lousy little creep and his weaselly accomplice who is so unversed in basic etiquette that she didn't even have the manners to introduce herself when we met. They can't get away with rejecting *me*. I rejected *them*, for heaven's sake. Didn't I tell them they could stuff their *Celebrity Diets* launch? Didn't I make it absolutely clear that I didn't want their lousy job? Is this how headhunters justify their existence? By demonstrating that they've turned down sufficient candidates to make the ones left on their shortlist look as though they got there through a process of exhaustive enquiry. Even my nose is hot. Since turning fifty, whenever I get cross, my nose goes red. I look like a lush. I could certainly do with a drink, but it's 9.30 in the morning, and I really don't want to go down that route.

Supposing this gets back to Jackson's MD, Craig. Although Craig Anderson knows exactly my capabilities — over the last decade we've lunched at least once a year and he's always hinted at wanting to lure me from Global if the right job came up — he'll still be infected by the revelation that I didn't sufficiently impress his new star publisher to get through to the second round (though what it says about Craig that Ms Annelise got to be his new star publisher is a worry in itself). And then no one, no one at all, will ever again be interested in giving me a proper job! No, not Hope, they'll say automatically, whenever my name comes up, she's a bit over-the-hill, don't you think, a bit *erratic*.

I could, of course, be gracious and let this go. Write it off to their inexperience. But there's something nagging at me, something bothering me that has nothing to do with Harry's undeniably crass and inappropriate email.

It's the feeling that even if I'd wanted the job — a job I could do with both hands tied behind my back — they would have turned me down. That they'd want someone younger. That by putting myself out of the running, before they had the chance to do it for me, I was subconsciously eliminating the possibility of rejection. Except that my safety net seems to have failed, and they've rejected me anyway.

I press the reply button:

Dear Harry,

I would like to put it on record that I withdrew my candidacy for the job at the interview. I made it absolutely clear that I was not interested in editing a magazine about Celebrity Diets.

It is unprofessional and potentially slanderous to reject me for a job for which I am not even applying.

I will be contacting Craig Anderson personally to make quite sure he is fully aware of the situation.

Yours sincerely,
Hope Lyndhurst

I still remember the number for Jackson International. The switch-board puts me through to Craig's PA who, when I tell her who I am, puts me straight on to Craig.

"Good to hear from you, Hope. How are you doing? I was thrilled to hear you've had another baby."

"Yes, I'm great thanks," I say, hoping I sound convincing. "Big misunderstanding about the baby, though. Your headhunter and your publisher thought I was referring to a baby, but I was actually referring to a dog."

Craig lets out a great guffaw. I can picture his considerable jowls juddering appreciatively.

"Priceless, Hope, absolutely priceless."

"Believe me," I say, "the way my life's going at the moment it would have to be immaculate conception for me to have another baby."

Craig guffaws again.

"You know, I love it when you talk dirty. We really should do lunch, you and I."

"Lunch would be lovely, but I'd like to put the record straight now. You must know I would be the worst possible choice as editor of Celebrity Diets. I'm just so not into that kind of thing. I made it absolutely clear to Annelise and the lad from the recruitment agency that I didn't want the job, but this morning I received an email which was effectively a rejection letter."

"You're really cheering me up today," says Craig, hooting with laughter again. "I've known you long enough, Hope, to know that you wouldn't be remotely interested in Celebrity Diets. You should never have been contacted by my people in the first place. I gave them some names to call — and you weren't even on my list. If you had been I'd have called you direct, you should know that. Bring me the head of the headhunter, I say. Honestly, I don't know why I bother with them."

"Well, at least you can rest assured that without me at the helm, *Celebrity Diets* will be your next big hit."

Everything I say seems to make Craig laugh.

"Look, Hope, I'd love to catch up, I really would, but I'm away for the last two weeks of August with the family, and then I'm travelling throughout September. And I know I don't have anything for you in the immediate pipeline. But let's fix something for October, by which time I may have some interesting little projects to talk about. And even if I don't, it would still be a pleasure to buy you lunch."

"I shall look forward to it."

"By the way, I hear *Jasmine*'s going swiftly down the pan. Not one of Simon's finest moments."

Simon, my old boss, and Craig are deadly rivals, and the two are always equally gleeful in their aggressive put-downs of one another. Each respects the other a great deal, but neither would admit it publicly. Their spats are great fodder for the trade journals, but I know for a fact that they dine together regularly. Craig would say *Jasmine* was going down the pan even if its circulation had trebled. But the thought cheers me anyway.

"Have a good summer, Craig, and I look forward to seeing you in the autumn."

"You too, Hope."

Susanna is trying to jump on my lap.

"Hang on, sweetie, just one more email to look at, then we'll go for our walk."

It's quite a momentous day for me and Susanna. She's had her twelve-week vaccinations, and it's safe to take her to the park. The dog bible says I need to get her used to socialising with other dogs. But how will I get along with the other mothers? Will I have to have them back for tea?

I neither recognise the name in the "from" box nor know what the message may be about from the words "Grand Hotel" which are written in the subject area. Junk or virus, I suspect, about to hit the delete key. But something stops me. Daniel Drake. There *is* something familiar about the name. Daniel. Dan. Could it possibly . . .? I never even knew his surname. My stomach does a little flip. In taking the chance of it being him, I risk the virus corrupting my computer. Sod the virus, I think, as I double click, my finger trembling slightly as it hovers above the mouse.

Hi Hope,

That was one helluva sudden departure back in May . . . If I'd known where you were staying, no way would you have got away without saying goodbye.

Now for a "Once-In-A-Lifetime" (Moss Hart and George S Kaufman, bet you got it right away) opportunity of making up for your disappearing act.

We're having a last-minute summer vacation in the UK, doing a house swap with a high-rolling Bostonian couple who moved to England ten years ago, and ended up buying some down-on-his-luck

247

lord's ancestral pile in Dorset. Wife plus kids, we'll be doing the whole Hardy hog for a two-week stretch. Trouble is I go stir-crazy after about forty-eight hours in Arcadia.

I've been reading your British critics on the net on the new production of *Grand Hotel* at the Donmar in Covent Garden, and they're raving about it. The pitch is this: you come as my guest to the show and dinner afterwards, and I leave the theatre booking and restaurant reservation to you.

I don't wish to be presumptuous, as you Brits are so fond of saying, but if, as we Yanks are so fond of saying, this idea floats your boat, then I'll be one happy guy. I have a hotel booking from 23–26 and hope you're going to be in town.

Say I can see you again. But if not . . . I guess we'll always have Paris.

Dan

We'll always have Paris! How corny you are, Mr Dan Drake. Pure *schmaltz*. Methinks you've maybe seen one movie and several hundred musicals too many. But you're a lot more cute than you are corny. A "helluva" lot more. This needs some serious thought.

Seeing Dan on home territory would be madness, especially while I'm trying to get Jack back. But supposing Jack won't come back, and I miss out on my "once-in-a-lifetime opportunity". *We'll always have Paris*. We could always have Paris *again*.

"Come on, Susanna, we need some fresh air. Let's go for a walk and talk this over."

★ ★ ★

I've bought a special extra-long training lead for our first few outings. I'm not convinced that my leadership skills are sufficiently intact for Susanna to obey my every command off-lead. Before I got a dog, I barely noticed other people's, unless one happened to crash into my legs during an over-exuberant play session with another pooch. Now it seems that almost everyone has a dog. And because mine is still at the adorable puppy stage, we are stopped every five seconds so she can be oohed, aahed and fawned over. Not even real babies have this effect on the British. I've made about ten new friends in as many minutes.

Although Susanna and I would love to walk for an hour or two, I'm under strict instructions to restrict the length of our outings until her bones have grown stronger. This means that I won't be able to take her on my training walks for the trek, but will have to leave her at home and then take her out for her own play session later. Jack was certainly right about a dog taking over your life. But at the moment I like having my life taken over, even though I know *The Future* has to be faced. Sooner rather than later.

Apart from the toilet training, which is not quite as advanced as I would like it to be, having Susanna has been beneficial in all sorts of unexpected ways. My mother is in love with her. In fact, she has expressed more affection for Susanna in the last couple of weeks than she has for me in fifty years. She allows Susanna to jump on her precious white sofas and the two of them snuggle up and take a nap together. Despite my mother's increasing frailty — and my father's concern that Susanna might be harbouring germs — she insists on allowing Susanna to lick her face, her neck, her hands and any other exposed body part. My mother talks to her — her voice is now a hoarse whisper — in the manner of a doting grandmother, exclaiming constantly at Susanna's beauty and brilliance. I can't help making comparison with her lack of interest in Olly. In truth, it sickens me. But it also lets me off the hook. With Susanna in her role of Peace Ambassador, there is a secure buffer zone between me and my mother. My visits have increased from three times a week to almost every day, and it's the presence of Susanna that has made them bearable.

Over coffee in the grounds of Kenwood House, I try to work out what to do about Dan. It seems to me I have three options. I can lie and say I'm busy or out of town; I can meet him for the show and dinner afterwards, and then go straight home — alone; or I can go back to his hotel for another night of the kind of fabulous sex I'd forgotten still existed. The kind of sex I only have to think about for a spontaneous pelvic contraction to occur. My gynaecologist would see this as very healthy — he recommends that all his patients practise their Kegel exercises at the bus stop to prevent the possibility of prolapse in later life . . .

I get the feeling Dan doesn't have to wrestle his conscience over this — unlike me. I wonder if he even has a conscience. My guess is that he's a pretty casual kind of philanderer. Which, leaving aside his wife, who's not really my business, is probably a good thing as far as I'm concerned. I know, from the word go, that this is strictly casual, something that has absolutely no possibility of a future, and is therefore a lot less complicated than a full-on affair.

Maddy and Mozart are coming for supper tonight. Fortunately, Mozart and Susanna are made for one another. He hasn't attacked her once. And, like most new lovers, they spend their time either kissing or sulking and deliberately ignoring one another. I'm going to have to confess Paris to Maddy. I'll go crazy if I don't talk to someone about it. I'd talk to Vanessa, but involving my son's mistress in my own extra-marital affairs is beginning to sound just too Jerry Springer for my taste.

I've cooked a half leg of lamb with a mustard and honey glaze, alongside roasted red peppers dressed with garlic, olive oil and balsamic vinegar, potatoes sizzled to golden crispness in the oven with goose fat, and broccoli *al dente* spritzed with lemon juice. And a chocolate and almond cake for dessert. I think Maddy was expecting spaghetti Bolognese, but she has still to absorb the fact of my new obsession with chopping, paring, slicing, grating, kneading, baking, reducing and every other culinary-ing.

"Mmm," says Maddy, patting her tummy after two portions of each course as I feed Susanna and Mozart the scraps from our plates. "She/he liked that. And so did I. Not sure I could ever walk out on someone who cooks as well as you."

"Cooking's just another of those avoidance activities, like the dog, which I've taken up since I got booted off

Jasmine. And in a funny way I think all this manic cooking was just one more thing that made Jack uneasy."

"How do you mean?"

"He liked me best when I was a working woman, independent. He's never wanted a *hausfrau* for a wife, and if I fuss over him in any way he feels all hemmed in and claustrophobic. He told me as much. He was once going off to a conference in Nottingham, and I offered to make him a sandwich for the train journey. It was as though I'd mortally offended him. Instead of saying something like 'Oh, that's really thoughtful of you,' he said, 'I don't want a sandwich, and if I did want one I'd be perfectly capable of making it myself.' He hates to be fussed over."

"Men are so weird."

"I need your advice, Maddy . . ."

"Shoot."

"You know my trip to Paris . . ."

"You mean the lingerie, the Picasso museum, the fantastic restaurant in St Germain. You were very perky about it all."

"More perky than you know."

"Meaning?"

"Meaning I slept with someone."

"You slept with someone! But you were only there for three days. Who? How? Where?"

"The restaurant. I met him in the restaurant."

"And you had sex with him?"

"Well, not there and then. After dinner. After walking for two hours along the Seine. After a couple of brandies."

"You old slag! How was it?"

"Incredible. Mind-blowing. Earth-shattering. Stupendous."

"Lucky old you. Was he a sexy frog?"

"An American. A professor. He teaches musical theatre. He loves old musicals."

"Handsome?"

"Very."

"Married?"

"Very."

"Kids?"

"Two."

"If you're going to tell me you've fallen in love, I might have to throw up. And after four months of throwing up every day, I'd really rather you didn't get me going again."

"Honestly, Maddy, I thought we'd never meet again. But I gave him my email address and he got in touch and he's coming over. *En famille*. Something to do with a house swap in Dorset. But he's coming to London on his own for a few days, and he wants to see a show and have dinner."

"So what are you going to do?"

"Exactly."

"Exactly what?"

"What am I going to do?"

"Bloody hell, Hope, I don't know. But it does sound awfully tempting."

"The thing is, I can't separate wanting to get back with Jack from my desire to go to bed with Dan. I'd like to put the two things in separate compartments, but they keep rubbing up against one another, blurring the boundaries."

"Well, it doesn't make you seem very committed to getting back with Jack if you're off screwing someone else in a swish London hotel."

"But what does one thing have to do with the other? Jack and I haven't had sex since last year. Dan made me feel desirable again. I've been wired all day since receiving his email. If he walked through the door right now I'd have to drag him straight up to the bedroom, leaving you to do the washing-up."

"It doesn't sound all that healthy to me."

"Meaning?"

"Meaning even if we're talking pure lust, it's going to muddle your feelings about Jack. On the other hand, there's always the chance that when you meet him again he might not appear nearly as attractive as he did first time around. Sometimes the one-night stand is best left at that, as I've learned from bitter experience."

"You mean, I might not even fancy him? I hadn't thought of that. And then instead of this great memory, it will be somehow sullied."

"But if you do fancy him, which is the more likely scenario, you could be heading for dangerous waters . . ."

"I'm feeling guilty about so many things at the moment, but, oddly, not at all guilty about having slept with Dan. It's the possibility of a replay that's pricking my conscience. I want to be with Jack, and I want to have fun with Dan. I have no illusions at all about a relationship with Dan. On the other hand, if it were the other way round, and I discovered Jack was making out with some popsie . . . Actually, I don't know how I'd feel, maybe I'd think he deserved the break . . . Oh, this is hopeless."

"When it comes down to it, you may just be playing one night of pleasure off against a lifetime back with Jack," says Maddy, no longer teasing but serious.

"But Jack doesn't have to know . . . and so far he hasn't even mentioned coming back. When I tried to bring up the subject he left the room."

"Oh, Hope, I really don't know. But my gut says don't do it — maybe later, if things with Jack don't work out, but not now. Not while it's all still up in the air."

"There may not be a later, but I'm sorry to say I think you're right. Look, Maddy, I've got an idea. When I was little and made a promise to someone, I didn't always keep it. But if I'd also said at the time of that promise, 'Cross my heart and hope to die,' nothing, but nothing, could have induced me to renege on it. So, I'm making a solemn promise to you now. I will meet Dan for the show and dinner afterwards, but I promise I will not have sex with him."

"Cross your heart and hope to die?"

"Cross my heart and hope to die. There, it's done."

"Hope, are you sure that this will do the trick? It seems rather random."

"Positive. But I have to admit that although I know it's the right thing, I'm really, truly, deeply disappointed."

"You do want Jack back, don't you?"

"Yes, I do. I mean, I'm really unhappy without him around, but I'm still trying to work out exactly what it is about him that I miss. And I'm beginning to think that I've spent the last eighteen years — ever since Olly was born — treating Jack like a vase, or a painting, that's been sitting in the same place all this time. Something you'd spot immediately if someone moved it to another position, or took it away altogether, but on a day-to-day basis you don't notice it's even there. Jack's always been so reliable, so accommodating. So involved with Olly, and always willing to listen to my problems. I think there must have come a point when I stopped appreciating him doing things and just expected it instead. Maybe I should have taken more notice, said thank you a little more often. Given back more. Although Jack always seemed so self-contained and cheery and un-needy."

"I don't know," says Maddy, sighing, "maybe this separation is a good thing. It's painful, I know, but at least it's forcing you to examine everything."

"I think that what's really felled me is the fact of everything hitting me at once. I can't focus on any one thing."

"Keep working on it, Hope."

"I'll try."

"And now there's something important I want to ask you." Maddy takes my hand and places it on her tummy.

"Go for it."

"I want you to be he/she's godmother."

"Oh, Maddy, I thought you'd never ask. I thought you thought I wasn't up to the job. I thought you thought I might be too old."

"Will you be godmother to my child, my friend?"

I could win awards for crying, I've done so much of it lately.

"I am honoured, privileged and over the moon," I blub. "I can't wait to have this baby of ours."

We're still hugging and weeping when Olly appears.

"What's this? A lesbian love-in cum dog orgy? Haven't I had enough shocks lately?"

"Congratulate me, Olly, I'm going to be a godmother."

"Congratulations, Mum. Maddy, you're enormous."

"Love you too, Olly."

"Have you eaten?" I ask.

"Yeah, I had pizza. But I'm starving."

"There's a whole plateful there left over. You can heat it in the microwave or have it cold."

That same little stabbing pain that occurs every time I think about Olly leaving home. Very soon there'll be no more starving boy in the house.

I turn my attention back to Maddy, and we talk about the baby and when we're going to go shopping for the pram, the cot, and all the rest of the paraphernalia.

When Maddy leaves, I call Ticketmaster and book seats for *Grand Hotel*. Then I ring the Ivy and book a table for 10.30p.m. after the show.

It's the end of another average day in my weird new world. A world that used to be full of certainty, and now the only certain thing is that I don't have a clue what's going to happen from one moment to the next. I've been turned down for a job I didn't apply for. I've gained a godchild. And I've waved goodbye to all possibility of a sex life. I finally drift off to sleep thinking of that night in Paris. Some people say women don't have wet dreams, but they're wrong. I wake up around 4a.m., having had delicious sex with a stranger. "Jack," I say sleepily, reaching out for my husband. Only Jack isn't there.

I book a manicure, pedicure, leg wax, bikini wax, facial, roots tint, wash and blow-dry. I am *not* going to have sex with Dan Drake. I go to Diane von Furstenberg in Ledbury Road and try on everything in the shop. I am *not* going to have sex with Dan Drake. I buy a simple sleeveless wrap dress with a hot-pink twig-like motif on a white background. And because the assistant insists I try it with a pair of dusty-pink suede Prada peep-toe shoes, which she brings in from Matches next door, and which have heels high enough to elongate and slim my legs but not so high as to make me walk like a duck, I buy the shoes as well. Cross my heart and hope to die. I am not going to have sex with Dan Drake. But I didn't say I wouldn't do my damnedest to make him want to have sex with me.

I've been buffed and polished like the very best antique silver. I don't look a day over forty-eight. I shall have to wear my glasses to the play if I'm going to be able to talk intelligently about it afterwards. I do have contact lenses, but I can't read the menu with them in, and I do find it embarrassing to have to ask diners at the next table to hold up the menu for me so I can read it long distance. Why am I fussing so? I'm only going to talk to the man. *Not* sleep with him.

Olly's working at the bar in West End Lane, but should be home by eight. And later he's going clubbing, but not until around ten thirty, which means he can walk the dog round the block before he goes out and before I get home, after which she won't need to go out until the morning.

It's a gorgeously warm night, I don't even need a jacket, but I take a cream pashmina to wrap round my shoulders in case it cools down. I am nervous, excited and slightly panicky in case I bump into anyone I know. I decide to arrive in style in a mini-cab, and then regret it. The cab reeks of stale tobacco and grease, and I fear that's how I'll end up smelling too. There is so little stuffing in the upholstery, I might as well be sitting on steel rods. Great black clouds are trailing from the exhaust. My cloud has given me the night off. In fact, there have been an increasing number of stalker-free moments since Susanna came into my life.

I step out onto the pavement outside the Donmar Warehouse.

"Hope, how great to see you. Wow, you look a million dollars. Not working clearly agrees with you."

Of all the people I never want to bump into, Exquisite Mark has to be right at the top of my list.

He's on a roll.

"DvF, of *course*. Once a woman's hit a certain age she really shouldn't wear anything else. *So* flattering to the figure."

Garrotting would be too kind an ending for Mark.

And then I spot him, ambling down the street in beige chinos, a bottle-green Polo shirt and a pair of brown brogues, waving a copy of *Time Out*.

"Wow, Hope, you look great," he says, stooping to kiss me lightly on the cheek.

"Just what I said," says Mark, extending a hand towards Dan, and fluttering those fabulous eyelashes of his.

My evening is being ruined before it has even begun.

"Dan, this is Mark, a former colleague of mine."

"Pleased to meet you, Dan, you sound like a Bostonian to me."

"Sharp guy. You've got a good ear."

Do something, Hope, and do it quickly, I tell myself, before the two of them disappear into the pub next door for a pint.

"Sorry to rush you, Dan, but I'd kill for a drink, and the bar's upstairs. Enjoy the show, Mark."

I grab Dan by the wrist and haul him inside and up the stairs.

"Is everything OK?" asks Dan. "You seem a little harassed."

"It's that man. I hate him."

"Hate. That's a strong word. I thought he seemed rather charming."

"Oh, yes, indeed, in the way that Brutus was charming right up until the very moment he betrayed

Caesar. In the way that Hitler could be really sweet and gentle with Eva Braun, even after slaughtering six million Jews. In the way that Cruella de Vil wanted to cosy up with those cute little Dalmatians at the same time as she was planning to flay them for a new coat."

"I'm beginning to get the picture. You don't like the guy."

"It's because of him I got fired."

"You didn't tell me you got fired."

"There's a lot you don't know about me."

"That's good. It means there's a lot for me to find out."

Unlike teenagers, grown-ups can't get away with groping one another the moment the lights go down in the auditorium. Which is very fortunate. Otherwise, despite my promise, I might be straddling Dan's lap right now. I've gone into a kind of static overdrive. Every time Dan adjusts his large frame in his seat, and his trousered thigh barely brushes against the flimsy material of my dress, sparks fizz and crackle through my body like an unchoreographed, amateur fireworks display. When he leans over to whisper a comment about the show, and his lips no more than graze my ear, a shiver shoots from my neck down my spine. There's a congested feeling in my pelvis, an ache inside my vagina.

The show is the perfect backdrop to my unaccustomed feelings. In its stage incarnation, the film that made Greta Garbo famous for wanting to be alone is a stunning evocation of pre-war Berlin — at once hedonistic, glamorous and sleazy. "Time is running out," the characters keep repeating — and we know that time is running out not just for these individuals, living decadently at Grand Hotel, but for Germany, as the economic crisis deepens and the slow descent to the Second World War begins. Time is running out . . . It feels a bit like that for me too. I'm fifty, for heaven's sake. My husband has left me. I'm sitting next to a man I fancy so much I am about to spontaneously combust. Shouldn't I be grabbing my chances while I can? Why be good when being bad, from where I'm sitting, looks so much more fun? Cross my heart and hope to die.

"Exhilarating," I say, as we slowly file out with the crowds.

"Exhilarating, sexy and sardonic," says Dan.

"Exhilarating, sexy, sardonic, louche, lush. I'm running out of adjectives."

"This is beginning to feel like *Supermarket Sweep*. Do you have that show here?"

"Sadly, yes, but I've never watched it."

"So where's dinner?"

"The Ivy. Otherwise known as the Celebrity Caff."

"Do you have influence? In Boston and New York you sometimes have to wait months for a reservation."

"I wouldn't call it influence, exactly. I just have a few semi-famous acquaintances. First time I tried to book they said they were full. I rang five minutes later giving my shoe-designer friend's name, and they gave me a table right away."

"But won't they realise that neither of us are her?"

"Maybe, maybe not. But they won't make a scene."

"Hope, did you feel horny in the theatre?"

"As a matter of fact I did."

"Me too. Horny as hell."

This is not going at all as planned.

The guy with the bookings book looks slightly askance when I say my name, or rather the name of the well-known designer who shoes A-list feet in her impossible-to-stand-upright-in, S&M fetish footwear. "She couldn't make it at the last minute, so I came with someone else," I mumble. He waves us through.

Gosh, that really is Gwyneth Paltrow and Chris Martin skulking in the corner. I give Dan a little prod and nod, "Over there."

"I'm impressed."

We're seated side by side at a kind of central banquette, laid with a traditional white tablecloth.

"Great camouflage," says Dan, slipping his hand under the tablecloth and making for the slit in my skirt with radar accuracy.

"Daaan! You can't do that here. Jesus, it's fucking Mark and his posse. If he gets wind of what you're up to, it will be all over town before breakfast."

Mark and three immaculately dressed male companions are led to the table to our right.

"Hi there, Hope. Dan. Very stylish, I thought. Now don't let me and the guys spoil your cosy chat. Just pretend we're not here."

If only.

"Behave yourself," I hiss in Dan's ear. "I can't tell you how bad this could get. Jack sorted out some sports injury of his a couple of years back. Now he rings Jack whenever he has a problem, and with his nerve is probably still doing so, despite having done me out of my job."

"This place is pretty cool. But maybe we should have gone somewhere less conspicuous."

"Maybe you're right."

"How about we have just one quick course and then back to my hotel for dessert?"

"You're a genius," I say.

When the waiter arrives, Dan says loudly, so Mark can hear: "We've only time for one course, I'm afraid. I'm flying out first thing and I have to pick my wife up in an hour from her aunt's house in Kensington."

Too much information, I'm thinking. But Mark's heard every word, and so long as he's fathoming whether to read anything into it or not he has no evidence whatsoever of anything illicit.

Over fishcake and spinach (me), bangers and mash (him), we dissect *Grand Hotel*, chat about the run-down but magnificent manor house in Dorset where Dan's been staying and discuss Dan's work. All non-controversial subjects that even if Mark were to be noting every word he'd have nothing to go on. I'm working hard on pretending that Dan is my bank manager — deeply boring and deeply unattractive. It seems to be doing the trick of curbing my tongue, if not my internal organs.

★ ★ ★

The air has cooled, and as we leave the restaurant I shake out my neatly folded pashmina.

"Here, let me do that," says Dan.

He shakes out the sheet of creamy cashmere and arcs it over my head like a skipping rope. Drawing the two ends of the scarf around and over my chest, he pulls me closer, burying his face in my neck and breathing in deeply.

"You smell so good, Hope."

I might dissolve, right here on the pavement, but I can't keep myself from glancing anxiously about.

"Not here," I say, not wanting him to stop, desire distilled to even greater potency by the danger of discovery. He moves away, his eyes narrowing in a knowing smile.

We walk towards his hotel, an invisible barrier keeping us apart, a no-go zone beyond which there's no going back. Once through the lobby doors of Dan's hotel, I feel relatively safe from prying eyes. We head for the wood-panelled drawing room and find ourselves a plumply upholstered sofa in a quiet corner.

"I think I'll just have coffee," I say. It's 11.30p.m., and I need to keep sober if I'm going to come to a rational decision. *Cross your heart and hope to die.*

"Dan," I say. "I don't think I should sleep with you."

"Yeuwre makin' a big mistake, honey."

Dan's mock-macho Southern drawl makes me giggle.

"It's just that my life's so complicated at the moment. I don't want to screw things up more than I've done already."

"Screw things up, no. Screw me, most definitely."

"Oh, Dan, you're not taking me seriously."

"Look, Hope, it's just a bit of fun. We're both married and we both have commitments and we live in different countries. I'm not going to try to steal you away from Jack. I enjoy your company, and I enjoy having sex with you. End of story."

For some reason I don't like Dan saying Jack's name as if he knows him.

"The thing is, Jack's left me, and I'm not sure sex with you is any kind of answer."

"Fired from your job. Left by your husband. Yeah, I can see things are a little complicated. A night with me is just what you need — to take your mind off things. Answers I can't promise."

"How many affairs have you had since you've been married?"

"Look, this isn't how it operates."

"Go on, how many?"

"Not very many . . ."

"Because the thing is, in twenty years you're the only guy apart from Jack I've ever slept with."

"I'm flattered. But it's no worse a sin to sleep with a man twice than it is once."

"But the first time was spontaneous. This is premeditated. It's calculated."

"Oh, so spontaneity's a lapse; premeditation's a deadly sin."

"Cross my heart and hope to die," I say, aloud.

"What's that you said?"

"Oh, just some silly, childish superstition to do with promises kept and broken."

"Are you superstitious, then? A believer in omens and portents?"

"Not at all."

"Me neither. In which case shall we hold the coffee and get a bottle of champagne sent to my room instead?"

"Yes, Dan, I'd like that very much indeed."

In the lift on the way up Dan stands behind me and clasps my body to his.

"Ever had sex in an elevator?" he asks, as his hands head south between my legs, and I can feel his hard cock pressing between my buttocks.

"I thought it only happened in the movies," I reply, wishing we could empty the hotel of guests and staff and do it right here.

We are in his room.

"I want to undress you," he says.

He sits on the bed, and I stand in front of him.

He pulls on the ties at the side of my waist and my dress unwraps itself. I have on the second set of underwear I bought in Paris, and I'm wearing hold-up stockings.

"I like this look," he says, slipping my dress from my shoulders so I'm left standing in my underwear and my high heels. He begins to trace my body with his hands.

Something's buzzing in my handbag. My mobile hardly ever rings. I glance at my watch. And certainly not at this hour.

"Ignore it," he says.

"I can't. Only a few people have my number, it must be important."

I was feeling so sexy. Now, as I have to walk in my underwear to the table to collect my handbag, I feel exposed and uncomfortable, his eyes scrutinising every inch of me. I open my bag and take out my phone. "You have one new message," it says. It's from Olly.

Emergency! Had 2 double shift at the bar, 1 of the guys ill. No time 2 take Su 4 a walk. U need 2 take her out as soon as u get home.

"Fuck!" I spit the word out.

"That was the idea," says Dan. "Is everything OK?"

"Dan, give me a moment to think."

I look at my watch again. It's five to midnight. Susanna hasn't been out since six. If I don't get back soon she will become distressed and start pissing and shitting all over the floor. Olly might not be back until four or five in the morning. The thought of hurrying sex with Dan, then dashing home to clear up Susanna's mess, is the perfect antidote to arousal.

"Dan, there's an emergency, I have to go straight home."

"What kind of an emergency?"

"A canine one."

"Are you kidding me, Hope? Is this some kind of a joke?"

"No, Dan, I promise. There is nothing in the world I'd rather do right now than go to bed with you and a bottle of champagne. But I've got this text from my son, and I have to go home."

268

Dan is shaking his head slowly from side to side, the bare hint of a smile turning up the corners of his mouth.

"It's what makes you special, I guess."

"What's that?" I ask, desperate to get back into my dress. I feel like a prostitute, parading in my underwear before a fully-dressed stranger.

"Your dedication to your dog."

We both laugh and it breaks the tension. He stands and pulls me to him, kissing me full on the mouth, prising my lips apart with his tongue.

"We'd have been so good together," he says, as I finally release myself.

"Yes, we would. I'm so sorry, Dan. Look, I'll call you. Maybe we'll meet before you go back down to Dorset."

"Let me help you on with that." Dan holds out my dress for me to put my arms through, like a coat, and then wraps me back into it. It's a gentlemanly gesture and helps me to feel less self-conscious.

"Thanks, Dan, for a lovely evening, and what would have been a lovely night."

I know at that moment that we won't meet before he goes back down to Dorset because I won't make that call. He accompanies me downstairs, and this time the lift is just a lift, stripped of its erotic appeal. The doorman hails me a cab, and Dan waves me off.

I'd made a solemn promise to myself and to Maddy that I wouldn't sleep with Dan. And I'd only been saved from breaking it by the ardour-dampening vision of Susanna's mess on the carpet. To all intents and purposes, I broke my promise the second I saw Dan coming towards me as I stood outside the theatre. I have all the will power of a Labrador faced with a bag of discarded chips on the pavement.

When I open the front door, Susanna bounds towards me, jumping up at my legs and snagging my stockings.

"Get off me, you monster," I yell, before patting and stroking her fondly.

There's no smell and no evidence of any mess.

"Give me two minutes," I say, and take the stairs two at a time. I kick off my new shoes, throw my clothes on the bed, peel off my new, now-snagged, stockings and grab an old pair of jeans, T-shirt and Birkenstocks from the cupboard.

The night is still full of stars. I nod at other dog walkers as our respective dogs sniff one another's bottoms before moving on. I watch a young couple returning from a night out, probably drunk, trying to kiss one another and keep walking at the same time. They stumble into a lamp post, provoking a fit of giggles. I see a woman walking rapidly, in the way that women alone do, pretending to look relaxed but on the alert for unnamed threats.

How strange life is. Right now I could be rolling around on a large double bed in a sumptuous hotel room with a handsome man between my thighs. Instead, I am scooping poop into a council-issue, green plastic bag. The ridiculousness of everything suddenly hits me, and I'm laughing aloud, wiping tears from my eyes. A young bloke in a hoodie — the kind I might normally think is about to mug me — rushes by, glancing sideways at me with a worried look on his face. It makes me laugh more, the thought of me scaring him more than he scares me.

"Oh, Susanna," I say, "you and your toilet training, you may have scuppered my sex life for good."

Susanna looks up at me and wags her tail.

I wonder if the opposite of "cross my heart and hope to die" might be "uncross my heart and hope to live". I carry that thought with me as Susanna and I continue our midnight ramble. Dan Drake was only ever going to be a moment. I have the whole of the rest of my life to consider.

Pleasure and Pain

I get a special, private pleasure walking Susanna across Hampstead Heath early in the morning on weekdays, throwing a ball for her over and over to run after and bring back to me. It's perhaps the only time I am fully focused on what I'm doing, lost in the moment rather than grappling with intrusive thoughts. Thoughts that ram into one another like dodgem cars, then back away and speed off in another direction, only to collide again a moment later.

This regular ritual is little different from an outing with an overexcited child, a child who wants to play the same game again and again and again before eventually collapsing in an exhausted heap. I have no need of other company, or the desire to stand around in gaggles with other dog owners. But I go along with the etiquette. I acknowledge every dog walker who passes, smiling and metaphorically raising my baseball cap. Sometimes Susanna strikes up a playground friendship with another dog and a vigorous game of chase ensues. In these circumstances, I politely chat to the other dog's owner, like a mother at the school gate organising play-dates. I never was at the school gate to organise play-dates for Olly.

I've bought myself a ball thrower, a red plastic contraption which claws the ball so I can pick it up from the ground without having to actually handle the offending object, covered as it is in Susanna's slimy saliva. The idea is that it throws the ball far further than I ever could by hand, making the game even more fun. It's the ball thrower's first outing, and it's taking me a while to get the hang of it. The first few attempts I get into a tennis-pro serve position and lob the flexible plastic handle over my shoulder like Venus Williams, or so I delude myself. Each time Susanna follows the trajectory of my arm, and runs off in what should be the direction of the ball. Then she stops dead, realising she's been duped, because of course there is no ball. The ball stays lodged, immovable inside its claw. I glance around. A group of four walkers, with rucksacks, mountain boots and climbers' poles — who have evidently mistaken Hampstead Heath for Everest — have stopped to watch my little sideshow. "Come on, you can do it!" one of them shouts, waving his pole at me. I am sweaty with embarrassment. I come here for quality time with my dog, and to be left alone, not to be the centre of attention and a laughing stock. After a few more failed and frustrating attempts I say very loudly to Susanna, but hoping my audience can hear: "Must be a fault in the manufacture, this ball chucker's a dud. We'll go for our walk and then take it straight back to the shop." Everyone talks to their dogs aloud, so it's not the fact of my doing so that has my little audience smiling knowingly at one another before moving on.

"You need to flick, not fling," says a friendly voice coming up behind me.

"Oh, Nick, it's you. I feel such an idiot."

"Here to the rescue. Remember when I stopped you from falling flat on your face? Just over there," he says, pointing in the direction of where I stumbled over my shoelace on my first Hampstead Over-the-Hillbillies outing. "You were so busy being an Alpha female, so determined to get to the front of the group —"

"Hey, you weren't supposed to notice." I laugh. "So what's the trick to this blasted ball thrower?"

Nick comes up close behind me and takes hold of my wrist, lifting my arm above my head.

"Like this," he says, manipulating my wrist backwards and forwards. "No need to put your full body weight into it, just flick with a crisp, controlled movement. Now show me what you can do."

I feel suddenly shy, and can sense myself blushing, like a child who wants to prove herself but is afraid of failing and being laughed at.

I flick. Or at least I think I do. The ball remains resolutely in its claw. I flick again. *Nada*. And again. This time more determinedly. The ball shoots out and heads off into the distance, Susanna in hot pursuit. I punch the air with my fist. I feel ridiculously proud.

"Well done, Hope, you'll be a champion dog-ball chucker yet."

I'm beaming.

"Can I join you?" asks Nick. "Unless you'd prefer to walk alone. I won't be offended. Sometimes I pray I won't bump into anyone I know when I'm out here. It's often the only time I get to think things through."

"In that case, I should be asking you the same question. Wouldn't *you* prefer to walk alone?"

Nick smiles his crinkly-eyed smile.

"Not at all, bumping into you has already made my day."

"You are such a gentleman." I feel myself blushing again. When I was a child, I could have blushed for Britain. I should have grown out of it by now. "It just so happens I was planning to put my celebrity fund-raiser plans on paper later today, but it would be great to talk them through first."

"Sally and I were lucky to find you, Hope."

"Mmm. Say nothing more until you've heard my idea. It's so off-the-wall you may live to regret those words."

"So hit me with it."

I glance behind me to make sure Susanna hasn't run off, and inhale deeply as we set off, conscious that this idea of mine is whacky in the extreme. "Well, I know it sounds unlikely, but this dog of mine has been an absolute inspiration. I'd never have thought of it if it hadn't been for Susanna."

Nick raises an eyebrow, says nothing.

"OK, here goes. The campaign title will be 'Dogs for Cat's', as in dogs for Cat's Place."

Nick's eyes aren't crinkling now, but his nose is. I can see I've got him worried.

"Dogs for Cat's. I see."

"No, you don't. Not yet. What I have in mind is a charity catwalk show. Oh, my God, that's brilliant, catwalk, Cat's walk! Look, I've only just thought of that, we'll get back to it later."

Nick's smiling again now.

"I think I'm beginning to see how the creative process works. Not linear, that's for sure. Not like us boring old accountants who work by rules and logic."

"You're not boring, Nick, you're lovely." What a surprise! I had no idea that's what I was going to say. And, judging by the look on his face, Nick's surprised too. "But back to where I was. A charity catwalk show in which celebrities parade with their pooches, followed by a dinner and auction. I've started writing down the names of well-known dog owners from Jodie Kidd and Julia Carling to Sara Cox, Sienna Miller, Joss Stone, Paris Hilton, Geri Halliwell and Caprice. Not one hundred per cent A-list, but A-list enough for the tabloids and the celebrity weeklies."

"Hope, do you really think you could pull off something like this?"

"I do, otherwise I wouldn't have suggested it. But we'll need a bit of luck to get us going. Probably the best way to start would be with dog-owning designers — people like Matthew Williamson or Philip Treacy. If the designers bite, then they'll rope in their celebrity, pet-owning clients."

"You mean, it'll be a bit like Crufts. Except the dog owners will be celebrities in designer frocks rather than wearing flat caps and blue rinses."

"Exactly. We'll also set up a photo booth and ask someone like David Bailey to take pictures of the celebs with their dogs. We'll auction the photos, signed by the photographer, and we'll give a second print to the celebrities as a thank you."

"And you can guarantee media attention?"

"The PR potential is massive because the photo-ops are so good, and great pictures are what the newspapers and magazines most want. Just imagine how fantastic the group shot will look, especially if, as I intend, I can persuade a designer to produce an exclusive range of dog jackets."

"Dog jackets I can live with. But what if there's a dog *fight* in the middle of the show?"

"Well, I can't guarantee the behaviour of the celebs! But the dogs will be fine. No one with an aggressive dog would dream of exposing it to such temptation. If you're concerned, we'll have a couple of dog handlers on hand in case of emergencies; that's easy to organise. So what do you think?"

"You're right about off the wall. But it's getting to me. It's exciting. And different. And kind of wild. And Cat always wanted a puppy, so it works in that way too. I think I'm on the verge of loving it."

I so want Nick and Sally to like this idea. It's the first time in ages that I've felt a real spark of creative enthusiasm. I'm used to working in a team, sharing ideas the second I have them, so planning it all on my own has been quite a challenge. If Nick likes my proposal, there's no obvious reason why Sally and the committee shouldn't like it too.

277

"I know it sounds a bit convoluted," I say to Nick, checking again that Susanna's coming up behind, "but I really believe it can work. The trick is to get the ball rolling and my hunch is that if someone of the calibre of Williamson supplies the clothes, and a photographer of Bailey's status agrees to take the pictures, the celebrities and their agents will start to take it seriously."

"And the timing?"

"There's no way this can be scheduled until around May of next year. A venue will have to be booked, party planners appointed, a producer for the catwalk show found, sponsors approached individually, a celebrity or professional auctioneer brought on board, items for auction donated. Plus, it's going to have to be someone's job to persuade the rich, the powerful and the famous to buy tickets and come along with their chequebooks on the night. Most important of all, we have to get the budgets right from the outset otherwise the whole thing could go disastrously wrong and the charity will lose a fortune."

"And who's going to make it all happen? You?"

"I'm happy to open my contacts book and hit the phone, but this is a huge commitment, and we need to call in professional event organisers. Unless I start looking seriously for a job the money will run out. My big, fat bank account of January, when I got my payoff, is already looking decidedly anorexic."

"It does sound amazing, Hope. Put it in your report, and Sally and I will go through it and then we'll meet up to discuss it."

"How is Sally?"

"Acting strangely."

"How do you mean?"

"Do you think you'd know if Jack was having an affair?"

I'm taken aback by the question, the directness of it. It's not as though I know Nick very well. We met only a few months ago, and mostly we've talked about Cat and the charity. But I have such warm feelings for Nick — and for Sally too — that I want to be considered about this.

"That's some question, Nick. But speaking personally, as we're not living together and I barely see him . . . if he were having an affair now, I almost certainly wouldn't know. But if we were still under the same roof . . ." I trail off, thinking of my own Parisian deception. "Well, no, not necessarily. I think it really depends on how much the person concerned wants to keep it from their partner. If they're really determined for it to stay secret they'll probably succeed. If, subconsciously, for whatever reason, they actually want their partner to find out, they'll make 'mistakes', tell stories that are inconsistent, leave clues . . . In which case it's probably a plea for attention, for recognition of what's wrong with the marriage, rather than a deliberate attempt at cruelty. On the other hand, it might be the only way that person can signal the end of the relationship — ensuring they're found out, rather than having the courage to say it to their partner's face. It's a difficult one, Nick."

279

"I don't know how to put this, Hope, and I don't even know if I should be saying this as it's not exactly fair to you and it's only a suspicion, but I think . . . I think that Sally may be having an affair. I think she may be having an affair with Jack . . ."

"But that's rid —" Before I can finish my word I am interrupted by the piercing sound, carried by the warm breeze, of a woman screeching and swearing and on the verge of hysteria.

"Get off me, you stupid dog, you vicious animal. Look, you've ruined my skirt. It's in shreds. Who's the fucking owner?"

I look around to see which ill-behaved, ill-trained dog is the instigator of this outcry, and I see Susanna jumping up, trying to grab a croissant out of a young woman's hand. The woman, probably late twenties, dressed more for work than a walk, is waving the croissant around above her head, and Susanna is getting more and more excited.

Ignoring Nick and all the other gawping dog owners, I run over towards Susanna shouting, "Susanna! Susanna! Come here, *now*." Susanna glances round, throws me a look of pure indifference, then turns her attention back to the croissant-waving woman. I'm panting by the time I reach her. I try to grab her by the collar but the woman is still waving the croissant, and Susanna is still determined to get hold of it.

"Drop that croissant *now*," I shout at the woman, forgetting that I'm talking to her and not the dog. The woman does a startled little jump and obeys. Susanna dives straight for the croissant, grabs it between her

280

teeth and scampers off to a quiet spot where she can have her *petit dejeuner* undisturbed.

"You are a very *bad* girl," I shout in the general direction of the dog, in complete contradiction to everything I've learned from the training manuals, since she is quite evidently out of my control at this point and my ticking off is counter-productive. If she can ignore me once, without immediate repercussions, she will ignore me next time as well.

"How *dare* you call me bad, you bitch," says the young woman who is trembling with rage and looks as though she is about to attack me.

"No, not you, the dog. The *dog!*" I can't help myself, I start to laugh. "I am *so* sorry," I splutter. "It must have been the croissant. And every time you raised your arm to escape her, she must have thought you were playing and wanted her to jump up and catch it. I can see," I say, cracking up again, "I can see from that paper bag you're carrying that it came from Maison Blanc — they're her favourite." I deliver one of my spontaneous signature snorts.

"So it's my fault, is it, for having the cheek to eat a croissant on public land? And now you're making a joke of it. It's not funny. You stupid, dried-up old cows and your bloody dogs. I hate the lot of you."

She has a right to be angry, this sour-faced young woman, but she's in danger of going too far.

"Just look. My brand-new Jigsaw skirt, it's ruined. Ninety quid it cost me, and it's the first time I've worn it. I'm on my way to a meeting at South End Green.

This was supposed to be a short cut. How the hell am I supposed to go to a meeting looking like this?"

I examine her skirt, which isn't in nearly as bad a state as she thinks it is. Two small brown paw prints — which will easily brush off as we've not had rain for a week and the ground is almost parched — and a half-inch tear. I refrain from saying any of this. Jigsaw woman looks about to pounce.

"I don't know what to say," I say, trying to keep a straight face. "She's usually so well behaved, but I was talking and I was distracted, and she's still a puppy and I clearly have a lot more training to do. Here, I'll write down my details and you can get in touch and tell me what I owe you. I'm sorry, I really am." I pull a pencil from my backpack and write my name, address and telephone number on the Maison Blanc paper bag.

"I'll be getting in touch all right. That dog of yours should be put down." Croissant woman marches off, not looking where she's going and stabbing dementedly at her mobile phone. I rather hope she walks into a tree.

I call Susanna. She's finished her croissant and trots happily towards me.

"Now *sit*," I say sternly, and she does, as I attach the lead to her collar. "You're staying attached to this until you learn to behave yourself, young lady."

Nick has been watching the proceedings from a safe distance. Now he walks over to join me.

"Two comic turns so far, and it's only a quarter past nine in the morning. I thought it best not to interfere. Are you OK?"

"Yes, but I didn't help my case by laughing. And Susanna did tear her skirt. I'd have been just as furious if the positions had been reversed."

Nick reaches out and touches my shoulder. "I got my timing all wrong, didn't? I should have thought more carefully about the implications of what I just said to you."

"There's really no need to apologise," I say, although I rather wish Nick had kept his suspicions to himself, at least until such time as he had some evidence. "I don't think there was ever going to be a good time for what just passed between us."

"I'm sorry, Hope, I really am, it could just be my imagination." Nick looks suddenly shrunken, smaller than I remember him.

"Ouch!" A stabbing pain in my stomach, just above my belly button, startles me.

"Are you really OK?"

"Yes, just a funny pain. Out of the blue. From nowhere. It's probably a stress-response. I feel a bit shaky, Nick," I say. "Would you mind if we cut the rest of the walk and went straight to Kenwood House so we can talk about this sitting down, over a coffee?"

"You've not even met Jack, have you?" I say as Nick comes out from the cafe bearing two coffees and draws up a chair next to me in what, in other circumstances, would be the perfect *al fresco*, late-summer setting. I'm trying to ignore the pain in my stomach.

"Not met Jack, are you kidding? He's over practically all the time. Sally insists on inviting him round — three

283

times last week! She says he must be lonely on his own and that she owes him so much for curing her back and shoulder. Don't get me wrong; he's a really decent guy, but three times in a week!"

How am I supposed to respond? Jack to dinner three times in a week? I feel on the verge of one of my counter-productive rants, but the pain in my stomach is containing me, slowing me down. I'm shaken by my encounter with croissant woman — making a joke of it was just a smokescreen; I often start cracking inappropriate jokes when I'm nervous. And now I have to try to focus on the possibility of a new drama in my life. I had no idea about how cosy Sally and Jack had become. Is that what she meant that night of the committee meeting when she thanked me for Jack? Surely not.

Should I suggest to Nick that if Sally really was having an affair she wouldn't be quite so blatant about it? Or that Jack's such an honourable man that even if he were to have an affair with another man's wife, he'd never be so unkind as to flaunt it in his face? But maybe I have no real idea of what Sally or even Jack is capable of. I didn't know what I was capable of until I did it in Paris — and nearly did it again in Covent Garden. I could say how hurt I feel that Sally hasn't thought about me or even invited me once for dinner — despite the work I'm doing free of charge for the charity and despite the possibility that I might be lonely too. But pointing out the contradiction in Sally's behaviour would make the "affair" between Sally and Jack seem even more likely in Nick's eyes.

So I decide to say none of these things. Instead, I ask, "How are things between you and Sally?"

"Not so healthy," he replies.

"And what do you mean by that?" The pain is really beginning to bother me.

"What glues us together is the memory of Cat, our determination to create this memorial to her short life. For Sally it's bordering on obsession. Without the charity I think she, we, would fall apart. Plenty of couples break up in these circumstances. One wants to talk about their loss, the other can only cope by not talking about it at all. But it's not like that for us. We talk of little else. That's what I mean by unhealthy. Our life is everything about Cat and nothing about us."

"Don't answer if you think I'm being intrusive, but why didn't you have more children?"

"It's no secret. Sally couldn't bear the possibility of it happening again. She wouldn't have another child because she was so very fearful of losing it. It was her decision, not mine."

"But you both always seem so relentlessly optimistic and upbeat. I am always so inspired by Sally's sunny outlook. And by yours too."

"Yeah, Oscars for both of us."

"Oh, Nick. I really don't know. I think perhaps Sally's just being kind. I really hope she is, for both our sakes." I've been thinking about this quite dispassionately. Trying to look at it from Nick's position. It's only beginning to dawn on me that if Nick is right, and Sally and Jack are having an affair, maybe Sally is the

285

real reason Jack left me. And if that is the case, then Jack and I are really finished. A picture comes into my head of the two of them in a candlelit restaurant, Sally opening her heart to Jack, Jack looking at the beautiful, proud, brave, tragic Sally and finding himself falling for her. So different in her elegant and vulnerable blondeness from dark-haired, klutzy, neurotic me.

"Have you thought about confronting her?" I ask.

"I already did. She said it was the craziest accusation she'd ever heard. Would you confront Jack about it?"

"Nick, I need to think about this, but right now all I can think about is this pain in my stomach, which is getting worse. I may have to go home and take something for it."

"And you thought we were just going to have a pleasant stroll and a chat," says Nick, sounding weary and defeated.

"Yes, Nick." I smile weakly. "You've ruined my day and given me a pain in the gut. And shouldn't you be at work by now?"

"My God, the time," says Nick, looking at his watch, and getting up from his chair. He blows me a kiss, promises to call later to make sure I'm all right, and is gone.

I head for the car park, not able to quite straighten up because of the nagging pain. Susanna is pulling on the lead, trying to make me go faster than I can. It must be something I've eaten or some kind of bug. Whatever it is, it's getting worse. And somehow I don't think Jack is the cause.

★ ★ ★

By the time Maddy turns up to see me at 9p.m., after late surgery, I am crying from the pain. She feels my stomach, which is hard, and has blown up like a balloon.

"Either you're trying to steal my thunder," says Maddy, "or you have some kind of blockage. We need to get you to the hospital, and we need to get you there fast."

"But surely . . ."

"There is no surely about it," she says, waddling around my bedroom and into the bathroom to gather up whatever I might need for an overnight stay. "Here," she says, flinging me a pair of sweatpants, a T-shirt and sweater. "Get these on. I'd call an ambulance, but as the car's right outside I can probably get you there faster."

I'm a complex web of post-operative tubes and wires. There's the epidural in my back, still feeding anaesthetic into the nerve routes from the spinal cord and blocking out the pain. There's the tube that goes up my nose and down into my stomach to drain bile into a bag. There's one tube filling me with antibiotics and another feeding liquids to rehydrate me. And of course a catheter until such time as I can make it to the toilet. I'm on a noisy ward close to the nurses' station with the rest of the "high dependency" patients. I am alive.

Anxiety is a contradictory creature. For months and months, I have been in a perpetual panic. From the moment the doctor said, "We'll give it seventy-two hours; sometimes if we rest the bowel these blockages clear themselves, otherwise we'll have to operate," I became as calm as the Dalai Lama. Life has never before struck me as quite so random. Anything can happen and often does. When you have absolutely no control over what's happening to you, letting go is your only option. All these months, when I've been unsuccessfully trying to make some order out of the chaos my life has become, I have been close to breaking point. Suddenly, I felt as though a great burden had been lifted. Through the pre-operative morphine haze, I found myself thinking, "What will be, will be."

Twenty centimetres of my intestine have been removed in an operation that most certainly saved my life. Otherwise, I would literally have exploded. Scar tissue from an appendectomy when I was fifteen had attached itself to my intestine and slowly strangled it, causing an impenetrable blockage.

I am as wilted as an English lettuce past its sell-by date. Three days of starvation before they decided to go ahead and operate, and up to a week's more starvation to go, depending on when my bowel decides to crank itself up and start functioning again. If before the operation my stomach was bloated, now everything is. My back when I touch it feels waxy and hugely puffed out, my ankles — never my best asset — are positively elephantine, my surgical stockings need to be replaced with a larger size. My hair is slicked back and greasy, my skin sallow and my nose covered with tape to hold the nose tube in place. I cannot eat, drink, or sleep —

the noise from other patients, the nurses clattering around their station, alarms and buzzers beeping, make rest impossible. I stare up at the ceiling and think, "So, I'm alive." I moisten my parched lips with a tiny sponge that I dip in a bowl of water on my bedside table. It's the closest I'm going to get to a meal for a while.

The first faces I saw when I came round from the anaesthetic were those of Jack and Olly. My eyes opened for just a few seconds, before my boulder-heavy lids dragged them shut again. I couldn't speak.

"You're going to be fine," said Jack, stooping to gently raise and kiss my hand, lying limply on the bed. "The operation was a complete success. I've just been speaking to the surgeon."

Olly took Jack's place and bent over to kiss my forehead. And then I was gone again.

When I opened my eyes for the second time, the two of them were still there, keeping vigil. My face felt strange. I touched it and discovered I was still wearing an oxygen mask.

My first words were: "Who's looking after Susanna?"

"Everything's sorted," said Jack. "You don't have to worry about a thing. Mike and Stanko have taken up residence in the spare room. Stanko's not working at the moment, so he's in charge of the dog. And Mike is taking a fortnight off after you get home to help you convalesce."

I smiled at the thought of Mike and his boyfriend moving in with me.

"Oh, goody," I said quietly, "it will be like *Will and Grace*." But then it dawned on me that Jack hadn't offered to move back in himself. I was already exhausted again.

"What about you, Ols?" I asked weakly.

"I'm fine. Doing lots of shifts at the bar, as I've only got a month to go."

One month and Olly will be gone. What did I expect? To wake up to a whole new world with a husband who was coming home, a son who wasn't going to go away, an interesting new job, a mother who was not dying and who loved me, and a new birth certificate to prove I'm twenty years younger than I thought I was?

"And you, Jack?"

"Stop worrying about everyone else, Hope. We're all fine. And now you need to rest."

I closed my eyes again. Actually, I wasn't worrying, I'd just wanted to know how he was.

There is an endless stream of visitors to my bedside. Jack. Olly. Sarah. Maddy. My cousin, Mike. Tanya. Sally and Nick. Mario. Vanessa. Sharon, my leg waxer. Even Anita, although trust her to bring chocolates when surely she knows I can't eat. I barely have the strength to talk to any of them at first, but it matters to me that they come. That they care.

On my first cautious foray out of bed, I feel like a refugee, all my worldly goods — the epidural, the catheter and urine bag, the drips — dragged along beside me. I am still bent right over. I make it perhaps twenty feet before I have to turn back and retreat to the safety of my bed. I slump back on the pillows, worn out. My stomach has been sliced down the centre, from the top of my belly button to my pubis. Alongside the appendix scar and the Caesarean scar, my body will look like a metropolitan road map. Sexy, huh?

All day long people come to do things to me — inject me to prevent blood clots, check my blood pressure, replace my drip bags, empty my urine bag, take my temperature. One of the toilets, I am told, has a big sign on the outside of the door — MRSA, Do Not Enter. Even this doesn't disturb my new-found equilibrium. I look at the inside of my right arm, blue from the wrist to the elbow — the bruising will go, I tell myself. Some of my veins aren't working as well as they should. New lines have to be set up. So what's a few sharp needles between an overworked nurse and a malleable patient?

I'm relentlessly upbeat. I do the breathing exercises as prescribed by the physiotherapist and every time I get up, I venture a little further down the corridor. Each day the number of tubes diminishes. First to go, after three days, is the epidural. Without it, the pain is less severe than I'd feared — it's kept under control with injections, and after another twenty-four hours, I manage to wean myself off the painkillers altogether.

"You're doing very well," the consultant says to me on his rounds, as consultants always do. "But we can't take this tube out of your nose until your bowels start functioning. Nothing to eat for a while yet, I'm afraid."

For the first time in my life, I'm not interested in food. "I'm planning on going on a trek at the end of November," I tell the consultant. "In the Atlas mountains. Shouldn't be a problem, should it?"

"Hmm. That's only about two and a half months from now. You've had major surgery, and although I wouldn't say it's impossible, I can't guarantee you'll be up to it. And it's certainly not something I'd recommend so soon. Let's see how well you recover and not make too many plans, OK?"

"OK," I say aloud. Not OK, I say to myself. Not even having half my insides out is going to stop me from going on that trek. I have to prove something to myself, though right now I can't think what that something is.

I'm no longer nil-by-mouth. Mike turns up with chicken soup.

"Since when did you become a Jewish mother?" I ask, sipping tentatively at my first sustenance for ten days.

"Since just before I poured the soup from the carton into this mug and popped it into the microwave at the end of the corridor," he grins.

"Oh, Mike, you and Stanko are perfect angels. You have no idea how grateful I am to you both for coming to stay."

"Well, since I'm your favourite cousin, it's the least I can do. We've already booked Sharon to come and give you a foot massage and a facial as soon as you get back. Now that your nose tube is out, I can see the damage that's been done under that nose plaster over the past ten days. Major extraction is called for."

"Please, Mike, don't make me laugh. It hurts."

"We're going to have lots of fun, sweetie. Stanko is the Jamie Oliver of Sarajevo. You will be so spoiled."

"I am already," I say, and I mean it. Except that at that very moment I start to retch, and Mike's chicken soup is regurgitated all down my nightdress.

Mike looks panicked and shouts for a nurse.

"Not to worry, love, this often happens at the beginning," says Amy, the staff nurse, as she arrives to take over. I know, for a fact, that Amy has been on shift for seven hours and hasn't taken her compulsory break yet, because she told me so ten minutes ago.

"Perhaps, Mike, you'd better go," I say. "Sarah's coming soon, in any case, and I need to clean up. Might have a little rest before she arrives."

Mike looks grateful for the get-out.

"Think of the fun we'll have," he says, waving and blowing kisses until he's out of sight.

"Goodness, Sarah, you look worse than me," I say, as my ghostly sister drags over a chair like a weary Sisyphus and sits down on it, red-eyed, puffy-lidded and with skin the colour of cement. I can tell she's been crying.

"Poor you," I say, "racing between me and Mummy like this. You don't have to come every day, you know. I'm so much better now. And I'm sure Daddy needs all the help he can get."

Sarah looks at me, but her eyes have no life in them. She's staring but not seeing. Her voice, like her eyes, is expressionless.

"I can't keep this from you, Hope, not any longer. It's all over. Last night Mummy took an overdose. She knew exactly what she was doing. She took just enough pills, but not so many as to make her sick. And when Daddy went to sleep, she must have washed them down with alcohol so she'd fall asleep herself."

Sarah's voice doesn't falter. "By the time Daddy woke up, she was unconscious, the empty pill bottle on the bedside table. If it weren't for the bottle, he might have thought she was still sleeping. Within twenty minutes of getting her to the hospital, she suffered heart failure. Right here, on the seventh floor, two below you. I can't stay long, Hope, I have to go back to Daddy."

Propped up against the pillows, I hold my arms open for my sister. "Just come here, Sarah," I say quietly, "come here." And then she's in my arms, sitting on the side of the bed with her head against my chest and huge, heaving sobs racking her body. I stroke the back of her head, over and over.

"Sarah, my love, it's over. And in the best way. The alternative — the long, drawn-out suffering — would have been too horrible. Too horrible for her and too horrible for Daddy. She did the right thing for both of them." Finally, my mother has done the right thing.

"It's just been too much to bear," she sobs. "I thought I might lose you too. Both of you in this same damned place. You look so fragile, you've almost disappeared. And then all the time trying to be strong for Daddy, to hold it all together. And now the funeral, and the shivah, and having to face all those people. And you not even able to be there. If it's bad for me, it must be even worse for you . . ."

"Oh, my sweet Sarah. My beloved sister and friend. It's not worse for me than it is for you. You see, you can't lose someone you never really had. I've been searching for the mother in our mother for most of my life. I don't have to look any more. It's not worse for me, because you loved her despite her faults. You forgave. I didn't. I've spent too much of my life mourning her absence, but these past few months I've realised I can live with it. And now that she's gone, she's no more gone than she was before." Sarah's still sobbing, but less urgently now. "I'm sad for Daddy, and for you, but that's it for me. I have you and William and your kids — you're my family. I still have Daddy. And Olly. I have Maddy and all my friends. And who knows? Maybe I'll even have Jack again one day if I can come to my senses and start behaving like a proper grown-up. And if not, I'll still have a life. Mummy gave us life, and she gave me you — I'm so grateful to her for that."

Sarah's sobbing is silenced now, her breathing less heavy. I continue to stroke her hair.

Somewhere in this building where lives saved and lives lost are common currency, my mother lies dead. I'm one of the survivors, and I'm glad of it.

In Jewish tradition, a funeral must take place as soon as possible following the death. While I lie in my hospital bed, dozens of friends and distant family members gather with the mourners to attend my mother's funeral in a cemetery on London's outskirts. The service, as is

295

also traditional, is short and austere in the company of the coffin. No music is played. The coffin is led from the prayer hall to the allotted burial space, further prayers are said, and the coffin is lowered into the earth. Those who come to attend the funeral file past the grave one by one, each shovelling a clod of earth onto the coffin.

It is not customary in the Jewish religion for women to recite the Kaddish, which is the mourner's prayer, but Sarah has brought into the hospital for me a memorial candle which will burn for twenty-four hours if the hospital authorities don't declare it a fire hazard. My mother's funeral is at noon. I light the little candle twenty minutes later, around the time the actual burial will be taking place. "Goodbye, Mummy," I say, as the wick lights. "May you rest in peace." I reach for my Walkman on the table next to the bed and slot in a cassette of Mozart's Requiem. Then I lie back against the pillows and take refuge inside the music. Like Cyrano de Bergerac, who wooed his friend's beloved with his poetry, I turn to Mozart to convey to my dead mother all the emotions I will never fully articulate. The yearning, the anger, the sorrow and the forgiveness — all there in Mozart's haunting mass.

I've been dozing in the chair next to my bed. I open my eyes and see a somewhat stooped, elderly man walking tentatively towards me. My eyes adjust their focus, and I can see it's my father, with Sarah following just behind him.

"Daddy, it's you!" I exclaim, my excited voice in sharp contrast to my frail physical condition. I haul myself up, slowly and shakily, like an old lady.

"Hello, darling girl." He smiles. "What a crazy old world we live in."

It's the first time I've seen him since before I came into hospital. And for the first time, he looks every one of his eighty-two years.

We hug, but gently, each aware of the other's frailty. "Daddy, Daddy, Daddy," I say, over and over, overcome by the emotion of seeing him again.

Sarah is dressed head to toe in black. They have evidently come straight from the funeral.

"You've lit a candle," my father says.

"Yes, it's from Sarah. Even at a time like this, she thinks of everything — she brought it in for me, though I fear a nurse will be round any minute to snuff it out. Come and sit down, both of you . . . I'll get back into bed to make more room."

"Thank God you're all right," says my father. "I couldn't bear not being able to get in to see you."

"The surgeon says I'm recovering incredibly well, and I even kept my lunch down today. But you must have come straight from the funeral. How did you get away with that?"

Everything feels unreal. My mother is dead. I'm playing gracious hostess from my hospital bed. And my father and sister, who according to custom should be back at my father's house, ready to greet well-wishers, have gone AWOL.

"I got the rabbi to announce that the shivah would begin at eight o'clock this evening, but that in the meantime we were unable to have anyone back to the house," my father tells me.

"You have no idea how pleased I am that you came," I say, welling up again.

"I couldn't wait a minute longer to see for myself that you're all right," says my father. "Your poor mother's gone now. I don't give a damn about doing what's expected. My daughters are more important than any damn protocol."

I've said nothing about my mother. I have to find the words, the right words.

"Daddy, isn't it better that she went this way?"

"I just wish she'd told me. I could have helped her. It must have been so lonely, planning it all on her own."

"I'm sure she did it to save you from any culpability afterwards," I say. "To be absolutely sure no one could accuse you of euthanasia. It was just another gesture to show how much she loved you."

The tears are gently trickling down my father's face.

"I shall miss her so much, so very, very much," he says simply.

"And so will I," says Sarah.

"Oh, look," I say, saved by the tea lady with her trolley. "Three cups, if you don't mind."

"We're not supposed to . . ."

"Yes, I know, but my father and sister have come straight from a funeral, so if it isn't too much trouble . . ."

"Glad to see you're getting a bit of your old spirit back," says my father. He turns to the tea lady with his most beguiling smile. "Two sugars, please." And she smiles begrudgingly back.

Home and Away

It's been two weeks since I left the hospital, during which time I have developed a special relationship with the postbox on the corner of my road. At first the glossy red marker of my recovery was frustratingly out of reach. By the time I had tied the laces of my trainers and put on my coat I was almost ready for a lie-down. Having shuffled not more than half the two hundred yards or so distance, I needed all my energy to shuffle home again. After about five days I reached the milestone of the box itself. For the next few days I counted how many paces beyond the box I could go, at the same time as reminding myself to conserve sufficient energy for the return journey. Today was another milestone. A red-letter day! I walked right out of sight of the postbox and round the entire block. It took me twenty minutes, double the time it would normally take. I got home and promptly fell asleep on the sofa.

I am shocked at the state of me. A stone lighter now than when I went into hospital. When I can steel myself, I look in the mirror at my naked and battered body, and examine the scrawny flesh which seems to have divorced itself from the bone and tendons and sinew beneath. I'm not certain there's any muscle left. My stomach is a war zone, criss-crossed with the scars of bloody battles, some faded, but one — larger and fiercer than all the others — still red and raw in defeat. The angry 8-inch vertical gash of the bowel resection; the diagonal slice of the appendix scar; the horizontal slash of the emergency Caesarean. It's as though I've been periodically attacked with a machete. Is this a body you could ever allow a lover to see? Would Dan and I still have ended up in bed if we'd met after this latest round of vivisection? How would Jack feel about me with this new fault-line through my centre?

There's nothing I can do about my latest war wound, but I can make a solemn oath never again to complain about being fat when I put on an extra pound or two. It's the kind of hopeless pledge I know I'll break the minute I'm well again, but for the moment I am convinced that for a woman of fifty there is definitely such a thing as too thin.

I am physically weak, so it surprises me that I feel so, well, robust, psychologically sturdier than I've been all year. Perky almost. No hovering black cloud, no mouse gnawing at my solar plexus. Instead of regarding this latest drama as yet another blow to my dented psyche, it's as though I've been jolted awake to the possibilities of living. Maybe a near-death experience was just what I needed to shake me out of my anxious self-absorption. My selfish, poor-me funk.

With Mike and Stanko in the house, it's been like one long party. I'm not sure exactly what we're celebrating, but the atmosphere at home has completely changed. Over the past few months, every time I've opened the front door, I've felt oppressed by the weight of air surrounding me. I would wander from room to room, wondering if this steadfast, Victorian house, which I once loved so much, was somehow to blame for my ever-darkening mood. It's as though Mike and Stanko have drawn back the curtains, opened all the windows and let the fresh air and sunshine stream in, when in fact it's cold and bleak outside and the windows remain resolutely shut. Olly is all smiles and even his footsteps on the stairs seem lighter, and it may be my imagination, but the music coming from his room seems more melodious, less thumping and aggressive than before.

I lie on the sofa in the conservatory, surrounded by newspapers and magazines, and while Mike's at work, Stanko tends to me and Susanna. He's feeding me back to health, and as he chops and whisks and sautés, he sings hilarious approximations of songs with English lyrics he doesn't fully understand and can't pronounce properly. I am astonished by the kindness of this man I barely know, nursing and nurturing me in this way, so careful to cook only things he thinks I will be able to digest easily — such as simple rice dishes, steamed fish, mashed potatoes, scrambled eggs. At first I could only peck at what he served, but now I'm tucking in with increasing enthusiasm each passing day. There are guests for supper almost every night. I help with a little bit of chopping or laying the table, and leave the rest to Stanko. We eat at the table in the conservatory, so I join in for as long as I have the energy, then retire to the sofa in the corner and listen to the conversation in the background while I rest.

One night, Olly's mates James and Ravi came round, bearing a bouquet of white roses. They were exaggeratedly polite in my presence, asking about my health and answering my questions about their exams and their plans with deliberate solicitude. After a beer or two they started to be more themselves. I love having these smart, young men in my home, so ready and eager to conquer the world. They talked animatedly about their gap years and where and when the three of them might meet up. I'm touched by their bravado and carapace of cool, and the way in which their manufactured facades seem to help them deal with the uncertainties of striking out into the world for the first time. Olly will be travelling solo for the most part. He's got some work lined up, teaching English at a school in southern India as well as a three-month research stint for the Murray–Darling Commission in Australia, an organisation which plans water and land resources for the vast area it serves.

Olly's imminent departure is the most difficult thing to bear.

Vanessa, practising her psychotherapeutic skills, has suggested I might view Olly going off as a kind of liberation, a release from eighteen long years of responsibility.

"You'll be free. Free to do exactly as you please."

"But I don't want to be free. I want to wake up knowing that Olly's dirty washing needs to be loaded into the machine and that the biscuit tin needs refilling. I'll even miss the mushroom-sprouting half-empty mugs and furry plates in his tip of a bedroom."

Olly. Olly. Olly. My true love. All through Olly's childhood I would hug him and say, "I love you so much I can hardly breathe." And he'd reply, "I love *you* so much I can hardly breathe." And then we'd both play this silly game, panting like puppies, to show how loving one another had interfered with our regular breathing.

"You're going to have to let go," says Vanessa bossily.

"Come *on*! I know I have to let go. And it's not exactly the case that I've tried to hold him back. I've encouraged this whole gap-year thing all along. I'm immensely proud of him for taking this first big step towards independence. Any parent would be. But for me it feels like a loss rather than a liberation. Honestly, it's worse than Jack going. I shouldn't say it, but it's true. I'll get used to it, of course, but this is not something I'm going to deny."

"Not denying is good." She smiles.

"Beware of therapists spouting psychobabble." I smile back.

It's hard to believe how much I loathed Vanessa, and how much I like her now. I just try not to think too much about her and Olly alone together.

"You're going to miss him too, aren't you?"

"That's for sure." There's a slight catch in Vanessa's voice, and I can see she's trying to hold herself together. "But this was only ever an interlude. I like to think of Olly as my Elastoplast Man. The one who's helped to heal me while I was getting over that bastard Derek. Olly and I will always be friends, no matter how many girls he has on his travels. And of course he'll never forget the tricks that his very first Mrs Robinson taught him." She actually winks at me. I wince. Vanessa notices and laughs.

"Too much information," I say. "But if he's helped put Derek six feet under, I'm glad for you."

I've learned from Vanessa that the bastard that is Derek walked out on her when she was eight months pregnant with Poppy, her second child. Maintenance payments go into her bank account once a month, but Derek lives in Spain now with his new wife and a new baby. He sends the kids birthday cards with cash inside but never visits because he told Vanessa it would be "too painful". Vanessa didn't get an answer when she asked, "Too painful for you or too painful for them?"

"I'd like to tell him where to shove his money," she told me, "and the minute I'm financially on my feet that's exactly what I'll do. In the meantime, I'm prepared to act grateful."

Vanessa pops by with the kids every day after school. While Damien and Poppy spend half an hour rolling around on the floor with Susanna, Vanessa updates me on what she's learned on her psychotherapy course.

Living with Mike and Stanko has reminded me of what a good relationship is all about. Mike is most certainly in love, and I believe it's reciprocated, even if up until now, before I was able to observe them at close range, there's been a nagging doubt about Stanko. I couldn't quite get out of my head that Stanko, who came to the UK two years ago, penniless and not knowing a soul, might only be after Mike for his money. At forty-five, Mike's a good decade older than Stanko. They met in a Soho coffee bar frequented by gays, where Stanko, who had been a chef in Sarajevo, was sweeping the floor around Mike's table. It was love at first sighting of Stanko's biceps, Mike told me, as Stanko swished his broom back and forth over the crumbs under Mike's feet. Physically, the two are David and Goliath. Mike is small — not more than five foot eight — and wiry, with close-cropped silver hair, a thin face and a prominent Semitic nose which looks all the larger against his bony cheeks. His eyes are as quick as his tongue, darting everywhere, missing nothing. Stanko is more than six foot two, with a Calvin Klein underwear ad body, high Slavic cheekbones and green eyes. And yet it's Mike's presence which commands attention. Once you've sighed over Stanko's beauty you are drawn to Mike's fizzing energy. You wouldn't think twice about the physical disparity if Mike and Stanko were a heterosexual couple, but as same-sex lovers they look almost touchingly incongruous. "Meet Stanko. She stoops to conquer," said Mike, when he first introduced me, as I gazed up into Stanko's uncomprehending eyes.

Thanks to his job as a commodities trader in the City, Mike is flush with money, and he's thinking of backing Stanko in business, starting with a small cafe, but one serving proper food, and seeing how it goes from there. Stanko's lottery numbers have come up, I once thought cynically, but now I'm beginning to think that perhaps the real winner is Mike.

Stanko talks with a great deal of passion for his beloved Sarajevo, the cosmopolitan city he grew up in as the child of a peace-loving family with a Muslim father and Serb mother, but when people ask him about the war he pulls down the shutters as fast as a bank teller due for his lunch break. Mike's the only one who knows the full story, but out of loyalty to Stanko he says nothing. The only information Stanko has given me is that he was working as a chef at the Sarajevo Holiday Inn in early April 1992 when the unarmed protest against the barricades set up around the city by followers of Radovan Karadzic was met with gunfire from the top floor of the hotel. This is the incident which sparked the four-year siege of Sarajevo and about which Stanko refuses to talk.

"Trust me," said Mike once, "Stanko is a brave and good man. He has really suffered, as you can imagine, coming from a Muslim–Serb family. His father died before the siege, his mother as a result of it. If landing me means he's landed on his feet, he deserves it."

"And he's gorgeous and a great cook to boot," I added, "so it looks as though you've landed on your feet as well. Would you marry him if you could?" I asked lightly.

"I *will* marry him when the laws are finally changed, that's if he'll have me."

"And can I be best woman?"

"Consider it confirmed."

The more I see the two of them together, the more my concerns about Stanko dissipate. They are both so thoughtful around one another. When Mike comes in stressed and exhausted, Stanko is ready with a drink. Not a meal has been served that Mike hasn't praised Stanko fulsomely for, asking him about the provenance of particular flavours, treating each meal Stanko prepares as a gift rather than a right. When Mike talks about his work, Stanko really listens, and asks the kind of questions that demonstrate a genuine interest in Mike's alien world, in which millions of pounds change hands at the press of a computer key. At weekends they go to the gym together or shopping in Borough Market and out looking for potential sites for the cafe. Stanko struggles to read the novels Mike enjoys so they can discuss them together. And I can guess about the sex because creaky bed springs and satisfied, only half-muffled grunts give the game away. I'm happy for Mike, I really am, but sometimes when I watch the two of them together, being so intimate and loving under my own roof, I start to ache so much I have to turn away.

I've come up with an interim career for Stanko — I wish I could do the same for me — and he's been spending the time when he's not running around me working on his marketing plan. Stanko is just brilliant with Susanna and adores all dogs, even Maddy's little monster, so I've suggested he starts a dog-walking business. Stanko and Mike think I'm a genius for suggesting it, and Mike's offered to buy him a second-hand van to transport the dogs to the Heath.

Stanko has designed the leaflets on my computer, printed them out and started to distribute them all around the area.

What's missing in this bustling household is Jack. Even when it's filled with people, there's a hole in this house where Jack should be. He's nowhere, and yet everywhere too — in his favourite books on the shelves, in the few clothes that still line his cupboards and drawers, in the way the wine glasses are stored rim up, when I prefer to store them rim down. Oddly, since his departure, I've been putting the glasses back on the shelf in the way that he prefers. All those petty disagreements. And for what? Twenty years of sex and love and family life reduced to a domestic power struggle over which way up to store a glass. Why is it so hard to articulate what we really mean? And now he's gone I have no trouble doing what he wants. It wouldn't exactly have amounted to a surrender if I'd done this before.

His scruffy old towelling robe still sits on the hook behind the bathroom door. I insert my hands deep into the pockets and press myself against it. What once was the softest Egyptian cotton has gone crisp and bristly, the result of hundreds of washing cycles. I make a mental note to buy him a new robe if he decides to come home. My hand curls around a crumpled piece of paper. I take it out and open it. There's the washed-out remains of what looks like a telephone number on it, and I replace it, without interest, in the pocket. Yes, Jack is all around and yet quite invisible.

So now I share my house with two gay lovers and a teenage boy while I recuperate from life-threatening surgery. Not at all how I expected my year of turning fifty to pan out. Tonight Jack's coming for dinner. Olly's working, Stanko and Mike are going out to a movie. In his role as domestic Adonis, Stanko has laid the table, lit candles and prepared some of Jack's favourite traditional English dishes, as briefed by me. A dinner of ham and pea soup, followed by Irish stew and bread-and-butter pudding. Enough calories and cholesterol in a single meal to bring on a heart attack. All I have to do is warm it all up and serve.

"Stanko, this really is beyond the call of duty," I tell him.

"No problem, I like practise English dishes for when I have restaurant."

"Mmm, but if the way to a man's heart really is via his stomach, I'm a tad concerned that Jack might fall in love with *you*."

Stanko smiles uncertainly, not sure if I've made a joke.

"Jack no love me. Jack love with you, I sure."

Mike and Stanko are moving out at the weekend. I so wish they'd stay longer, but I can just about make it to the shops on my own now, and I really don't need nursing. They go on Saturday and the following Thursday Olly will be off. Then it will be just me and Susanna.

Although Jack has popped in lots of times since I've been home, there have always been other people in the house. This is going to be the first chance I've really had to talk to him since Nick raised his suspicions about Jack and Sally. Do I/don't I broach the subject, I ask myself as I apply the first make-up I've bothered to put on since before the operation. My eyes look hollow. On the plus side, my skin has a kind of translucent quality and my eyes are bright, the result of my enforced, ten-day fast. A detox my former beauty editor would fully approve of. But I shan't be trying it again any time soon.

I've put on two or three pounds but still almost nothing fits me. The only thing I can wear is a pair of jeans that I bought a size too small last year and never again managed to zip up after trying them on in the shop on one of my "thin" days. I dress to give myself a bit of bulk. Over a white vest I wear a chunky, shawl-neck, cable cardigan cinched with a wide belt. It definitely helps to make me look less skeletal.

My hair seems to have laid down and died, but I wash and blowdry it as best I can and hope the candlelight will be kind. Mid blowdry, an uncomfortable thought pops into my head and propels me towards the bathroom and Jack's towelling robe hanging on the hook behind the door. The number on the scrap of paper in his pocket. I don't know what made me think of it just now but the washed-out numbers, even with one or two bleached out altogether, seem familiar. I retrieve the paper and go straight back to my computer and to my Outlook address book. As I thought. An avalanche of anxiety envelops me. I look at my hands and they are trembling.

I had promised myself that I wouldn't jump to conclusions, but it's proving hard not to. I wanted to use tonight to build a bridge to Jack, not to blow one apart. As I stare at the hastily torn scrap of lined paper with Sally's number on it, another notebook from another time comes sharply into focus. I am on the tube on the way to work, in the earliest days of my relationship with Jack, and pulling out the little lavender suede notebook with lined paper that I carried around everywhere with me at the time. Balancing the notebook on one thigh of my crossed legs, somewhere between Swiss Cottage and Bond Street, I wrote the heading: WHY I THINK I LOVE JACK and underneath a list of all his qualities that sprang spontaneously to mind.

I turn away from the computer and start riffling through the drawers in my desk, slamming them shut as I fail to find what I'm looking for. From the bottom drawer, where it is buried beneath packets of photographs, postcards purchased at various galleries and museums and a miscellany of stationery, I pull out that scuffed old lavender notebook. It feels urgent that I find the list, now, before Jack arrives. I fan the pages like a card sharp, passing scribbled names and numbers, ideas for the magazine I was working on, random jottings. The page I'm searching for jumps out at me. WHY I THINK I LOVE JACK it says, written with a thick black felt-tip pen, and three times underlined. I lean back in my office chair and swing it round away from the computer, scanning the page.

Charm without smarm reads the first line. This with double asterisks. I read on.

Never tries to impress anyone
Completely without pretension
Such healing hands
His favourite novelists are women
His quirk of tunelessly crooning lyrics — mostly the bad ones
*That first ever present he gave me — a supersize bar of Cadbury's milk chocolate, rather than a beribboned box of Godiva champagne truffles
How he fits with my friends and family
His trousers
Because the first time we made love I cried and the second time we got the giggles
And because I don't think I'll ever want to make love to a man other than him for the rest of my life

I finished with the words . . . *to be continued* . . .

It was the first thing on my list, the unselfconscious charm, that attracted me most of all. With his natural affability and almost old-fashioned courtesy — Cary Grant without the corny come-ons — Jack could win over complete strangers. He'd meet someone for the first time and within ten minutes he'd be receiving an invitation for dinner or a drink. And it was a charm that worked equally well on both men and women. I once watched in awe as a belligerent drunk knocked into him in the street. Within moments the two of them were

313

exchanging anecdotes rather than the blows I'd been expecting. I suppose what Jack had was a kind of low-key glamour. Inside his aura you felt somehow sparklier and more animated, although his own manner was quiet and playful.

His lack of pretension was something I just felt grateful for. Jack had none of the petty snobberies of the people I met through my work as a journalist. He was as comfortable in a caff as he was at the Ritz. He read highbrow novels and trashy detective stories and appreciated them both for what they were. He never regarded himself as a superior being, nor as an inferior one. He thought himself good enough. He had self-esteem by the bucket-load.

I was impressed by Jack's refusal to try to impress anyone. He was so different in this respect from any man I'd ever dated. Men with their ambitions written across their foreheads in 48 point bold Bodoni. Men with egos as blatant as the Trump Tower. Men who talked at you rather than to you, who bounced ideas off you like you were the back wall of a squash court. Most people warmed instantly to Jack, and if they didn't, he never tried to make them like him or put on a show to win them over. I remember thinking: *When I grow up I want to be like Jack.*

So perhaps the real reason I fell for Jack was that he was everything I wasn't. I never stopped worrying about what other people thought of me, whether I measured up, made the grade. The result was that most people liked Jack a great deal, me less so — or at least not until they got to know me, after which I seemed to grow on them and they stuck. Whereas Jack made people feel instantly at ease, I seemed to make strangers fidget, not, I think, out of boredom with my company but because my own initial twitchiness transmitted itself, spreading mild agitation like a virus. There was a fluidity about Jack that enabled him to fit in everywhere, to negotiate around the trickiest people and situations.

"So what *exactly* is it about Jack?" I remember Maddy quizzing me one day. I showed her the list and attempted to amplify.

"It's hard to explain, Maddy, but he seems to glide through life. Things touch him, of course they do, but they don't seem to scar him. So he's never bogged down in self-doubt or guilt or regrets."

"So what's he doing courting a neurotic fruitcake like you?"

"I often wonder myself. But I do seem to make him laugh. And we always have so much to talk about. I also think he's reached a point where he needs to nest. He recognises my homing instinct, the bit of me that's a Jewish mama bursting to get out. After spending so much of his childhood moving from one country to another, and despite his ability to be comfortable anywhere, he wants to put down roots. And excuse the boast, but it's also occurred to me that my incredible sexual allure and Olympian athleticism in bed might have something to do with it."

"Really? That good?"

"I wish. But I think it's a balance thing. He doesn't have to prove himself by getting to the top of some career ladder. He's not interested in being the boss or being famous or making a pot of money . . . there's not a competitive bone in his body. Even when he wanted to act, it wasn't fame he was after, just the love of what he was doing. In the end he probably wasn't hungry enough. And although he's prepared to work hard, he doesn't expect his work to define him, like so many men — or like me. On the other hand he seems to approve of me and my ambition. And he likes my independence. Being with him is so comfortable; he mops up my anxiety and deposits it somewhere way beyond reach. We're different, but we add up."

"So it's not so much the hurly-burly of the chaise longue as the deep, deep peace of the double bed?"

"Well, since we're in quoting mode, I prefer Rilke to Mrs Patrick Campbell. 'Love consists in this: that two solitudes protect and touch and greet each other.' It's funny, but you know how I described Jack's healing hands? Well, I think he has a healing presence too. He doesn't just have this ability to untie the physical knots. When I'm with him, all the mental kinks seem to smooth out as well. I can let down my guard, because he makes me feel safe. Safe and cherished."

"So you're really and truly in love."

"Yes, but not in the way I expected it would happen, or at least not how I expected it would be in the beginning. There's been no pain in my belly, no sick feeling in my throat, no melodrama, no jealousy, no fear that he's going to abandon me, no explosive rows followed by passionate reconciliations. I thought falling in love had to be agony, now I see it as meltingly pleasurable. Isn't that enough?"

"I guess so, but maybe it doesn't sound . . . I don't know — exciting?"

Maddy was right. It wasn't about excitement. I didn't fall dramatically in love with Jack. I kind of slid into it, gently and easily. There was never a question of whether we would or wouldn't be together. After Jack returned from Venice the Christmas following our meeting, we were a couple. We were together all the time when we weren't working. Within weeks Jack had moved out of his rented flat and in with me, to the flat I'd proudly afforded a down payment on from my own savings. And Jack fitted in so fast. Even my mother liked him. My dad, my sister and Maddy adored him. I didn't have to make any decisions. Jack and I just got together and stayed together.

It's only when it all starts to go wrong that you begin to wonder whether what you felt at the beginning was enough . . . enough for things to last.

What would I say if I were to try to write that list again from scratch today? No time for that now. I slip the scrap of paper with the phone number on it into the back pocket of my jeans. There's a ring on the doorbell. It can only be Jack.

I've cleared away the soup and put the steaming pot of Irish stew onto the table. Jack automatically picks up the ladle next to the pot and starts to serve. He burrows the serving spoon deep into the dish, scooping up meat and potatoes and onions and pearl barley and transfers it into a wide soup bowl I hold out for him. It's typical of Jack's natural grace that nothing slops onto the rim of the bowl. As I watch Jack perform this mundane, everyday task, something stirs inside me and makes my own hand falter.

"Steady there, you've got the shakes," says Jack, reaching out to hold the bowl with his free hand and saving the contents from spilling all over the table.

"Jack, I need to ask you something." I hesitate, the words won't come out.

"Yes?" says Jack patiently.

"Are you . . . are you . . ." It's no good, I can't do it. "Are you planning to take Olly to the airport when he leaves on Thursday?" Coward!

"Well, yes, I was planning to. Are you going to come too?"

"I don't think so. It's probably better if I say goodbye to him here. I don't want to start blubbing at the departure gates. No, you see him off on your own."

Jack smiles at me.

"'Leaving on a jet plane. Don't know when I'll be back again . . .'"

"Don't laugh at me, Jack, please . . ."

"I'm not laughing, Hope. But he's only going on an extended holiday. He hasn't taken out the emigration papers yet."

"It's not so much this trip, but what it represents. It's an emotional journey he's going on, and although he'll come back, I guess he'll never need me again in the way he has up until now."

"That's what parenting is all about, Hope."

"OK, I admit it. I'm a clingy, moany, whiny, overbearing, possessive, stereotypical Jewish mother. But if one more person tries to lecture me about letting go, I may have to thump them."

"I think you're right not to come to the airport, Hope, it will be easier all round. But what I've been wanting to say is that you and Olly seem to have really got it together since I left."

"It hasn't been easy, but I suppose I finally got off his case, as he puts it, and it's made the hugest difference."

"He says that you've been quite amazing over the operation, especially considering how awful it's all been."

"Thanks for telling me that. It means a lot."

"I assume the trek is definitely off."

"You assume wrong."

"But it's only six weeks to go."

"Yes, but I've already been out of hospital for two weeks, and I reckon if I walk a little further each day, in a month or so I'll be absolutely fine. The doctor says I'm recovering remarkably well, and I can only put that down to the fact that I was fit before the operation from going to the gym three times a week and walking Susanna every day in addition to the training walks."

Jack refills my wine glass and takes the dinner plates over to the sink.

"Do you want to wait a while before the bread-and-butter pudding?" I call over.

"That Stanko is a bit of a find, isn't he?" says Jack.

"An angel," I agree.

Jack returns and sits back down opposite me.

"Jack, would you consider coming back?"

"Would you want me to?"

I pause. "It hurts not having you around, but — and I'm surprised to find myself saying this — I don't think this is the right time. I've got so much sorting out still to do that if you came back now I think we'd go straight back to where we were before. And I don't think you'd accept that. I'm not even sure I would."

"We both need more time to sort ourselves out."

This is my chance. "Jack, do you have someone . . ."

Jack is staring at me intently.

"Do you have someone . . . someone who can fix the table leg? It's gone quite wobbly."

"Talk about butterfly mind. But yes, I'm sure I do. I can call you tomorrow with a number." We're playing games. I'm quite sure Jack knew exactly what I was about to say.

"Thanks, that would be great."

It's all too polite, too damned adult and civilised. I want something real to happen. I want him to reach over the table and cup my face in the palm of his hand. I want to pound my fists against his chest and demand he tells me whether or not he's having an affair with Sally. I want him to declare his love and ask to come home, or I want him to tell me it's over and he's never coming back again.

"Jack, I'm exhausted. It's been really lovely having you for dinner in our own house, but now I'm knackered. Blame it on the operation or blame it on the fact that suddenly I can't deal with you being here but not being here and the uncertainty of not knowing what the hell's going to happen to us. Please go now before I say something I'll regret."

Jack stands and sighs.

"We were doing so well, I thought."

"We were, for a bit. And we will again. But no more, not now."

"Look, why don't you go upstairs to bed, and I'll clear away the dishes and let myself out."

Every bit of my body is crying out for the cocooning comfort of my duvet, the escape of sleep. "I won't say no to your offer, Jack, I'm far too tired for dishes, and if I'm not in the room I can't possibly say the wrong thing. Oh, and help yourself to the bread-and-butter pudding. Goodnight."

I turn my back on Jack and walk slowly out of the room.

Maddy's on the sofa, lying feet up to relieve the pressure on her swollen ankles.

"The baby's still breech, and the chances of it turning of its own accord are pretty remote. I saw the obstetrician this morning, and we agreed that I'd elect to have a Caesarean."

"There goes the birthing pool and the scented candles."

"Big baby. Small me. Breech. Old as God. A Caesar does seem sensible."

"Of course it does. And I'm glad you're making the decision now rather than possibly ending up with an emergency C-section after a long labour."

"You know, you don't still have to be there. It's one thing holding my hand while I'm moaning and groaning and shouting abuse at you, another to see me sliced open in the operating theatre."

"Me down at the sharp end? No way, but I wouldn't miss this show for the world. Just remember where you'll be in the war-wound pecking order — two scars behind me and not a chance of catching up. So when's C-day?"

"Monday morning, nine o'clock. A week before I'm due, so hopefully I won't go into labour early."

"Only four days to go! I'd better get into training. My first major outing, and back to the place I've just come from. My favourite hospital, my home-from-home."

"Shut up, Hope, and make me a camomile tea. You don't look that much of an invalid to me."

"Give me the update on Ed and the boys."

"The boys are practically bursting with excitement. Their beloved aunt Maddy having a baby means they'll have their first first cousin. If they knew I was expecting their brother or sister, I have a feeling there'd be less enthusiasm. A cousin is fun, a sibling just an attention-seeking rival."

"And Ed?"

"He seems quite relaxed with me, as though he really wants us to be friends. I don't get the impression that he feels at all guilty about what happened between us, although I can't be sure. He started to say something the other day, and I cut him right off."

"And what was that?"

"He said he wished the baby were his."

"He did? And what did you say?"

"I said, 'Well, it's not, and I wouldn't be happy at all if it were.'"

"And then?"

"He just looked rather crestfallen and didn't say anything. But before he left, he kissed me on the cheek and said, 'You and Ru, I miss you both.'"

"And you said . . ."

"'But I'm here,' and he said, 'Who are you trying to kid? When Ruth died, because of what we did, I lost both of you. It doesn't seem fair.'"

"Oh, Maddy," I say. "If only you'd —" I cut myself off mid-sentence. Now is not the time to lecture Maddy on why she ought to tell Ed the truth. "Let's just concentrate, shall we, on giving birth to this little person inside your tummy?"

While I boil the kettle for Maddy's tea, I am struck with a notion that has all the clarity and brilliance of the Koh-i-noor diamond. It is so spectacularly simple that I can't believe I haven't considered it before. I'm suddenly impatient for Maddy to go home. There's something I need to do. Simple as my task is, it involves taking a huge risk which I may regret for the rest of my life. On the other hand, if I don't do what I'm about to do I will regret that for the rest of my life as well.

"Ed, darling," I say, when he picks up the phone, "I haven't seen you for ages. And I'm going stir-crazy stuck at home. Get a babysitter and come and see me. You'll have to forgive me my ravaged appearance but it would be so wonderful to catch up and hear how you're getting on."

I don't really give Ed the chance to say no.

"My minders move out Saturday, so Saturday evening — if you're not busy — would be great. Look forward to it. Bye."

Maddy's been allocated one of the side rooms off the end of the main ward. She has given birth to a beautiful baby girl, weighing 8lb 2oz, a very big little girl indeed for someone with as small a frame as her mother. I held Maddy's hand — and my breath — throughout the proceedings. Until the actual moment that the doctor lifted the baby from behind the screened-off section below Maddy's waist and we heard her first cry, it had all felt pretty clinical. Once the epidural was working, the whole thing took only about twenty-five minutes. The operating theatre was crowded with people — the obstetrician and his assistant, the anaesthetist with his, two nurses, a midwife, the paediatrician. But without the emotional build-up of labour itself, I almost forgot about the fact that Maddy was being opened up to get a baby out, and all my concern was focused on whether Maddy was reasonably relaxed and pain-free. Which she was.

But the look on Maddy's face as the baby was placed in her arms said all I needed to know. "Look at her," she said, over and over. "Just look at her."

I looked and for a tiny instant, through the muslin of tears that made the scene before me as misty as a Monet painting, I thought she was mine. I even reached towards Maddy to pluck the baby from her arms and into mine, jolting myself back before she noticed.

"Emma, my love," Maddy whispered. "Emma, my sweet, my precious gift."

Emma. The title of Ruth's favourite book.

Emma is asleep in the perspex hospital cot, swaddled in a soft, white, satin-trimmed baby blanket. Maddy is still numb from the epidural but smiling from ear to ear.

"Why do you keep looking at your watch?" she asks me. "Do you have another appointment?"

"Of course not," I stutter. "I'm just thinking you might like a little quality time with your baby."

"What do you think of my baby?"

"She's perfect."

"And again."

"Perfect."

"And one last time . . ."

There's a knock at the door, followed by the sound of someone fumbling with a doorknob. A sweating, panting man, with his jacket wrongly buttoned, stumbles through the door like a drunk, clutching a vast bouquet of red roses that almost obscures his face.

"I had to drop off the twins at school . . . and then I raced straight here . . . but the traffic was awful . . . and . . . Maddy . . . Maddy, my love, are you all right . . ."

Maddy didn't look at all frightened before giving birth. Now she looks terrified. Her eyes dart from Ed to me to Ed and back to me again.

"Hope, what the hell . . ."

"Maddy," says Ed, "I know everything. I know . . ."

"What have you done? What have you fucking done?" Maddy's eyes pierce me with such contempt that it hits me like a physical blow.

"How could you? How bloody could you?"

"Maddy —" I begin.

"Not a word. I don't want to hear a single word."

I feel dazed, as if from a blow to the head. In slow motion I reach for my bag from the floor, raise myself from the chair next to Maddy's bed and turn slightly to lift my coat from the arm rest. I look again at Maddy. She is wild-eyed, and her face is clenched like a fist.

"Can't you see what you've done? It's as much a betrayal as my betrayal of Ruth. We're the same, us two. Despicable."

"Maddy, please . . ." says Ed, but he's looking at the floor.

"I'm so sorry, Maddy," I say. "I thought it was for the best, I thought it would bring you together. I thought it was the right thing to do."

"You've ruined everything. Everything. I hate you."

The baby has started to cry. Ed is standing at the foot of the bed, head bowed, roses in hand, like a supplicant. Maddy is screaming. "Get out of here. Get out of here. You too, Ed. I'm sorry, but I can't have you here, not now."

"But she's my baby too," says Ed. It's more of a plea than a statement. "Isn't she?" he adds, as though having just been told by me that he's the father, he's no longer quite sure.

The baby's howls are no match for Maddy's.

A nurse bursts in. "Everything all right? I've just come on. Says on my chart that you've had the baby, but from the racket it sounds like you're in labour. What's up?"

"I want them out of here," sobs Maddy. "I want to be alone with my baby. Surely it's my right to be left alone with my baby."

As I flee down through the main maternity ward, the lower right-hand side of my stomach, around the site of the operation, is cramping in agony.

"Hope, wait," calls Ed after me. "Wait."

But I don't. The other day Maddy said to me, "The day my baby is born will be the most important day of my life. Nothing before or after will ever mean as much."

However much Maddy hates me right now, I hate me even more.

Ain't No Mountain High Enough

Olly's gone. Jack's gone. Maddy's out of my life. I can't talk to anyone about Maddy because no one knows the story and it would only be heaping betrayal upon betrayal. I call her, email her, put notes through her door. She won't respond. I've left messages for Ed too. It would appear I'm on his blacklist as well. I thought of standing in wait outside Maddy's home until she came out with the baby in the buggy, but that would amount to harassment, which she surely doesn't need. I should be with her, helping her, shopping, cooking, practising my rusty nappy-changing skills, anything to see her through these first few weeks alone with her baby. I feel impotent and a failure. Jack is my only conduit to Maddy.

"What the hell has happened between you?" he rang to ask me.

"I can't talk about it," I said.

"Maddy won't talk about it either," said Jack. "You're like children, you two. She's on her own and in dire need of help. Why don't you just turn up?"

"Because she wouldn't open the door. Or, if she did, she'd slam it right back in my face."

"So you're talking to her, but she's not talking to you. Is that what you're telling me?"

"That's about it." Jack emits an odd sort of grunt.

"How's she doing?" I ask. "And Emma. Is Emma OK?"

"The baby's thriving. Maddy looks exhausted, as though she hasn't slept a wink. Her neighbour has been getting her some shopping as she can't lift much after the Caesarean. Stanko takes the dog out twice a day and the same saintly neighbour who does the shopping walks it once around the block in the evening. Home for a whole week and so far Maddy and Emma haven't left the house."

I grimace. "Jack, you have to believe me, I was only trying to help. I thought I could wave my magic wand and everything would be wonderful."

"There's not much point in you telling me what you hoped to achieve if I've no idea what you're talking about and if I can't be let in on the big secret. All I know is that you went into the delivery room as Maddy's best friend and came out as her worst enemy. I don't get it. Anyone would think you'd tried to steal the baby."

"Maybe one day I'll tell you, Jack, if ever this awful business gets resolved, which I doubt."

I can hear Jack's sigh down the phone. Another reason for him not to come home to his dysfunctional wife. I seem to have lost the knack of hanging on to what's precious to me.

"You probably think it's all my fault, don't you?"

"I didn't say a word."

"You didn't have to. But, actually, you'd be right. It was all my fault."

"Olly texted me last night." Jack's voice is lighter now, the mere mention of Olly lifting a burden from his vocal cords.

"Me too. Says the school is modelled on an English public school, only they eat curry instead of turkey twizzlers. Do you miss him?"

"Not yet, he's only been gone a week. I was just happy to hear from him."

"I missed him even before he'd left."

"You're impossible, Hope."

"I know. Are you free for dinner?"

"Sorry, no. I've already made arrangements."

"Oh. Anyone or anything special?"

"Hope, you promised not to do this."

"I know I did. But I slipped up." I can't help the sarcasm creeping into my voice. If only Jack knew how well behaved I'm being. I still haven't mentioned Sally once to him. I'm not sure if I can hold out much longer.

"Better be going," says Jack awkwardly. I can feel Jack itching to get away from me.

"Just one small favour. Pleeease."

"Go on." The heaviness has crept back into his voice. It's what I do to him. Weigh him down.

"Will you look in on Maddy every couple of days? Just to make sure she's OK and has everything she needs. Honestly, I'd be there round the clock if she'd let me."

330

"I was planning to anyway, so no favour required. Don't forget she's my friend too. Funny how I used to think I was in touch with my feminine side. Now I realise I don't understand women at all."

"Me neither," I reply. Was that a chuckle I heard faintly down the line? Or just wishful thinking on my part?

After putting down the phone I wander upstairs into Olly's room. I suppose I should have tidied it up, put all his magazines into neat piles, put his books and CDs into some kind of order, stripped the mattress bare to air it. I've done none of these things. I want this room to stay just how it was when Olly left it until I've got used to the idea of him not being here. Like a shrine, albeit a dishevelled one in desperate need of a dust. Or a crime scene, in which nothing must be moved until all the forensic evidence has been gathered.

It helps that Olly's room looks as though he might walk back into it any minute, as though he's just popped out to the shops or been out for a beer with his mates. There's a torn and crumpled T-shirt flung over the back of his desk chair. I pick it up, intending to drop it into the laundry bin. But I can't bring myself to do it. Instead, draping the T-shirt across the palms of my hands like a flannel, I cover my face with it, imbibing Olly, breathing him deep inside me. It feels as though I'm doing something forbidden. Something a mother isn't supposed to do. Olly's scent, sweet and sour, sweat and aftershave, envelops me. If Olly were to walk in on me, he would be horrified. But why should I feel guilty? Just as a baby derives comfort from the smell of its mother, I need Olly's scent to reassure me now. I reluctantly close Olly's bedroom door behind me, taking the T-shirt with me and scrunching it into a ball. Once in my own room I look around for a place to put it. I find myself glancing over my shoulder, as if expecting to be caught out, before settling it carefully under Jack's pillow, as though I'm handling a precious talisman rather than a grubby rag. It will be my harmless little secret, something to hug when I wake at 3a.m.

Now what?

I ring my father.

"Daddy, it's me, Hope. Do you fancy a film and something to eat this evening?"

"Not tonight, poppet, I've got the boys over for bridge."

"Good for you."

"I work on the principle that whisky and activity are the best antidotes to grief."

"How about tomorrow?"

"Tomorrow I can do. But would you mind if we skipped the film? I'd far rather eat and talk."

"Me too, I just thought a film might be a better distraction than me."

"Nonsense. A good bottle of claret and a proper conversation will cheer us both up."

"Sorry to be sentimental, Daddy, but I do love you."

"The feeling's mutual, you silly girl."

I put down the phone and turn to Susanna, who's standing outside my study door, waiting for permission to come in.

"Looks like it's just you and me, babe," I say. "Don't suppose you'd say no to a play in the park?" Susanna wags her tail and looks up at me with a look of pure devotion. For the moment I'm prepared to overlook the fact she gazes at anyone who's nice to her in exactly the same way. I'll take my devotion where I find it.

I think my father's right about the importance of distraction. With less than four weeks to go until the trek, I'm focusing on building up my strength and stamina.

And shopping.

I would never have thought that a morning in Field and Trek could make my heart beat faster. Not compared, say, to splashing out at Harvey Nichols in the days when one of the perks of my job was a large clothing allowance. There is just so much gorgeous kit to choose from. The world of trekking even has its own iconic brands. Fashion, for example, has Prada; trekking has Brasher, named for the mountaineer's famous lightweight boot. And while Giorgio Armani favours colours such as taupe and greige, the Saloman Women's Adventure Trek 7 boot goes one better, featuring a bestseller in the fetching colour known as swamp.

I have more accessories than Victoria Beckham. I just hope I can breathe at altitude as well as my jacket boasts it can. Also in my kit are thermals for nights, various layers from T-shirts to fleeces to waterproofs for days. I have a pair of trousers that can be transformed into shorts by undoing the horizontal zips located just above the knee. A look I doubt will hit the catwalk, but wonderfully practical when you're trying to cool down halfway up a mountain in a heatwave. After much deliberation, I've purchased a three-seasons or four-seasons bag. It's like learning a new language, this secret code of adventure sportswear. I've also bought one large rucksack — which will hold everything I don't need with me while I'm walking and which our Berber guides will strap to their fleet of mules during the day — and a mini rucksack to hold my essential day kit such as water and energy bars. And lipstick. I wonder if all the women on the trek are as vain as me.

My most prized possession is what I refer to as my miner's lamp. Battery-operated, it goes round your head like a bandana. I can use it for finding my way round the campsite at night if I need to find a rock to pee behind and for reading when my tent companion is asleep. So far I've not been allocated a tent companion.

Thanks to some arm-twisting of friends and relatives and the generosity of some of the big-name advertisers who used to buy space in *Jasmine*, I've raised about three grand in sponsorship money. Like every novice trekker, I'm more worried about the toilet facilities than I am about falling into a ravine or not being able to keep up with the rest of the group.

Outside, way above the clouds, is a vermilion setting sun, offset by an almost-full moon. Inside, clogging up the aeroplane aisles, is a motley mob of seventy fellow trekkers, mostly strangers to one another, gathered from Cornwall to Fife and ranging in age, I would estimate, from around twenty to sixty-something. The mood has changed from uncertainty to excitement and the airline staff are having to try to contain the crowd, ordering everyone back to their seats. In half an hour we'll be touching down in Casablanca, before catching our internal flight for a one-night stopover at a hotel in Ouarzazate, close to where the trek proper begins in the remote Jebel Sahro, which lies between the Sahara and the High Atlas mountains. Sally, like the mother of the bride at a wedding reception, has been combing the aisle checking that all her guests are comfortable and enjoying themselves and have had enough to eat.

"Everything OK, Hope?" She stops next to my aisle seat, looking even taller and more willowy than usual. The more attractive Sally looks, the more uncomfortable I feel.

"Just look at that sunset," I reply, pointing at the luminous sky through the window. "But I can't say I'm not nervous."

"It's always scary the first time. But you'll be fine. Even with your recent surgery you're well above average fitness. By the way, you and I are sharing."

"Sharing?"

"The tent. Not tonight at the hotel, but for the duration of the trek."

I'm hoping I misheard. "But what about Nick?"

"No way. He snores like a warthog, and the altitude only makes it worse. He's bagged himself one of the single tents. I hope that's all right with you."

Sally flashes one of her sincerest smiles and gives a little toss of her head, causing her streaky blonde hair to swing in a credible approximation of a l'Oréal model in a shampoo ad. It occurs to me that saintly Sally might just be one of the most coolly calculating people I've ever met. I don't buy this snoring business. Sally wants something from me, and this is her way of making sure she gets it. At first I had naively thought Sally's loss had conferred on her a kind of impregnable goodness. But what I'm wondering now is whether her pain has simply hardened her, made her tunnel-visioned in her ambition to achieve her goals. Or maybe she was always that way. But what exactly are her goals? Cat's Place, for sure. But what does she want from me? And from Jack? If it really is Jack she's after then sharing a tent with me in order to find out just how much of a rival for his affections I still am, would be sheer cruelty.

This is not at all what I planned, although, come to think of it, not a single thing I've done all year has gone according to how I've planned it. So I'm going to have to either plan a whole lot better or give up making plans altogether. My intention had been to focus my energy on the physical challenge ahead, and I had been rather hoping that this whole experience would clear my head, not addle it further. Not a chance, it would seem.

"Sharing with you would be great," I say, wondering if my hesitance — or rather my hypocrisy — shows, but certainly not about to have a confrontation at 30,000 feet. I'd far rather have shared with a complete stranger, one whom I could be absolutely certain wasn't screwing my husband. *Know thine enemy* is the expression that comes to mind as the seat belt sign comes on, and I wonder if perhaps I can't turn this to my own advantage. *Don't be such a suspicious cow*, I chide myself a moment later.

As the co-pilot announces, "Ten minutes to landing," I close my eyes and hope that coming to Morocco was a good decision.

Coming to Morocco *was* a good decision. I am elated, exhilarated and exhausted. And too hyped-up to sleep. It's midnight, and apart from the sonorous snoring that punctuates the peace of our wilderness settlement, all is still. I have decided to bring my mat and sleeping bag and miniature pillow out into the open. It must be close to freezing, but I'm layered up against the elements with thermals and gloves and a warm hat pulled low over my forehead and ears. The sky is so big and the stars so bright that I can't resist making my bed outside the claustrophobic atmosphere of the tent I share with Sally. I intend to lie here until the discomfort of the cold outweighs the pleasure of the cloudless night. Every now and then, among the myriad glittering diamonds, a single star shoots across the endless sky and makes me catch my breath.

Out here in the wilderness I don't feel fifty. I don't feel any age at all. My age has simply floated away and settled itself on a distant, snowy peak. For hours at a time I find I am simply able to free my mind of everything other than my surroundings. I am conscious of the straining of my calves and thighs, a niggling ache in my menopausal hips, and a certain crankiness in my knees. The balls of my feet are sore and stinging. But

337

none of these physical sensations trouble me. I welcome them, in fact. It's a relief to allow my body rather than my mind to drive me on. I'm revelling in this feeling of being fully physically engaged.

I'm beginning to feel the chill in my sleeping bag under the stars when I'm startled by the sound of crunching stone, and sit bolt upright with a thumping heart.

"Is that you, Hope?"

I breathe a sigh of relief at the sound of Nick's voice.

"Thank God," I whisper. "I thought it was a rattlesnake or something. Sally's fast asleep, you'd better not disturb her."

"I wasn't planning to. I had to get up for a piss, and I spotted a large lump on the ground right outside your tent. Thought I ought to come and investigate."

"And the large lump was me." I giggle. "Want to come and join me for a while, before I freeze to death?"

"Is that an invitation to get into your sleeping bag?"

"It most certainly is not."

"That's a shame, we could have warmed one another's toes."

"How about you going and getting *your* sleeping bag and coming straight back? Have you got any supplies? I'm starving."

"I have one gross of Tracker bars, six bananas and a flask of brandy in my rucksack. Will that do?"

"You can hold the bananas. But yes, please, to a Tracker bar and a swig of the hard stuff."

Nick disappears once more into the darkness. I breathe out a chill mist and smile up at the night sky.

How odd it feels to be tucked up in a sleeping bag like this, on a late November night in Morocco, inviting this charming man I've only recently met to come and lie next to me, and not caring at all how funny I must look lying here in my woolly hat with a miner's lamp strapped around my head.

As soon as I hear the sound of stones crunching again I switch on my lamp, sending a beam of light in Nick's direction.

He looks so comic on tiptoes in his long johns, fleece and bobble hat, with his walking boots untied, his sleeping bag trailing against the ground and clutching what must be Tracker bars between his teeth.

"Oh, goody," I say. "A midnight feast."

He leans down towards me, proffering the snack bars still lodged in his mouth. I pluck them from his lips and he sets about arranging himself. His teeth are chattering.

"Hurry up and get into your sleeping bag," I say, "before frostbite sets in."

"Bugger, I forgot my pillow."

"No worries, you can share mine, even though it's barely big enough for my own head."

"We're going to be knackered tomorrow."

"Yeah, but it'll be worth it."

Finally Nick is sorted, but sharing such a tiny pillow is quite impossible.

"How about I have the pillow and you rest your head on my manly chest?" Nick suggests.

"You can't get pregnant that way, can you?" I ask.

Nick snorts. "Well, I suppose there's always a first time. You know, you'd look a lot more attractive without that lamp thing on your head."

"But I'm not trying to look attractive," I say, slipping it over my head with a grin. "Now, where's the brandy?"

For the next few minutes we lie there in companionable silence, my head resting on Nick's chest, the two of us munching on our Tracker bars and passing his hip-flask to and fro, staring up at the stars. The brandy suffuses my insides with waves of warmth.

"Life is a mystery to be experienced, not a riddle to be solved," says Nick, sighing gently.

"Fine words, but easier to say than live by. I'm so glad you and Sally talked me into this."

"Me too." Nick lifts his head and plants a little kiss on the top of my woolly hat.

"Hey, pal, what was that for?"

"For making me forget myself."

"That's not me, it's the mountains."

"It's partly the mountains, but it's you too."

"Nick, I've been dying to ask you something. Why do you think Sally wanted to share with me?"

"Because I sometimes snore, I suppose. Isn't that what she told you?"

"Yes, but I didn't believe her."

"But I do snore."

"That bit I believed, just not the reason. Is Jack still playing third corner of the triangle in your marriage?"

"I don't know, Hope. Maybe it was all my imagination. He hasn't been round so much lately, although she's definitely met up with him a couple of times that I know of. She makes such a point of telling me, kind of casually throwing it into the conversation . . ."

"Like . . ."

"Like, 'Oh, I bumped into Jack yesterday and we had a bite for lunch,' or 'I'm going to have an early supper with Jack to talk about some of the alternative therapies we're thinking of offering at the centre.' The more she insists on telling me, the more I think it might be a smokescreen. But up here in the mountains, in this incredible place, it just doesn't seem to matter. Nothing does."

"That's what I love about it too. I've spent so much of this year going over the mistakes I've made, and worrying about the ones I'm about to make, that this feeling of being in the here and now is totally liberating."

"Hope, you do know that you're quite a special person, don't you? You're always so down on yourself, which, considering how talented and funny and attractive —"

"You're only saying that because I look so sexy in my thermals and my woolly hat and because my miner's lamp is the last word in chic," I interrupt before he can finish. There's a kind of longing in Nick's tone that I can't deal with right now. "Now would you mind shutting up while I contemplate the wonders of the universe." I shift my head into a more comfortable position.

"Here, you take this for a moment," says Nick, raising himself up again and moving the pillow to a position where I can lie back against it.

"But what about you?" I lower my head and snuggle still further down into my sleeping bag.

"Ssh, I'm on the case," whispers Nick. And in the next instant he has rolled onto his side and half on top of me. His hands are cupping my face, and his lips are on mine before I'm even aware of what's happening. I'm strait-jacketed inside my bag, my arms effectively pinned to my side. The only thing I can move is my head, and I attempt to shake it vigorously, like a dog with itchy ears. As I try to get my lips away from his and Nick refuses to give up, our noses rub against one another's as though we're over-excited Eskimos.

"No, Nick, no," I splutter as loud as I dare. "Have you gone mad?"

"I can't help it, Hope," he says, drawing back a couple of inches from my face, looking at me with an intensity that shocks me. "Aren't you feeling it too?"

"If you mean the cold, yes. But this isn't a sensible way to warm up. Just how drunk are you?"

"I didn't mean the cold, and I'm not drunk at all," says Nick forlornly, rolling off me and onto his back. "Shit!" Without my pillow as a buffer, Nick's head hits something stony.

"Nick, are you all right? You'd better not be bleeding." Now it's my turn to roll onto my side, releasing an arm from my sleeping bag so I can prop myself up on my elbow, head on hand.

Nick runs his hand across the back of his head.

"Doesn't feel wet. No blood. So I guess I'll survive. Hurts like hell, though."

"But what came over you? Aren't our lives complicated enough already?"

"I'm an oaf. I'm sorry."

"You're not an oaf, and don't be sorry, just don't do it again."

"I guess that up here under the stars anything seems possible. Ever since I saved you from falling flat on your face on Hampstead Heath you've been featuring in my fantasies. What happened just happened. It wasn't premeditated. If I hadn't needed a piss, I'd never have known you were out here."

I stifle a laugh. "Oh, Nick, you are so adorable. In other circumstances I know I could fancy you too. And I'm grateful for the fact that you fancy me. But I simply won't allow myself to have sexual feelings for you. You've become a friend, and I want it to stay that way. In any case, how can I possibly feature in your fantasies looking like this?"

Nick isn't playing along with my taking it lightly. "Sally and I haven't slept together since Cat died," he announces. It's a statement delivered deadpan, without emotion.

"Since Cat died!" I'm shocked. "That's six years, isn't it? I knew she wouldn't have another child. But are you telling me that in six years you haven't once made love?"

"Not once."

"But that's horrible for you. For both of you, I suspect."

"Exactly. And you're the first person I've tried to —"

"In six years? That's the kind of loyalty that deserves a medal."

"To be honest, Hope, I know my marriage to Sally is over. And a bit of me even wants her to be having an affair with Jack, as it would give me the excuse to leave. But that would hurt you, and I don't want you to be hurt."

"I had no idea. You seem so connected, so committed."

"Committed to Cat's Place, yes. But without that, there'd be nothing. Nothing at all."

"And if you separate?"

"Cat's Place will still happen. It's always been more Sally's baby than mine, and if she didn't want me to still be involved, we could always find someone else to look after the business side. We've fulfilled our unspoken bargain, and now seems the right time to part."

"I'm so sorry, Nick, but I'm really not your answer."

"I think you could be."

"You're going to have to take my word for it. What I'd really like to do now is put my head on your chest again."

"Be my guest. But no funny business, I promise. The brandy's making me sleepy."

"Me too."

"Do you think we should go back to our tents?"

They're the last words I hear Nick say before I fall asleep.

344

When Sally emerges from our tent at 6.30 a.m., her first sight is of the two of us lying on the ground together, fast asleep, rolled on our sides facing one another, noses touching. I've no idea what went through Sally's mind when she saw us there, but she's her cool-as-usual self, as though my sleeping all night curled up with her husband isn't even worth commenting on. "Hey, you two reprobates, time to get up if you don't want to miss breakfast."

It takes me a moment to remember where I am and what went on last night. "Hi, Sally," I say, trying to sound equally casual. "I think the altitude is having the opposite effect on Nick's snoring. He didn't wake me once."

"Glad to hear it, Hope. See you in a few minutes." With an elegant wave of her hand she steps daintily over us in the direction of the already gathering group at the far end of our encampment.

Nick gives me a sheepish, sleepy grin. "Morning, sexy."

My mouth is dry. The tip of my nose is freezing. I have a nasty hangover and the last thing I'm in the mood for is an eight-hour walk uphill. I could do with a hot shower and a hair wash. For some unaccountable reason I feel ridiculously optimistic.

It's the fourth night of our trek, and we are camped on a flat, almost circular tract of land, like the stage of an amphitheatre. Instead of tiered seating, we are surrounded by pink "Pitons" or needles, natural rock formations which stand on guard, upright and austere,

345

arranged like soldiers encircling an enemy encampment. As we arrived at our resting place, it was already a hive of activity, with some of the team of Berbers unloading the mules and erecting tents for us, others baking bread in makeshift ovens inside clumps of rocks. Relieved of their burdens of equipment, tents and rucksacks, the mules were eating their supper, while the muleteers lay resting on colourful rugs spread out on the gentle slopes leading towards the Pitons.

We have feasted on meat stew cooked in huge metal pots with fresh tomatoes, peppers and onions. There is fresh-baked flat bread, cheese and hard-boiled eggs. Our gentle Berber guides have lit a spectacular fire and are circling it, playing their drums and tambourines. Fortified by generous gulps of brandy and whisky, which have appeared from yet more hip-flasks secreted deep in anorak pockets, we join the Berbers in their dancing.

I am no nearer to discovering the truth about Sally and Jack. Sally continues to be her cool, enigmatic self, even after discovering Nick and me sleeping together nose-to-nose. Sally, I'm depressed to discover, is one of those people who wake up looking wonderful. Hair not matted, eyes not puffy, thoroughly refreshed and acting as though the dawning of a new day is a gift. It's enough to make you hate a person. If you were Jack, on the other hand, I suppose it could be almost enough to make you fall in love. It can't be much fun to wake up to me with my eyelids blown up like balloons, my hair knotted and sticking out at odd angles like Worzel

346

Gummidge, the nearest thing to the spoken word a grumpy grunt.

Sharing a tent with Sally has revealed nothing about her relationship with Jack. We are too tired to talk by the time we wriggle into our sleeping bags and during the day we are split into separate walking groups. Tonight, however, when I awake around 2a.m. and need a pee, Sally is woken too by a sharp yelp as I hit my head on one of the tent's metal struts.

"I'm coming with you," she says sleepily, slithering out of her sleeping bag. "You've no idea the creatures you could bump into alone out there. Like my husband, for example." I'm grateful for her instinctive acknowledgment of my nervousness.

As we stumble around the campsite, tripping over stones and crashing into one another, we break into giggles which start quietly and grow louder and louder until the entire campsite reverberates with the sound of shushing.

"Shut the fuck up," roars a basso profondo voice.

"Shut the fuck up yourself," responds another.

"It's not funny, mate," counters the basso profondo.

But it is, and now the laughs can be heard inside other tents too, and soon more bodies emerge eerily into the darkness, looking, now that they've been woken, for a suitable spot to relieve themselves. Sally is weak from laughter and breathlessly clinging on to me. It's the first time I've seen Sally really loosen up, and my first glimpse of the girl within the woman. Despite my doubts about her and Jack, I find a huge surge of sympathy welling up inside me, and a warmth towards her that takes me by surprise.

Back, finally, in our tent, Sally whispers, "Are you in the mood to talk?"

"Sure, if you want to," I reply.

"Has Nick said anything about us?"

Not wanting to betray any confidences I reply, "Not much. But long-term relationships are hard enough when they haven't been touched by tragedy. I guess it must be even tougher when they have."

"To be honest, Hope, it's over. Nick and I are finished."

"Have you talked to him about it?"

"We never discuss us. We never even refer to us. It's just a business relationship — we're running a charity, and we just happen to live under the same roof. We're unfailingly polite, we never row, we try never to hurt one another's feelings, we're barely human."

"And if Cat hadn't died?"

"If Cat hadn't died we would have been divorced years ago."

"Oh, I hadn't realised," I reply. "I'm not sure I understand. I'd assumed, if anything, that it was Cat's death that put pressure on the marriage, but that also made it strong." I'm at a loss as to what to say that might possibly be helpful.

"That's because, like so many others, you have this romantic view of loss. Loss is crap. It doesn't make you a better person — it makes you angry and vengeful and envious."

348

"But I don't get it. I can see why you might have pulled together for the sake of Cat while she was alive. But she died six years ago, and you're still together."

"Guilt, I suppose. We've been staying together to punish one another for Cat's death."

"But that's an awful thing to do. Cat's death wasn't your fault."

"Of course it wasn't. But that doesn't stop me thinking every day that I should have done more to help her. That it should have been me, not her, who died. Only the charity has given us a united sense of purpose. Now we've almost achieved our goals, I can't see the point of our staying together any longer."

"That's so sad, Sally, but maybe it's also for the best. If opening Cat's Place lifts the burden of guilt, and you go your separate ways, maybe you'll both be able to find some happiness again."

"So now you know why I wanted to share with you rather than Nick. I just couldn't bear to be in such close proximity."

On the one hand I want to take Sally in my arms and comfort her, on the other I want to grab hold of her roughly and demand to be told the truth. I can't work Sally out at all. Neither can I bring myself to ask the Jack question. Not up here, where there's nowhere to run to.

"Sally, you're going to have to talk to Nick. You seem to have both reached the same conclusion. What's the point in delaying any longer?"

"The mountains do seem to bring everything into sharper focus, don't they?"

"Try to sleep," I say, more gently than I feel. "Tomorrow's our last — and longest — trekking day."

No wonder Sally has turned to Jack. I get the feeling she wants me to understand, to forgive her for a crime I'm supposed to guess she has committed. I sleep fitfully, dreaming that I climb the tallest peak and Jack's standing at the top waiting for me. But just when I'm about to reach him, another figure emerges from behind the summit. A woman with blonde hair that glints in the sunlight.

There's been no mountain-top epiphany for me here. No *Aha* moment when everything I need to do about my life has suddenly become clear. But I can feel a shift. And it has something to do with size and scale. The bigger the landscape, the larger the sky, the taller the mountains we see in the distance, the deeper the gorges we pass through, the brighter the sunlight during the day and the stars at night, the greater the kindness and sensitivity of our Berber guides, the more affecting the life-stories of our fellow trekkers, so many of whom are supporting the charity because their own lives have been touched by personal loss, the more insignificant I feel. And the more lacking in importance and smaller I feel, the more I realise that it's this very insignificance that should be my spur. In a landscape that's been here for millions of years before I came tramping over it in my trendy trekking boots, and is likely to remain here for millions more, fifty and fed-up seems a pretty feeble excuse for not getting on with life.

If I've only got this nanosecond of allotted time, I'd better start making something of it before it's over.

The Jebel Sahro has put a glint in everyone's eye. We are going home with a new sense of purpose, with the thought that decisions have to be made, problems faced, changes considered. In my more cynical moments I suppose it's a bit like going on one of those intensive group-brainwashing courses, with a guru who promises you enlightenment in a single weekend. A kind of updated Est training for the twenty-first century, but instead of a hotel ballroom with flocked wallpaper and someone standing on a stage telling you you're an asshole, you get the unspoiled beauty of a rugged wilderness and work out your asshole rating for yourself.

It's our last day and as we walk our final few hours back to where we began, my thoughts have turned towards Jack again. If I can't confront Sally, the time, surely, has come to confront Jack.

I know a lot of what's gone wrong between me and Jack has been my fault. And yet I'm not prepared to take all the blame. My so-called brilliant career, before it so suddenly slipped away from me, afforded us the kind of lifestyle that Jack's laid-back physio practice could never have supplied. And it's not as if Jack didn't enjoy the luxuries my job allowed us. Holidays wherever we wanted, dining out in the top restaurants without having to select the cheapest items on the menu, the best seats in the house at the theatre. I'm not saying Jack needed all this stuff, but he did participate with enthusiasm.

For me, it was always about so much more than the money and what it could buy. I loved my work, looked forward to it almost every single day until my year of approaching fifty. And there was something about being economically independent, mistress of my own purse-strings, that I never wanted to let go of. The thought of having to ask a man for money, even now, makes me shiver. Early feminist imprinting, I guess.

A high-powered, full-time job, a small child, a home to run. Is there any way in those circumstances that a relationship isn't going to become a victim of neglect? It's so easy to simply stop paying attention to one another. I was so busy I didn't care. Jack was so easy-going, he didn't seem to mind. Except he did. And as I became ever more anxious, more manic, more self-absorbed, more wrapped up in what I regarded as the hideous notion of turning fifty, the more the distance between us grew.

And maybe I should have been less honest about the sense of loss I've been feeling about Olly leaving home. How would I feel if it were the other way round and Jack were acting like it was a death in the family? Wouldn't I be thinking, yes, of course it's natural to feel it as a wrench, but hey, you've still got me? Me, your wife, remember her?

But I still won't accept that to have a truly strong marriage you have to put your partner first, above everyone and everything else. Like my mother, for example, who always favoured my father over me and Sarah, and over me in particular. At least I've learned something. I've learned from my mother's mistakes, rather than fallen into the trap of repeating them. And if I've overcompensated with the love I've lavished on Olly, and overreacted about his growing up and going away, then at least he knows he's truly cherished. Even if Jack and I are finished, I'm not going to regret the attention I've paid to Olly. Of that I am certain.

We've touched down at Heathrow just after midnight. There's much hugging and kissing and promising to stay in touch between people who only a week ago were complete strangers to one another. I wasn't expecting a hero's welcome with banners and bunting, but there's just a second or two as I walk through the corridor marked "Nothing To Declare" when I wonder, or rather hope, that Jack might turn up. Sally and Nick maintain their usual masks, expressing their gratitude to everyone for taking part, looking absolutely united. Rather than face the prospect of sharing a carriage with them on the Express to Paddington, I slip away quietly.

The last thing I do before falling into bed is send a text. "Ain't no mountain high enough . . . I'm back. Love Hope". Jack will appreciate the lyric, and he'll know that what follows are the words "to keep me from getting to you". But will he, I wonder, as consciousness falls away, appreciate the sentiment?

Christmas Already

I'm woken by the sound of a doorbell ringing and a dog barking. Susanna! I look at my alarm clock. My watch says 10.00. I throw back the duvet and fail to leap out of bed. Every bit of me is stiff from six days of trekking. And it's not helped by the fact that I've been sleeping on the ground inside a zip-up bag, suffering Jewish Princess and the Pea syndrome. So instead of leaping, I hobble. With a struggle and much huffing and puffing I raise the ancient sash window.

"Stanko! Susanna! Be with you in a tick."

I try to run my fingers through my hair but they get stuck in the tangle. It makes me think of Sally and her unfair advantage over me. Not that it will make much difference to Stanko or Susanna.

When I finally open the door, still in a pair of flannel pyjamas, Susanna practically mows me down with excitement. "At least someone loves me," I say, laughing as she licks my face.

Stanko, laden with dog paraphernalia, is looking more handsome than ever.

354

"Come in, come in." I relieve Stanko of a large bag of dog food and a dog bed. "No one has the right to be as good-looking as you."

Stanko doesn't register my remark. "First, you look my new van, then I come," he says, grinning.

"Give me two minutes to pull on some jeans. I'm sure your new van wouldn't want to see me looking like this."

Susanna bounds up the stairs on my behalf as I trail behind, my thighs resisting every painful step.

The van, a gleaming white Ford Transit, is every bit as gorgeous as Stanko's beaming face suggests. Emblazoned on the side in black is the name of his new company, Walkin' the Dog, and a mobile phone number.

"Congratulations, Stanko. Looks like you're in business."

Over black coffee, because there's no milk in the house, and toast made with some old sliced bread stored in the freezer for emergencies, we chat about Susanna's behaviour — impeccable, of course — during my absence, and Stanko's plan to become a dog trainer as well as walker, all while continuing to search for premises for his cafe/restaurant.

"When I get restaurant I make yard for dog playground. Special sell point."

"I like it. That would be a genuine first — and great for publicity purposes. Are things good with you and Mike?"

"The best. How you say? True love. When I come to England I think I be unhappy always. Now, only when I think the war and my parents. I have good friends. You are my friend, like my mother."

"Thank you, Stanko. But do you mean that I remind you of your mother, or that I'm a friend, just as your mother was your friend?"

"I no understand. But you make me think my mother because you love your son very strong. Jack is stupid man to go away. You clever and kind. Mike say, I say also."

"Stop right now, Stanko, before I crumple."

"I go quick. Maddy waiting for me take Mozart."

The mention of Maddy deflates me instantly.

"Tell Maddy . . . No, don't bother, there really isn't any point," I say glumly. But instead of the usual surge of guilt that floods over me at the thought of Maddy, a new thought pops into my head that perhaps this isn't entirely my fault. That in depriving Emma of both a father and a godmother, both of whom would cherish and love her, she is giving her precious daughter, the child she longed for and never thought she'd have, the worst possible start in life. Maddy is thinking only of her shame in sleeping with her dying sister's husband, and not at all of what's best for Emma. Me not to blame! Or at least not completely. Not all my fault! What's happening here?

Susanna and I escort Stanko to the door and wave him off. He waves an arm out of the window and smiles into his rear-view mirror.

I haven't showered or unpacked, there's shopping to do, and I need to check my phone and email messages. The old anxiety is hovering around me, like dust that's been disturbed by movement but slowly starts to settle itself again. But I will not, must not, allow it to take hold. In the mountains of Morocco, I seemed to re-find my spirit. What will it take to hang on to it now I'm home?

Under the shower I turn the water on full blast, wash my hair for the first time in ten days, slough off the dead skin with a loofah and note that my scar is looking slightly less angry than before I left. I finish with a blast of icy cold water that makes me scream as loudly as if I'd discovered a black-widow spider scurrying across the tiles. It's a trick I'd learned from *Jasmine* — providing the shock doesn't send you into cardiac arrest, the bone-chilling finale will boost your blood circulation and make your skin glow. Maybe.

I emerge energised, with another of my immaculately thought-through plans. Or, depending on your point of view, a typically rash and instinctive decision that's likely to land me in the mire.

"Hi, Hope, how was the trip?"

"Oh, Jack, you'd have loved it. The Berbers who looked after us were incredibly gracious. The landscape was stunning, the night skies awesome, even the painful bits going up and up for what seemed like for ever were mostly pleasure. Remind me, some time, to tell you my toilet-tent story."

"I'm sure it will be fascinating. So no broken bones for me to fix?"

"Just a couple. Nothing serious."

"You sound great."

This is my cue. My sounding "great" is just what I need for what's coming.

"Jack . . . are you busy on Boxing Day?"

"I've not given a second thought to Christmas. Nothing planned so far."

"Will you come away with me?"

"'*Come Away With Me*'? That's the title of a song by Norah Jones. She's my new heroine."

This sounds more like the Jack I know and think I still love. The one with an annoyingly appropriate lyric for every occasion.

"Yes, Jack, I have heard of Norah Jones. I've even got her CD in the car. But will you come away with me?"

"Where to?"

"Is that a yes or a no?"

"It's a maybe. Do you think it's a good idea?"

"Of course I think it's a good idea, or I wouldn't have asked." I can feel the irritation entering my voice, so I change tack. "The truth is, Jack, I don't know if it's a good idea. In fact, it may be a terrible idea. But I'm prepared to take the risk."

"OK, girl, let's go for it. But only if you're paying."

"Of course, darling. Wasn't it ever the case?"

"Bitch! So where are we going?"

"It's a surprise. To be honest, I haven't even thought. Somewhere exotic. Somewhere to blow the last of my savings before I'm obliged to apply for a job as a Waitrose checkout girl. They all know me in there, and most of them are at least as ancient as me, so I should fit in, no problem. And the discount on shopping will be extremely useful."

"Very funny."

"Actually, not funny. The money is almost all gone."

"You do sound a lot more cheerful than before you went away."

"That's because I am. Impending bankruptcy notwithstanding."

This is the first conversation I've had with Jack in ages that hasn't ended with a palpable tension in the air. After putting down the phone I go straight into the study. Just as soon as I've checked my emails I intend to search for winter-sun deals on the Internet.

I'm still logging on when the phone rings again.

"Hope, it's Tanya. You'll never guess what's happened."

"They've fired Mark and they're closing *Jasmine*."

"You must be psychic. How on earth did you know?"

"I didn't. It's just one of those vengeful fantasises I've been having all year. Is it really true?"

"Apparently, sales have been plummeting issue by issue, the advertisers have lost all confidence, and rather than do a re-relaunch, Simon has decided to cut his losses and shut the whole thing down."

I'm sort of smiling, but not nearly as gleeful as I would have expected myself to be in the circumstances. "What are *you* going to do, Tanya?"

"Oh, I'm not worried. I'll either get another job in the company or have enough redundancy to tide me over until I find something new. Mark was becoming more and more of a monster, and I couldn't have stuck it much longer anyway. Last week he sent me out — in *my* lunch hour, can you believe? — to buy all the food he needed for one of his soirées. And then he had the nerve to tell me off for having been gone for too long. When I mentioned I hadn't even had the chance to get myself a sandwich, he told me I'd have to wait until later as he had so much for me to do. It was pure abuse. And even I've been getting fed up with all those articles on stain removal. To be honest, it's the best news I've had for months."

"Typical Tanya, you always did look on the bright side. Unlike your neurotic former boss."

"Neurotic, maybe, and demanding, but always fair and always sensitive."

"So has Mark already gone?"

"He seems to have disappeared into thin air, even though it was announced only half an hour ago. In theory, he needs to clear out his office, but if yours looked like a vision of hell as painted by Hieronymus Bosch, his would make a Mondrian look cluttered. Everything Mark requires in life is on his BlackBerry. So I'm rather hoping I may never have to see him again."

"This is going to look pretty awful for Global. Firing editors happens all the time, but actually closing down a magazine is something much more serious. To take the decision to close down what was at least still a profitable magazine when I left, the sales must have seized up altogether. I'd like to see Simon wangle his smarmy way out of this one."

"Remember how everyone cried when you left?"

"Even whatshername who was only there to research her novel and was thrilled because it gave her something interesting to write about for a change."

"Well, no one's crying now. They're all just furious that it could be allowed to happen."

"Thanks for calling me, Tanya. How's James? When can I see you?"

"James is fine, which is the other thing I wanted to tell you. We're getting married."

"Hey, that's wonderful news, congratulations. *Mazel tov*."

"*Mazel* who?"

"It means good luck. It's Hebrew. But it also means congratulations. James is such a *mensch*."

"What's going on here? Why are you speaking to me in tongues?"

"It's weddings. I'm just hopelessly sentimental about them. And when I get sentimental I get incredibly Jewish. *Mensch* is a Yiddish word, from the German. And it means a really good human being, someone to respect. Someone like James."

"Hope, there's something I want to ask you before you lose me altogether."

"Sure."

"As I don't have a mother any more, I wondered if you might come with me to help choose the dress."

"That's one of the best offers I've ever had. Are you thinking meringues? I'm mad about meringues, although not necessarily for weddings."

"Meringues, cathedral-length veils, duchess satin, I want the whole fairytale. And I did wonder if you might be able to help me organise the wedding as well. But you have to say if it's too much."

"Sweet Tanya, when will I ever get another chance to play mother of the bride? I don't suppose Olly's going to be tripping down the aisle in yards of tulle. I'm so happy for you — it puts the news about *Jasmine* quite in the shade."

And I mean what I've just said. When I put down the phone I find that I have no interest in gloating over the demise of *Jasmine* and of Mark. Helping to plan Tanya's wedding seems to me an endeavour far more worthy of my attention.

While I'm dreaming wedding flowers and favours, I glance at my as-yet unopened emails and the phone rings again.

"Craig Anderson here. Is that you, Hope?"

"It is indeed." Craig Anderson, the boss of Jackson International, the man I spoke to following my headhunter debacle. This must have something to do with the closure of *Jasmine*.

"You've not been responding to my emails, and I've been trying to get hold of you for the last ten days."

So it can't be to do with *Jasmine* after all.

I glance at my inbox and between the updates from Amazon and eBay and the cheap airlines and all the other companies I've subscribed to in the past and who've been hounding me ever since, I can make out two or three emails with Craig's name on them.

"I've been climbing mountains, Craig, and only got back last night."

"So you and I were right about *Jasmine*. Simon must be kicking himself."

It's funny, but a year ago I would have entered into this conversation with gusto, crowing about Mark's comeuppance, cracking jokes about Simon's disastrous reading of the women's magazine market. But now it just seems like a waste of breath.

"Yes," I reply. "It is a shame about *Jasmine*. It was such a strong magazine for so long, it should never have been allowed to just lie down and die."

"You're being very gracious. I'd love to see Simon's face right now."

I say nothing.

"But the real reason I'm ringing, Hope, and if you remember I said I'd be in touch — things just took longer than I thought they would — is that I've got a proposition to put to you. You must be aware that the market is absolutely crying out for a magazine aimed at the feisty woman of forty-plus. Forties, fifties and beyond, it's where all the spending power is. It's not with the singles in their twenties, or the cash-strapped parents in their thirties that *Jasmine* was aimed at. And you can forget this baking business that Simon thought was going to wow the readers. Fifty-year-olds are more interested in sex than sauces. What do you think?"

"I think you're absolutely right, Craig," I say, conjuring up Dan and me in Paris, Nick and me up a mountain, a surge of excitement, the old adrenaline coursing through me.

I'm also thinking, how come, if we fifty-year-olds are all so feisty and fabulous, Craig only last month dumped his feisty, fifty-year-old wife for a thirty-two-year-old art director on one of his magazines? And what would this magazine be anyway, other than just an excuse to sell more stuff to women that they don't actually need? Like anti-wrinkle and cellulite creams, and cosmetic surgery holidays in South Africa and Spain.

"We should definitely talk," I continue, trying to sound both casual and enthusiastic at the same time. My mind is racing over the pros and cons. A chance to empower women of my own age would be pretty attractive. To prove George Bernard Shaw's maxim that youth is wasted on the young. An opportunity to celebrate real women leading exciting and fulfilling lives and taking on new challenges and . . . and Tanya could come back and work for me. And I could put together a brilliant team and become an award-winning editor once again and show the world that I'm not a write-off. But why do I need to show the world I'm not a write-off? What I need to do is show myself. My year of turning fifty has been one long nightmare. And how could I launch and edit such a magazine if I didn't believe in it? And yet . . . Something Simone de Beauvoir once wrote has been haunting me all year. It was in a collection of three stories, on the theme of growing old.

The door will open slowly and I shall see what there is behind the door. It is the future. The door to the future will open. Slowly. Unrelentingly. I am on the threshold.

But for the first time I think how you have to change only one word from this passage to alter its meaning entirely. Remove the word *unrelentingly*, and the future can be seen in a whole new light. Maybe just a word is all it takes.

"You still there, Hope?"

"Sorry, Craig. I just had about a million ideas all at once."

All I'd planned to do today was some rather mundane chores. It was going to be an ordinary day. So far it's been anything but.

"Have you thought of a title?"

"Not yet. Thought I'd leave that to you."

"How about *Spirit*, or perhaps *New Spirit*?"

"I *love* the sound of *New Spirit*. What's the thinking?"

"Oh, it's just a theme I picked up on in Morocco. It kind of fits my mood. But we can go into that later."

"Well, as you said, we need to talk. Let's put something in the diary as soon as possible. Will next Monday work for you?"

I wander out with Susanna to do some shopping. Passing a newsagent, I go in and scan the shelves. I'm already picturing *New Spirit* beaming out at me, nestled between, say, *Vogue* and *Good Housekeeping*. I start to gather together a whole pile of the latest glossies. If I'm going to talk to Craig I need to know what the magazines are up to as I've barely been able to bring myself to read one all year. But something stops me. I'm not somehow in the right frame of mind, and I find myself putting them back on the glossy piles from which I've taken them. Instead, I scoop up three bridal titles and plan my evening of going through them with a stash of Post-it notes to attach to anything I think Tanya might like the look of.

I'm going through my emails, deleting all the junk, when I come across one which reads "not good enough" in the subject box. Then I note the sender. Dan Drake is the last person I was expecting to hear from. It's been months since I ran out on him in Covent Garden, and I never wrote to fully explain myself. I hesitate before opening it. But it's goading me like a glinting gold box of creamy truffles. What does "not good enough" mean? Where's the harm in opening it? Surely I can't become contaminated — I think I mean intoxicated — by a single email.

> Dear Hope,
> It's been bugging me since August. What on earth was that stuff about a canine emergency? I guess you realise it's the second time you've run out on me unexpectedly . . . and I'm hoping it's not getting to be a habit.
> A lot can happen in a few months — and has. For a start my wife's walked out on me. And I thought I was the one who had the monopoly on bad behaviour. Turns out our second child may not even be mine. She's been having an affair with a co-worker ever since she went back to work after Monica, the elder of our two kids, was born. She's not saying Molly's the other guy's child, but she

can't be certain. I've been thinking of going the paternity-test route but it seems a helluva thing for the kid to have to live with, and it may just be better to keep quiet about it. On the other hand, if my wife's setting up home with this other guy and he *is* the father, then I guess he — and Molly — have a right to know. He also has a right to pay. It's a pretty big mess.

The other news is that I'm coming back to London on a visiting professorship to teach an American literature course. I feel I hardly know you, Hope, and I'd like to get to know you better. You owe me one, don't you think?

I arrive in the New Year. You'll be the first person I call . . .

Dan

PS I can still picture you slipping out of that cute wrap dress you were wearing. I get horny every time I think of it.

Why does he have to do this to me? I thought I'd microfiched Dan and stored the film in my memory bank. I know full well he's just a charismatic chancer, and presumptuous with it, but he's so upfront about it that it's thoroughly disarming. There must be hundreds of women a man as attractive as him can screw. And I can't believe he's just too lazy to go looking. So, why me? Dan coming to London, not just for a fleeting visit, but to stay for months, possibly a year or more, he didn't make it clear, is the last thing I need right now.

But it's so bloody tempting. I'd been determined to expunge Dan from my system. I'd got the rationale all sorted in my head. First, because I knew I wanted Jack back and didn't want Dan to get in the way. Secondly, because I thought Dan wouldn't be remotely interested in me after my not exactly winning performance in the summer. And thirdly, since the operation . . . well, if I can hardly bear to look at my body, why on earth would anyone else want to?

Damn you, Dan Drake. I suppose we could always have sex through a hole in a specially commissioned designer shroud. I need time to think about how to reply. Dan alone and separated is a far more dangerous proposition than Dan semi-attached to his wife.

On the other hand, if my make-or-break holiday with Jack is more break than make, then dallying with Dan in the new year might be justified. Can you still be callow at fifty? What's got into me today?

So much is happening and so fast that an evening on the sofa curled up with a bunch of bridal magazines seems like the ideal activity for lowering the temperature. I ring Tanya just in case she wants to join me. She does.

"I'll order in some Chinese if you like," I suggest.

"Perfect. See you around seven."

Tanya and I have tucked into Peking duck and pancakes, scallops with ginger, noodles with three kinds of vegetables, barbecued pork ribs and a mound of special fried rice. We've been poring over *Brides* and

You and Your Wedding while we've been eating, and the pages are smeared with grease and morsels of food. Tanya's been persuaded out of frothy meringues and is now thinking streamlined and strapless. Her dad is extremely wealthy so a Vera Wang or Monique Lhuillier at three to four thousand quid a throw won't pose any problems.

Now we're seated on opposite ends of the sofa, facing one another, legs up and entangled, eating Minstrels. We're talking venues and camellias versus roses and bridesmaids and honeymoons and have just opened a second bottle of wine when the doorbell rings. I automatically look at my watch.

"Who can that be? No one pops round unannounced at this time of night. And I think I've had enough surprises for one day."

"Well, we could sit around debating it for an hour or two," giggles Tanya, "and by the time we've finished, whoever it is will be gone."

"Maybe it's one of those scary blokes selling dishcloths at ten quid each."

The bell rings again, longer and more insistently. Reluctantly, I get up from the sofa, peering through the spyhole before I open the door.

"I don't believe it," is all I can say. "I just don't believe it."

"Well, aren't you going to let us in?" chirps a familiar voice.

Standing in my doorway are Maddy, with Emma curled fast asleep in a papoose on her front, and Ed and the twins. Ed is grinning and clutching a bottle of

369

champagne. Maddy is grinning and clutching a big bunch of white lilies.

I'm already drunk, so when I stand on a chair to reach for the champagne glasses on the top shelf of the kitchen cabinet, I sway alarmingly. And as the chair rocks onto its back legs, I almost fall off.

"Careful there," roars Ed, grabbing hold of the chair to steady it.

"There had better be a good explanation for all this," I say, looking down from a great height at the unexpected gathering in my kitchen. Although I already know by the looks on Maddy's and Ed's faces, and of course the bottle of champagne, that I'm no longer in trouble.

The twins are flat out on the carpet with Susanna, who doesn't at all mind being disturbed from her slumbers. Emma, though, has suddenly woken up and is starting to whimper. Maddy's breast puts in an instant and very prominent appearance and Emma latches on greedily. Tanya, for want of knowing what to say to anyone, has started rinsing out aluminium cartons instead of throwing them straight into the bin.

The champagne glasses are filled.

Ed raises his first.

"I would like us all to raise a glass . . ." I raise my glass. "Not you, Hope." I lower it again. "I would like us all to raise a glass to Hope Lyndhurst-Steele, the woman who knew the right thing to do and who brought Maddy and me together at last."

"And I would like to raise my glass," says Maddy, from her position on the sofa, Emma sucking contentedly at her breast. "I would like to raise my glass, if only I could manoeuvre it around these enormous bosoms of mine, to the very best friend a woman could have."

"And while we're at it," says Tanya, leaving the sink to come and stand at my side, "I would like to raise a glass to the best boss I've ever worked for."

And then, predictably, I cry. And I can't stop. But I'm laughing too. And I'm hugging everything that moves and I don't need any explanations of anything, I don't even want any explanations. All I know is that Maddy has seen what's right, and what really matters, and that Ed must love her even though he loved Ruth too, and that they're all going to be a family, and that the twins will have a mother again, and Emma will have a father and I'll have my friend back and can start being a proper godmother, and that we can wheel Emma in the park with our dogs by our sides, and that fifty, fuck it, is no worse than forty-nine, and although it's a helluva lot worse than thirty, and somewhat worse than forty, it may well be better than sixty, which is ages away, and what's age got to do with anything that's important anyway?

"I've been such an idiot," Maddy says, when I've eventually calmed down sufficiently to be able to listen. "And I've behaved so badly towards you."

"Yes, my friend, you have. But I've been an idiot too. Which is probably why we're so compatible."

"And you forgive me?"

"Nothing to forgive, mama Maddy, just so long as I can now, finally, hold that baby of yours."

"Emma, sweetheart," says Maddy, "I'd like you to meet your godmother. Properly this time. Until yesterday you only had me. Now you've a daddy, two brothers and a godmother. You are such a lucky girl." She plucks her, tiny and perfect, from the papoose, and places her tenderly in my arms.

I'm sitting with Vanessa in Mario's, telling her everything that's happened — except about Dan. I can't quite bring myself to share my sex life — albeit a measly one and a half sexual encounters — with a woman who's been sharing her sex life with my son. Even though I now count Vanessa as my friend, it doesn't mean she has to know *everything*.

"How's the counselling course going?" I ask.

"It's hard; it's not like I ever went to college or anything. But I'm sticking with it, and I've found myself some extra-curricular help."

"And what does that mean exactly?"

"It means I've met someone."

"Another toy boy?

"No, I'm not usually into cradling-snatching, you know. Olly was a one-off. No, this guy's one of the teachers. He's a psychologist and he's really smart and he's got a great ass and he isn't even married."

"Not even divorced?"

"Not even."

"And how old?"

"He's thirty-four next week, and he's invited me away for the weekend. I wanted to ask you the most enormous favour, Hope. Is there any chance at all that you could look after the kids? You won't have to do much for them, they'll never get bored playing with Susanna."

"I'd love to do that for you, Vanessa. Have you heard from Olly?"

"Yes, I got a long letter from him the other day. I think he's really enjoying himself. Says he's palled up with this other teaching assistant — a girl — and they're going to go travelling together. But reading between the lines, I think he's trying to tell me she's more than just a pal. I don't mind. That episode is over, but it will always be a lovely memory."

"You have a generous heart, Vanessa. I had a letter too, waiting for me when I got back from Morocco. It was full of wonderful descriptions of the school and the boys and the teachers and what little he has seen so far of his surroundings. But no mention of the girl."

"And how are things between you and Jack?"

"Well, we're going away together after Christmas. It's funny, I wanted this to happen so much, and now I'm not so sure."

"Because . . ."

"Because when he left I thought I was entirely to blame. Just as I thought I was entirely to blame for Maddy's response when I told Ed about the baby. But now I think that Jack's got to take some responsibility too. It's all very well him saying he supported me all those years, and that he always gave me more than I gave him, but the truth is I was the one trying to keep

373

everything going, juggling the job and Olly, and running the household and making lots of money. And I may not have given him my full attention, but that's normal when you're married and working and have kids. And when I started to implode he just couldn't take it, even though that was when I needed him most. And as for sex, well, who wants sex when they're worn out and feeling lousy about themselves?"

"So you're thinking of going alone? Or cancelling?"

"Well, neither really. I'm just hoping our holiday doesn't turn into a battleground. Perhaps it's unrealistic of me to think we can work things out on a romantic desert island if we can't work them out here. And whereas before I saw this holiday as a kind of apology, a peace token if you like, now I'm less in the mood to put myself down and apologise. I'm thinking that in the wife stakes I've not scored too badly down the years."

I look out of the window. The Christmas decorations are up, fairy lights strung between the street lamps. The wine bar opposite is spilling girls in high heels and bare legs out onto the pavement, and young men clutching bottles of beer. They're laughing and drunkenly tripping off the pavement into the road, as cars roar by tooting horns. A figure wearing a familiar stripy scarf is walking past the restaurant on this side of the road. He has his arm round a woman's shoulders, protecting her from the biting wind. I can see only the top of the woman's head, burrowing into him. It's a very blonde sort of head. The scarf there's no mistaking — it was a present from me to Jack.

My hand, which holds a wine glass, is trembling. "Did you see what I just saw?"

Vanessa fiddles with a ring on her middle finger and looks at her empty plate.

"Hard to tell in this light," she says, looking up.

"Not that hard, actually," I reply. "That was definitely my husband and the woman he was with was definitely blonde. I'm thinking Sally."

"I've never met her, remember?"

"I really don't get it. Why would he agree to go away with me at Christmas if he's having an affair with Sally right on our doorstep? Why would Sally be calling me about her blasted charity every five minutes if she was having an affair with Jack? And now I've gone and invited her and Nick to Christmas drinks."

"I thought they were splitting up."

"They are, but I didn't know who to choose, so I told them to decide among themselves and the decision was that they'd both come."

"And Jack?"

"No, Jack's not coming. We agreed it would be weird to have everyone round with us pretending to be a normal married couple. So Jack's going to his sister, the dreaded Anita. It will be the first time in twenty years that she's had to make Christmas lunch."

"Is she really that bad?"

"Actually, she's worse. She came to see me only once while I was recuperating. She stayed less than ten minutes, and spent the entire time telling me that it was setting a terrible example to Olly having two openly homosexual men sharing a bed in the same house as an impressionable young man. I asked her if she thought it was catching, and she just snorted and said I was being deliberately controversial as usual."

"Hope, you're burbling. We were talking about Jack, remember? You've just seen him walk by with a woman who may — or not — be Sally, with whom he may — or not — be having an affair."

I gulp down what's left in my wine glass.

"I'm burbling because I don't know what else to do."

"You could try to tell me what you're feeling."

"An absolute fool, for starters. Betrayed — by both of them. But am I eaten up with jealousy? Can I bear the thought of Jack touching another woman? A few months ago I might have said yes to the first question and no to the second. And now I think it might be the other way round. Does that mean I no longer love Jack after all? I'm really not sure. Will I fall to pieces if he doesn't come back? I fell to pieces when he left in May, but no, I don't think I'll fall to pieces again if he doesn't come back."

"So why haven't you confronted either of them before?"

"I suppose because I couldn't face up to the truth. Didn't think I could handle it. But seeing the two of them together like that, well, I'm going to have to face it. I'm going to put it to Jack on the flight out."

"That doesn't sound like great timing to me."

"As far as I'm concerned, no time is a great time. But at least, trapped inside his seat belt, there's nowhere for him to run."

★　★　★

We've had an indifferent meal, watched an indifferent movie, and Jack is removing his book from the pocket of the seat in front of him. I'm feeling sick, and it's not the altitude that's causing it.

"Jack, I don't want to ruin our holiday or anything, not before it's even begun, but I have to ask you something. If I don't ask it will hang over me the whole time we're away, and I just don't think I could bear it. In fact, I know I couldn't bear it, so I'm just going to have to ask it anyway, even though the timing's lousy and —"

"Spit it out, girl. You've got me cornered anyway." Jack half-smiles, indulgent or long-suffering, I'm not sure which.

"You and Sally. Are you or are you not having an affair? I've suspected it for months, and I saw the two of you huddled up together the other week and I know that you're always going round and Nick —"

"I thought you asked me a question. Do you want an answer or not?" And then Jack laughs and I'm about to be furious when he says quite simply, "No, we're not having an affair. We never have had an affair and we never will."

I'm more shocked than I would have been if he'd said that they were going to move in together in the New Year.

"But . . . but . . . Nick thinks you are, and I was having dinner with Vanessa and I saw you go past Mario's — last Thursday it was — and you were wearing that scarf I gave you. If that wasn't Sally, who the hell . . ."

"Actually, that was Sally."

"So you're lying."

"No, I'm not lying. We actually had a drink together to talk about you."

"About me?"

"Yes. she wants to offer you a job. But she wasn't at all sure you'd accept."

"So why didn't she ask me herself?"

"Because Sally's the sort of person who needs to know all the angles. And she thought if she offered it too soon, before you'd decided for yourself the kind of thing you wanted to do next, you'd turn her down. So she wanted my opinion on how best to approach you."

"So if you've not been having an affair, why does Nick think you were? Why were you round there so often? Why did you keep going out for drinks with her?"

"Because she kept inviting me, because she needed someone other than Nick to stare at across the dinner table every night and because I listened to her troubles. We physios are a bit like hairdressers — people tell us their troubles."

"So you haven't been having an affair with Sally."

"No. I've been having an affair with Daniella and also with Evie."

"With *whom*?"

"Two women I met — one in a wine bar and the other on a bus."

"Two women! Both at once?"

"No, not both at once. First one, and then the other. And now neither. Satisfied?"

I'm smiling. I don't know why but I'm smiling. I'm about to ask how good they were in bed, but I shut myself up. Of course Jack hasn't become a born-again virgin since our break-up. Why should he have been? But he hasn't been having an affair with Sally.

"What kind of job?" I ask, grabbing Jack's hand and kissing the back of it.

"Director of Communications, something like that."

"Can she afford me?"

"Not at the rate you've been getting."

"You know Craig wants me to launch a new magazine for him?"

"Back to square one then, Hope, exactly where you wanted to be."

I say nothing. We must be halfway to our island paradise in the Maldives. Suddenly, I can't wait to get there.

Paradise Mislaid

We've been here four days and nights and we still haven't made love. But there's a companionable closeness, and it's growing. At night we sleep in a big double bed together, sometimes snuggling in a spoon position. During the day, Jack goes off on diving trips and I swim closer to home, snorkelling around the bay where there are more than enough fish for my taste, or reading on the deck of our over-water bungalow.

This hideaway island in the Maldives is little more than an amoeba in a vast turquoise ocean. You can walk around it, barefoot in the sand, in little more than twenty minutes. I do it in the mornings alone, and in the evening, as the sun goes down, we walk together. We hold hands, and it feels good. Can we be the only couple on the island not on their honeymoon? The only couple more interested in what's on our dinner plates than looking into one another's eyes? We make jokes about it, and if sometimes I feel a little wistful, it doesn't make me wish I could go back, because that would take away so many of the good things I've experienced since meeting Jack. We talk easily, and sometimes not at all. I look around and am surprised by how little some of the honeymoon couples have to say to one another.

"Was I really so awful, Jack? Turning fifty, hitting the menopause, losing my job and my mother — even if we weren't exactly close — was quite a lot to shoulder all at once. And with Olly leaving home as well. Isn't the test of a good relationship how you deal with the hard times, not just the good?"

"Of course it is. But I'd been feeling for ages that I didn't exist for you. Sure I was handy to have around, but that was about it. I was furious with you. Even when you were so low, I felt more furious than sympathetic."

"I'm quite prepared to admit that I was whiny and self-pitying. But I was close to a breakdown as well. You should have been there. Even after my operation you didn't offer to come and look after me."

"It just seemed the wrong basis on which to start over. If Mike and Stanko hadn't stepped in I would have done so myself. But you did OK with those guys."

"I did more than OK. I learned again what a good relationship looks like. But I did miss you."

"You asked me about my affairs. What about you?"

"Too busy collapsing on the pavement outside Waitrose and having general anaesthetics for that kind of thing." So I tell a lie. And just as I didn't feel guilty about Paris, I don't feel guilty about denying it.

"It's nice being here with you," says Jack. "I'm not sure I'd rather be here with anyone else."

I could be having sex on every corner of this island with a man like Dan.

"Mmm," I reply, non-committally. *Nice*. Nice? Is that something I'm supposed to be grateful for at fifty?

More in the spirit of irony than romance, I've booked the "Exclusive Hideaway Sleepover" Package for New Year's Eve, which is our last night on the island. At five in the afternoon a small Dhoni, a traditional Maldivian fishing boat, pulls up outside our water villa, and we chug over to another island which is no more than 100 metres in length and barely half that in width and which is to be our private quarters for the night.

Outside our four-poster canopied bed on the sand, with its gauzy muslin curtains billowing gently in the breeze, a waiter — who was already standing on the shore ready to greet us when we arrived — has set up a table for dinner on the sand with a white cloth, gleaming silver and glass, candles in glass lanterns and frangipani flowers floating on water in glass bowls. A champagne bucket sits on a silver stand in the sand next to us.

As I raise the glass to my mouth, Jack says, "Since you've arranged all your birthday treats yourself so far, it's my turn to surprise you."

He pulls an airline ticket out of the back pocket of his trousers.

"Your return ticket," he says.

"Thanks, Jack, but I've already got one of those."

"Yes, but I've changed it."

"What do you mean? We're going home tomorrow."

"I am. But you're not."

"Don't tell me you're shipping me off to Australia like a convict?"

"Not quite so far. You're going home via Colombo."

"Sri Lanka? Whatever for?"

"For a few days. There's someone who wants to see you."

"Jack, I don't get it."

And then suddenly I do.

"You mean Olly? You mean I'm going to spend a few days with Olly? Oh, Jack, that's the best birthday present in the world."

"I thought you'd think that. Olly was about to leave India for Sri Lanka anyway, so it just meant a bit of juggling with the dates."

"But why aren't you coming too?"

"I wasn't sure how it would work out, the two of us being away together."

"And how has it worked out, do you think?"

"Shall we just do it rather than talk about it for the time being?"

"Yes, a good idea. Thank you so much for this, Jack."

Our waiter has departed. It's just the two of us on the island. There was a brilliant moon before, but it seems to have disappeared. The gentle breeze has turned into a succession of gusts, coming closer and closer together like labour pains, until they join together in one long agonising blast. Then the first plop of rain settles on my head. And then another. And another. Soon it's torrenting down, and we're running for the refuge of our canopied bed with its wooden roof. Our candle snuffs out, and we're plunged into darkness. The curtains, designed more to keep the mosquitoes out than the rain, are protecting us from neither. The sea and the wind are roaring now, and I'm really scared.

"Jack, I think the sea's getting closer."

"Well, it's bound to, a bit, with all this wind and rain."

"When will it stop?"

"You're asking me?"

"I'm scared. You need to investigate."

"Why me?"

"Because you're the man."

"Oh, yes, I forgot."

"Here, take the torch, which they so kindly left. This is madness, it must happen all the time — why didn't they warn us?"

"Calm down, Hope, I'm sure it does happen all the time and nothing bad ever results. I'm sure it sounds much worse than it is."

Jack goes to investigate. I'm too frightened to move. He comes back, looking deadly serious.

"Close. Incredibly close."

"What, the sea?"

"Of course the sea, what else? We may have to try to swim back to the main island."

"In this? Are you kidding? We'd both drown."

I'm starting to whimper.

"Only kidding, Hope. It's blowing over. Half the sky is filled with stars. It's going to stop any second."

"Well, I'm a wreck. Come back to bed, *please*."

Jack's laughing now, and he pulls back the covers and sits on top of me, pinning my arms above my head.

"Whose idea was this anyway?"

"OK, OK, I admit it. I give in." Now I'm laughing too.

Jack leans over me and kisses me on the tip of my nose. And then on my forehead, and my eyelids, then my cheeks and mouth and neck and down and down. He lifts the hem of my short nightdress which I've been wearing because I felt shy of exposing my scar. He hasn't seen it yet.

"It's not pretty, Jack, it's really not pretty."

"No, Hope, but it's you, it's still you, Hope Impossible Lyndhurst-Steele."

And soon we are making love, gently, playfully, tenderly, and I don't mind so much about the scar. And it feels good. And it feels right. But there's something missing. I can sense that Jack is close to coming, but not me, I'm way off. I think of Dan and of Paris and my back against the door and his hands all over me, and I'm suddenly so hot I cry out and now I'm as ready as Jack is and when the surge overtakes me I don't know who I'm making love to and it doesn't really matter any more. Afterwards, I lie there wondering. Is thinking of another man when you make love to your husband as much of a betrayal as actually making love to another man? Or is it an acceptable way to keep passion alive? Are there any rules any more? Or do we simply make them up as we go along?

"Hope, my love," says Jack sleepily, "I think it's time I came home." I don't reply.

On the flight to Colombo, I ponder the decisions still to be made. Do I go to work for Craig as *le grand fromage*

385

in a glossy, high-profile job? Or do I work for a relative pittance in Sally's charity and help get Cat's Place the support it needs? Do Jack and I make a go of it? Or do I take a chance on Dan or some other man I've not yet met? Or could I contemplate a life with no man at all? Actually, I've already made my decisions, but I'm on my way to see my son, and everything — and everyone — else can wait.

I walk through the arrivals gate at Colombo. Behind the barrier there's a tanned and long-limbed boy in khaki shorts and flip-flops and a sleeveless vest that's seen better days, waving and smiling. My heart soars. And then I notice the girl next to him. She's holding Olly's other hand, the one that's not waving at me. She has long, dark, ringletted hair, and comes barely to Olly's shoulders. She's skinny like him, and she's also wearing shorts and flip-flops and a vest — and a nervous smile. This I wasn't expecting.

Olly and I hug.

"Olly, you look amazing. I don't need to ask, I can see you're having a wonderful time."

"Happy Birthday, Mum. I should have told you in advance that I wouldn't be alone, but it was all so last minute. This is Alicia. We were at the school together. She's . . ."

I swallow. This was supposed to be the two of us. I swallow again. Olly wants me to meet this girl. It's important to him. He wants me to like her.

"She's far too beautiful for you, Olly. Delighted to meet you, Alicia."

Olly's shoulders visibly relax. He grabs my bag and the three of us head for the exit.

"Where to?" I ask Olly. "You're in charge."

"Me in charge? As you will discover, Alicia, there is only one person in charge when my mother's around."

"That was then, Ols. People can change, you know. You'd be amazed what happens when a woman gets to the age of fifty."

"You're not fifty, I don't believe it," says Alicia.

"You're right. I'm fifty-one. Let's go and celebrate."

ISIS publish a wide range of books in large print, from fiction to biography. Any suggestions for books you would like to see in large print or audio are always welcome. Please send to the Editorial Department at:

ISIS Publishing Limited
7 Centremead
Osney Mead
Oxford OX2 0ES

A full list of titles is available free of charge from:

Ulverscroft Large Print Books Limited

(UK)
The Green
Bradgate Road, Anstey
Leicester LE7 7FU
Tel: (0116) 236 4325

(Australia)
P.O. Box 314
St Leonards
NSW 1590
Tel: (02) 9436 2622

(USA)
P.O. Box 1230
West Seneca
N.Y. 14224-1230
Tel: (716) 674 4270

(Canada)
P.O. Box 80038
Burlington
Ontario L7L 6B1
Tel: (905) 637 8734

(New Zealand)
P.O. Box 456
Feilding
Tel: (06) 323 6828

Details of **ISIS** complete and unabridged audio books are also available from these offices. Alternatively, contact your local library for details of their collection of **ISIS** large print and unabridged audio books.